W9-DEB-783

MICKEY ZUCKER REICHERT

THE
RETURN
OF
NIGHTFALL

DAW BOOKS, INC.
DONALD A. WOLLHEIM, FOUNDER
375 Hudson Street, New York, NY 10014

ELIZABETH R. WOLLHEIM
SHEILA E. GILBERT
PUBLISHERS
http://www.dawbooks.com

First Paperback Printing, September 2005

1 2 3 4 5 6 7 8 9

DAW TRADEMARK REGISTERED
U.S. PAT. OFF. AND FOREIGN COUNTRIES
—MARCA REGISTRADA
HECHO EN U.S.A.

PRINTED IN THE U.S.A.

To Jody Lee,
friend, artist, and loving mother—
from her biggest fan.

Acknowledgments

I would like to thank the following people:
Sheila Gilbert, Mark Moore, Sandra Zucker,
Jonathan Matson, Tim Larson, Jackie, Koby, and Carly.

Also, to all the persistent fans of Nightfall for
demanding a sequel—sorry it took me eleven years
to get the message.

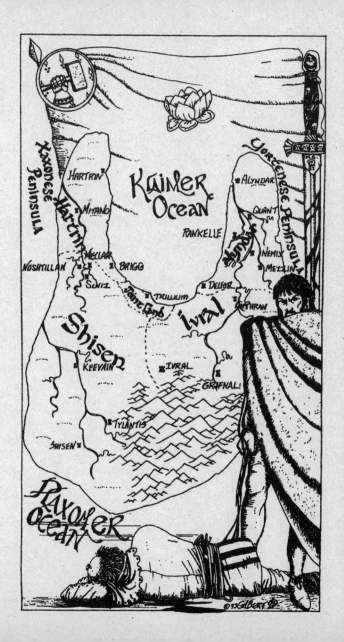

The Legend of Nightfall:
A Nursery Rhyme

A demon wakens with the night,
Reviling sun and all things bright.
Evil's friend and virtue's foe—
Darkness comes where Nightfall goes.

Eyes darker than the midnight shade;
Teeth sharper than the headsman's blade.
When he smiles, a cold wind blows—
Darkness comes where Nightfall goes.

When shadows fall and sunlight breaks,
What Nightfall touches, Nightfall takes.
Lives and silver, maids in bows—
Darkness comes where Nightfall goes.

A demon cruel; a monster stark,
Grim moonlight, coldness, deepest dark.
Nightmares come to those who doze
In darkness where old Nightfall goes.

Nightfall laughs, and death's ax falls.
Hell opens wide and swallows all.
He rules the depths where no light shows—
Darkness comes where Nightfall goes.

Lock up your children after dark,
Lest Nightfall find an easy mark.
For safety ends at twilight's close—
And darkness comes where Nightfall goes.

Razor claws and fiery eyes;
Leathern wings to cleave the skies.
His soul within stark midnight froze—
Darkness comes where Nightfall goes.

*Those who brave the night will find
Horror, dread, and demon kind.
He slays them all and rends their souls—
Darkness comes where Nightfall goes.*

*Birthed within the black abyss,
His silent gift a deadly kiss.
Gone before the rooster crows—
Darkness comes where Nightfall goes.*

*Counting years like grains of sand.
Countless fall beneath his hand.
Time, his minion; night, his clothes—
Darkness comes where Nightfall goes.*

*Where Nightfall walks, all virtue dies.
He weaves a trail of pain and lies.
On mankind heaps his vilest woes—
Darkness comes where Nightfall goes.*

*Wolves and bats and beasts of night,
Spirits black that flee the light,
Cringed in fear when he arose—
Darkness comes where Nightfall goes.*

*He feeds on elders and children,
On soldiers, kings, and beggarmen.
He never stops and never slows—
Darkness comes where Nightfall goes.*

*The Evil One, the demon blight
Who hides in day and stalks the night.
He steals the stars and drags them low—
Darkness comes where Nightfall goes.*

Alternative verses:

*Three kings and their armies rode
To hunt the demon in the cold;
But where they've gone, no mortal knows—
Darkness comes where Nightfall goes.*

*A dragon laughed at Nightfall's fame,
Rained curses on the demon's name;
The dragon's bones now lie in rows—
Darkness comes where Nightfall goes.*

*A wizard hoped to slay the beast.
He conjured up a poisoned feast.
The demon fed him to the crows—
Darkness comes where Nightfall goes.*

*A gambler bet the tales were lies
And scorned the wisdom of the wise.
The odds were not the ones he chose—
Darkness comes where Nightfall goes.*

*Six princes fought him in the night.
Their fortress of unequaled might
'Twas gone before the sun arose—
Darkness comes where Nightfall goes.*

*The Evil One, the demon blight
Who hides in day and stalks the night.
He steals the stars and drags them low—
Darkness comes where Nightfall goes.*

† Prologue †

NIGHTFALL AWAKENED to the first rays of sunlight trickling through the open window of his room in Alyndar Castle. As always, he woke without stiffening, without changing the pattern of his breathing, without providing any hint to anyone who might be watching that the level of his alertness had changed. He assessed the status of his injuries from weeks-long habit; and, to his delight, found nothing amiss. For the first time since he had fallen the equivalent of nine stories, locked in battle with a flying sorcerer, nothing hurt.

Nightfall opened his eyes. He knew every detail of the room by heart, secure in the knowledge that, if anything had changed in the night, he would immediately be aware of it. He lay on a real bed, its ticking softened by thick, fuzzy blankets fit for royalty. His furniture consisted of a massive wardrobe, currently containing exactly two changes of clothing and sparse toiletries. An empty chest took up most of the space at the end of the bed, and a chamber pot sat in the corner.

Nightfall ran a hand through tangled mahogany-brown hair that no longer was covered in grime, dust, and dyes. Once a master of disguise living regularly as seven different men, and occasionally as several others, he had spent months adjusting to his given name, Sudian, and the one appearance he had not used since childhood: his own. Doing so obviated the need for him to assume postures that made his slightly less than average height seem taller or shorter, his slender and sinewy frame seem muscular, lame, or bulky; but it also left him feeling naked and vulnerable. Clean-shaven, Sudian had no way to hide his strong chin and cheekbones, his fair skin; and no shadowing or squints masked eyes the dense, dark indigo of blackened steel.

Now free of splints, bandages, and the ache of healing bones and muscles, Nightfall felt driven by the sudden urge to *move*. His life usually kept him in constant motion, in body and mind. He felt withered by the healing and resting, in desperate need of a reckless run or climb. His gaze went naturally to the window, and memory caught him in a sudden and frantic crush. Once again, he felt himself surging through the air as he attacked Chancellor Gilleran in a blood-maddened frenzy, his hands scrabbling for the sorcerer's throat. Using magic, Gilleran flew, dragging Nightfall with him, through the seventh-story tower window. The sorcerer's fingernails raked Nightfall's face in crooked lines of fiery pain. Gilleran kicked and flailed to free himself, soaring ever higher to assure that when Nightfall's grip failed, the fall would kill him.

Now, as then, Nightfall hid fear behind desperation and will. His mind was inescapably drawn back to that fateful encounter, and his vision gave him only whirling pictures of treetops, guards leaning from the tower windows, and the courtyard far below them. Gilleran's struggles, and his own previous blood loss, impaired his coordination and threatened his hold on the sorcerer. Given the choice of dying alone or taking the chancellor with him, Nightfall chose the latter. He tapped the talent that had come to him at birth, driving his weight upward, beyond Gilleran's ability to support. And both of them had plummeted.

It was a plunge Nightfall could never forget, seconds of utter panic that passed like an hour of shrieking agony. Gilleran's screams had shattered his hearing, and the struggle to break free of Nightfall's hold became lashing, pounding, and desperate. In the final moments, Nightfall had abruptly lowered his weight, propelling his body to feather-lightness with a thought. He could not reverse the deadly momentum, but it gave him the top position over Gilleran and allowed him to grab a tree limb to slow his descent. Ultimately, the landing killed Gilleran and left Nightfall with a shattered left hand, a dislocated shoulder, a badly bitten thumb, several broken ribs, and deeply unconscious.

He considered himself lucky to have survived at all.

Now, Nightfall pushed aside the detailed pictures his mind still so easily conjured. His life had always depended upon quickness in thought and action, deadly accurate skill, and split-second timing. He could not afford to develop a fear of anything. Hesitation would spell his doom, no matter how normal that delay or unwillingness might seem to the rest of the world. He had no time to spare for second thoughts when his only escape lay beyond a second-, or seventh-, or millionth-story window.

A knock on the door dragged Nightfall fully back to the present. He flipped open the wardrobe and grabbed a set of clean clothing: a shirt, tunic, and breeks in royal Alyndarian purple and silver. Noble's clothes.

"Who is it?" he called, while he swiftly pulled off his nightshirt and donned the proper garb.

The muffled male voice was unintelligible.

Nightfall smoothed the cold fabric of his silks, shook back his hair, and opened the door to a young male guard with a sword at his belt, dressed in similar colors over mail.

Apparently expecting more conversation shouted through the door, the guard retreated a step, then bowed. "My lord, King Edward Nargol would like to know if you're well enough to join him in court today."

King Edward. The title still sounded bizarre to Nightfall. King *Edward.* He wondered if he could ever see more to the eighteen-year-old monarch of Alyndar than the impetuous, idealistic prince he had escorted around most of the world. Using Chancellor Gilleran's magical "oath-bond," King Rikard had bound the deadliest assassin in the four kingdoms to his dangerously naive younger son. Nightfall had been charged with the task of keeping Edward alive and getting him landed within a rapidly dwindling time period, all without the prince knowing his mission or his identity beyond that of the dutiful squire, Sudian. If Nightfall failed at any part, the magic assured Gilleran would take Nightfall's soul and, with it, his natal weight-shifting talent.

And failure seemed a certainty. No matter what approach Nightfall had taken, Edward's raw and innocent zeal mangled his best-laid schemes and plans. In the end, Gilleran had undone himself by murdering the elder prince and the king, thereby granting the crown to Edward, landing him through inheritance. Had Nightfall not interfered, Gilleran would have slaughtered Edward as well and would now rule both Alyndar and Nightfall's soul.

Nightfall lowered his head. He would rather chew off his own fingertips than sit through a morning of highborns' griping. "Please inform His Majesty pain kept me awake most of the night." It was a lie. Nightfall could not remember a better sleep. "I'm still not quite ready for court."

"Yes, my lord." The guard bowed again, turned, and retreated down the hallway.

Nightfall closed the door, sighing as he did. The excuse would not hold up much longer. Two weeks had passed since the month-long grieving period for King Rikard and Crown Prince Leyne had ended, and the royal healers now proclaimed Nightfall fit. Twice, he had attempted to sit upon the chancellor's seat at Edward's side and perform his promised duty, but even dawdling had not rescued him from the tedium. Both times, he had arrived late enough to avoid all the fussy preparations, but he still had to face the proceedings. The first time, he fell asleep amid the ramblings of some knight about honor and family. Nightfall had blamed the lapse on pain medication, though he had taken none in days. The second time, he found his mind wandering and his body in perpetual, fidgeting motion.

Hoping to fulfill another need, Nightfall returned to the window and looked down the three stories into the inner courtyard. The sun had barely crested the horizon, and no one yet tarried or frolicked among the statues, flowers, and benches. Most had just awakened, and the autumn morning chill would keep them away at least until the approach of midday. Certain he had no audience, Nightfall sprang to the window ledge, then swung down onto the stonework of the tower wall. From habit, he easily found finger-and toeholds in the mortar.

A breeze caressed him, bringing with it the memory of wind surging around him as he tumbled helplessly toward the ground, locked with Gilleran. He banished the image fiercely. Fear would not have him. Instead, he concentrated on the feel of the cold stone against his hands, feet, and cheek, finding chinks from long habit, and shinnying down the side as if born to the process. This time, he did not even need to rely on his natal talent. Custom and practice alone allowed him a perfect downward climb.

The moment his feet touched ground, Nightfall shinnied back up, dodging the windows in the first and second floors. It would not do for the castle regulars and help to see the king's adviser scurrying up and down walls like a spider. Soon, his stomach unclenched and his muscles loosened, falling into the familiarity of their task. The memories of his fall would stay with him, but they could no longer hurt him. One more climb and he would purge the feeling of desperation from his system, would escape the natural inclination to avoid any situation that might remind him of his latest brush with mortality.

For a man like Nightfall, escaping death was as routine as breathing; and he would not allow one incident to haunt him. His new position, as Edward's adviser, protected him from many of the daily agonies he had known in his prior life. He no longer had to scrounge or steal to eat, no longer had to dodge predators in dark, shit-stinking alleys, no longer had to hide from the whims and rages of the street folk who had unwittingly raised him. But even the magnificent army and navy of Alyndar might not keep him safe from sorcerers.

Nightfall had learned in childhood to avoid using his natal weight-shifting talent whenever possible, worried about discovery. Sorcerers gained their magic only by slaying those rare people born with such an ability, and their method required tortuous ritual slaughter and taking possession of the victim's soul. Any sorcerer who knew of his power would hunt him as fiercely as Gilleran and others had, and many people would sell any Gifted's secret for the rewards a sorcerer would pay for such a tip. The Alyndarians still whispered about the gods, happenstance, or demons that had rescued Nightfall from sharing Gilleran's fate; but few spoke their concerns aloud. To do so might belittle the sacrifice that had rescued King Edward from the fate of his father and brother.

Reaching the sill, Nightfall reversed his course again, needing one more wild climb to placate his internal demons. This time, he skittered like a squirrel, performing broad zigzags and looping circles, clinging sideways and upside down, reassuring himself that his wounds had claimed nothing permanent and his trepidations would never own him. He was Sudian now and forever, but no one had yet demanded that the king's new adviser become as stodgy and ham-fisted as the others. In his many guises, he had scaled fortresses and mountains, scuttled across riggings and lines, and found his way through tunnels and mazes. He had even escaped the great prison of Alyndar.

Nightfall headed upward again, prepared to clamber back into his room and start his day with the rosy glow of exertion still on his face. As he reached the sill, a hand clamped over his, pinning it in place.

Nightfall froze as possibilities ticked through his mind. A sudden jerk might free him but would also send him tumbling to the ground. He would live, but he saw no need to risk injury, or reveal his talent, unnecessarily. Then, righteous indignation filled him. He knew of no law preventing him from climbing to his own bedroom window. He glanced upward to the young, plain features of his betrothed. Short hair, as white as an elder's, feathered around her fine cheeks and green-brown eyes narrowed in clear irritation.

"Kelryn." Nightfall hefted his other hand to the ledge. "You startled me."

Taking his other wrist, she hauled him toward her.

Nightfall allowed her assistance, though he would have done better without it. Concerned he might inadvertently drag her out the window, he kept his weight on his legs and used only toeholds to work his way inside.

Once there, the lovers faced one another in silence. Nightfall made the first move, reaching for her.

Kelryn dodged his embrace. "Sudian, what are you doing?"

Nightfall smiled innocently. "Trying to hug and kiss the woman who promised to marry me."

"Now what fool woman would agree to that?" Kelryn bantered, but an edge in her tone took the humor from her words.

Nightfall would have liked to give a witty reply, but he could not ignore the obvious. "You're mad at me."

That opened the floodgates. No longer attempting to hide her disappointment, Kelryn spilled the reason. "Of course I'm mad at you." She turned away, a move that did nothing to lessen his desire for her. Once a dancer, she had a captivating grace that drew him every bit as much as her slender, muscular body. "Ned has treated us with such amazing kindness." She used the nickname Edward preferred from friends, when formality did not exclude it. "How can you act so blatantly ungrateful?"

"Ungrateful?" Nightfall blinked, surprised by the accusation. "I am grateful. I'm grateful as hell." Though perhaps not the best choice of words, Nightfall meant them. Gilleran had revealed Nightfall's identity as the shadowy demon of legend to Edward. The new monarch had been all but honor-bound to execute Nightfall, yet had promoted him instead. Few would have the gall or desire to place an assassin in the ultimate position of trust, yet Edward had. He had also kept Nightfall's secret, even from his inner circle of guards. The trust the king of Alyndar had placed in Nightfall would have seemed ludicrous and fatally misplaced had it not been so absolutely and utterly correct. In pretending to protect and venerate the guileless, mettlesome prince, he had come to respect and like him, much to his own surprise. "I nearly died saving his royal hide. Isn't that grateful enough?"

"No."

The answer caught Nightfall off guard. "No?"

"No, Sudian, it's not enough." Kelryn glided to the bed and sat, which only continued to fuel Nightfall's desire. He had known her for years, yet his hunger for her never seemed satisfied. She had become his shining star, his very definition of beauty. "Graciousness isn't a one-time thing. Edward is a friend, and you should treat him like one. Always."

Nightfall did not bother to argue. Right or wrong did not matter; he could never win against Kelryn. "I've had exactly three friends in my life, and you're one of them." He crouched in front of her but did not reach to touch her again. "Perhaps I just don't know how to treat them."

"You do."

Nightfall was not so sure. "Treat me like I don't."

Kelryn sighed and pulled her legs onto the bed, folding them. "Let's start with this: You don't make promises to friends you have no intention of keeping."

Nightfall knew exactly where this was going. "You mean the adviser thing?"

Kelryn gave him a penetrating look. "The 'adviser thing,' as you so interestingly put it, was your vow to serve Alyndar and her king to the best of your ability. You agreed to become nobility, and it's time you took up the responsibilities of your position as well as reaped the benefits."

Nightfall continued to stare. He had never heard Kelryn use so many long words nor speak so expressively. Now twenty-four, she had spent close to half of her life in a dance hall. "But I know absolutely nothing about anything that happens in court. Ned has good advisers there already, men who served his father and grandfather. What could I possibly add?"

"Entertainment at the very least." Kelryn finally smiled.

Nightfall rose and looked longingly toward the window. He wanted one more chance to assure himself he could make a quick escape if it became necessary, without an assault of memory mangling his concentration. "I don't recall agreeing to become a jester." Nightfall had become competent in all the things that mattered to him; his survival had depended upon it. If arrogant, pretentious highborns laughed at him, he might not manage to keep himself from slicing up their pretty, powdered faces.

Kelryn shifted position, rustling the ticking. "Then, perhaps it's common sense you can add to the proceedings. As I recall, Ned said you could help him judge the masses because you have real knowledge of their plights."

"I'm not ready . . ." Nightfall started slowly, knowing the tired excuse would not work on Kelryn.

"If you can climb a tower, you're ready for court." Kelryn added pointedly, "And you know you really shouldn't be doing it at all. The nobles are already questioning your past. You don't need to supply them with the sling stones and arrows."

"I know." Nightfall lowered his head, wondering if he might have made the biggest mistake of his life. It was the dream of every commoner to live in a palace, waited upon by diligent servants and trusted by the king. Yet, now that he had those luxuries, Nightfall could not help worrying about their price. "But . . ." He turned, giving Kelryn a pleading look. "Have you ever sat through court?"

"Many times."

"You have?"

"I have."

Nightfall fell silent, staring, trying to make sense of what he heard. "You . . . you understand . . . what . . . ?"

"Just because I'm lowborn and a woman doesn't mean I can't understand—"

Nightfall waved a dismissive hand. "I just meant the couple of times I went, I didn't get half of what they were saying. Bores me to a stupor." He became painfully honest, the way he could be only with Kelryn. She was the sole one he had ever told about his other persona and his natal talent. When King Edward's father had captured him in the guise of Marak the Nemixite sailor, the very identity under which Kelryn had known him, Nightfall had wrongly believed her his betrayer. "I can't stand it, Kelryn. If that's what I committed myself to, I'd rather go back to starving in the streets."

Kelryn rose and caught him into the embrace she had earlier shunned. Her expression revealed only compassion, but he read a hint of alarm in her eyes. "Sudian, it's not that bad. After a week or so, it all starts to make perfect sense. The local nobles can get preoccupied with some strange and trivial matters, but the politics between kingdoms is fascinating." She actually sounded excited. "And you have as much knowledge as anyone when it comes to the commoners, more than most."

Nightfall doubted even that. "I still don't understand what Ned needs me for."

Kelryn spoke into his ear, her body warm and her hair like velvet against his cheek. "The king finds comfort in your presence. He wants you in his court to advise him. Isn't that better than wanting you in his court on charges of murder and mayhem?"

Kelryn's closeness was driving Nightfall to distraction.

"Right now," she murmured as if divulging sexual secrets, "Ned is headed for a conference. Fourth floor, East Tower. He asked for you specifically. He says he needs you."

"And I need you." Nightfall leaned in to kiss her, and his hands slid along her sides toward her breasts.

Kelryn raised her chin and caught his hands before they reached their destination. "If you're not well enough to help a friend, then you're not well enough to have me either."

Nightfall groaned but did not argue. His yearning for her was painful. "Fourth floor, East Tower?"

Kelryn squeezed his fingers. "I'll be here when you get back."

"To torture me some more?"

"No, Sudian." Kelryn performed an alluring little dance, ending with a curtsy. "To *please* you, my lord."

Nightfall could not have scrambled out the door any faster.

Nightfall had no trouble finding the proper room. Guards stood at parade-ground attention in front of the doors, and a variety of noble men and women milled outside, clearly wishing they could join the secret discussion. Though he ignored them, Nightfall noticed them all. He could not have done otherwise. No matter how preoccupied he appeared, his senses remained instinctively alert and attuned to every movement around him. His lifestyle had required him to remember every word uttered in his presence, to recognize every face and the guise in which he saw it, but mostly to take immediate notice of any action that might signify a threat. Now, nothing jarred his senses enough to concern him, though he knew they all visually followed his walk to the door. The guards stepped aside to allow him entry. Nightfall tripped the latch and pulled the door open.

An unfamiliar voice wafted into the hallway, full of pathos and frustration, "But, Sire, it's just not done—"

Nightfall's entrance interrupted the discussion, and the assembly fell into instant silence as every eye found him.

Discovering that the room was much more crowded than he expected, Nightfall hesitated in the doorway, still bracing it open a crack that allowed the mob on the landing to stare at the interrupted proceedings. A large table took up most of the space, and well-dressed and -coiffed men filled all of the seats around it. Others, mostly guardsmen, crouched, sat, or stood on the periphery. Nightfall knew several by name and many others by brief association, but none well. He felt more comfortable among Alyndar's staff and servants, though his presence clearly unnerved them. Since the day Edward had promoted him from squire to adviser, Alyndar's lowest class no longer considered Nightfall one of them. The maids presented him with curtsies, and the pages addressed him as "sir" or "my lord."

Nightfall's gaze went automatically to the most dangerous man in the room, at least in his assessment. Though not the largest warrior present, Chief of Prison Guards Volkmier stood out from the rest. Unlike the other titled commanders, he stood among the elite guards rather than sitting at the table, and he wore gray and lavender to the others' purple and silver. A compact redhead with a no-nonsense bearing, Volkmier had a history with Nightfall he would rather forget. Four times, they had clashed, twice in Nightfall guise and twice as Sudian; Volkmier had won every time. Bull-muscled, yet swift, cool, and competent, the chief of the prison guards had proved sharp-witted and remarkably dangerous. He wielded sword or crossbow with an expert's lightness, and he grasped the intricacies of situations with a quickness rarely associated with men so dedicated to the fighting arts. King Rikard had trusted the man completely, more than even his elite bodyguards; and Nightfall had seen him make snap judgments with remarkable competence. Luckily for him, direct orders had prevented Volkmier from killing him in two instances, and wise decisions in the other two. Though fate had pitted them on opposite sides, Nightfall held a grudging respect for the chief of Alyndar's prison guards. He only wished circumstances would stop bringing them together.

Seated at the head of the table, King Edward Nargol grinned at Nightfall, genuinely glad to see him. It seemed wrong to Nightfall to see the adolescent monarch looking exactly the same as the impetuous, idealistic prince he had escorted for several painful, dragging months. Like the guards, Edward wore Alyndar's colors and crest, a powerful fist clutching a hammer. Brilliant golden hair offset his round, handsome face. His tall, muscle-packed frame exceeded nearly all of his guards', yet his friendly blue eyes betrayed the dangerous naïveté that had nearly gotten them both killed on so many occasions. "Sudian! So glad you could make it after all." His voice held raw excitement, without a trace of sarcasm. He patted the chair at his left, though it contained a tall, slender man with ebony hair and dark brown eyes.

Though it placed his back to the door and to Captain Volkmier, Nightfall went to the indicated spot. The man already seated there rose less than graciously, executed a casual bow, and offered the chair to Sudian. "Chancellor."

Nightfall stiffened. He had never heard that title applied directly to him, though the castle rumors had given him reason to believe the adviser position he had accepted was the same vacated by Gilleran's death. Since King Edward seemed undisturbed by the reference, Nightfall did not question it. Edward would never allow a lapse in protocol to go unmentioned or unpunished. Nightfall sat, and the man who had occupied his chair found a position along the wall with the guards.

Edward cleared his throat, granting his full attention to Nightfall. "Sudian, I was just explaining to my council, advisers, and guards how I violated law and propriety by escaping from Duke Varsah's incarceration in Schiz."

You told them . . . Though practiced at hiding emotion, Nightfall could not keep his nostrils from flaring. *You stupid, prattling moron!* He recalled details of their encounter with Duke Varsah from the time he had served as Edward's adoring and steadfast squire, when the need to rescue his soul from magical bondage had driven his every action. *You blitheringly ignorant prettyboy!* One of his attempts to get Edward landed had involved trying to form a romance between Prince Edward and the duke's daughter, Willafrida. Instead, Nightfall had gotten Edward in trouble for sneaking into a highborn lady's bedroom at night. The duke had trapped them neatly, insisting on a virginity test to prove the young prince had violated his daughter. Restitution, Varsah insisted, would have to come in the form of marriage, and he had had his eye on Edward's brother, Crown Prince Leyne. Certain Willafrida would fail the test, through no fault of Edward's, and crushed by the burden of limited time, Nightfall had fast-talked Edward into escaping the duchy.

"We need to apologize to the duke and pay him restitution."

Nightfall stared into the king's keen blue eyes, seeing nothing that would suggest he was joking. "But, M—" He stepped himself from saying "Master," once a condition of the oath-bond. He had despised calling any man such a thing, but it had become ingrained habit difficult to shake. "Sire, the duke was wrong to have taken you prisoner. He's the one who should apologize."

Murmurs swept the room.

A frown scored Edward's handsome features. "You are wise in many ways, Sudian; but, in this case, you are sorely mistaken. Duke Varsah found me in his daughter's bedroom. He had every right to hold me."

"You didn't touch her."

"That is immaterial, Sudian. I gave him reason to worry for her safety. He imprisoned me properly and appropriately under the laws of every kingdom. He and my father had a right to negotiate punishment."

Nightfall rolled his eyes. The rules and ethics of nobles seemed lunacy. "She called you into her bedroom. Which is worse? Refusing the request of a noble lady or crossing a random threshold?"

The prince's cheeks reddened, and his eyes narrowed in clear agitation. Nightfall found most people easy to read, but no one more so than King Edward. The inexperienced, virgin king felt flustered and embarrassed. "I've already explained my poor decision, Sudian. There's no need to call more attention to it."

It was not the point Nightfall had intended to make. "I only meant—" Worried he might make the situation even worse, he glanced around the room for assistance from the many men who watched the exchange in silence.

A stranger stepped in to rescue him. "His Majesty has described his intention to return to Schiz . . ."

Nightfall closed his eyes. *Please don't tell me this innocent, overly moral fool plans to put himself back in Varsah's custody.*

" . . . to make a personal apology and rectify his . . . um . . . error with monetary remuneration."

Relieved his assumption had proved wrong, Nightfall released a pent up breath. He had seen the king do too many insane and dangerous things in the name of propriety and refused to underestimate Edward's ability to get himself, and everyone around him, in trouble. "I see."

Another man took up the explanation, in the voice Nightfall had heard when he first entered. "And I was explaining to His Majesty that we should send an emissary in his place. It's just not done. In all of Alyndar's history—"

Edward interrupted in a voice that made Nightfall cringe. "I know Alyndar's history, Dacyl. Just because something's never been done before, doesn't render it wrong or immoral."

Nightfall knew that tone too well. Edward saw the situation as a point of honor; and, when it came to his principles, the entire army of Alyndar could not sway him. The whole situation seemed nonsensical to Nightfall. The so-called imprisonment had consisted of placing Edward into a fancy room in the duchy tower, one they had easily escaped. In fact, it had taken Nightfall far more time and effort to talk Edward into leaving than it had to physically accomplish it.

Edward continued, "No king of Alyndar has ever broken kingdom law before either. Compensating a crime of that magnitude requires swift and direct attention."

"Yes, Sire." The man Nightfall had replaced spoke next. "But an emissary can provide both."

Another cut in. "Khanwar's absolutely right. We need you here, Your Majesty. The mourning period's only half a month gone, and there is much to do."

Edward turned his gaze to this new speaker. "And our long hours in court have paid off. We've cleared the docket. Anything that comes up while I'm gone can either wait for my return or pass the judgment of my . . . regent."

Nightfall suddenly felt as if the entire room had shifted its focus to him. Pressed to say something, he spoke the words his role as Sudian the Faithful required, "Sire, you know I will remain loyally at your side whenever and wherever you go." He hated the guise circumstance had forced him to take, despised the fool's mission to which he might just have committed himself. He doubted expensive gifts and a long-winded speech would pacify the sly and selfish duke of Schiz. Varsah had seen a kingdom in his daughter's future, and Nightfall doubted gemstones and pretty words would distract him. Worse, Nightfall suspected Edward might give in to Varsah's demands in the name of fairness, locking himself into a loveless marriage to a graceless, homely woman and an insufferable father-in-law.

Nightfall expected the discussion to continue for hours. Surely Edward's top councillors and advisers would not give up until they disabused their new king of this irrational and idiotic notion. Yet, to his surprise, once he pledged his support the others fell silent.

A soldier of gigantic proportions rose and bowed with a graceful flourish. "Your Majesty, if you insist on going, I will assemble my best men for your escort."

Nightfall held his breath, concerned Edward might find some reason to refuse the offer.

Edward nodded at the massive warrior. "Thank you, General." He threw up a hand in a grand display, as if responding to the cheers of a multitude. "Ready my gear and destrier! We leave on the morrow." He sprang from his chair.

To a man, the others leaped to their feet, except for Nightfall who marveled at their awkward speed.

The king bashed through the door and onto the landing, followed by his guards and councillors.

Volkmier remained in place stationed, Nightfall noticed, between himself and the door. Suddenly wishing he had remained at Edward's side, he studied his fingernails and pretended not to notice his only remaining companion.

Several moments passed in silence, then Volkmier cleared his throat.

Grudgingly, Nightfall swung his gaze toward the chief of prison guards.

"Sudian." Volkmier spoke softly, but his tone held a hint of menace. "Please. Bring our king safely home."

More confused than troubled by the words, Nightfall rose. Though nearly a full head shy of Volkmier's height, he felt more comfortable in a fully defensible position. "Why tell this to me? The general's men—"

Volkmier interrupted, "The guards will keep His Majesty safe from highwaymen and anyone who might wish him ill." He pursed his lips. A comma of ginger hair slipped onto his forehead, well short of his eyes. He would never allow such a thing to spoil his deadly aim. "You, Sudian, might be the only man who can keep him safe from himself."

The somberness of Volkmier's expression precluded Nightfall finding any humor in the comment or resorting to a sarcastic response. The guardsman's pale eyes held a glint of terrible warning. His words were more than dire request; they were also a threat.

Resorting to the bold and blind allegiance he had pledged to Edward on the day of their meeting, for the purpose of irritating King Rikard as much as winning the prince's trust, Nightfall raised his head and spoke with feigned sincerity. "I'll do my level best." *And with the help of luck and gods and circumstance, I might even succeed.*

† Chapter 1 †

When you willingly choose another's troubles as your own, you just stop surviving and start living.

—Dyfrin of Keevain, the demon's friend

IN THE WESTERN quarter of Schiz, Duke Varsah's city, a fire danced in the hearth of the He-Ain't-Here Tavern, casting scarlet and amber designs across the diners. Nightfall sat in the corner chair of a corner table beside King Edward Nargol of Alyndar. Guards ate and drank around the periphery, arrayed in Alyndar's purple and silver. Commoners and travelers swarmed the nearby tables, keeping the help in constant motion. Nonetheless, a barmaid or serving boy remained always beside the royal table, prepared to wipe up any spill, to relay their least request.

Nightfall kept silent tabs on everyone in the tavern, an ingrained and wary instinct he could not have shaken if he wished to do so. His every movement was casual, masked as a thoughtful gesture, a fidget, a hair-rearranging head toss; but each shift in position granted him an unobtrusive means to observe every person and anticipate danger. He knew many of the patrons from his other guises; they were mostly Schizians mixed with visitors from the neighboring cities of Meclar and Noshtillan. They all drank, talked, and laughed; but Nightfall absorbed the strange underlying stiltedness, the not-quite-surreptitious looks his party earned amid the open stares of ruder folk, and the preponderance of those men most prone to curiosity and gossip.

When not cooking or cleaning, the pudgy proprietor Gil stood in the doorway between kitchen and common room, wringing his hands. He was not accustomed to royalty in his simply furnished red-stone building, constructed for meeting and drinking rather than hostelry. The upper class normally took lodgings in the south-end inn that Nightfall had gotten to know well in his persona of Balshaz the merchant. As the polio-stricken odd-jobber, Frihiat, however, he had grown familiar with the He-Ain't-Here's few rooms, now booked solid. Nightfall took some guilty pleasure in the usually unflappable proprietor's discomfort.

In the best position for surveying the entire room, Nightfall noticed the two men approaching before any of the guards so much as rolled a glance in their direction. In his mid-twenties, the younger one sported an overlarge head topped with muddy curls, a crooked nose, and broad lips. The other appeared middle-aged, tall and thin with a mop of sandy hair and a scar running from the outer corner of his right eye to his chin. Nightfall recognized both. The first was Brandon Magebane, a gifted man with the most dangerous career Nightfall could imagine: hunting sorcerers. The second, Gatiwan, had accompanied Brandon on some of his forays, risking his life to rid the world of its greatest evil.

Quick as a cat, Nightfall rose and held out his hands in greeting. "Brandon. Gatiwan. Good to see you both again."

Guards' hands went to hilts, but the exuberant greeting of the king's adviser kept them from standing or making any overt threat.

Brandon bowed appreciatively to the king, then addressed Nightfall. "Sudian. How wonderful to see you again. I presume you've come to fulfill your promise?" It was a ludicrous assumption. No king would travel halfway around the continent merely to escort a servant. As fast as the thought arose, Nightfall quashed it. *Edward would.*

Edward turned a beetle-browed look on his adviser. To most of the world, Sudian had sprung from nowhere, the next in line to replace the thirty-six previous stewards who had abandoned the job of protecting and educating the brash young prince. For these men of Schiz to know Nightfall as Sudian, they had to have become acquainted in the months he had traveled with Edward; yet the king had never seen them.

In fact, Nightfall had met Gatiwan in a tavern while Edward slept, and the older man had referred him to Brandon Magebane. Nightfall had visited Brandon in secret, seeking one of the magical stones the Magebane created with his natal talent, which could thwart a sorcerer's magic for a single spell. Brandon had given Nightfall the stone with the stipulation that, one day, Nightfall would assist the magehunters on one of their ventures. It was a rash promise made in desperation, one he had no intention of keeping, then or now.

Nightfall smiled. As one of the natally gifted, he appreciated what the Magebane and his rotation of volunteer followers did. But he had finally found a happy life, friends, a fiancée he loved, and had no interest in becoming part of a suicide mission. "Not today, Brandon. But thanks for the offer."

Looking over, Nightfall found King Edward staring at him and knew what had to follow.

"Did you make this man a promise, Sudian?" In Edward's tone, Nightfall heard the same damnable nobility that had caused the king's late father to bind the boy to an assassin despised as an otherworld demon, named for the night-stalking creature of legend who terrified children's dreams.

"Well, yes, Sire," Nightfall admitted against his better judgment. "But just as a general 'maybe someday' type of—"

Edward would hear none of it. "If you promised . . ."

"Ned . . ." Nightfall warned, aware the king had no way of knowing to what dangers he was about to commit his adviser. By using the diminutive form of Edward's name, he also hoped to remind the boy-king that his companion, at thirty-four, was nearly old enough to be his father: older, wiser, and far more experienced.

Edward ignored the unspoken advice. "A man of honor holds dear even the least of his vows."

Nightfall crooked a brow. No words were necessary. Of all the men present, Edward alone knew his previous guise as the demon of legend, a vicious assassin who was anything but a man of honor.

King Edward's blue eyes held that fiery gleam of a personal crusade, a look that brooked no compromise. For whatever reason, he believed his adviser's actions reflected on him and on the esteem of Alyndar itself. Once those things came into play, nothing Nightfall had to say would accomplish more than angering his king.

Nightfall sighed, then turned his gaze back to a smiling Brandon Magebane. "Apparently, I'd love to help you. What would you like me to do?"

The healer's one-room cabin smelled of myriad herbs, some as sweet and pungent as nutmeg, others as overwhelmingly bitter as onion. Nightfall glanced around the windowless space at the four dingy chinked-log walls and the thatch ceiling. An eight-year-old boy lay on piled straw, his small pale body enveloped in a patchwork of bandages. One circled his forehead, encasing his ears in salve-smeared, bloodstained cloth. A fringe of fine, page-cut sandy hair surrounded a heart-shaped face, and large brown eyes peered back at Nightfall. The room's only piece of furniture, a small table, held a basin filled with medical supplies.

"Sudian," Brandon said, "I'd like you to meet Byroth."

The child continued to stare at Nightfall, managing a weak smile.

Nightfall nodded cordially, heart rate quickening. "What happened?" Though he intended the question for anyone, he continued to look at Byroth.

Apparently believing himself the target of Nightfall's inquiry, Byroth responded, "I don't remember." Looking at Nightfall's livery, he added, "Sire."

Having become accustomed to the "sirs" and "my lords" of the castle regulars, Nightfall remained unrattled by the excessive label of respect. "I'm just a servant, Byroth. No need for fancy titles." It was not technically true. Since his promotion, the help refused to claim him; and he could no longer move invisibly through gentried circles. He did not know exactly where his advisory position fell on the social spectrum, but he was certainly no longer a servant. He did not, however, wish to explain his abrupt and rapid advancement to Brandon and Gatiwan. Away from royalty and its stuffy pretension, he preferred to remain just one of the boys.

Byroth nodded. "I keep trying to think what happened, but I can't remember much. Someone grabbed me; I know that. Then, a lot of pain." He stiffened, then grimaced at the discomfort that small movement caused him. "After that, my father hugging me, my mother screaming. Lots of blood." He shrugged. "That's it."

"Thank you." Nightfall looked askance at the Magebane and his assistant. He despised sorcerers at least as much as anyone, had spent much of his life dodging them, and had nearly fallen victim to two. He particularly hated those who targeted children, though nearly all of them did. Simpler prey, the young were also more likely to accidentally or innocently reveal themselves as one of the natally gifted.

Brandon avoided Nightfall's questioning gaze to address Byroth. "Would you mind if Sudian examined your wounds?"

Byroth gestured assent. "So long as you don't . . . hurt me."

Nightfall declined the invitation. "I don't need to see them. Thank you."

Brandon Magebane glanced from man to child and back, then waved toward the door. "Why don't you try to sleep, Byroth. We'll come back in a little while."

Byroth's expression turned stricken. "You won't leave me alone, will you?"

"We'll be right outside," Gatiwan promised. "If we do leave, we'll post a guard."

With a nervous nod, Byroth closed his eyes as the men filed from the room.

As soon as the door clicked closed, Brandon rounded on Nightfall. "What do you think?"

Nightfall glanced around at the familiar city bathed in twilight. Narrow streets flowed between the wood and thatch cottages. His alter ego, Frihiat, had often limped out to earn drinks in the He-Ain't-Here with stories, a quiet simple existence detached from the knife's edge life of "the demon." Crickets screed their high-pitched song while the people scurried about finishing their work before sunset. Seeing and feeling no one near enough to overhear them, Nightfall turned his attention to Brandon's question, which held many possibilities. "What do I think about what?"

"The wounds." Gatiwan took over impatiently. "Do you think a sorcerer could have inflicted them?"

Nightfall blinked, lacking some of the information and not completely certain of the intention behind his companions dragging him to visit a wounded child. "Does Byroth have a birth gift?"

"Not that he's admitted," Gatiwan said. "But we haven't pushed that hard."

"What do the wounds look like?"

Brandon's scrutiny grew more intense. "You just passed up the chance to see them."

Though an expert on wounds and their infliction,

Nightfall shrugged. "You didn't give me a reason to." Not wishing to disturb the boy any more now than then, he added, "What does the healer think they are?"

"Stab wounds." Brandon also searched the dimly-lit streets. "Simple stab wounds, she thinks, from a regular old knife."

"Nothing weird and magical-looking? No burns or oddly shaped bruises?"

Brandon shook his head. "They look like stab wounds to me, too. But we can't be sure."

"No," Nightfall admitted. "You're never sure with magic." He had once faced a sorcerer who could freeze a man's head, then shatter it like the ice it had become. With a distant motion, Gilleran had opened an agonizing gash from Nightfall's hipbone to his buttocks. At a man's throat, that same spell might prove immediately fatal. The natal talents spanned beyond his imagination. The so-called "gifted," like Brandon and himself, each had only one special ability; but the sorcerers could juggle an assortment, limited only by the number and type of talent-cursed souls they could steal from their victims' writhing bodies. They especially enjoyed hunting down one another, as the ritual slaughter of another sorcerer meant gaining all the harnessed souls of the loser. That was the Magebane's salvation. It meant the sorcerers dared not reveal themselves or band together, even to destroy such an obvious and self-proclaimed threat.

Nightfall continued, "Besides, it doesn't matter how a sorcerer creates panic and suffering in his victim. Any type of severe emotional distress or excruciating pain brings the soul and its talent to the surface."

Brandon and Gatiwan stared at Nightfall, who suddenly wished he had not said anything. "What?" he demanded.

"You speak," Brandon said, barely above a whisper, "like a man with firsthand experience."

Nightfall did not like the Magebane's implications.

He had spent all of his life hiding his talent. Even Alyndar's king knew only that Nightfall had some sort of birth gift that sorcerers wanted. Nightfall would not reveal himself to two men he hardly knew. "Are you accusing me of having a natal gift? Or of being a sorcerer?"

Brandon's homely features opened questioningly. "You tell us which."

"Neither," Nightfall lied, then added, "but if either were the case, you know I'd have to give you the same answer."

"So just tell the truth," Gatiwan suggested.

Nightfall noted the serious expressions on the men's faces and mentally tracked the locations of the throwing knives he always carried. "How do you know I'm not?"

Brandon kept his voice steady and intense, though low. "Because when you first came to me, you needed something to help you fight a sorcerer who had attacked you and your master."

Gatiwan took over, the somberness of his expression highlighting the scar across his face. "If King Edward the Enthusiastic had a natal talent, he'd have displayed it for the world in the excitement of righting some injustice."

Nightfall tried to divert the conversation. "He prefers King Edward the *Just*."

Brandon managed a smile. "When he's old enough to temper some of that zeal with wisdom, he'll probably earn the nickname he wants. Until then—" Apparently recognizing Nightfall's successful tactic, Brandon returned to the matter at hand. "Are you a sorcerer or gifted?"

Gatiwan did not wait for an answer before adding in a voice like the crackle of old parchment. "Because it wouldn't be the first time Alyndar chose a sorcerer for a chancellor."

Nightfall knew the truth of that statement only too well. Though accustomed to being considered a murderous demon, comparisons to that heartless, conniving monster called Gilleran made even Nightfall ill. "I'm not a sorcerer."

"If you were a sorcerer, you'd say the same." Gatiwan reminded Nightfall in his own words.

"If I were a sorcerer," Nightfall corrected, "I'd kill my hell-damned, disgusting, slimy, hideous self."

Brandon laughed. "Believe it or not, I actually met a sorcerer with the self-control to never act on his birthright. And I didn't kill him." As if to catch Nightfall unaware, he asked quickly, "So what's your talent?"

"Even if I had one, I . . ." Nightfall started.

They finished in unison, ". . . would have to deny it."

With clear reluctance, Gatiwan returned to the case. "Byroth's the fourth child in a month."

That caught Nightfall's attention. As rare as the natal gifts were, it seemed highly unlikely a small city like Schiz could harbor four children with them. Of course, since those with the talents hid them for their own safety, no one really knew exactly how frequently they occurred. The best and most often quoted estimate was one in a thousand people bore natal gifts and, perhaps, one in five thousand had a bent for sorcery. "Tell me about the others."

Brandon ran a hand through his dark curls. "First one happened a year or so ago. Playmate of Byroth's, seven years old, drowned in the creek."

Though tragic, it seemed fairly commonplace. "What makes you think a sorcerer was involved?"

"I didn't at the time." The Magebane continued to finger-comb his hair, dislodging bits of bark and sand. "In hindsight, I noted a couple of suspicious things. The boy had a nasty head wound. The healer thought it might have happened afterward, when the current drove the body into a rock, but they found an awful lot of blood on the bank for it to have come from a corpse already dead. He had many bruises, but the ones around his neck seemed impossible for jutting rocks to have caused."

Nightfall was impressed. "You really delve into the details, don't you?"

Brandon's fingers stilled. "I do this for a living, remember? And these killings happened on my home territory."

"And the second one?" Nightfall tossed his own hair, cut short and plastered in Alyndar's style. He no longer missed the wild, filthy tangles he had worn in Nightfall guise and as Marak, nor Frihiat's bleached curtain, nor even the merchant Balshaz' neat locks. He had learned to appreciate the accuracy not having to peer around a chaotic frenzy of snarls added to his already deadly aim.

"An infant." Gatiwan cringed, and his face screwed up as if he might cry. "Stolen from its crib in the night and found mangled nearby the next day."

Brandon lowered his head.

Nightfall examined the facts critically. He had suffered and inflicted too much evil to feel anything for a baby he knew only in the abstract. "Did it have a talent?"

Brandon raised his shoulders. "We don't know for sure. Proud parents. First baby after years of marriage. They took him to a lot of gatherings. They think he must have done something in front of someone—could have been anyone. An uncle believes the baby might have given him a wicked pinch, and an aunt says he could have caused a flash of light." Brandon let his shoulders drop. "All after the fact, of course, so it's hard to know if they really remember these things or are just searching for some logic to a hateful act."

"Or telling us what they think we want to hear," Gatiwan added. "Wouldn't be the first time."

Brandon nodded. "They just want to help."

"Some help." Nightfall wondered how many ignorant people would prefer to believe a loved one died for the wicked desires of a sorcerer rather than without any cause at all. They had no way of knowing how the sorcerers bound the souls to their bidding, how the natally gifted suffered even after death until the sorcerer either died or the soul "burned out" and the sorcerer lost that particular talent. "And the third one?"

"Eleven-year-old." Gatiwan fully regained his composure. "Had a knack for getting her little brothers and sisters to sleep." He added suggestively, "An inhuman knack."

"A clear talent," Nightfall guessed.

"It's a wonder she made it to eleven." Brandon removed his hand from his hair, the curls popping back into disarray. "Though sorcerers tend to avoid coming this close to where I live."

"Except the really stupid ones." Gatiwan gave Nightfall another searching look, as if to remind him they had not yet ascertained whether or not he might be one.

Nightfall ignored the insinuation "Was she stabbed, too?"

"Stoned, apparently." Brandon shifted from foot to foot. "Found her wedged in a ravine covered with bruises and surrounded by rocks."

"Brutal," Nightfall said. In all his days as the demon, he had never murdered a child and no one in such a cruel fashion. "But there's only one way to know whether these killings might be related."

When the other two men just stared, Nightfall finished.

"Find out if Byroth has a talent. If at least two of the children did, that's a pretty clear sign."

"He won't tell us," Gatiwan reminded.

"Then," Nightfall said, "we might want to start with his parents."

Though tidy and sparsely furnished, the main room of Byroth's family cottage felt dangerously closed in to Nightfall. He had let Brandon take the most secure position, a stool pressed against one wall that granted him a full view of the fireplace, both windows, and the door. Nightfall understood the Magebane's need to see any danger before it struck and did not want to seem similarly hunted. Consequently, he found himself peering out the window at his back at intervals, unable to grant the parents his full attention. Gatiwan had chosen to sit on a storage chest between one of the windows and the door, while the mother hunkered on a rickety stepladder leading to an overhead loft. In two places, the main room opened onto children's bedrooms. Byroth's five sisters slept in one. The other still held the bloody straw pallet that had served as his bed.

Byroth's father had chosen a seat on the floor where he rocked himself like a fearful toddler. A large man with work-callused hands and strong arms, he now looked more like a lost child. His wiry hair lay wildly snarled, and he had not shaved in several days.

The mother had clearly made more of an effort to appear presentable in front of important company. Her black hair was neatly pressed, braided, and twisted on top of her head; and she wore a clean, if simple, shift. Her hands twisted in her lap, never still. "What can I tell you?" she asked expectantly. Though she had relived the terror more than once, she obviously hoped these professionals might find answers where others had failed.

Gatiwan's usually gruff manner softened. "We know this is hard for you, madam. We're just wondering if you could tell us what happened three nights ago."

The woman looked at her husband, who continued to weave back and forth, eyes unfocused. "Jawar's not handling this well," she explained. "Five daughters and only one stillborn son till Byroth came."

Nightfall nodded encouragingly. To a manual laborer, having strong assistants was important, and none came cheaper than one's own male offspring.

"He doted on the boy. Best friends, they did almost everything but sleep together."

Jawar murmured to no one in particular. "Nothing, nothing on this fair earth is precisely as it seems . . ."

All eyes jerked to the father.

Byroth's mother apologized. "He's been babbling since the attack."

". . . the placid plow horse, the deadly mosquito growing on a crystal pond . . ."

Politely, the visitors ignored the father's ramblings while the mother returned to the unanswered question. "We had gone out that night, as we often do, to the docks. That's where would-be storytellers, poets, and philosophers try out their ideas."

It was a long-standing tradition, Nightfall knew. As Frihiat, he had come there often, and the bartenders frequently attended, hoping to discover new talent. Occasionally, they did find someone worth paying, in coin or board, to entertain their customers. Frihiat had never made the cut, though Nightfall had used the persona to tell good enough stories to earn drinks from fellow patrons.

"The children were all fine on our return. All peacefully asleep." The mother gestured at the two rooms leading off from the one they now occupied. We went up to bed." She made a sweeping upward motion to indicate climbing the ladder on which she now perched. "Later that night, Jawar said he heard something outside and went to investigate. I had fallen back to sleep when I heard Byroth scream. I was scared, so I waited for Jawar to handle it. But when the screaming continued, I sneaked down to see. She swallowed hard, and tears obscured her eyes. "I saw . . . I saw . . . oh, Byroth—" She folded her face into her hands, the rest of her description muffled. "I heard a scuffle, a shout. By the time I dared to tear aside the doorway covering, Jawar had chased the assassin out the window and was cradling our little boy. Both covered in blood. On the walls, the straw, the floor. More on the window ledge, and I thought I saw a man's shadow disappearing into the night."

"You're sure it was a man?" Brandon interjected, their only clue thus far to the identity of the sorcerer.

"It could have been a large boy or woman. A trick of shadow." The mother heaved a heavy sigh. "I was too focused on my loved ones to pay much attention." Finally, she looked up. Moisture still blurred her eyes, but they held a deep hardness, a glint of hatred. "Whoever did this must be caught and punished." She turned her attention to her husband, and her look softened. "I believe Jawar saw the man who tried to kill our son, maybe even wrestled with him. But he's too distressed to talk."

Apparently believing himself addressed, Jawar muttered, "The bond between man and daughter is sacred; but the son, the son, is his true reflection."

"To talk *coherently,* " she corrected.

Gatiwan directed his gaze fully upon Byroth's mother. "So he's not making sense to you either?"

She sucked in another lungful of air. "Not since the . . . incident. He just sits there, quoting the poets and philosophers from the docks." She added, clearly to provoke her husband to anger if not reason, "I had always believed him a strong man who could handle terrible things better than me."

Brandon Magebane swooped to the father's defense. "It may not be his fault. The sorcerer might have inflicted some sort of spell on him."

The mother stiffened. "Sorcerer," she said weakly. "You think it might have been—?"

"We don't know." Gatiwan stretched his legs out in front of him. "We're here to try to figure that out." He did not mention that, if not, their interest in the case would evaporate. At the least, it would free Nightfall from his obligation.

Brandon added, "Do you know if Byroth had a talent?"

"Many." The mother gave her husband another glance. He had reason to know the boy better than she did. "But nothing magical. Not that I ever noticed." She shook her head. "No. No, I'm sorry. Byroth didn't have . . . a birth gift. Nothing a sorcerer would . . ." She trailed off, her head rocking harder, as if to convince the world of her certainty.

The father babbled, ". . . the placid plow horse, the deadly mosquito, the crystal pond." He glanced at Nightfall with vacant, hollow eyes. "The bond, the bond."

The woman waved at Byroth's bedroom. "I haven't gone in there since. Haven't touched anything. The knife's still there; he just dropped it. You're welcome to look."

"Look, look," Jawar echoed. "But why? That most obvious is hardest to see."

Liking this case less and less, doubting they could gather enough information to find the sorcerer if, in fact, one was even involved, Nightfall followed Gatiwan and Brandon to the bloody bedroom.

The scene yielded no useful clues, at least to Nightfall. The unadorned knife, well used and sharpened many times, might belong to anyone. The bloody footprints could have come from either parent as easily as from the attacker, and the scattered straw revealed nothing but an understandable struggle. The frowns scoring his companions' faces told Nightfall they found nothing more significant than he had. So, they returned to the healer's cabin and dismissed its guard, needing to confront the victim one more time.

Byroth seemed stronger to Nightfall this time, a testament to children's ability to bounce back from the worst of trauma. He handled nearly getting mauled to death better than either of his parents. "I knew you'd come back," he said.

Brandon sat on the edge of the bed. "Byroth, we're trying to help you, and your family, too."

"My father's gone insane," Byroth pronounced with the forthrightness only a child would dare.

"Not insane," Gatiwan corrected. "Just very distraught. We believe it will pass."

It was essential truth. Uncertain if shock, loss, or magic had unhinged the man, they could only guess whether time would cure him. The natal talents spanned such a gamut, Nightfall could only wonder if such a spell would last for days, weeks, or forever. If the sorcerer had such a power, he had not used it against Byroth. Further consideration brought an answer for that. Driven from his rational mind, Byroth might not react properly to inflicted pain; and the sorcerer might lose his soul. Nightfall shook off the thought, not yet convinced a sorcerer had attacked Byroth.

"But to help them and you," Brandon continued, "I need the answer to a question I already asked. Don't be frightened. We're here to help you and others like you, to keep you safe."

Byroth looked from man to man. He looked longest at Nightfall. "You want to know if I have a birth gift."

Brandon nodded. "Because, if you do, you'll need our protection. Perhaps forever."

Nightfall wondered just how many people Brandon warded and how he managed to keep them all safe.

Byroth said nothing, gaze still straying between them. Finally, he pursed his lips and nodded. "I ... can tell ..." He seemed to be measuring their responses as he spoke each word. "... if someone else ... has ... a birth gift."

Brandon and Gatiwan exchanged looks. "You can?" Brandon pressed, laboring not to strangle on his words.

Even Nightfall, the master of role-playing, could not stop his nostrils from flaring. To a sorcerer, it might prove the ultimate talent, the one he would risk everything to get.

"Like," Byroth continued. "I know you have a talent." He met Brandon's gaze. "But he doesn't." He gestured at Gatiwan, then turned his attention to Nightfall. "And you've got one, too."

Exposed, Nightfall kept his features a blank mask, ignoring the triumphant smile spreading across Gatiwan's lips.

"Do you," Brandon started, then paused to swallow hard. "Do you know what those talents are?"

"No. It just tells me you have them."

Now, Nightfall would not have given up the mission for anything. He had little choice but to commit himself fully to Byroth's safety. If a sorcerer got hold of that power, the talented, including himself, had no place to hide. One by one, the spell would expose them, and the sorcerer would feast upon them.

"Thank you," Brandon said. "I know that was hard, and I'm going to tell you something extremely important, then we will never mention this again. *Do not, under any circumstances, ever tell anyone else that you, or anyone you sense, have a birth gift.* Yours is a powerful talent, and there's not a sorcerer in any part of the world who wouldn't give his own . . . favorite body part to have it."

"Oh," Byroth said, dark eyes growing round as coins. Nightfall could feel his gaze on all of them as they exited. And, though he knew the boy was as much a victim of his natal talent as the rest of them, he could not help feeling like prey.

For the first shift, the Magebane assigned Nightfall to stay with the boy, Gatiwan to sleep, while he patrolled the outside. That suited Nightfall well enough. He could not have slept yet, not with Byroth's revelation hanging over him. The sentry position seemed better suited to him, given his background; but he had no intention of surrendering another of his deep dark secrets. So he accepted the assignment Brandon gave him, pausing only to leave word of his whereabouts with King Edward before settling in with Byroth.

The power of Brandon's words clearly had a daunting effect on Byroth as well. As the room plunged into a darkness the windowless room only enhanced, he rolled and pitched on his pallet, sleepless.

Hunkered near the door, Nightfall understood the

boy's restlessness. He fiddled with the stone in his pocket, one of Brandon's spell-breakers. It took the Magebane months to place his natal ability into an inanimate object, during which time he could not use his talent for anything else; and each stone just worked once. Since Brandon had not preplanned this particular hunt, he had made only two since his last outing and had given one to each of his companions. "Are you all right?"

Byroth's voice floated out of the pitch. "Just scared, I guess. I . . . don't want . . . to suffer like that again. You understand?"

"I understand." Nightfall sought movement, a shadow amidst the darkness, a wariness awakened by something he could not quite sense. "I understand. No one wants to suffer." Preferring quiet, he added, "Try to sleep. You need as much as you can get."

Byroth stopped talking, but he continued to flop around on the pallet. "Maybe if you sang to me?"

Nightfall rolled his eyes and shook his head, both movements the boy could not discern. His prostitute mother had never softened the night with lullabies, and the bawdy bar songs he knew did not seem appropriate. "I don't sing."

"Oh." Byroth slumped into a new position on the ticking. "Would you mind if I did it, then?"

Nightfall shrugged, still trying to make out objects through the gloom. He wanted it dark enough that any sorcerer who got past Brandon would not notice him, but he would need his own vision well adjusted. "Go ahead, if you think it'll help."

"Thanks." Byroth's thin, reedy voice floated into the cold, night air. "Hush, my darling, my sweetest babe—"

Nightfall ignored the boy, thinking of his encounter with Byroth's parents. They had seemed so broken, so utterly devastated by the near-loss of their son; they both clearly loved him fiercely. Nightfall had not lamented his own empty upbringing for many years: the mother who had alternately beaten and cried for him, the men who came and went, the father who could have been any one or none of them. *The bond between man and daughter is sacred; but the son, the son, is his true reflection.* Nightfall was once the true reflection of the men to whom his mother had sold her body, including the one who had battered her to death. Now, he had found a way beyond the poet philosopher's claim. *How much better have Byroth and his father fared?*

It was a question that needed no answer. Nightfall found himself trapped in recollection, the world fading into a dark void around him. His watchfulness withered, replaced by a mental world where word and sound came only from within. *Nothing, nothing on this fair earth is precisely as it seems. The placid plow horse, the deadly mosquito growing on a crystal pond.* In the world of the dreamer, nonsense can become a statement of vivid brilliance. *Nothing is what is seems.*

Suddenly, Nightfall understood. He closed his hand over the stone Brandon had given him. His fingers tightened with awkward slowness, seeking the laxity of sleep. He felt his head sagging, heavy as lead; and the welcoming darkness erased the significance from all but his dreamworld thoughts. But those focused him well enough. A wholly mental pursuit, he called on his talent to overcome the heavy inertia magical fatigue forced upon him, driving down his weight to a sliver of normal. Lighter than feathers, his fingers obeyed him. He drew out the stone, which now seemed more like a boulder, and hurled it toward the boy. It cut a glowing scarlet arc through the air.

The singing broke off in a high-pitched squeak, and Nightfall's senses returned in an overwhelming rush. He scuttled aside, and something sharp jabbed into his thigh instead of his privates. Restoring his mass, he kicked at his attacker, rolling as he moved. His attack also missed, and he dropped to a crouch, realigning, waiting for the other to reveal himself. It all made sense now. He knew who had attacked Byroth, and he also knew why.

A shadow lunged toward Nightfall, and a knife glinted in the slivers of light leaching through cracks in the construction. Concentrating fully on the weapon, Nightfall sprang for his attacker, Byroth himself. He caught the thin wrist, twisting viciously. The knife thumped to the floor. The boy screamed, pain mixed with frustration. His arms and legs lashed violently, wildly, toward Nightfall. Several blows landed with bruising force, but Nightfall bulled through the pain. He dropped his mass again and hurled himself at Byroth. The instant he felt the boy beneath him, he drove his weight to its heaviest. Air hissed out of Byroth's mouth, in a crushed and muted screech.

Expertly, Nightfall sorted limbs and parts until he had Byroth fully pinned and one of his own hands free. He flipped a dagger from his wrist sheath and planted it at Byroth's throat.

"Wh—" the boy started, forcing words around the tremendous burden crushing him to the ground. "What are you going . . . to do to me?" The voice sounded soft, pitiful, the plea of a confused eight-year-old.

Nightfall bit his lip. Even in his most savage days, he had never enjoyed killing. He could afford to choose his victims with care, and he based it upon his own judgment of their worthiness. He had never murdered a child, yet this was no regular child. Byroth was a sorcerer, one who had already shown a cruel streak far beyond his years. The first talent he had stolen, from a seven-year-old friend, had given him the means to detect the gifted from birth. He had callously slaughtered an infant, probably for the ability to heal more quickly or to make the huge leaps he had taken to attack Nightfall. He knew some people who could kill an eight-year-old without compunction, but most could never conceive of such a thing. *Brutal at eight; merciless by twenty.* Nightfall took solace from Jawar's words: *Noth-*

*ing on this earth is precisely what it seems. Byroth is no
child; he's truly the demon so many named me.*

"What are you going to do with me?" Byroth whispered again.

"I'm going," Nightfall said coldly, "to finish the job
your father began."

By the time Brandon Magebane and Gatiwan arrived, Nightfall had completed the deed. The two men
stared at the little body on the floor, the rumpled sheets,
the peaceful look on the corpse's face.

"I couldn't save him," Nightfall said, crouched beside
Byroth. He let grief touch his voice, not wholly feigned.
Though the others would misinterpret what he said, his
words were grim truth.

Brandon crouched beside Nightfall. "Don't blame
yourself. The sorcerer got by me, too. I'm not sure how."

Gatiwan grunted. "Some sort of teleportation spell,
I'd warrant."

Nightfall lowered his head. Lying came easily to him,
though not always for so noble a reason. No one but
him ever needed to know that Jawar had tried to kill his
own son. If the boy's father could eventually forgive
himself, at least he would avoid the condemnation of his
wife and neighbors. He had done the right thing, and
Nightfall planned to tell him that.

Brandon's hand dropped to Nightfall's shoulder. "At
least you managed to prevent the ritual. The talent died
with Byroth, and he doesn't have to suffer the limbo of
a harnessed soul."

Nightfall nodded philosophically. The ability to become a sorcerer was as innate as the gifts. That curse
had destroyed Byroth's soul long before Nightfall had
dispatched it to whatever afterlife it warranted. In the
process, so many innocents had been saved.

Gatiwan sighed heavily. "Let's go report this death to
the authorities."

Nightfall and Brandon rose together. "I think," the

Magebane said, winking at Nightfall, "at least the king of Alyndar will forgive us."

Nightfall was less sure. Though Edward's journey through other kingdoms with a demon for a guide had softened the world's colors, he still clung to a morality of crisp blacks and whites. To the king of Alyndar, all humans had an essential core of goodness; and their every action made sense in the proper context. At times, Nightfall appreciated his master's innocence. Any other monarch, knowing his adviser's identity, would have seen that Nightfall suffered a slow and infinitely painful death for the many crimes attributed to him. In his own inexplicably simple way, King Edward had instead placed the world's most notorious criminal directly at his side. *Actually, King Rikard did.* Nightfall could not forget that Edward's shrewd father, and his conniving chancellor, had initiated their relationship.

Over the last two months, Nightfall had come to grips with the startling realization that he had, in fact, genuinely earned Edward's trust. The extreme loyalty forced by Gilleran's magic, the over-the-top allegiance that had started as a facetious game had flared to bizarre and unexpected reality. Edward's effortless compassion had won over a demon who had once believed himself incapable of caring. Nightfall's mother had never merited even the innate love and trust of a child for his caretaker. Only three people had ever found Nightfall deserving of friendship: Kelryn, Edward, and his childhood friend, Dyfrin. The latter, he now knew, had saved him from becoming the conscienceless killer he, along with the rest of the world, had once believed himself to be.

Though only nine years older, Dyfrin had become like a father, guiding Nightfall with kindness and words of gentle wisdom. A natal mind reader with ethics every bit as solid as Edward's, Dyfrin had kept himself alive with odd jobs, entertaining sleights of hand, bets, and minor scams that preyed always on the greedy. He had harbored a soft spot as wide as a country for the needy and gave what little he had freely, without expectation of repayment or gratitude. *Until that bastard Gilleran killed him.* Nightfall's mind went instantly to the image of his best friend writhing against the ultimate agony, the gruesome rending of body from soul, the harnessing of his talent to the will of a sorcerer. His mind sparked to a fiery anger hotter than hellfire. His vision blurred, his fingers clenched to bloodless fists, and his heartbeat became a frantic pounding. He shoved the thought away with an effort that seemed heroic. Contemplation of Dyfrin's death always made him crazy.

Brandon Magebane reached for Nightfall's arm. Still more accustomed to violence than comforting, Nightfall jerked away, wildly spinning to a crouch.

Brandon stared. "Sudian, are you all right?"

Nightfall waited until his heart fell back into its normal rhythm before trusting himself to speak. "I'm . . ." He skipped platitudes in favor of something with a grain of truth, ". . . very tired." Not wanting to discuss his recent train of thought, he pressed back to the words that had brought him there. "King Edward won't hold us responsible for Byroth's death, but it'll disappoint him to know we couldn't protect an eight-year-old."

Gatiwan shrugged. Brandon said nothing, clearly weighing his words so as not to increase what must have seemed like Nightfall's feelings of guilt and responsibility.

"But it's not Alyndar's king I'm worried about," Nightfall continued, though he knew Brandon had only mentioned Edward's reaction as a joke. "We're way outside Alyndarian jurisdiction."

Apparently misinterpreting Nightfall's distress, Gatiwan huffed out a laugh. "King Jolund won't concern himself with the matter of a single death, and Duke Varsah gives the Magekillers wide discretion . . ."

Nightfall forced a smile. He did not worry for his current companions. Only a foolish ruler would alienate a man of the Magebane's power, and Varsah was no fool.

At the least, Brandon's presence would keep most sorcerers from Schiz. Hearing the duke's name aloud reminded Nightfall of the reason Edward and his entourage had come to the city, and the irritation that had haunted their two weeks of travel from Alyndar returned. Kelryn would have flayed him if he had fought too hard against something so important to Edward, but he wished the councillors and ministers had not given up so quickly. Handling Byroth seemed easy compared to the juggling act ahead of him. *Varsah's greed and Edward's damnable honor versus my wits.* He groaned. The odds of this battle seemed overwhelming, especially given his ignorance of noble's law and protocol. He only hoped that, when the time came, he would find the words to rescue the king from a life-altering mistake.

Still misreading Nightfall's discomfort, Brandon again reached for his arm, this time with slow caution. Nightfall forced himself to remain still as the long fingers closed around his forearm in a gesture of compassion. "Don't you go worrying about what anyone thinks of what happened. We'll handle the authorities. And we'll never so much as mention your name."

Though still not his concern, Nightfall assumed an expression of relief. These two men could do nothing to address his actual worries, and he did appreciate that they would keep the information to themselves. Anything that might be seen as an Alyndarian indiscretion became fodder for Duke Varsah, and Edward would undoubtedly feel responsible for any dubious action of his adviser. "Thank you. I'd like to go with you to speak with Byroth's parents."

"You're sure—" Brandon started, forestalled by Nightfall's raised hand.

"No fun, I understand. But I feel responsible." Breaking the news of a young son's death to stricken parents did not appeal to Nightfall, but he might never have another chance to put things right with Byroth's father.

"Then, I'd like to fall into anything reasonably soft that might serve as a bed."

Gatiwan coughed deeply, then spat on the floorboards. "About that bed. You're staying at the He-Ain't-Here?"

Nightfall nodded at information they clearly already knew.

Gatiwan grinned, his scar turning the expression wicked. "I'm afraid you'll have to settle for unreasonably hard."

Nightfall wondered what Gatiwan would think if he knew some of the places Nightfall had slept. He yawned to emphasize a tiredness not wholly feigned. "Right now, I could sleep on a bed of nails."

† Chapter 2 †

A fool fears nothing and calls it courage.
A hero conquers what he fears.

—Dyfrin of Keevain, the demon's friend

NIGHTFALL STEPPED into cool night air that carried the familiar scents of city nights. The last, acrid vestiges of cook fires still clung to the narrow roadways, tainted with thick meat smells, oils, and spices. A metallic tang mingled with the others, along with the odors of garbage, urine, and unwashed bodies that always clung to the alleyway debris. A quarter moon grazed the darkness, though clouds hid most of the stars and dawn had not yet added its pinkness to the sky. Insects hummed a steady chorus, pierced by irregular high-pitched chirping. In the distance, a polecat yipped like the cry of a lonesome baby.

Brandon and Gatiwan joined Nightfall in the roadway, closing the door on the grisly contents of the healer's cottage. Its click roused Alyndar's adviser to a realization just beyond understanding. Something felt wrong, out of place. Nightfall froze.

Brandon took the lead, heading into the threadlike

roadways with the confidence of a man who owned the dark streets. It was a bearing Nightfall knew well, one that would put off all but the fiercest, most desperate predators or those with no concept of danger. A man who regularly fought sorcerers had little to fear from common thugs. Gatiwan glided after his companion, clearly no stranger to the perils of any city's night. Neither seemed to notice the jarring suspicion that held Nightfall rigidly in place. Nevertheless, he did not dismiss his unease. He had learned to trust instincts that rarely failed him; and his reading of movement, sound, and shadow had always proved more acute than even the most cautious, the most hunted of other men.

"Let me do the talking this time," Brandon said, a hint of warning in his voice.

Gatiwan spread his hands in innocent question. Clearly, his direct manner had gotten him into trouble in the past.

"Wait," Nightfall said.

The other two men stopped and turned to look at him. "Listen."

Obediently, Brandon cocked his head, and Gatiwan went utterly still beside him.

Nightfall seized upon the silence to try to sift out what bothered him. He could still hear the up-and-down chorus of insects, the rare piercing cries of far-away animals. Every sense told him they were alone. Safe.

"I don't hear anything," Brandon whispered.

Gatiwan shook his head with a frown. "What is it?"

Nightfall hid his own discomfort behind an expression of intent focus. "I don't know," he admitted. "Maybe ... nothing."

Gatiwan made a gesture of dismissal, but Brandon took Nightfall's concerns more seriously. "What did it sound like?"

Nightfall shook his head. He could not yet define what was bothering him, was not even sure why he had identified it as a noise. "Paranoia." He allowed for a crooked smile. "My own." He tilted his head toward the parents' cottage, a strand of red-brown hair sliding across his brow.

Brandon led the way, but he shortened his steps and lost some of the cocky swagger of his earlier movements. That suited Nightfall as he and Gatiwan followed. Too much confidence might draw the meanest of the night folk, the ones who saw self-assurance as a challenge. The streets seemed much the same as Nightfall had known them. The character of Frihiat had had a distinct limp, slowing his walk and allowing a scrutiny of the streets that few of his other personae accorded him. Barrels lined the thoroughfares and alleyways, catching rainwater for drinking; and gutters guided the excess, along with wastes and refuse, toward the lower, northern edge of town. The shadows lay empty, the dimly lit crevices and puddled rooftops barren of thieves, street kids, and skulkers. Some of the homeless huddled in dens of piled thatch, shattered crates, and trash heaps; and Nightfall realized what had bothered him. No direct sound or movement had roused his suspicion. The normal dance of the night streets had gone off-kilter.

Nightfall froze in his tracks, his internal alarm growing more insistent. He found himself cringing without reason. Not long ago, he would have worried about Edward's safety, and the magic of the oath-bond would have spurred him to desperate action.

Allowing harm to come to Edward would have shattered the oath-bond, and Nightfall's soul would have become the property of Gilleran. Now, his heart hammered, anticipating the agony of the magic that no longer bound him to the prince-turned-king. The pain did not come, but the accompanying terror did. Danger in the city big enough to empty the streets of riffraff and send ruffians cowering into their holes likely involved the hasty, impulsively virtuous king of Alyndar.

It took Brandon and Gatiwan several paces to realize Nightfall had stopped. Both came to a halt and turned to face him.

"Coming?" Gatiwan said.

Nightfall shook his head.

Brandon tossed a nervous glance around the cottages, his usual arrogant courage lost. Few things disarmed a streetwise man more than mistrusting his own instincts, knowing something has gone amiss, yet finding himself unable to sense or calculate it. "What is it, Sudian?"

"I don't know." Nightfall continued to study the night, seeking solace in familiar rhythms. "But I have to get back to His Majesty."

Gatiwan grunted his understanding, but the Magebane showed a better appreciation. Brandon had more experience with the natural wariness of the natally gifted. Gatiwan did not have to worry for his life and soul every moment of each and every day. "We'll send along your condolences."

Though driven to leave, Nightfall fulfilled his duty. "Condolences, yes." He hoped he sounded more convincing than he felt. He no longer felt a bit of remorse for the killing. "Be sure you tell the father that his wounding of the sorcerer rescued many other men's sons and daughters."

Brandon tapped his broad lips thoughtfully. "You mean because the sorcerer's injuries made him too weak to take Byroth's soul?"

Nightfall hoped the Magekillers would continue along that line of thought. They would believe that, had the sorcerer come at Nightfall and Byroth at full strength, he would have killed Alyndar's adviser and taken the boy's soul. Though no stranger to deadpan lying, Nightfall hedged. "The father will know what I mean. Be sure they both realize Byroth's fate was sealed the moment he got his power. No one could have protected him—"

Gatiwan jumped in. "Brandon could have—"

"With that talent?" Nightfall frowned. "The Almighty Father could not have protected him, nor the sorcerer who obtained it, nor the one after him. The ability Byroth . . ." Exhaustion wore down Nightfall's caution. He wanted to say, "obtained," wished he could share the burden with his companions; but he dared not trust them. No matter the appropriateness of or the reason for the slaying, Nightfall would not willingly stand before the judgment of Duke Varsah nor place Byroth's father in that position. As much as he had come to enjoy camaraderie, Nightfall could never risk giving another man, especially one like Varsah, the upper hand. He started over, "That ability Byroth *had* was one of the greatest curses anyone could bear."

A light flashed through Brandon Magebane's pale eyes. "I could have stopped hunting. The sorcerers would have come to me. On my territory."

"Your territory; their terms." Gatiwan made Nightfall's point for him. "And what kind of life would Byroth have had? Living bait for the Magebane's trap?"

Driven to check on Edward, Nightfall finished his piece. "And make sure the mother realizes that, though she lost a son, she still has the father . . . if she shows him some compassion." *And forgiveness.* Without awaiting further comment or questioning, Nightfall fled into the night.

Amid the cloaking darkness and the cool night air, Nightfall felt at home in Schiz' threadlike byways. Huddled alone in shadows was the only place he had ever felt safe, hidden from his mother's bitterness, the cruelty of her clients, the predators who assaulted those lost children who did not learn how to cover fast enough. Then, a dark empty street had seemed like paradise. Now, he worried over the lack of rogues who normally owned the night alleys. Clearly, something troublesome had happened, dangerous enough that the people of the night feared to get involved or caught in the guardsmen's retaliatory sweep. *It's Ned. It has to be Ned.*

For an instant, the past overwhelmed Nightfall. Every instinct screamed at him to run and hide with the other monsters. He was the demon of legend, a creature unworthy of love or friendship, a survivor who tied himself to nothing and nobody. These moments of self-hatred had come upon him less frequently over time. When they threatened to overwhelm him, an image of Dyfrin always came to mind: the heart-shaped face, the tangled mop of sand-colored hair, the soft dark eyes that pierced the fiercest, most desperate facade. Dyfrin the brother; Dyfrin the father; Dyfrin the friend, truer than truth itself. The same Dyfrin who had rescued Nightfall from a conscienceless, soulless existence in life often came to him in memory after death, to save his humanity again and again. Nightfall now realized the feelings he had for Dyfrin were the same as those for King Edward Nargol, ones he now recognized as genuine friendship. And, though Nightfall once scorned ties to other people as a weakness, he now found himself as powerless to resist them as the feeblest victim. *Ned, you guileless dizzard, what have you gotten yourself into this time?*

Nightfall composed himself as he slipped from the end of an alley onto the main road housing the He-Ain't-Here. He took up the character of Sudian effortlessly, as he had so many others, so many times. He straightened purple and silver silks, speckled with road mud and plastered with grime. A hole gaped in the left thigh of his britches, the ragged edges streaked scarlet with his own blood. Only now he recognized the pain throbbing through the wound, the exhaustion weighting his limbs and forcing his thoughts to wade through his skull like lead.

Beside the red stone tavern, horses nickered and pranced in the paddock, uncharacteristically nervous.

Even Nightfall's usually calm bay stood with planted hooves, head high and nostrils sifting the wind. The amorphous, crudely lettered bar sign cast a shadow against the common room. A thin column of smoke wafted from the chimney, indicating a dying hearth fire, poorly tended.

Suddenly, the door was wrenched open with a shrill squeal of hinges. Two men dressed in black tunics with yellowish-brown trim meandered outside, one examining the door, the other scanning the streets.

Nightfall overcame an urge to melt into the shadows. He had every right to approach the He-Ain't-Here, and the presence of guardsmen only fueled the propriety of his actions. He hurried toward the men, both of whom looked up at his approach.

The taller of the two, lean and hungry-looking, spoke, "Excuse me, sir. Are you with Alyndar?"

Nightfall went utterly still. All speculation fled his mind, replaced by the grim realization that his worst suspicions had been confirmed. He instinctively shoved aside panic with strength of will, drawing up beside them before daring to answer. "I'm Sudian, King Edward's adviser. What's going on?"

The guards exchanged glances; and this time, the short, squatter man replied, "There's been a . . . happening, sir. We're trying to get the details."

"If you'll please wait here . . ." the other started.

Nightfall did not let him finish. Quick as thought, he slipped between the guards to look inside the He-Ain't-Here. The fire had died, leaving glowing logs coated with ash. Several massive lanterns lit the room like daylight revealing most of the tables lying on their sides, including the large one Edward and his entourage had used. Sword strokes scarred the edges. Several bodies lay in awkward disarray on the floor, one on the bar, and another draped over a three-legged chair. Blood and beer dripped from the walls, and scarlet puddles stained the floor beneath the bodies. A terrified huddle of men and women stood behind the bar, watching several other guardsmen sift through the wreckage. Seeing no sign of Edward among them, Nightfall headed toward the bodies. His heart rate quickened with every beat. *Ned. Where's Ned? Where in the blackest hell is Ned?* He ran his gaze over the carnage, seeking something on which to ground his understanding, any sign of Alyndar's king.

One of the guards caught Nightfall's arm. Nightfall gritted his teeth, fighting the urge to remove the hand at its wrist. Instead, he whipped his head toward the guard, wearing his sternest glare. Those blue-black eyes had stared down some of the most dangerous men in the world.

The guard dropped his gaze, appropriately cowed. "Wait, sir. We're still figuring out what happened."

"King Edward?" Nightfall said through gritted teeth. Even from a distance, he recognized several of Edward's bodyguards among the corpses: strong men, fierce fighters. A frantic, icy agony stole over him, and he channeled his terror into anger. He could not afford to act like a desperate mother seeking a missing toddler, and he did not dare entertain the possibility that Edward was dead.

"We . . . don't know," the guard admitted.

Nightfall wanted to throttle the man. At the least, it might startle someone into telling him something useful. Instead, he disguised building rage behind a tone of flat composure. "What *do* you know?"

The guard released Nightfall's arm, rubbing his hands together self-consciously while his willowy partner addressed the question. "It all happened fast. Over before we got here." He gestured toward the people behind the bar. "These folks were hiding under tables, behind the counter, tangled in chairs."

Nightfall flicked his attention to the witnesses, all of whom avoided his gaze. He recognized them, including the proprietor, his staff, a musician, and a handful of locals. "What do they say happened?"

The taller guard shrugged. "You're welcome to ask them. See if you can get better answers than we did." Frustration tinged his voice, and he visually swept the room through narrowed eyes.

Another pair of guards appeared from one of the two large back rooms that served as sleeping quarters. One spoke in a gruff voice as he entered the common room. "Nothing seems disturbed back there. There's a large chest still locked and undamaged in the secondary room. It—" He broke off at the sight of Nightfall, head bobbing as he studied the livery. "Who's this?"

The shorter guard answered for Nightfall. "King's adviser. He was out when all this happened."

"Was he, now?" The speaker examined Nightfall more closely, taking in the torn and bloody britches, and a hint of suspicion was evident in his tone. A large, well muscled man, he had a neck like a bull, topped by a jowly, red face. His partner looked as wiry as any thief, his movements quick, jumpy, and nearly constant. "What a lucky coincidence."

Not liking the turn of the conversation, Nightfall ignored the guards to concentrate on the witnesses. The Schizians might just as well hurl themselves against the red stone walls as investigate him; it would do nothing to help King Edward. He held out his hands in a friendly gesture, trying to look like one of the masses. "So, what did happen?"

The patrons and staff turned their gazes to the grimy floor, to the ceiling, to the supply room, anywhere except toward Nightfall. Some muttered their ignorance. Others shrugged or simply stood in miserable silence.

A fire seemed to light in Nightfall's chest. As the demon, a vicious snarl into any of their faces would open the floodgates of memory. As Sudian, the dutiful adviser, he could only coax and hope. He turned his attention to Gil, the proprietor, using an appealing tone intended to imply a bond had developed in the short time they had known one another. "What happened, *donner*?" He used a jovial term just shy of "friend."

Gil shook his head, sparse hair sweat-plastered to his freckled scalp. "I'm sorry, sir. I didn't see anything."

Nightfall fell silent, not allowing himself to surrender to desperate concern. He considered his options. He knew of few men capable of terrifying so many people into silence, and nearly all of those lived in the city of Trillium on Hartrinian, Shisenian, and Ivralian joint land. The huge crossroad city lay outside the jurisdiction of any of the four kingdoms, thus fostering lax laws and harboring the worst criminals. He found several solutions, many ways to open the mouths of men who chose silence; but none of them worked in his current identity. Frustration buzzed through his head, a bigger nuisance than the fatigue that came from missing a night's sleep. He had to remind himself that King Edward and his father had granted him a new life by declaring the demon dead, all of his crimes fully punished. Nightfall could effortlessly bully out the information unavailable to Sudian and the Schizian guards, but only at the price of undoing his pardon.

Nightfall played his role. He had never crossed personae and could not start doing it now. "Please, Gil. You must have seen something." Real desperation softened his tone. A senseless urge seized him to run in a wild, searching spiral until the whole world fell under his scrutiny; instead, he maintained composure. He would have plenty of time to worry. For now, he had to keep terror in check, to gather facts with calm dispatch.

Gil's plump features lapsed into irritated wrinkles, and he dropped to the floor. He assumed a position with his rear end in the air toward Nightfall and his head tucked between his arms and his chest. "I was like this. Like this!" He swiveled his head toward Nightfall. "Do you see any eyeballs in my ass!"

At the moment, Gil's ass looked more like a tempting target for the heel of his boot. Nightfall bit his lip, not trusting himself to speak until Gil regained his feet. "Eight or ten people died in here. Violently." He looked from person to person. "Your ears don't have to be sewn to your ass to hear something."

Gil pursed his lips. "I heard nothing." The group murmured assent, and the proprietor added. "No one heard anything. No one saw anything."

Nightfall whirled toward the four guards, who now stood together, watching his attempt with amusement. "What does that mean?" He tried to sound guileless and confused rather than accusatory.

The short, stout guard's brows rose in increments.

Nightfall's fists clenched at his sides. "What . . . does . . . that . . . mean?"

"For which word, sir, do you need further explanation?"

Nightfall did not need anything explained. He knew exactly what they meant, that someone had intimidated these people to the point where lying to the authorities seemed safer than speaking. He wanted the guards to tell him who wielded enough power to accomplish such a thing. "I want you to explain how an army burst into this tavern, causing so much death and destruction, in utter silence. How can so many people simultaneously get struck dumb and blind?" His own words brought another possibility to light, and he shuddered. *A sorcerer?* He dismissed the thought as unlikely. If magic had rendered the entire group innocently senseless, they would appear more confused than frightened, more talkative and less evasive. "But, mostly, I want to know the whereabouts and condition of my liege, King Edward Nargol of Alyndar."

The bullnecked guard ran a hand through short, brown hair ruffled to spikes. "We haven't found him yet. Either he left the tavern before the fighting started or . . ."

Nightfall knew the heroic young king would take exception to the words the guard had not yet spoken. "King Edward would never run from a battle."

"Then," the tall, thin guard said, "he might have gotten captured. We've seen no sign of him, dead or alive."

Nightfall drew some solace from those words. At least, Edward might still be alive. He doubted Edward's bodyguards would have allowed the king to leave the He-Ain't-Here without them, even just to relieve himself. If he had managed to go off alone, he should have returned when he heard the commotion in the tavern. Urination was not usually a lengthy process, especially for a young man. Nightfall spoke carefully, trying not to sound too worldly, "Let's assume, for the moment, that someone did abduct him. Why would they do that, and what's likely to happen next?"

The guards glanced at one another. The crowd behind the bar shifted warily. Finally, the tall, thin guard spoke. "Sudian, since you appear to be the only locatable living representative of the kingdom of Alyndar, I think it would be best if you brought your questions directly to the duke."

Suddenly seized in a grip of ice, Nightfall momentarily froze. His last discussion with the duke of Schiz had ended in angry shouting, imprisonment, and the threat of execution. Though it seemed as if he held all the cards this time, Varsah could turn that advantage against him in an instant. In his own element, the duke could threaten nearly anything, and Nightfall would be hard-pressed to call any bluff. As the cold prickles ebbed away, Nightfall cleared his throat. "Very well." He glanced down at the rumpled, stained, and bloody silks he had worn for a day and a night, through a fight and several walks through dusty streets. "Let me change my clothes first."

The guards drew together, exchanging looks but no words. Finally, the wiry one said in a voice like flint, "Of course, sir. We think everything's intact back there." He gestured vaguely over his shoulder toward the sleeping quarters. "But you can tell better than we can if anything's missing. We'd like to know what you think."

Nightfall nodded. No matter the appearance of the back rooms, he had little idea what he should think. It frustrated him that the one thing that might gain the information he needed to help Edward, retaking demon guise, would also destroy the bond between them. The gallant king would never forgive him harming, threatening, or killing anyone to assist in such a rescue, nor could any ruler keep on an adviser linked to the demon. Without another word, he headed for the quarters he shared with Edward and a rotation of bodyguards, feeling the eyes of every guard, worker, and patron boring into his back.

Nightfall slid the door open a crack, glad to find these hinges well-oiled. Surely, the hardware on the main tavern doors would be no harder to maintain, and Nightfall guessed the patrons had come to like the high-pitched squeal that announced every entrance or exit. Apparently, even an irritating noise could soothe when it became familiarly associated with a place of comfort. It was a notion not altogether foreign to Nightfall. He had returned unhesitantly to the mother who cursed and beat as often as cuddled him, though he did learn to read her moods, and eventually even those of strangers, with flawless accuracy. He slipped inside and soundlessly shut the door.

The room looked nearly the same as when Nightfall had last left it, the few changes reasonably attributable to the king and his bodyguards having spent most of a day and night in there since. A glimmer of moonlight trickled through the only window, and the heavy curtains hung still, unstirred by a breeze carrying the scent of fire. The proprietor had brought in three reasonably comfortable pallets: the ticking firmly wrapped in cotton thick enough to dull the sharp edges of straw. Neatly draped blankets covered the pallets. Piled straw lay against one wall, the usual makeshift accommodations of the He-Ain't-Here now reserved for an extra sleeper or a comfortable roost for an alert sentry. Aside from a change of clothing, now spread across one pallet, Nightfall carried no gear he could not fit on his person at all times. A guardsman's dusty pack lay beside the piled straw. A battered chest supplied by the proprietor stood at the foot of Edward's bed, and a man-sized shadow flickered beside it.

The movement seized Nightfall's instant attention. He crouched, waiting.

Nothing happened.

A draft from the window stirred through Nightfall's hair, cold against sweat-dampened skin. He remained in place, keeping his own breathing silent, his every muscle still. Like most predators, humans were drawn to motion.

Still, nothing moved. Only the musical sounds of the night touched his hearing. Nevertheless, Nightfall remained in position past those critical moments when most men believed themselves safe. Hopefully, his silence would convince the intruder that a guard had only glanced inside, then retreated.

The other took the bait. Nightfall again saw movement near the end of the king's bed. With wary slowness, the chest's lid lifted in increments.

Trained to caution, Nightfall barely noticed the pain cramping through his injured leg, the protest of sinews too long in one place. He kept his gaze locked on the activity, scarcely bothering even to blink.

At length, a head poked cautiously over the lowest edge of the chest to peer inside it.

Stock-still in the shadows, Nightfall now held the advantage. His eyes had adjusted to the scant moonlight funneling through a window set nearer to the stranger than himself. He watched as a darkly gloved hand settled onto the edge of the chest, and the other man's head tipped downward to study the contents more closely. The profile gave Nightfall an image of shaggy, short-cut hair, a pointed nose, and a scraggle of beard.

His attention wholly on the stranger, Nightfall freed one of the throwing daggers at his wrist. The other man shifted, raising his head to sweep the room with a glance. Apparently blind to the lurking danger, he returned to his task. One hand dipped into the trunk to rummage through Edward's personal effects.

"Be still," Nightfall said.

The man made a graceful leap onto Edward's bed.

Nightfall threw the dagger. It grazed the fabric of the stranger's breeks, just short of the inner thigh, then embedded in the wall with a satisfying thunk. Before it did, Nightfall snapped another hilt into his hand. "A finger's breadth higher, you're a eunuch. An arm's length, you gurgle. Want to take your chances I missed on purpose?"

The man froze. His position now fully revealed him as a stranger: a young man only just mature enough for the beard. His gaze slipped toward the window, measuring.

Nightfall wanted to dare the boy to test his quickness against Nightfall's, but he held his tongue. He had already pressed to the edge of his character. Instead, he moved his hand slightly to allow moonlight to gleam from the second blade. That would serve as warning enough. "What are you doing here?"

The boy licked his lips with nervous flicks of his tongue. He said nothing.

"Look," Nightfall started, watching the other for the slightest tensing that might betray an attempt at escape. "I'm usually a tolerant man. But the folks in the common room won't tell me anything, and I'm going to get answers one way or another."

The stranger swallowed hard. "I . . . I . . . don't know what you're talking about."

It was a lie, and Nightfall knew it. As always, he read the unspoken nuances in expression, gesture, posture, and movement as well as word. That skill had kept him alive every bit as much as his natal talent for weight shifting. "What happened in the He-Ain't-Here tonight, and where is my master?"

"Your–your master?"

The boy was stalling, and Nightfall had no patience

for it. "King Edward of Alyndar." He added a deliberate knife edge to his voice. "Where is he? You've got to a ten count to answer." He started immediately. "One. Two . . ."

"Wait!" the young man said with soft force. "Stop counting."

"Three. Four . . ."

"All right!"

Now, Nightfall did stop. He gave the youngster a two count for throat clearing and fidgeting, then continued, "Five!"

The words tumbled out in a squeak. "There was a big fight here. I thought . . . I thought I could take some things without anyone noticing."

Though a plausible explanation, it was nonetheless untrue. Nightfall sensed the deception as easily as breathing. "You work for the killers!"

"No!"

"What do they want from King Edward? Where did they take him?"

"I don't know." The stranger's gaze gave him away, divided between Nightfall and the window. "I don't know anything."

The similarity between his claim and those in the common room clinched the connection. Nightfall's free hand tightened, and he willed himself calm and in control, of himself and the situation. He wanted to warn the young man that talking served him better than silence, that Nightfall could inflict worse than the man or men his silence protected, that loyalty to these killers was not worth dying for. But those were the demon's words and would have to remain unspoken. "Tell me," he said with a slowness that verged on a Grifnalian drawl, "what you *do* know."

A slight stiffening revealed the younger man's intent a split second before he moved. Though there was plenty of time for Nightfall to hurl his dagger, he did not. He simply watched as the stranger made a wild leap for the window and surveyed lethal targets as he scrambled through it. In Nightfall guise, he would have had to kill the youngster, if only to maintain his reputation as a supernaturally informed demon: conscienceless evil with uncanny reflexes. Now, he relished the choice allowing him to let the boy go free. If he needed to, he could find the youth again and use whatever means necessary to force out the truth.

As Sudian, Nightfall flipped the dagger and replaced it in its sheath. Crossing the room, he eased the other blade from the wall, still pinning a scrap of fabric from the stranger's breeks. He replaced that, too, attention on the window. The intruder might return, or another come, to find whatever had drawn the first. Keeping his head low, he glanced outside. Darkness faded before the rising sun, and rainbow bands of color touched the far horizon. Candlelight flickered in the nearby cottage windows.

Swiftly, Nightfall changed his clothes, then pawed through Edward's things searching for the object that might have drawn the thief. It seemed like a hopeless task. Edward always brought more gear with him than Nightfall could imagine needing. On their last excursion, he had made it his mission to surreptitiously lighten the load, while Edward insisted on crafting palisade defenses every time they stopped to camp. He shoved aside myriad pieces of heavy armor, creams and vials he now recognized as toiletries, and a mass of purple and silver clothing. Smaller objects sifted through the mass to clunk against the wooden bottom. He examined these: a comb, a brush, a hand mirror, and a ring.

Nightfall dropped to his haunches and shook his head. He could only guess at the purposes of the thief, the kidnappers, and the killers. Too many ideas bombarded his mind, and he needed more information to sensibly sort them. Though he dreaded it, his conversation with Duke Varsah might give him some clues. When the duke had taken then-Prince Edward prisoner,

Nightfall had made a desperate and wild run through the dungeons to save him. Only later he discovered highborns do not imprison royalty in dungeons but in furnished quarters that could dazzle a peasant family. Ignorance of the upper class turned his considerations of this new crime into unsophisticated nonsense. If the thugs intended assassination, they would surely have left Edward's body in the tavern or, at least, in some highly prominent place.

Nightfall wound the ring through his fingers as he considered. Though crafted of fine gold, with small rich-purple stones nestled on either side of a flat setting, it did not seem as valuable as most of the items in the chest they had brought to appease the duke of Schiz. Its contents included platinum coins and diamond jewelry, a far more likely target for thieves; but the guards had proclaimed it safe.

Nightfall examined the ring more closely. A competent jeweler had drizzled and engraved the flattened central surface to form an intricate picture of Alyndar's mailed fist clutching a hammer. Six tiny amethysts sat in semicircular patterns on either side of the image. He had seen Edward wear the ring to court or affairs of state, though he had never looked at it closely before. Now, guessing it to be the thief's target, he pocketed it.

"Are you ready in there, sir?" The voice of the burliest guard wafted in to Sudian.

To meet with that bastard, Varsah? Nightfall readjusted his fresh tunic. *Never.* He headed toward the door, smiling sweetly. "I'm finished. Sorry I took so long, but you did ask me to check on our possessions." He stepped back into the common room. The bull-necked guard and his partner met him nearly at the opening, while the other two stood with the crowd behind the bar. "I think I foiled a thief," he said, not bothering with details. "You should probably keep a guard on that locked chest in the second room."

Gil finally spoke coherently, "I had a bouncer stationed there until the guards herded him in here." He glanced toward Hervandis, a solid, no-necked Schizian who could not turn his head without moving at the waist. "I could put him back on duty."

Nightfall added ice to his tone. "I'd rather one of the town guard. Someone brave enough not to cower behind his own ass, deaf and blind, while assassins slaughter innocents in the tavern."

Gil clamped his mouth into an angry white line, though he said nothing more.

The first guard who had spoken to Nightfall moved toward the center of the room, barely hiding his own smile. "We'll get right on that, sir. Thank you."

It still felt strange to Nightfall to have men scurrying to obey his orders, without the need for intimidation. Though he liked the power, he hoped he would not have to become used to it. He preferred the quieter, more unobtrusive role of adviser at the king's side. As much as he appreciated his freedom, he did not enjoy having people parsing his every utterance, nor the realization that any mistake could cause ill will to an entire kingdom, perhaps even a war. He looked forward to handing over the mantle of control to Edward or, at worst, to his successor. "Then I'm ready to go. Who's my escort?"

The guard's smaller partner stepped up. "Me, sir."

Nightfall gestured to the door, then headed toward it himself, the other man rushing to his side.

They stepped out into a morning that smelled of cook fires and lamp oil. People shouted to one another across distances, the common folk as yet oblivious to the goings-on in the He-Ain't-Here the previous night. Nightfall knew that, once the guards released the tavern's patrons, the news would spread swiftly. Schiz' lowest class had already adjusted its patterns to suit the tragedy, and the effects would ripple outward and upward to every corner of the city. It wasn't every day a king's entourage got murdered and the man himself went missing, and most would not even know the best way to react.

For now, the chilly walk through threadlike city streets felt strange at the side of a guardsman. Nightfall fell into step beside the smaller man, observing how the bronze-colored stripes on his cuffs and sleeves bunched with every step. Sandy hair fell in a straight sweep to his ears, sliding onto his forehead at intervals. The cool air turned his cheeks to pink circles, and he kept his mouth clamped tightly closed.

Shortly, they came to the cobbled streets surrounding the duke's citadel. Neatly tended plots held scraggly vegetables, their stalks touched brown with autumn. The flower beds lay barren, the dying stems plucked and bulbs buried deep within the dark soil. From the center rose the stone-block citadel that served as a home for the duke and his family. Some of the lower-story windows were shuttered, and others bore glass to keep out intruders and the elements. Most of the second-story windows lay open, some with lacy or heavy patterned curtains fluttering in the breeze. Lanterns lit several of the rooms.

The guard led Nightfall to the front porch and its heavy oak door. He knocked vigorously.

The door eased open. A young, female face poked out, round-eyed and heavy-featured. When she caught sight of the guard and his companion in Alyndarian silks, she curtsied. "What can I do for you, sirs?"

The guard spoke for them both. "Please inform the duke that Sudian . . ." He hesitated, apparently expecting Nightfall to fill in the rest of his name. Alyndarian highborns usually had a family name or, at least, finished their formal title with the name of their fathers and "'s son."

Nightfall said nothing. Coming from the lowest of the low, he had no family name, could not even begin to guess the identity of his father.

The guard finished anyway, ". . . adviser to *missing* King Edward . . ." He stressed the significant word, surely to direct the girl to inform the duke about the problem as well. ". . . is here."

It seemed odd to Nightfall that the duke might not know about such a significant happening in his domain. Word spread through the underworld in moments, and any ruler worth his weight in salt should have equally valuable sources. Clearly, his guard force had learned of it and come to investigate. Then, Nightfall remembered how the guards had peered through the doorways during their last conference, clearly worried he might let slip their inability to stop his crazed and fruitless rush through the empty dungeon. They had not reported it to Varsah, presumably because he overreacted to mistakes. Nightfall could see how the guards and servants might hesitate to awaken their lord, even with news of import.

The girl seemed to take no notice of the oddly emphasized word. She simply curtsied again. "Follow me, please." She led them through the familiar wide entry hall to the immaculate, white-walled meeting room with its three doorless entries. "Please make yourself comfortable. I'll let Duke Varsah know you're here."

Nightfall glanced around the room. It looked much as he remembered it from his last visit. A fire danced on an ashy pile of logs in the fireplace, sending shadows flickering along the rectangular-cut blocks that formed its outline. Occasionally, wood shifted, and sparks exploded from the movement. The mantel held an array of intricately carved warrior figurines engaged in a miniature battle. Above them hung a flattering portrait of Duke Varsah dressed in glimmering bronze mail, draped flamboyantly in a cape of midnight black. His figure seemed more muscled than stout, the jowls and wrinkles smoothed from his face, and his frizzled graying hair a youthful black. Cradling his helmet, he stared into the distance, his chin raised regally and his dark eyes strong and full of wisdom. Framed with notched daggers, the picture stood out boldly, a remarkable accent to an otherwise drab room.

Nightfall glanced at the two plush couches facing a

matching chair he knew belonged to the duke. He debated taking Varsah's seat only for a moment. The guard would surely not allow it. Though the arrangement of the furniture would grant the duke some power, it seemed preferable to the superiority he would gain by throwing Nightfall out of his chair. When dealing with crooks and killers, position could spell the difference between obedience and attack, but he doubted royalty worried about such mundane things.

Between the sitting areas, a rectangular table held a chessboard, its ivory and alabaster pieces in their starting positions. Nightfall walked around it to take a seat in the center of one of the couches. He had not bothered to disarm himself this time, and the guard had not asked him to do so. Nevertheless, he became abruptly aware of the many throwing daggers he carried: in wrist and boot sheaths as well as secreted in his clothing. Though Edward had offered it, Nightfall did not carry a sword. He had too little experience with close fighting to bother with something as likely to trip him up as save him. He relied on his wits, his stealth, and his long practiced ability with hurling daggers.

That thought brought memories of Dyfrin. The two had spent countless hours flinging things at one another: initially wooden blades, then blunted ones, then lethally sharpened steel with deadly accuracy. Named "dagger catch," the game had become their greatest threat and their salvation. At first luck, then skill, had kept them both alive. Nightfall had even discovered a trick Dyfrin could never master, one the older man had labeled the "razor rebound." It involved Nightfall catching, rather than dodging, a hurled dagger and sending it instantly and precisely back upon its wielder. That move had nearly ended the game, until Dyfrin learned to anticipate it and Nightfall to deliberately miss. It had rescued Nightfall's soul in an inn in Nemix called Grittmon's, where he had caught a dagger intended for Edward. Unfortunately, he had grabbed it by the blade, opening a gash in his hand. The next dagger had found him in better position, and he had razor rebounded it, saving both of their lives.

Now, Nightfall opened and closed his left hand in remembrance. The scar had become lost in the normal creases of his hand, though colder mornings reminded him of it with a dull ache. He tossed the thought aside, working to hone his wits to the sharpness of a blade. Against Duke Varsah, words would prove the more important weapons. *Words and knowledge, and I'm pitifully low on ammunition there.* That realization brought Nightfall full circle, and he smiled at another favorite saying of Dyfrin's: "You know, Marak . . ." He knew Nightfall best in his Nemixite sailor role. ". . . I'm sure we're learning something useful with this game; but doesn't it seem foolish to practice disarming ourselves in battle?"

The guard cleared his throat nervously. "I'm sure Duke Varsah won't be much longer."

Nightfall waved dismissively. "No hurry. I'm shy on sleep and enjoying just sitting here without demands made on me." Though based on truth, it was a lie and a dodge. The idea of facing off with the shrewd and loathsome duke kept exhaustion at bay. He dreaded the moment the man walked into the room, and the battle of wills and words that would follow; yet he also wished this business already finished. All he really cared about was finding the king alive. If Duke Varsah could help him reach that goal, he had to think of the old man as an ally.

Figures gathered at two of the entryways, whispering amongst themselves. Apparently, word of his arrival had spread swiftly among the guards and servants.

Nightfall leaned back against the plush cushions of the couch, fighting the urge to rest his boots on the chess table. He had learned highborns considered it rude to place one's feet, even shod, anywhere except the floor and one's own pallet.

A pair of guards entered through the empty doorway, taking positions at either side of the duke's chair. Nightfall's escort stiffened, which cued Nightfall to stand. A moment later, Duke Varsah appeared between two more of his guards. The duke wore blue silks trimmed with lace, which stood out brilliantly against the guards' black uniforms and their muted, tawny cuffs. Though approaching seventy, he walked with the straight-backed ease of a much younger man and without the aid of a steadying hand or walking stick. His steel-colored hair lay slicked back so tightly with perfumed oils that Nightfall could barely detect a hint of its usual frizzled texture. Dark eyes burned brightly in a creased and jowly face, full of a learned wisdom Nightfall would never understand. His own came fully of experience and street smarts.

One of the guards introduced him, "Duke Varsah of Schiz."

Nightfall bowed, as custom demanded. He knew from his previous encounter that the duke expected him to speak his own name and title. "Sudian, adviser to King Edward Nargol of Alyndar." He finished to find Duke Varsah utterly still.

The duke's eyes grew wide, and his lids seemed to disappear among the wrinkles. "You!"

Nightfall banished a smile, hardly daring to believe how easily he had gained the upper hand. He turned his attention to the duke, awaiting a command or question.

A heavy silence followed. Nightfall searched his mind for some indication he had missed some obvious detail of manners and protocol. He could think of none but did not trust himself to believe that meant none existed.

Duke Varsah thrust a finger toward Nightfall. "You belong in my dungeon! Not only for insubordination, unbefitting language, and threats against royalty, but for jailbreak and kidnapping as well."

"Kidnapping?" That one caught Nightfall by surprise.

"You . . . you stole a prince from my confinement."

"Ah." Now Nightfall understood. Varsah considered it a crime that he had taken Edward with him when he had escaped the duke's custody. Since that had been Nightfall's intention from the start, he found it difficult to tweeze the tidbit from the rest of his crimes.

"I could have you executed!"

Nightfall's heart rate quickened. He could feel it pounding against his ribs. *Could he?* He had considered many possibilities, but not that particular one. He kept his tone composed, a perfect contrast to Varsah's puffing, and played a hunch. "No, Lord, you couldn't."

The duke took a backward step, clearly unused to being contradicted. "What?"

Nightfall used exactly the same low tenor, "No, you couldn't."

"I couldn't?"

If you could, you obnoxious bastard, you'd already have me in your dungeon. "I'm not a servant any longer. You'd need Alyndar's consent to execute the king's adviser."

Rumbling laughter erupted from Varsah's throat. He headed toward his chair, though he did not sit. "If that's what you believe, you make a poor adviser indeed."

All right. Missed that one. Nightfall scrambled to save face. "Duke Varsah, King Edward finds me capable enough." Another lie. He knew Edward had promoted him from a sense of friendship, gratitude, and loyalty, not because of his ability to evaluate royal situations. When it came to affairs of house or court, Edward turned to wiser consultants; and Nightfall would rather sleep through the boring intricacies of the king's day. He took another tack. "And how would it look to Alyndar to find the king missing, his guards dead, and the only surviving member of his entourage killed by your hand?"

Duke Varsah went silent, gaze distant. He lowered himself into the plush chair without bothering to glance at it.

Nightfall could practically see the windmills and waterwheels of the duke's mind spinning as he contemplated that idea and took it in his own personal directions. *Uh-oh. What did I start?*

The duke snapped out of his reverie with a wide flourish of his hand. "Go! Go all of you. I'd like to speak with Sudian in private."

Nightfall considered swiftly, seeking the motivation behind such an odd decision. It had to bode ill for him. "No!"

The guards paused in mid-scramble. Every gaze snapped to Nightfall.

Varsah licked his lips. "No?" he repeated, his cheeks turning scarlet. "No? Now you also presume to command my guards?"

"No," Nightfall repeated, though he did not specify whether he had answered the question or merely reinforced his own order. "If they leave, I leave, too." He did not fear for his physical safety. He could outrun and, certainly, outfight a seventy-year-old man. He guessed the duke had more dangerous intentions. Likely, he would claim Nightfall had done or confessed something during their private conversation that would lead to his imprisonment or city-sanctioned murder. "My lord, with all due respect . . ." It had become Nightfall's favorite phrase. The highborn seemed to consider it polite, while the word "due" left him license to believe the amount minimal. "My liege is missing, plucked from your city; and you seem to care more for old insults than a king's disappearance."

The guards gasped in a nearly collective, audible breath.

Duke Varsah tensed to speak, but Nightfall did not give him the chance, continuing swiftly. He deliberately drew the blame onto himself so the duke could take no offense. "I'm afraid I don't trust myself alone with you, armed and angry. I might do something we both would regret." He shook his head while the duke considered his own next words. "No, Lord, your guards must stay, or I must leave."

Anger flashed through Varsah's dark eyes. Nightfall

had cornered him. "Very well, then." He made a reluctant gesture. "Stay." He turned his gaze directly onto Nightfall. "But realize we cannot speak of . . . personal matters."

Yeah, fine. I'll keep my bed and toileting habits to myself. "My lord," Nightfall started, uncertain of the best way to finish. "I understand. All I really wish to know is what has become of my master."

Duke Varsah blinked, then formed a tight-lipped smile. "You mean, your liege, don't you? As you reminded me, you're not a servant anymore."

Nightfall made a broad, acknowledging nod. When King Rikard had first placed it in the oath-bond that Nightfall refer to Edward only as "master," he had despised the very idea. Titles confused him. He was not even sure "lord" was right for a duke, though Varsah had not yet corrected him. Clearly, it was no insult. *Ned.* He pictured the young king, his golden hair flying as he stormed off in pursuit of justice for some overworked slave or underappreciated peasant. He looked every bit the part of a prince: jarringly handsome, his silks and armor always pristine, his head tilted in that faraway position that suggested he always had something of great import on his mind. Though guileless in his simplicity, he had had manners bashed into him since infancy, and he did everything with a clear strength of purpose. Though he preached peace, and meant it, he could hold his own in a battle with the best warriors. That last had caught Nightfall wholly by surprise when he had cheated to try to make Edward the winner of a tournament the young man had then proved he could handle by himself.

Nightfall had once believed himself incapable of trusting anyone. He considered bonds of love and friendship a weakness for enemies to manipulate. Nevertheless, he realized Dyfrin's kindnesses in his youth had left him vulnerable. He cared what happened to Kelryn and to Edward. He knew a devotion to both of them transcending the boundaries of his previous world: Kelryn as his lover and soon-to-be wife and Edward as a friend as close as any brother. He finally allowed the deeper realization of the king's disappearance to sink in. He might never see King Edward of Alyndar again. The thought brought deep despair, and all the fatigue he had held at bay seemed to assault him at once. "Please, Duke Varsah. I just want to find my . . . my king." He looked up, too tired for more games. "Your guards said you might know the best way for me to find him."

The sudden change in Nightfall's demeanor seemed to unbalance the duke as well. The rage left his eyes, and he stared in silence at his apparently demoralized visitor. "I . . . it's . . ." He cleared his throat and started again. "Sudian, it's surely money his captors want, the treasures of a kingdom. My suggestion: you return to Alyndar and await a demand for ransom. Depending on how long and carefully they planned this, it may already have arrived."

"Thank you," Nightfall said, meaning it. The duke's insight went a long way toward helping him understand this situation. "But, my lord, who would do this?"

The guards shifted, and a few whispers showed that, clearly, they thought the question foolish, the answer obvious.

Nightfall did not agree. If the most notorious criminal in the world had never heard of such a thing, it was clearly not the realm of common thugs.

"Another kingdom?" Duke Varsah guessed. "A barony in need of money? It's hard to say."

Stunned, Nightfall had to work to question. "But isn't that an act of . . . war?"

"Not necessarily. If it's done without casualties and the prisoner is detained in a way appropriate to his status—"

Apparently shocked beyond thought of consequences, the guard at Nightfall's side interrupted his leader. "But there are casualties! Ten Alyndarian royal guardsmen—"

Varsah jumped in as quickly, a frown deeply scoring his face. "Yes, this one is different. A war could ensue, but we know Alyndar's council is wise enough to establish the enemy before risking innocents."

Now Nightfall finally understood the duke's discomfort, his need to approach in attack mode. Varsah worried fury might drive Alyndar's army against the place that had harbored the king at the time of the kidnap, and he might pay dearly for the crimes of a group of vicious killers. Nightfall could not help considering the possibility that Varsah had played a role in the slaughter. It might explain why the witnesses chose silence while in the presence of his guardsmen; yet Nightfall dismissed the possibility. Varsah had every reason to want Edward and his entourage safe, at least until after their meeting. The naive, bachelor king with his guilt-riddled conscience seemed perfect fodder for a wily duke with designs on advancing his lineage to a kingdom, especially since Edward traveled with only his most inexperienced adviser. Nightfall wished Varsah had had a hand in the murders and abduction; it would have meant he could wipe the insolent grin from the duke's face with the full force of Alyndar behind him. Yet, he felt disappointedly certain of the old man's innocence.

Either because he guessed the natural direction of Nightfall's thoughts, or simply to accentuate his own, Varsah added, "Alyndar must understand we had no role in these terrible events, nor did we have any foreknowledge of them. If we had, we would have done everything possible to protect King Edward Nargol."

Though he preferred to let Duke Varsah suffer, Nightfall spoke the words he needed to. "Lord, I know." Even as he appeased the duke, Nightfall continued to work through the problem. No logical mind could have predicted Edward's abrupt and emphatic decision to ride to Schiz and personally apologize to a duke who better deserved a punch in his arrogant, jowly face. Edward's entourage had stopped in several towns along the way, yet news could travel only so fast compared to a mounted party. Killing ten of Alyndar's most able soldiers and capturing her warrior king required coordinating a vast number of swift and skilled assassins, as well as time to organize and practice the blitz. Nightfall knew enough about crime, both major and petty, to feel certain the kidnappers had to have known the destination of the king and his escort at least a week or two in advance.

Nightfall frowned. The entire trip had only taken a fortnight, which meant the killers' information could have come from only one source: Castle Alyndar. *A traitor?* Nightfall pursed his lips, suddenly afraid for those loyal to King Edward, but none so much as his betrothed. A rational portion of his mind urged him to stay in Schiz, to explore every possibility while the trail of the missing king remained warm, but his heart overrode all other necessity. He could not leave Kelryn in possible danger.

Clearly unnerved by Nightfall's long silence, Varsah leaned forward. "When your king is ransomed and restored, I pray he will return to the duchy and enjoy the comforts of my guest room."

It occurred to Nightfall that Duke Varsah had become more helpful and direct after Nightfall had dared to reveal some weakness. All of his life, he had associated power with strength and control. When he needed information, he bullied it from its sources. When he wanted something, he took it by stealth or force. He had brought it all together into a single black-eyed stare of the demon, known to turn violent men into obedient informants. The legends far exceeded his dangerousness, but those who believed needed no demonstration. Knowing Varsah awaited a more substantial reassurance, Nightfall complied. "I'll let those in charge know of your regret and, when I can, inform His Majesty of your invitation."

"Thank you." Duke Varsah smiled, but his eyes revealed calculation. "I'll send two parties to Alyndar: one by sea, which is faster, and the other by land to return Alyndar's horses. You can choose which group to join. My men will help carry belongings and see to it you arrive safely." He added, as if in afterthought, "And I'll table the king's past crimes, and your own, until his return visit."

Weighted by exhaustion, tired of the game, Nightfall saw how he could end it with a simple nod. He had disposed of Varsah's notion of execution, of turning a few moments of private conversation into some world-shattering and horrendous lie. They had even chatted calmly, each daring to expose a bit of vulnerability to the other. For now, that should have been enough; and yet, to Nightfall's mind, it was not. "Lord, I appreciate the escort, and I'm sure Alyndar's ..." Forgetting the term the duke had used for the gathering of highborns, he substituted, "... gentry will appreciate your efforts." He left his tone open for a challenge. "I hesitate to contradict ..."

The wrinkles deepened on Varsah's hoary face, and all sign of worry and weakness disappeared.

" ... but I believe, given the circumstances and location of King Edward's kidnapping ..."

The red circles reappeared at the duke's cheeks, and a vessel pulsed in his temple.

" ... that all of our so-called 'past crimes' ..."

The duke's fists clenched, and the scarlet gained an edge of violet.

" ... should be put to rest." Nightfall added, in case his attempt at flowery language had not been completely clear, "Forgiven. Forever." Then, as it seemed a long time since he had spoken a title, he added, "Duke Varsah."

The duke looked about ready to explode. Veins now pounded at both of his temples, and his face had gone positively dark, his eyes narrowed and his brows arched low. He ground his teeth, saying nothing.

Politely, Nightfall waited. The last time the duke had looked like this, Nightfall had wound up imprisoned. Then, Varsah had called him ill-mannered and lowly bred, some of the truest words ever spoken. Now, however, the tables had turned. Whatever Nightfall's past, he walked in royal circles, trusted by a king. The city of Schiz needed to curry favor with Alyndar. It was one thing for Nightfall to return with the news that the mission which had sent them to Schiz never got completed, quite another for him to report that, despite the king's kidnapping, Duke Varsah had refused it. Almost by accident, he had cornered the duke and earned himself a strong enemy in the process.

"Without restitution? Without a wedding for my humiliated and violated daughter?"

Nightfall knew he could tell the duke's men to bring the loaded chest to Varsah, knew that would placate some of the man's anger. But, at the moment, he savored Varsah's discomfort. Nightfall had despised the duke when the first condescending words dropped from his lips at their original meeting. He had wanted to best the obnoxious duke of Schiz since the idea of marrying Willafrida to Alyndar's king had first crossed the old bat's mind. Dyfrin would advise him otherwise; Edward would revile his tactics. This time, however, Nightfall stayed true to himself, turning the words of those highly ethical examples against Varsah. "A man of principle needs neither blood nor money to do what's right."

Varsah's fists cinched the plush arms of his chair so tightly, he left indentations in the shape of every finger. "Very well," he spat. "You're free to go, and my men will join you in the morning for the journey back to Alyndar." He leaned forward, brown eyes seeking Nightfall's attention.

Nightfall let him have the full effect of his evil blue-black stare.

"Sudian . . . if I never see you in my court again, it will be sooner than I care to do so."

It was a clear threat, softened by the fact that the glare did its work.

Duke Varsah looked away first.

† Chapter 3 †

*Learn men by deeds, not words. It is the most evil
who generally believe themselves most good.*

—Dyfrin of Keevain, the demon's friend

A HALF-DAY'S JOURNEY brought Nightfall and the
duke's men to the Hartrinian port city known as
Brigg. Though none of his personae had based themselves here, Nightfall knew it reasonably well from his
time as Marak the sailor and as Balshaz the merchant.
Those two traveled in very different circles, allowing
him to familiarize himself with all parts of the city. As
Marak, he had stuck to the northern half, concentrating
on the docks and the nearby businesses that sprang up
around them: mostly rundown shops, inns, taverns, and
bawdy houses. Balshaz had claimed the more civilized
southern areas housing the richer folk, a higher class of
accommodations, and more expensive goods. The jew-
elers kept their best wares here: the perfect diamonds,
rubies, and sapphires in settings of finely polished metals, while the dock shops sported the cheaper uncut,
flawed, or lesser valued stones. He had learned to find
bargains near the docks as well, where even the fresh-

est food, the finest wares, could not command as high a price.

Nightfall had gotten to know his Schizian escort mostly indirectly. A host of ten guards answered to a nobleman of uncertain rank whom they addressed as Sir Ragan or, simply, sir. He wore silks of olive green with a ghastly orange trim at hem, collar, and cuffs; and tooled leather shoes swaddled his feet. To Nightfall, he looked like a field of autumn gourds. His hair nearly matched the trim, its color only a bit more natural and cut into a layered style that scarcely managed to thicken it. He bore a nobleman's proper girth, and he buried a rash of freckles beneath a heavy coating of too-pale cosmetics.

The guards spanned a broad spectrum, from their massive leader with his shock of russet hair to a scrawny blond with the bleached skin and soft hands of a noble's son, which he probably was. The group kept to themselves, speaking to Nightfall only when absolutely necessary and with the utmost respect. They called him "lord" as often as "sir," and some bowed when addressing him, dodging eye contact. So far, Nightfall appreciated their distance. Left alone, he had time to sort through the crush of emotions he had earlier kept at bay, to think about how best to address King Edward's disappearance, and to handle his own situation. As a servant, he had appreciated that same lack of interaction, yet he found a major difference here. The guards did not talk freely around him as they would around a stable boy. Instead, they clung to silence in his presence or to conversations lacking any depth or opinion. If he wanted to know their gripes, thoughts, and intentions, he would have to actively snoop for them.

A handsome bay mule hauled a cart on which the men had placed the remaining effects of Alyndar, including the chest of gold and jewels intended for Duke Varsah. As this left little room for supplies, the men carried their own in worn leather packs slung across their backs. Aside from a single change of clothes, Nightfall's minimal things fit on his person; he kept the ring he had rescued from the thief in a close and secure inner fold of whatever he was wearing at the time. Ragan had strapped his pack across the withers of the mule.

A lanky guard with a hawklike nose and huge gaps between his teeth dipped his head at Nightfall. "Sir, we've a ship waiting for us at the docks. Does it suit you well enough to eat on board?"

Nightfall saw no reason to act disagreeable. Marak had always been his favorite personae, the one in which he knew Dyfrin and Kelryn. Dining on deck seemed as familiar as on land. "Certainly." He tried to recall where he had seen this man before.

Leaning against the cart, Ragan apparently overheard. "Sudian, have you ever dined on a ship before?"

Nightfall considered briefly. Overseas travel tended to be expensive and dangerous. Pirates ruled the seas; and one could get anywhere, albeit more slowly, overland. The pirates had learned to leave the military ships alone, and most of the regular merchants paid for their safety. Any other ship was an open target. "No," he lied, as much from curiosity as consistency with his character. He wondered if Ragan's response would display some empathy he had, thus far, wholly concealed.

But the nobleman simply nodded and turned as if to leave.

Nightfall gave the sneering noble a second chance. "Why do you ask?"

Ragan stepped back around to face Nightfall, but he said nothing. He appeared to be thinking.

Nightfall knew what the other man ought to say. Many became ill just climbing aboard a ship; the rocking motion of an unstable bow caused vertigo, nausea, or both. Eating usually worsened the effect. Even those not prone to seasickness tended to slop food over themselves with every unexpected movement. "Perhaps you were going to warn me about the differences between eating aboard and on land?"

Prompted, Ragan managed a smile, though crooked and unfriendly. "Differences, yes. I just wanted you to know that sailors can get a bit coarse with their language. And the fare will tend toward fish, sea plants, and suchlike."

"I like those," Nightfall said, still waiting for Ragan to mention the ill effects of traveling by ocean. Even those who had never set foot upon a deck had heard tales of men green-faced and vomiting over the rails. Nightfall had seen it firsthand many times. Sometimes an experienced sailor, who had weathered many meals in motion, could grow queasy or muddleheaded on a particularly stormy voyage or on a day when he could not quite center his balance. Nightfall had never personally suffered that fate. His natal weight-shifting ability allowed him to adjust his mass to every subtle movement. Instinct and time had trained him to do so in a manner that kept his step light and his faculties fully under his control. "And I've heard more than a few rude words in my lifetime."

"I'm sure you have." Though muttered darkly, Ragan's words were still faintly audible to Nightfall. He cleared his throat and spoke more directly. "Then, it shouldn't be a problem. I just thought you ought to know." Once again, he turned on his heel; and, this time, Nightfall watched him go.

Nightfall looked at the hawk-nosed guard who had remained quiet throughout the nobles' conversation. "It doesn't take the great brain of Harandy to figure out he doesn't like me."

The guard nodded briskly, flushing at the address, "No, sir." As his head descended, Nightfall remembered where he had previously seen the man. When he had dodged and darted through the duke's defenses seeking Prince Edward, he had flung himself on top of the dungeon cells to avoid a mass of pursuing guards, including this one.

Nightfall smiled. "Drop the 'sir,' please. We're old friends."

The corners of the guard's lips twitched despite a clear attempt to hold any expression from his face. "Old ... friends ... sir?"

"Surely you haven't forgotten. You can't chase some lunatic through the duke's dungeons every day."

No longer able to hold his emotions at bay, the guard smiled broadly, fully revealing the checkerboard of gaps and yellowed teeth. "What ..." He studied Nightfall's face as he spoke, clearly worried to overstep his boundaries. "What were you thinking?"

Nightfall encouraged the man with a grin of his own. If the noble who led this expedition had decided to hate him, he would need the goodwill of the guards. Too many things could "accidentally" happen to him on a five-day sea voyage. "I'm a promoted lowborn, new to the quirks of nobles. Didn't realize highborns consider a plush room an adequate prison for one of their own." He winked at the guard. "It's a wonder they're not committing crimes all the time."

The guard glanced around, presumably to ascertain that Ragan could not overhear. "I'd love a few hours or days of that kind of lockup. No responsibilities. Surrounded by comfortable furniture and rich food."

Both men stood in silence for several moments, the guard apparently contemplating the details, Nightfall biding his time.

The guard spoke first. "You're Sudian, right?"

Nightfall nodded.

"Name's Harvistan. You know, you're quicker than snot from a rheumy nose."

Nightfall had never heard that particular expression before. "Is that a compliment?"

"Slicker, too."

Nightfall's brows shot up. "Apparently not a compliment."

Harvistan shook his head, sandy hair flying. "No, no. I do mean it as a good thing. You're fast and really hard to catch."

"Thanks," Nightfall said, believing his forced companion meant his words as praise. "I'm really just very loyal. And, at the time, very desperate."

The guard grunted, a sound Nightfall would have liked defined; but he knew it was not yet time to test the fragile friendship with such questions. He would have plenty of time on the voyage.

Harvistan excused himself. "Need to get back to work, sir."

"Right." Nightfall ignored the guard's return to formality. Harvistan would consistently drop the title of respect when he felt comfortable enough to do so. To press now would only delay that moment. "Which ship should I be boarding?"

Harvistan turned his dark gaze toward the mule cart. "It's called *The Sharius,* named for the captain's wife, I think. Just get yourself there. We'll bring Alyndar's things aboard for you."

Nightfall nodded his understanding, hoping he had never worked with any of this ship's crew. It was a relatively small consideration. Kelryn, alone, had ever recognized him across aliases, and then only one time. He found himself thinking of her now: the slender dancer's body with its perfect firm curves and almost unnatural grace, the plain features surrounded by short white hair cut into feathers, the soft hazel eyes that seemed to see right through his hard exterior to his every discomfort and hidden insecurity. Like Dyfrin, she seemed to know him better than he knew his own self, but she did not have the mind reading talent that had proved Dyfrin's strength and his downfall.

Leaving the mule cart in the guards' capable hands, Nightfall headed toward the docks.

A double-masted, square-rigged ship, *The Sharius* bobbed at her mooring while Ragan, Nightfall, and the Schizian guardsmen shared a meal mid-deck. The nine-man crew did not join them, busy checking the lines, canvas, studs, and riggings, calling to one another in the language of their creed. Nightfall enjoyed their chatter, a soothing familiarity that gave him something to concentrate on while his own escort ignored him. Two of the Schizian guardsmen hugged the rail, gazing longingly at the city beyond the docks. Neither ate a bite of chowder, nor even the coarse brown bread the others broke into hunks and tossed into their bowls to soften.

Shortly, the nobleman set his chowder aside, half-eaten, and ran a sleeve across a brow spangled with sweat. His face held a greenish cast as he stumbled across the deck to the two guards and whispered something to them. Both managed weak smiles, and all three men headed aft.

Though amused by the irony, Nightfall continued to eat in silence. For now, Ragan and his two companions could hold off seasickness by disembarking; but *The Sharius* would cast off that night, separating the men from their haven. It seemed only fitting the man who had chosen not to warn Nightfall of the discomfort some feel on a rolling ship now suffered it himself.

Nightfall watched the sailors work as he continued to eat, enjoying the salt tang in his nostrils, glad for his utter lack of responsibility toward the ship. Because of his slightness and dexterity, he had suffered the task of handling the topsail, including reefing; which, in foul weather, often meant hours of wind-whipped labor. He had sailed with many captains and helmsmen: some as old and steady as salt, others as moody and fickle as the winds, and still more tough and unyielding. The sea, too, could be gentle as a kitten or raging as a monster, often within the same hour; and, no matter their personalities or proclivities, the captains could not afford any mistakes by their crews. The Hartrinians made the worst bosses. They tended to overwork and mistreat their free-hires much like their slaves, though they rarely had trouble recruiting sailors. They commanded sleek, fast ships carrying spices and perfume for trade. Few sailors could resist the easy responsiveness of a well-made craft, and the pay tended toward the generous given the expensive cargo and the fewer number of hands with which to split the take. The slaves were unpaid, and the well-built ships did not require as many crewmen as most.

The helmsman called for a hoisting of the sails. As the sailors hauled the clew tackles and bowsprit lines, Nightfall could see the triple squares of the main canvas held no official standard. Pale yellow, they bore only the abstract image of a plump and curvaceous woman, painted with a few wavy lines on the lower yard. Apparently a private ship, it bore no ties to any kingdom.

Finished with his dinner, Nightfall set aside his bowl. The chowder left him contentedly full and warm despite the rising evening wind off the ocean. The lap of waves against the hull, and the dulling of the sky, brought a welcome sense of comfort he had not known in the last few days. Exhaustion blunted his thoughts but could not overcome the wariness that had kept him alive this long. He looked forward to sleeping, rocked by the rhythm of the swells, and wondered about the quarters. The crew usually bunked in the forecastle, the captain and the helmsman aft. Guests stayed below decks, and their comfort depended on the ventilation and the ship's last cargo. If he found the lodgings unsuitable, he knew he could haul a blanket out on the deck and sleep beneath the stars with the chill night air ruffling over him and the skitter of wind through the sails.

Three of the Schizian guardsmen approached Nightfall; the scrawny blond with the noble's hands, a compact swarthy man, and a graying redhead who went by the name of Ivin. The blond cleared his throat. "Harvistan says you're quick."

"Quicker than quick," the swarthy guard added. "Like a squirrel."

Uncertain how to respond, Nightfall shrugged. "I guess I can be . . . squirrel-like . . . when I need to be."

He glanced at Harvistan, who displayed his gap-toothed grin. Four more Schizians watched the goings-on with clear interest. The last two guards, including the leader, ignored them. The latter seemed engrossed in sharpening his sword, while the other had not yet finished eating.

"Show us," the young blond said. "Please."

"Show you?" Nightfall gathered his legs into a crouch, uncertain where this request might lead. He watched the blond for any sign of impending attack, but nothing in the young man's demeanor suggested he intended his words as a threat. "Show you . . . I'm fast?"

"Like a squirrel," the blond reminded. "Do something zippy and tricky. Interesting. Like, like you did—" Now the boy swiveled toward Harvistan. "Like when you ran all around . . ." He faced Nightfall again, and his voice grew louder, more assured. ". . . the duke's citadel."

Nightfall glanced at the other men, trying to brush off the youngster's request as the overexuberance of a child. The men bobbed their heads sympathetically, but in every eye Nightfall read a desire to join in the prodding. They all wanted Nightfall to perform, and it discomforted him. He had rarely considered using survival skills and his talent as a way to influence people or to make a living, only in the most desperate situations. The idea of leaping crazily through stays and spars just to entertain his escort seemed ludicrous. He had never cared what anyone thought of him, had never understood Dyfrin's incessant desire to have people like him.

Yet, Nightfall also knew that gaining the guards' respect could work to his advantage. At the least, he might find out why the nobleman poised to address Alyndar's council about the king's disappearance disliked him so much. At the most, one of the Schizians could give him some important clue that might lead him to Edward and the kidnappers. Men of the guards' abilities tended to look down on people without definitive talent, to see them as a lesser form of humanity not worth a moment of their time.

Nightfall glanced around the familiar confines of the ship, knowing his time as Marak gave him great advantage here. The sailors continued to scurry about, cheeks flushed, brows damp despite the autumn chill. They wore bright yellow shirts to match the sails and linen pants stiffened with salt. He had no intention of doing anything that might interfere with their work, especially so near cast off, yet he knew how to dash around and even through them without so much as brushing an arm, slowing a step, or touching a running line they might need to prepare.

Without warning, he flung himself between the guards, spinning through them before they had a chance to react. He came up in a leaping sprint, covering the ground between them and the gunwale in an instant. Dropping his mass gained him more speed as he sprang to the rail and danced across it as lightly as a mouse. Exertion swept a thrill through him. He had never bothered to move so fast with no one in pursuit, nothing imminently deadly weighing upon his mind and heart. For that short space of time, he existed only to amuse; and the troubles that had distressed him since returning to the He-Ain't-Here seemed leagues and lifetimes distant.

Nightfall caught the railing with his hands and swung down to the docks. Weaving effortlessly between passengers and dockhands, he dashed across the planking without leaving a single solid footfall. As soon as each bare foot hit, it rose for the next movement, guided always by his ability to anticipate and reroute his balance without the need for thought. He jumped atop a box, then a stack of precariously piled crates, back to *The Sharius'* bulwarks. Somersaulting over the railing, he landed on the deck, restoring his mass for a satisfying thump. The moment his toes struck planking, he was off again.

Nightfall knew the spar plan of similar ships like the creases on his palms, yet he had not often had the chance to use the riggings as his playground. He knew better than to touch the footropes and stirrups the sailors were using to loosen the billowing canvas from its gaskets, to check the tackle, and to ascertain the worthiness of the sails. The sudden change in the distribution of weight could pitch one or more to their deaths on the deck or into the sea. Instead, he shinnied up the mainsail shrouds and stays, dodging the running rigging, the buntlines and clewlines the crew would need free to set the sails. He kept himself dangerously light, both to quicken his movements and keep him from jerking anchoring lines or yards.

"Hey!" someone called in a harsh Shisenian accent. "You topside!"

Nightfall froze, one arm wrapped around the yardarm and both feet braced against the mast. He found the speaker not far below him, adjusting the iron ring at the tip of the upper yard. A heavy-set, bearded man with skin like leather, he glanced at Nightfall through dark, hooded eyes. "While you're aloft, could you clout that topgallant stay a mite port?"

Nightfall had to stop himself from following the request unquestioningly. "Huh?" he returned, pretending not to understand.

"That stay. The topsides one, mate. Can you give it a knock a bit to port?"

Nightfall looked upward, in the direction the man had indicated. He could see the uppermost stay quite easily, and it did seem off-balanced. "I'd be happy to help you, but you'll have to speak one of the world's known languages."

Balanced by his underarms over the yard, the sailor finished his job and looked up at Nightfall. "You a lubber?"

"If you mean 'not a sailor,' " Nightfall said, knowing exactly what the man had meant. "That's me." In usual circumstances, it was probably easier for the sailor to do the job himself than to explain the nomenclature; but this involved a job at the highest point of the ship.

The sailor grunted. "Damn, what a waste."

Nightfall fought a smile. He scrambled up the futtock shroud and swung onto the topmost yard. He had nothing to cling onto here but the tiniest protrusion of the mast and the backstays that held the fore and aft lines. The wind whipped through his hair, the gentle roll of the moored ship amplified by height. He added mass, worried a gust might take him down, though he had little to fear from a fall, so long as he angled himself for the water. His low weight would ease his descent, and the ocean would cushion the impact. He closed his mind to memories of previous, recent falls, ones that had nearly resulted in his death; his climbing exercise on Alyndar's castle tower had done its job. Nevertheless, he usually preferred not to test the extremes of his talent.

The sailor inclined his head. "That there! That . . . iron . . . thingy." He struggled to shake the jargon. "Near your right hand. Can you . . . push it . . . summat . . . left . . . ward."

Nightfall obeyed, performing the task precisely while feigning ignorance. "Like this?"

"Good enough, thanks." The sailor resumed his own work, then shouted up to Nightfall again. "You know, you don't belong up there. You could get hurt."

Nightfall threw back his head, letting his hair ride on the wind. The salt air smelled like perfume. The mild toss of the ship felt like the soothing rock of a mother's arms. The cries of the sailors were music. As Marak, he had never bothered to savor those pleasures. He had found only discomfort in skin baked to leather, hands as rough as sandpaper and more callus than skin, fingernails shattered to the quick. Now, those seemed like forgotten joys from a younger, happier time. He wondered if he had discovered the secret to highborns' happiness: without the responsibility, he could find thrills in other men's drudgery.

On an impulse, Nightfall gauged the distance and proper arc to the water. Keeping his weight relatively low, he flung himself out and over the deck. Regret struck instantly. His heart pounded as the mast and riggings sailed past him. A maneuver meant to fill him with giddy excitement, to simulate flight, instead brought a sense of wild terror that bordered on panic. Action usually focused him, brought the world into vivid clarity that slowed time and enhanced thought. This time, mind and body screamed together that he had made a fatal mistake. In midair, he had little control of what came next. The memory of his last fall overwhelmed him, bringing back muffled memories of agony: his shoulder, his hand, the stabbing shock of every breath.

Nightfall waded through the strange sensation of fear overtaking logic, forcing himself to tuck and drive his weight downward as he struck the foaming water. The impact barely hurt. Cold water closed around him, muting hearing to a dull rumble and stinging his eyes with salt. Shocked free of the mind-numbing dread, he swam easily to the surface, searching for the same exhilaration that had brought him to this position. As soon as his head broke the waves, his ears filled with clapping and cheers. Sailors and guards alike stood near the rail, applauding an act he could only consider stark insanity.

For a moment, Nightfall froze, again assailed by fear. He had drawn attention to himself in a way he never would have dared in the past. It did not matter that he had gained admiration rather than notoriety or terrified obedience. He had deliberately lived his life in the shadows. To do otherwise, he knew, might spell his death. He had dodged his mother's rages by disappearing when she sought a target, by remaining quiet and docile to avoid further fueling her ire. He had survived the wild streets by dodging predators whenever possible. Quickness and cunning had served as better tools. Even the demon had never needed bluster. The populace feared the mysterious figure of darkness, his subtlety more terrifying than any outright threat.

Nightfall forced himself to move. The seawater dragged the heat from his limbs, slowing body and wits. He had wanted the guards' respect, and now he had it. Circumstances had changed, and he needed to change with them. If the part of Sudian required grand displays of mischievous whim, then he would play that role with the same seriousness with which he did every other. Perhaps he might even learn to enjoy it wholly, without the worries dredged from the more practical, deeper parts of his being.

Rather than force the sailors to unburden rescue lines, Nightfall changed his course for the docks. He caught the planks, dropped his weight, and effortlessly hurled himself over the railings. Though meager here, the wind chilled him to the bone. He shivered wildly, restoring his weight. *Smart. Kill yourself with fever showing off for a bunch of men you'll never see again.* Before he could take a dozen steps, five of the Schizian guards surrounded him, draping him with woolen blankets.

The scrawny, young blond ducked under the folds as they walked toward the ship. "That was splendid! Amazing! Did you do all that for me?"

Nightfall did not reply, savoring the mass of the blankets across his back, head, and shoulders and the instant warmth they provided.

The blond did not seem to notice he had gotten no response. "My name is Dawser, by the way. Can you teach me to climb like that?"

The other guards ignored Dawser. They clapped Nightfall on the back with the hearty greetings of an old friend.

"Well, done, donner," Harvistan said, his mouth against a fold of wool directly over Nightfall's ear.

"Impressive."

"Stupendous!"

"Astounding performance. Ever think of becoming a

guard?" That last question, from graying Ivin, struck Nightfall as so funny he sucked in a mouthful of salty saliva, sending him into a round of desperate coughing.

Dawser withdrew. The back pats continued, and a swarthy, middle-aged man with eyes dark as coals said, "Now what'd you have to go and say that for, Ivin. Becoming a guard. What a terrible thought. Why would you want to wish our lot on anyone?"

They all shared a laugh, then, which gave Nightfall time to regain his composure.

"You know," Harvistan said, still grinning. "A little dance on the side pieces probably would have sufficed."

"Hear, hear!" three said simultaneously, though one added, "Though not half as fun."

Arriving at the ship, they bundled Nightfall back aboard. A cabin boy met them as they stepped aboard, bowing vigorously and repeatedly. Blond and densely freckled, he appeared to be about ten years old, probably the captain's or a sailor's son. "Excuse me, my lord. Please, my lord. I thought you might like to go to your cabin now."

My *cabin?* Nightfall nearly walked right past the boy in his astonishment. "Me?"

The boy's cheeks flushed, and the freckles leaped into bold relief. His bowing became more agitated. "Yes, my lord. You, my lord." He paused mid-bow. "You are the Lord Chancellor Adviser to the King of Alyndar, are you not?"

Though Nightfall heard way too many syllables in that title, he could not wholly deny it. "I suppose that's me."

"Follow me, my lord." The boy headed midship, shoulders tensed, walk stiffened by nervousness.

The guards gave Nightfall a few more pats, and several took back their blankets, leaving only one. He pulled that last around his head like a cloak. Though sodden, it seemed better than nothing.

As the boy led Nightfall around the main sail, several of the sailors paused to give Nightfall an appreciative whistle, a word of impressed encouragement, or a touch. Wrung out by the attention and the wariness it raised, he appreciated the cabin boy's timing. He usually shied from touches, never certain which hand might hold a dagger or when one might turn from a friendly grip to a blow or imprisonment. The boy paused at the hold and gestured Nightfall over the coamings and down the wooden rungs of the short ladder leading between decks.

Accustomed to sleeping on the upper deck, Nightfall hesitated. The 'tween looked dark and dingy, though he could see unlit lanterns hanging from gimbal rings. Plank dividers had been thrown up, forming makeshift walls to the left and right. Another hole, smaller and offset from the first, led down to the cargo and storage areas on the lowest deck. Nightfall went below, and the boy followed.

"This room is yours, my lord," the boy said, gesturing at the second door on the starboard side. The first, Nightfall guessed, would belong to Ragan, while the guards would sleep in layered bunks on the port side.

Nightfall pushed open the door to his cabin. Though the walls had clearly been tossed together quickly, it seemed roomy and surprisingly comfortable for a ship's hold. A single cot took up most of the far corner, covered with fresh-smelling straw and blankets. A plain clay chamber pot sat in one corner, a wooden chair in another. The chest King Edward had ordered brought to Schiz filled the space between the bed and the seat. Nightfall's other set of silks lay in a neatly folded pile on the floor near the pot, his boots cleaned and oiled beside them. Soaked to the skin, clothes sodden, water dripping from his hair, he would have traded his best dagger for fresh warm linens and a hearth; but fire aboard a ship was far too dangerous to place into the hands of landlubbers. Even the sailors rarely allowed for such luxuries, dining on raw sea fare as often as cooked.

The boy waited in silence until Nightfall entered the room and turned. "Is there anything else I can get for you, my lord?"

Nightfall drew the blanket more tightly around him. The boy could not provide what he really wanted, and he already had more than he needed. *Power and knowledge,* Dyfrin had often told him, *live in unexpected places.* On a whim, he gestured the boy inside. "Yes. I need to talk to you for a moment."

The boy's nostrils flared, and his lids rose to reveal large, innocent brown eyes. Nevertheless, he dutifully followed Nightfall inside where he stood stiffly, awaiting an order.

Since the boy seemed concerned about what Nightfall wanted, he kept his distance and motioned the child to sit.

The boy perched on the edge of the chair. Only then, Nightfall closed the door and walked to the bed. He remained standing, however, not wanting to soak the straw and make it unsuitable for sleeping. "What's your name?"

"Danyal, my lord." The boy looked at his boots, avoiding Nightfall's gaze.

"Mine's Sudian," Nightfall said. He crouched to the boy's level.

"Yes, sir."

Nightfall read fear in every coiled sinew. He tried to put the cabin boy at ease. "I'm not going to hurt you, Danyal." When the boy still did not relax, he added, "I'm not going to touch you. I just want to give you this." Reaching into his pocket, he took out three silver coins, more than Danyal had probably seen in a lifetime.

Now the boy looked up, though his gaze went no farther than Nightfall's hand. He rose, approached, and started to reach for the money but stopped mid-movement. His attention finally flicked to Nightfall's eyes. "Thank you, my lord. But what would this be buying?"

Now Nightfall understood what he should have realized sooner. Most sailors believed a woman aboard bestowed ill luck upon an ocean voyage. When the rare female did embark, it was always in the company of a husband or guard. Weeks ship-bound could make any man hungry for intimacy; and if he could not reach the dock whores, a cabin boy might suffice for some. Nightfall's blood ran cold, and memory assailed him from his years on the street. Foul-smelling fingers clamped over his face. A hand shoved into the rags that served as his trousers. He had escaped that rape and slaughtered the man who had attempted it, but the outrage and humiliation lingered even now. He no longer believed Danyal the son of someone aboard. More likely, yearning for adventure, he had run away to the sea, only to find the drudgery aboard as ghastly as whatever he had escaped. Nightfall forced emotion from his voice, "Let's just say I know what it's like to be very young, alone, and at the bottom of the world. I'm not there anymore by the grace of the Father. If this buys you something better than you have, I've paid back some of my debt."

Though still wary, Danyal scooped the silver from Nightfall's hand. "Thank you, my lord." He spoke in the same respectful monotone, a hopeful light appearing in his eyes. He still clearly expected Nightfall to demand some service of him.

Though Nightfall had lied, it was not for the reasons the boy expected. He had stopped believing in gods when he found himself alone on the wild streets at eight. He owed nothing to the great and heavenly Father whose will Edward served. Dyfrin had steered him right on many occasions, but none had proven so true as his admonishment to treat servants with the same respect he accorded the highborn. Overtipping had gained him lifesaving allies: many a stable boy had tended their horses and gear with extra care and seen to it their belongings remained where Nightfall left them. Child servants overheard things no adult ever could, and they had an innocent way of misdirecting those they did not like and informing those they did.

Danyal shuffled toward the door. "May I go now, my lord?"

"Of course." Nightfall took the vacated chair.

Danyal reached for the door rope.

"Danyal."

The boy stiffened but dutifully turned. "Yes, my lord?"

"If you're feeling overwhelmed with work and need a place to hide for a while, just come to me. I'll pretend to give you some service to do here, and you can sleep or just relax."

Still clearly suspicious, Danyal said nothing.

Nightfall went to the root of the boy's concern. "I don't . . . 'use' boys, if that's what you're worried about. I've been there . . ." He paused, letting the words sink in. He had never confessed that to anyone other than Kelryn and wondered why he had done so now. "I wouldn't inflict it on anyone else."

Danyal finally relaxed, his shoulders dropping visibly. A smile tugged at the corners of his lips. The direct approach had finally broken through the last of his resistance. "Thank you, my lord."

"Thank you, Danyal."

Though Danyal clearly wanted to bolt from the room to fully dispel the tension, he faced Nightfall directly instead. "You're an uncommon noble, my lord. I hope . . . I hope you always . . ."

Nightfall tried to help. ". . . remember where I came from?"

Danyal bobbed his head happily.

"I'll try," Nightfall promised. "Though, sometimes, all I ever want to do is forget."

"Yeah." Danyal seized the rope and pulled open the door. "I can understand that, too, my lord." He disappeared through the crack, and the door banged shut behind him.

Nightfall rose and crossed the room. Taking up his dry silks, he dropped them onto the pallet, trying not to leave wet spots on the fabric. His interaction with the cabin boy pleased and unnerved him. Usually, when he sought to gain the confidence of someone, he had an ulterior motive, some scheme in mind. Though he told himself he had merely said what he needed to in order to gain the trust of someone who might know or hear something useful, he could not wholly fool himself. He liked Danyal, and the realization he had helped the boy suffused him with a warm satisfaction he could not escape.

Deal with it, Demon. You did something nice. Nightfall dragged apart his dry clothing, separating a soft leather undergarment from the tunic and breeks in Alyndar's purple and silver, all the while shaking his head. *What has that world-ignorant, guileless pretty-boy turned you into?* Thoughts of the king, even an insulting one, raised another stab of compassion. The most amazing part of the entire exchange was how easy it had proven. He did not have to make some wondrous and deft run through the riggings of a ship and freeze himself near to pneumonia, as he had for the guards and sailors. He had beguiled the boy with nothing more astounding than a shared truth.

As Nightfall changed from his wet clothing, using the remaining blanket to blot up the sea water, he realized Dyfrin had long ago told him what it had taken thirty-four years to figure out on his own. The parts of Dyfrin he had considered weaknesses, the actions he thought he would never comprehend, gained clarity. He wished he could tell his old friend, long his only friend, this great revelation. He could picture the soft, dark eyes in Dyfrin's heart-shaped face willing him to understand, holding the hope that others, including Nightfall, had long ago surrendered. "Deep down, Marak, you're a good man." All this at a time when the only "good" he would dare apply to himself preceded the word "killer."

Warm and dry, Nightfall lay upon his bed and studied

the rescued ring. Though small, the amethysts appeared flawless, flashing tiny purple highlights around the swaying ceiling. The fist and hammer symbol of Alyndar matched the many images arrayed around Alyndar Castle, strikingly perfect for such a tiny image engraved in gold. Accustomed to assessing value from his merchant role, Nightfall realized it might prove more valuable than he first thought. Clearly, it held great significance, not only to Edward but also to his captors.

With a sigh, Nightfall returned the ring to its secure position. He missed Dyfrin terribly, and now, also, Edward Nargol, king of Alyndar.

† Chapter 4 †

*You have to trust some people sometime. You may
make it without friends; but, with them, you can do
anything.*

     —Dyfrin of Keevain, the demon's friend

TENNETH KENTARIES yawned and stretched luxuriously in the high-backed chair perched on the dais
of Alyndar's Great Hall. Lines of peaked windows admitted muted afternoon sunlight, which played through
the hair of the few remaining nobles seated on the
benches in front of him. The purple carpet of the aisleway currently held no one, indented and muddied by
the footfalls of the guards, peasants, and courtiers who
had stood in question or judgment that day. A familiar
array of tapestries covered the stretches of stone wall
between the windows, depicting the same scenes they
had throughout King Rikard's thirty-eight-year reign. A
shield adorned with Alyndar's fist-clutching-a-hammer
crest hung over the entry. No one hovered beneath it
now. The double doors lay shut; the day's business, apparently, had concluded.

Tenneth knuckled his fingers through his neatly
trimmed beard, satisfied with his decisions and results.

Though never faced with a huge amount of dealings in the king's absence—anything of import that could wait for his return did—it still ran a respectable gamut. With the king away, and his chancellor/adviser with him, the task fell to the members of Alyndar's High Council. The five men took turns as arbiter, as the law commanded, so no one would get ideas about usurping the throne. Nevertheless, Tenneth believed himself the most worthy successor and imagined most of the others did also. Some made their opinions clearer than others, muttering darkly over the circumstances that left a younger son, barely capable of handling his own small affairs, wearing the crown of Alyndar.

With a flick of his long, lean fingers, Tenneth gestured the spectators from the Great Hall. He wanted to sit alone for a few moments, to enjoy the feel of the king's strategically padded chair, the view of the long, double line of tapestries he could choose to rearrange at a whim. He imagined himself as King Rikard, his own watery hazel eyes sharpened to the king's shrewd darkness, his pale skin and flabby musculature hardened to the tanned steel of the greatest king Alyndar had ever known. He wished his hair into the king's leonine curls, his own sandy strands cut short to hide their limp colorlessness. He harbored no real thoughts of treason; his idle life as Alyndar's second largest landowner, inherited through generations, suited him just fine. He only savored the chance to hover over the Great Hall for a time and to feel like a king.

The seat to Tenneth's right hand lay empty, as it usually had since Edward had ascended to the throne of Alyndar. Unlike his father's sorcerer chancellor, Edward's rarely bothered with affairs of court. A servant elevated by the new king's decree, he seemed dangerously ignorant of the affairs of courtiers, even bored by them. When he did deign to join Edward in the Great Hall, he always came late, with clear reluctance, and fidgeted like a child trapped in a tutor's long-winded lec-

ture. Evil-eyed and ever-vigilant, he seemed to expect
an army to burst through all of Alyndar's defenses and
into the Great Hall itself without a hint of warning.
Clearly ignorant of the amount of power his new status
granted him, Sudian made little attempt to mingle with
the highborns, excusing himself from their conversations to chat with the hired help.

Tenneth twirled his beard with a finger. Alyndar's navy
lord admiral, Nikolei Neerchus, had twice tried to broach
the subject of his poorly chosen chancellor with King
Edward, but the young monarch had politely brushed
aside the older and wiser man. Overwhelmed by the
grief of losing his father and brother within a short space
of time, injured by Gilleran's sorcerous attack, and
dropped abruptly into rulership of a quarter of the
world's land, Edward had no patience for such discussions. True, Sudian had saved Edward's life and nearly
lost his own in the battle; and such fierce loyalty deserved rewarding. Tenneth would not begrudge Sudian
that: high praise, a monetary prize, a bit of land, an hon-
orary title, perhaps. But to grant a servant performing his
duty, even so well, a position that placed him over so
many with far deeper ties to king and kingdom seemed
rashly imprudent at best. And some were grumbling.

Tenneth took his hand from his beard and placed it,
and the other, behind his head. As the gentry disappeared from the Great Hall, he luxuriated in the chair's
soft plush, warmed by the heat of his body. The chair beside him deserved a man of breeding and wisdom, perhaps Tenneth Kentaries himself: someone who cared
deeply about the goings-on in Alyndar, about the relationships between this great kingdom and the world's
other three, about the long-term goals of a realm that
must remain strong for his children, grandchildren, and
even more distant descendants of his line. He had no
idea of Sudian's origins. In fact, he realized, no one did;
but he knew the younger man had no deep ties of blood
to Alyndar.

A gruff voice cut suddenly through Tenneth's reverie. "Are you quite finished wallowing in the king's chair?"

Startled, Tenneth leaped to his feet to confront the short, round figure of Baron Elliat Laimont, the only man in Alyndar, besides the king, to own more land than he did. "Wha . . . ? How . . . ?"

Elliat responded to the question Tenneth could not quite force out in his surprise. "I walked right through the main doors and up the carpetway. You would have heard me had you not been writhing about like a cat on silk."

Tenneth felt his cheeks warm and tried for an air of indignation. "I wasn't wallowing." He placed his hands on his hips. "I happened to have a hard day, and I fell asleep."

Elliat grunted, lips twitching into a smile. "Hopefully *after* you finished sentencing the last of the peasants." He held up his beefy right arm to display a strip of parchment clutched in his fist. "Emergency meeting of the High Council. In the Strategy Room. Would you care to join us?"

Tenneth sprang from the dais without bothering with the steps. Though well into his fortieth year, he prided himself on remaining spry. "Of course." He joined Elliat at the base of the dais and followed his heavy tread up the soiled carpet. As soon as they exited the double doors, he knew, servants would scurry in to clean up the mess left by the day's business. By tomorrow, General Simont Basilaered would take his place on a spotless chair to sit at the end of a brilliant purple carpetway. The windows would admit clean sunlight, sparkling in the polish of the spectators' benches.

The four sentries stationed in front of the Great Hall barely moved as the two men burst through the doors and into the main corridor. Together, they headed up the spiral staircase leading to the upper floors of the west tower in silence. Though gripped by curiosity, Tenneth knew better than to question the other in the open corridors. Matters of the Council must remain secure. Servants scurried to the banisters to grant the nobles the central, most richly carpeted, portion of the oaken stairs, most giving short bows, nods, or curtsies of respect that Tenneth scarcely noticed. Shortly, they came to the fourth-floor landing, turning left toward the thick, steel-bound door that opened onto the Strategy Room. Two guards with spears and swords snapped to stiff attention as they came into sight.

The door opened, as if of its own accord. A page started through the crack, then froze with a gasp as he caught sight of the two important men headed toward him. Caught in the worst possible position, he attempted to bow, nod, and scurry simultaneously and wound up on the floor. Ignoring his antics, Elliat stepped over the quivering boy and into the room, Tenneth a stride later. At his back, Tenneth heard the scuffle of the boy, then the door crashed shut behind him with more force than a servant would usually allow. Apparently, the child was more concerned about a swift exit than propriety.

Maps lined the strategy room's windowless walls. An enormous eight-armed chandelier swayed in the breeze left by the hard and sudden closure of the door, flinging chaotic slashes of light and shadow across the papers, the room's other three occupants, and the massive table and chairs taking up most of the space. A silver tray at the center held white, doughy biscuits and mugs of pulpy juice, apparently brought by the departing page.

As the highest-ranking council member, Baron Elliat took the position at the head of the table. At either hand sat Army General Simont Basilaered and Navy Lord Admiral Nikolei Neerchus. Whale-boned and muscled like plowhorses, both of the fighting men dwarfed the others at the table. Simont was a giant of a man, a head taller than even their massive king, with sable curls perched thickly atop his head, tapering into bushy sideburns, and fusing into his heavy beard. Eyes as dark as his hair lay recessed beneath wide brows, and a prominent nose gave him an air of presence. No matter where he went or how still he stood, a man's eyes could not help but go to him. In battle, his mere presence could terrify an opponent, and he fairly radiated a charisma that kept his men in line and perfectly under his command. A decade younger than Tenneth, he had held his post for only nine years, yet the nobleman found himself nearly incapable of remembering who had served before him.

Though the navy's lord admiral bore only the resemblance of size, he also commanded respect and obedience. He kept his wheaten hair cropped short and his face clean-shaven. Large green eyes beneath wispy brows gave him a gentle appearance that belied a smoldering temper. He moved at ease through many circles. His chiseled features and powerful position made him a favorite among the women, and he had a soft-spoken wit that earned him friendships despite his imposing size and his famous rages. That sense of humor gained an edge as annoyance flared and could become sharp and sarcastic in an instant. He could turn a man to jelly with a few bellowed words, yet he never allowed the worst fit of pique to upset a well-thought-out strategy. He knew how to fight a battle, whether with words, fists, swords, or ballistae; and he knew how to win.

Alber Evrinn perched on the chair beside General Simont. Though at least an average-sized man, he looked small and dainty beside the warrior. Tenneth took the seat across from him, certain that Lord Admiral Nikolei dwarfed him just as much. Titled a knight, like himself, Alber was the third largest landholder in Alyndar. A tasteful red and yellow hat tamed his mop of brown hair, but it accentuated his long face and small, sharp nose. The slope of his light-brown eyes gave him an eternal look of sadness, broken only by his frequent smile. A man of few words, he was on a constant mission to find himself a worthy wife, one his appearance and quietness doomed to failure.

Elliat wasted no time calling the meeting to order. When alone, they had agreed to forsake formalities. "Thank you for your patience. I'm sure you're all wondering why I called this emergency meeting."

Murmurs swept the table and heads bobbed, including Tenneth's.

The baron dropped the piece of parchment to the tabletop. "I received this message, brought by Hartrinian courier dove."

Every eye went toward the parchment, but Simont moved first. It disappeared into his enormous fist, and his eyes scanned the words. For a large man, he showed an unexpected grace and quickness that unbalanced Alyndar's enemies.

The source of the message was significant. The rare, long-winged sea doves had a penchant for locating ships. Smarter than pigeons, they could fly out to designated places with a message before returning to their established roosts with a reply. Living on a peninsula, Alyndar owned some of the birds, though they were considered too valuable to risk for any but the most significant missions. King Idinbal of Hartrin used them regularly to identify approaching vessels, his supply larger as the birds were native to his climate and kingdom. A few other wealthy nobles also kept a few birds, which occasionally came up for sale. The last time Tenneth could recall Alyndar sending one was when they had demanded a sailor named Marak from the ketch *Raven*. Marak, it had turned out, was really the notorious criminal, Nightfall.

Simont cursed, then tossed the parchment back to the table where it was immediately snatched up by Nikolei.

"It's from Duke Varsah."

Tenneth sat up straighter. None of them had felt comfortable with the king's sudden and madcap decision to personally march off to Schiz. Had Alyndar's chancellor had the good sense to stand against the notion with the rest of his advisers, the inexperienced king would surely have abandoned his foolish notion.

Nikolei slammed his fist on the table so hard, juice sloshed from the untouched mugs. Alber jerked away from the table, and Tenneth suppressed a shiver.

Baron Elliat explained, "I'm afraid King Edward is hostage."

Tenneth's heart seemed to stop beating, and an imminent feeling of death stole over him. A shock of heat flashed through his entire body, followed by a dense prickle of ice. "What?" he managed, though his throat felt strangled.

Alber leaned forward, also sounding hoarse. "Duke Varsah has taken the king hostage?"

"No." Having had more time to digest the contents of the message, Elliat corrected for those who had not yet read it. "King Edward was taken from the city against the will of the duke." Anticipating Alber's next question, he added, "We do not yet know by whom."

Seized by a sudden need for movement, Tenneth shoved his chair from the table and rose. "Why? How can this happen?" Already knowing the answers, he did not wait for anyone to give them. "Who would do such a thing?"

"Bastards," Simont growled, though whether in answer to Tenneth's query or as an epithet, he did not specify.

Tenneth began pacing along the unoccupied side of the table.

Alber sought a more significant detail. "What about his entourage? Where were the men supposed to guard him?" A hint of accusation entered his tone, and the general immediately pounced upon it.

"Good men, all of them. Slaughtered defending him."

Tenneth paused in midstep, and another shiver traversed him. "All of them?"

Elliat sighed. "Every one."

Heads bowed around the table, and the conversation lapsed to silence. Tenneth closed his eyes in a quiet prayer to the Holy Father to watch over good men's souls. Then, he swung around to resume his pacing.

"Except one." Lord Admiral Nikolei Neerchus spoke in a low-pitched voice resembling a growl.

Tired of learning the details one by one, Tenneth snatched up the parchment from in front of the general. Immaculately penned in a strong, flowing script, it read:

To the Esteemed High Council of Alyndar
From Varsah Partinyin, Duke of Schiz

With the greatest of regrets, I inform you that King Edward Nargol of Alyndar was taken hostage from my city by fiends not yet identified. These thugs came upon him in a tavern under cover of darkness, killing all of his brave sentries. My best men are engaged in finding these villains; and, when they do, we will bring them to you for sentence. We hope to return your king safely home as soon as possible and will make every effort to see this done.

I am sending a diplomatic party with Alyndar's belongings and the sole survivor, who names himself the king's adviser. Forgive me my suspicions, but it seems odd that he happened to be away on some mysterious and inexplicable "mission" at the time of the king's disappearance, while the men he claims to have assisted deny any knowledge of him. Afterward, his demeanor in my court was grossly inappropriate for the seriousness of the situation. Although I would never disparage a trusted member of the king's circle, I think it well advised to delve into the background and intentions of this man, Sudian.

Please hold Schiz and myself blameless for this crime, as we are. We will cooperate in every way in seeing your great and benevolent king safely returned, and those involved in his capture will find death

*or your judgment. I regret that I never had the opportunity to meet
with King Edward and feel greatly humbled by his decision to honor
my city with his most august presence. I have since discovered the
reason for his visit and assure you it was entirely unnecessary. Of
course, all past crimes of the king and his squire are forgiven; and
all of the tribute found among the king's effects is being returned.*

My sincere apologies and sympathies go with you,
Duke Varsah Partinyin

Tenneth dropped the parchment in front of his own
seat. "Is it possible . . . ?" He could barely comprehend
the idea. "Could the duke be behind such a terrible . . . ?" Unable to finish, he looked askance at the
baron.

"Varsah?" Elliat shook his head, frowning. "Angry,
perhaps. Greedy. But murder and kidnapping?" The
corners of his mouth twitched farther downward, leaving a tract of creases across his chin and brow. "I don't
see it."

The only one who had not read the parchment, Alber
claimed it now.

"Madness." General Simont's gaze followed the message. "If he wished to claim credit for the atrocity, he
would have done so. If he wanted to hide it, he would
not have allowed it to occur within the borders of
Schiz."

Alber spoke in his usual soft manner. He did not usually say much; when he did, they all listened despite the
volume. "A greedy, guilty man would not return gold
and jewels within his right to keep."

Tenneth nodded. "You're right, Alber. He would have
waited until after his meeting with His Majesty, once he
wheedled as many concessions as the young king would
spare."

Elliat clearly also agreed. "If he were corrupt enough

to murder guardsmen and take a king, he'd have found a way to keep the offering, even if he had not yet met with young Ned. At the least, he could have claimed the same fiends stole it."

The admiral slammed his fist on the table again. "This is utter nonsense! I know Varsah, and he's anything but stupid. I have no doubt at all he's innocent, and we should honor his suspicions."

Tenneth saw where this was going. "You mean Sudian?"

"Of course, Sudian." Simont's dark eyes turned icy. "I've never trusted that scoundrel."

Elliat presented the other side, "King Edward trusts him, not wholly without cause. And King Rikard—"

The admiral interrupted in a voice so loud it seemed to pierce the walls. "King Rikard trusted that bastard Gilleran too. Twenty-some years that sorcerer whispered his poison in the king's ear, longer than our current king has been alive."

Nikolei did not need to finish. They all knew how that had ended, with Alyndar's greatest king bleeding great gouts of blood on the chapel floor, his head shattered into glasslike fragments by Gilleran's ice spell. Nearby sat the gold-inlaid coffin holding the remains of Crown Prince Leyne, killed in tourney, also at the whim of Gilleran's magic. Edward, too, would have died that day if not for Sudian's interference. Given time to hide the evidence, Gilleran might even have perched upon the throne of Alyndar, gleefully stealing the lives and talents of the natally gifted, adding to his own power until no one could have stopped him.

Softly, Alber reminded them, "Sudian saved Edward's life and killed the sorcerer."

Tenneth remembered. They all did. Nevertheless, he considered the possibilities. Nikolei had made an excellent point regarding Gilleran, who had worked his way into the king's trust and the same position of power by also appearing selflessly loyal. "At the time, Sudian was only a squire. He needed an act that grand to earn his promotion to a position of ultimate trust."

Alber tented his fingers over the parchment. "But he could have died. Should have. What would that have gained him?"

"Should have," Nikolei repeated, raising his craggy head. "But didn't." His eyes became wary slits. "Just how did he survive that fall anyway?"

It was a long-standing debate. Most believed the Almighty Father had intervened, slowing Sudian's fall to reward him for protecting the sacred line of kings. Had Gilleran succeeded in slaughtering Edward along with his father and brother, the bloodline of the Nargols would have ended that day. Less religious folk attributed Sudian's survival to the tree branches he had seized to slow his landing, to the dumb luck of landing on top of Gilleran, or to a combination of both.

No one spoke any of the tired arguments now, but Nikolei raised a new one. "Only magic could have saved him." He lowered his wheaten head, hatred clearly stamped across his features. "What do we know about Sudian's past, anyway? Is it possible we have another sorcerer for a chancellor?"

From his studies, Tenneth knew events in history had a habit of recurring. Both of the warrior commanders had expressed their distrust of and dislike for Sudian in the past. Edward's well-known exuberance and unsophisticated innocence in combination with Sudian's suspiciously excessive loyalty raised troubling doubts about the chancellor's long-term intentions. "That's an excellent question, Admiral. What exactly do we know about Sudian's past?"

"Not much," Elliat said, head bobbing at the implications.

"Then," Simont finished with warrior finality. "It's time we find out what we can."

*   *   *

The Sharius rocked gently over the swells of the Klaimer Ocean, under the smooth control of her crew. Though he had decided to spend most of the trip in his quarters, Nightfall found the actual execution of this plan unbearable. Alone, he brooded, worrying about rescuing the missing king without the proper information or any known direction. He felt helpless, which drove him to terrible, fierce fits of anger. He hated the situation, his ignorance, and his inability to tap the many information sources he had once kept at his disposal. He wanted to grab every man in existence by the throat and shake until one of them delivered King Edward, alive and unharmed, or at least the facts he needed to find the king himself.

Instead, Nightfall spent his days topside, listening to the guards' stories and regaling them with some of his own. His time as Frihiat had taught him how to capture and hold attention, as well as to tell when his audience needed a change. He reveled in the riffle of salt air through his hair and the ceaseless slog of water against the hull. He even took some malicious pleasure in the occasional sight of the nobleman, Ragan, flopped over the railing, vomiting into the sea. Unlike Nightfall, the Schizian did spend most of his time in his quarters, until driven out in need of open air. Occasionally, he joined his men for a meal or to discuss mission matters, but he always avoided Nightfall. His rare glances vividly displayed distrust and hatred, a detail not lost on the guards.

On the sixth day of the crossing, the young blond, Dawser, approached Nightfall, who had his back pressed to the main mast, legs stretched out in front of him. "I think you're incredible," the boy said, sitting cross-legged beside him. "Why doesn't Ragan like you?"

Nightfall glanced up, sweeping the deck with his gaze from long habit. A few of the guards and sailors milled about, some within earshot; but they seemed intent on other things. He did not care if they overheard. "I don't know. I thought maybe one of you could tell me."

Dawser ran a hand through his hair, leaving the short strands standing up in its wake. "I don't know either. He seems to think you had something to do with the murders and your king's disappearance."

Nightfall appreciated the direct response. Though that possibility had sat foremost in his suspicions, it helped to have someone in the know clarify it. He snorted. "That's nonsense."

"I know."

Though Dawser could not possibly know, Nightfall appreciated his loyalty, even if it did serve little real purpose. "I'm as faithful to and protective of King Edward as any man can be."

"I know."

Nightfall swiveled his head to look directly at the younger man. "How do you know?"

Dawser cleared his throat and spoke with a certainty beyond his years. "Because no one would do what Harvistan says you did in Duke Varsah's dungeon unless he really cared for the person he was looking for."

"And," a wavy-haired, heavy-set guard added, joining them, "you fret way too much to be celebrating a calculated victory." Nightfall remembered his name as Chintylin.

Ivin, who had been conversing with Chintylin a moment earlier came, too, to put in his piece. "And you've been a noble for too short a time to already think the way they do."

Nightfall's brows bunched, and the other two guards looked equally confused.

Chintylin questioned first. "What do you mean by that?"

Ivin made a noise deep in his throat. "I mean most commonfolk won't dare harm nobles for fear of punishment, but the highborn take to slaughtering one another for status. Sudian's not been privileged long enough to start using such tactics."

Though Chintylin had come up with his own reason for

Nightfall's innocence, he dismissed Ivin's. "Tactics like murdering a whole roomful of people?" He waved a hand. "Please. That doesn't take a strategist."

Ivin pressed his back to the side of the ship and slid to the deck. "Oh, it's not subtle, but it worked. How's Sudian supposed to get the clout or the money to hire the Bloodshadow Brotherhood in the three days he's had to learn how to be a highborn?"

Though moot, and dangerously wrong, the question raised others. Nightfall could not believe an organized underground network existed that he knew nothing about. "The Bloodshadow Brotherhood? What's that?"

Dawser jumped back in, "It's this really mean bunch of thugs."

Nodding, Chintylin elaborated. "Rumor is they're demons, one grown from every droplet of blood spilled during the execution of Nightfall."

Nightfall forced a shiver. "Creepy."

"Quick and total destruction." Ivin grunted. "Without a hint of humanity or guilt. They're good at what they do, and they're the only ones I can think of who could render an entire room of witnesses silent."

Nightfall finally had his answer, though it merely served to raise more questions. He considered these, limited to the ones that would not make it clear he understood the workings of criminals.

At that moment, a cry wafted from above. "Pirates!"

Nightfall's blood ran cold. Before he could think, he darted past the guards, leaped to the boom, and shinnied up the riggings. Even the off duty sailors scurried to the railings.

"Starboard!" the lookout shouted. "Black sails!"

Nightfall looked out over mild seas to the rapidly approaching ship. Sleek and light, it moved before the wind with a quickness *The Sharius* could never outrun. Double-masted with three triangular jibs, it flew two different flags from the topmasts, both jet black. The main mast's bore a white hourglass against the dark fabric, and the mizzen's displayed a human figure and a treasure chest, with arrows pointing each way between them. Nightfall recognized the meaning of only one. The hourglass cautioned them to surrender swiftly, before time ran out and bloodshed became imminent. He did not recognize the second; his ships had never used or seen it. Men swarmed the pirate ship's railings and riggings, and sunlight glimmered from the blades of their thick, curved short swords.

Professionals. Nightfall scampered down the lines to the deck.

Danyal appeared at Nightfall's side. "Quickly, my lord. You need to go below."

Dread prickled through Nightfall. He had faced pirates once before, as Marak, had watched them gleefully slaughter every sailor for the pittance of money they carried and the cargo in the hold. Then, the pirate's captain had appreciated Nightfall's deadly aim and allowed him to live on as a member of the pirate crew. It seemed unlikely Nightfall would find two brigand captains enthralled by his ability to throw knives, and he had no better plan for survival this time. He could only hope the guards and crew could overpower the pirates and not too many would die.

"Come! Come, my lord!" Danyal hauled on Nightfall's hand. "Quickly."

With no plan of his own, Nightfall followed Danyal across the deck, to the ladder, and into the hold. Plunged into sudden darkness, Nightfall did not wait for his eyes to adjust, trusting his memory and the cabin boy to lead him safely to his quarters. He knew they would find only temporary safety there. Once the pirates killed the guards and sailors, they would come first to find any goodies stored below. With blood frenzy at its height, they would search every corner, steal or burn the ship itself, and take a grim and ferocious pleasure in tearing apart any man they thought to be noble.

Danyal came to a sudden halt at the door to Nightfall's cabin. When the boy made no move to open it, Nightfall whirled to face the first mate, a spare, balding man with a crusted beard and piercing blue eyes who stood against the wall between the two cabins.

"Sudian," the man said, as if seeing right through the cabin boy, "sir."

Danyal's hand slipped from Nightfall's, and he sidled toward the exit.

Feet rattled on the deck, and the shouts of readying guards and sailors blended into a hum punctuated by shouts.

"That's me," Nightfall confirmed. "Were you looking for me?"

"Yes, sir." The mate continued to train his sharp gaze on Nightfall, though he shuffled his feet with clear uneasiness. "I'm afraid pirates are swiftly approaching the ship."

Nightfall nodded. "I'm aware of that."

"Yes." The first mate fell into an edgy silence that unnerved Nightfall more than the stare.

"How can I help?" he prodded. If someone had a reasonable idea, he felt more than ready to consider it. All of their lives depended on it. When pirates turned their minds to plunder and slaughter, no one survived unless he seemed worth more money sold into slavery. A slight, sinewy thirty-four-year-old man did not fit that category.

"The pirates have proposed what they call a 'hostage barter.'"

Nightfall narrowed his eyes and shook his head slightly to indicate the words meant nothing to him. For once, he did not have to feign ignorance. He could not recall his pirate company ever employing such a tactic, but he guessed the second flag announced their intentions, since the other ship had not yet drawn close enough for direct communication.

"If we surrender the highest-ranking man on the ship, they won't fight us. No one dies."

Nightfall remained in place, and his expression did

not change. It made no sense for pirates to accept some soft-handed, sweet-smelling noble like Ragan instead of whatever treasures the ship might hold. "Then . . . ?"

"The hostage barters for his life, promises a reasonable amount of silver or gems or jewels to equal his worth. If the pirates accept the blood price, the exchange is made. The agreed upon amount goes to the pirates, and the man returns to his rightful ship."

"If not . . ." Nightfall prompted.

The mate's face flushed, barely noticeable in the darkness of the hold. Danyal tried to look busy, now behind Nightfall. ". . . the hostage is killed. The pirates board the ship, slaughter every man aboard, and take whatever they wish."

Nightfall considered the arrangement. Though different than what he had known as a sailor or a pirate, it made a certain amount of sense. So long as the pirates held the highest-ranking passenger, the crew would not attack. The brigands had a nobleman to terrorize without risking their own lives in any way. The pirates might not get all the moneys aboard, but they would not settle for any pittance. The hostage seemed likely to promise anything, if properly "persuaded," and would likely hold his life worth a significant amount of treasure. In time, one's worth in barter to pirates might even become a symbol of status among the highborn. The pirates would get their money, the ship might keep at least some of her goods, and no one had to fight or die. Guessing the first mate's next question, Nightfall said, "You may feel free to use the chest of money, gems, and jewelry I brought aboard as you see fit for barter."

"Thank you, sir." No taller than Nightfall, the first mate met his gaze levelly. "But I'm not the one who'll be doing the bartering."

Nightfall dismissed the comment with a wave. "Then tell Ragan he can use the Alyndarian treasure." Though he did not care for the nobleman, he saw no reason to put the guards and crew at risk for an unnecessary battle. Money meant nothing to him, especially when it was not his own. "All of it, if he believes he's worth it."

"Yes, sir." The first mate's gaze returned to his shoes, and he shuffled his feet in a nervous gesture. "But Alyndar's lord chancellor and adviser outranks a Schizian knight."

As the implications suddenly became all too clear, Nightfall felt his chest squeeze tight. "Me?"

"You, sir." Now, the first mate dodged Nightfall's gaze. "You are the highest-ranking man aboard *The Sharius*. You are the one the pirates want."

† Chapter 5 †

*Given a chance and a little ingenuity, most men will
hand you their money.*

—Dyfrin of Keevain, the demon's friend

The *Sharius'* canvas snapped and rattled in the winds
as she lay at anchor in the Klaimer Ocean. Nightfall
stood near the main mast, with one booted foot
propped against the rail, studying the other ship. Above
him, a sailor in the lookout post flashed a flag indicating
agreement to the terms. The Schizian guards, fully armored, stood around him, offering words of advice and
encouragement that Nightfall did not bother to heed.
He did not need their sympathy; the arrangement suited
him. If lives had to hinge on the skills of one man
aboard, he preferred it to be himself. He had survived
too long by trusting his own instincts; and the idea of
waiting in ignorance while Ragan, or one of the sailors,
bartered for him might have driven him to madness.

Although the first mate, a man he now knew as
Bermann, had told him any monetary exchange would
occur after the bargaining, Nightfall had crammed his
pockets with gems, jewelry, and silver. He did not want
to give the pirates any reason to board *The Sharius* or

an opportunity to violate their promise by claiming some man had offended them. Tensions would remain high on both sides, and neither guards nor pirates were known for holding their tempers. He had hidden Edward's personal ring deep in the change of clothing he left lying casually across his bed. The ring clearly held significance beyond its obvious value, and he could not allow it to catch a pirate's fancy.

Bermann stood beside Nightfall now, the only man he bothered to listen to. "We're not usually a sea-crossing ship. We prefer jobs nearer to Brigg, so most of the crew has a family. The captain and I prefer to bring them all safely home."

Nightfall nodded once, saying nothing. He had no intention of squandering lives, his own included.

"Thank you." Bermann rested a hand on Nightfall's shoulder. "The sailors, they love the sea. It's not a well paying job, but—"

When Bermann did not continue, Nightfall tore his gaze from the pirate ship to look directly at the first mate.

"The men have scrounged together seven silvers they can add to the coffer. The captain says he'll contribute two of his own as well."

It was a fortune to workingmen, and Nightfall appreciated their generosity, though he refused it. "Thank you, Bermann; it's a generous offer. But if it takes more than the treasures of Alyndar to appease these killers, nine more silvers won't make a difference."

Now, Bermann nodded, and Nightfall returned his attention to the sea. A detail niggled at his thoughts, and he frowned. The impending ordeal had nearly pushed it from his mind, but he needed to mention his suspicions to the first mate in case his discussions with the pirates failed. He pitched his voice too low for anyone to overhear. "Bermann, you need to look to your men."

The first mate drew a step toward Nightfall, though it put him nearer than proper social boundaries demanded. "Excuse me, sir?"

"You have a traitor aboard. Or else one on shore who knew your mission."

Bermann jerked away, clearly shocked by the accusation. Then, curiosity overcame surprise, and he returned to their conversation. "Why . . . ? Why do you say so?"

A small boat slid down the side of the pirates' ship, and two men scurried down a hatchwork of sisal lines to settle into it. For a few moments, they adjusted their paddles, then started rowing for *The Sharius*.

The apprehension around Nightfall seemed to treble in an instant. He could sense the coil of guardsmen's hands around hilts, and even sailors' fingers disappeared into their tight-fitting shirts, where they kept a utility knife or two. As his eyes adjusted to the sea mist, Nightfall carved out details that distance and salt-grained air had kept at bay. Though sleeker and smaller than *The Sharius,* the pirate ship looked weathered, its caulking dull and overdue for repair. The bowsprit held a trinket shimmering with amber highlights that defined it as gold, and it appeared to have the shape of an animal head. Nightfall's imagination filled in gem-encrusted eyes. He put his mind to its significance. If the pirates could afford to put such a great piece on display, without fighting over its ownership, it meant they had fared well in the past few days or weeks. Heavy with treasure, battle weary, they would understandably choose a ploy such as their so-called "hostage barter." Likely, they were already short several men and ready to return to whatever city or hidden atoll they called home. Someone with more ship experience than these bloodthirsty bandits-at-sea needed to handle repairs before their slipshod maintenance sent them all to a watery grave.

"I'm assuming from what you told me of *The Sharius'* usual route you don't carry noblemen regularly."

"That's true." Bermann still clearly had not found the connection that seemed so obvious to Nightfall.

"Yet those pirates knew you had at least one titled

man on board to barter and, probably, that you had a boatload of armed and armored guardsmen they would do better not to challenge."

Bermann stroked his stubbly chin thoughtfully. "That's . . . true." He glanced around at the hovering guards and sailors as if to pick out the betrayer at a glance. "You do realize those armed and armored guardsmen will sink faster than boulders if knocked overboard."

Nightfall lifted and lowered one shoulder. "You and I know that. The pirates know it, too. Even the guards might." He glanced around, not at all sure of his last statement. More accustomed to the weight of their defenses than to overseas travel, such a thing might not occur to the fighting men. "But it'll make them look that much more dangerous to the pirates. To drown a man, you have to move him to water first. Dead pirates can't do that."

Nightfall turned his attention to the approaching craft. Though small, it could fit three men, four uncomfortably. The two inside it now appeared to outweigh Nightfall's baseline by at least a quarter again. Both wore rags across their brows, one bald, the other with a mane of stiff, wheaten hair held from his eyes by the hastily tied cloth. Breeks hugged their legs, and their tucked shirts billowed at narrow waists. They wore light linen shoes that were surely stiffer at the soles so they could climb the lines without bruising their arches. Neither had shaved in several days.

Bermann tossed a cleated rope ladder over the side. It plunged downward, flapping against the planks, and the end disappeared beneath the water. "May the gods bless your task."

Nightfall smiled. The gods had never bothered to assist his narrow escapes, his thefts and killings, and he had no use or need for them now. He considered other necessities as the boat rowed toward them. Aside from two well-secreted throwing blades he could afford to lose, he had disarmed himself. If the pirates chose to search him, they would not find anything suspicious about his carrying a couple of utilitarian knives. Anything more might look like an attempt to sabotage the proceedings. He was almost ready. Raising a hand with a sudden grand gesture that seized the attention of sailors and soldiers, and sent Bermann scurrying to a more appropriate distance, Nightfall addressed every man aboard. "Listen up!"

The group fell utterly silent.

"No matter how tempting, no matter what they say or do, don't harm those men coming to get me except in defense." He glared at Dawser, the youngest and most impulsive of the guards. "And don't try to goad them to attack either. The satisfaction of jabbing a sword through one of their black-hearted guts isn't worth all of our lives . . ."

Dawser nodded.

. . . *yet,* Nightfall added silently. Unaccustomed to others placing their well-being into his charge, he wondered if his usual strategies might fail here. *Damn Dyfrin. Damn Edward.* Nightfall longed for those simpler times when only his survival mattered and no one dared to rely on him for anything. Earlier, the captain had suggested substituting a guard or sailor for the real adviser to Alyndar's king, but Nightfall had dismissed the suggestion. Not only might one or more of the pirates know his appearance, it would mean trusting a stranger to negotiate for his life.

The pirates rowed toward the rope ladder, their eyes narrowed and never still. Two against a ship left them vulnerable to tricks and traps. But, though the guards and sailors hung over the railings glaring at the pirates below, no one spoke or made any hostile gesture. Apparently, they took Nightfall at his word.

Nightfall assumed an air of aloof confidence as he clambered down the rope ladder toward the tranquil sea below. Though devoid of storm swells and wind-whipped wavelets, its dark depths hid the dangers living below: tides that could suck a man to the core of the world, the sharks, massive-jawed fish, and giant Alyndarian lobsters that would feast on his remains. He deliberately avoided staring at the pirates, trying to look unconcerned. If they did anything dangerous, he felt certain the men aboard *The Sharius* would warn him.

The odor of salt grew thicker as Nightfall descended, and a light breeze threw pinpoints of water into his face. As he came nearly to the level of the ocean, he finally glanced casually toward the longboat. It sat exactly where he had last seen it, the length of two men from his own current position. Hanging on with one hand and both feet, he glanced expectantly at the pirates, who made no move to row nearer.

For several moments, they waited in perfect stalemate, Nightfall clinging to the ladder while the longboat remained too far away to board. A murmur rose from *The Sharius*, but no one shouted anything coherent toward the pirates. Nightfall glanced between the pirates and the water separating him from them, trying to understand their motivation.

The bald pirate showed a gap-toothed smile. He jerked his head to beckon Nightfall to the longboat.

Nightfall looked at the dark ocean directly beneath him. He could swim, and it seemed unlikely a predator could find him in the time it would take to reach and board the small craft; but he had no intention of drenching himself again or of giving the pirates the upper hand. "Come closer."

The bald pirate laughed, and the wheaten-haired one grinned now, too. "Swim."

"I don't swim." Nightfall kept his point vague. The pirates had no way of knowing whether he meant he could not or chose not to swim. Surely, they would not let him drown.

The pirates conversed briefly. Still grinning, they both

called out, "Then, jump, nobleman." They spat out the last word like a dire insult. "Jump!"

"Jump," Nightfall muttered.

"Bastards!" someone shouted from above.

Nightfall jerked his head in warning to the guardsmen and crew above. *Let me handle this.* He cleared his throat. "Jump?" he repeated.

The pirates laughed hoarsely. "Yeah, jump. Jump, silversucker." The bald man used a harsh term for the upper class, derived from their use of rare precious metals for such everyday items as tableware. "Jump!"

Be careful what you ask for . . . Nightfall grasped a rung of the rope ladder in both hands, freeing his feet to plant them against the hull. Dropping his weight, he pushed off with his legs. The rope swung easily on its cleats, building momentum, rocking him back toward *The Sharius*. Keeping his hold, Nightfall shoved himself from the planking again, adjusting the height and distance of his arc from long practice. Releasing the rope, he drove his weight upward, enhancing a somersault that should have launched him to a perfect landing in the longboat.

Instead, Nightfall careened toward the pirates, balance disrupted by the mass of coins and jewels he had forgotten to take into account. Instead of alighting as delicately as a cat amid the pirates, he plowed into the younger blond with enough force to send him tumbling over the side. Flailing wildly, the pirate crashed into the water with a splash that soaked his companion and Nightfall simultaneously. *So much for staying dry.* Nightfall rescued his balance before his own graceless maneuver carried him over the side as well.

Sputtering, the younger pirate flung water from his hair and swam a single stroke back to the longboat. He tossed an arm over the bow. "You hell-damned, dirty, silversucking, son of a—"

The bald man laughed as hard at his companion's

dilemma as he had at Nightfall's, though he did catch the other pirate's hand. "You did tell him to jump, Paskhon."

"So did you, ya scurvy bastard; but I don't see you floundering." The younger pirate's epithets turned to grumbles as he lurched back into the craft. It swayed dangerously sideways, saved by a sudden movement by Nightfall. He kept his expression innocent, giving no indication he gained the slightest amusement from the antics he had accidentally caused at their command.

Paskhon made a sudden motion that sent Nightfall's hand instinctively to one of his knives, though he resisted the urge to draw it. He should not need to defend himself. The other pirate would have no choice but to protect their charge from violence.

But no weapon appeared in Paskhon's hand. Instead, he howled a wordless noise of rage, his face captured by a blood wrath that turned it nearly scarlet. "You ugly, spoiled little *bastard*!" He glanced over the side at the unforgiving ocean. "You lost me my best sword! I ought to fling you to the bottom of the sea to fetch it!" He lunged toward Nightfall, only to leap nearly into the bald man's arms. "Arturo, get out of my way! Don't make me have to kill both of you!"

"Control your temper, Paskhon." Arturo spoke softly but with impressive force. He jerked his head toward *The Sharius.*

Paskhon finally deigned to look over his shoulder. The armored guards aboard the ship looked down on them with leveled bows.

Nightfall had never seen any of them use a bow. He had not even known they traveled with quivers in their packs, and he hoped none of them would have to shoot. He doubted he would survive the barrage, either.

Paskhon grunted and sat in his proper seat, a scowl pasted on his broad lips and his arms folded across his chest. Nightfall remained still as Arturo returned to his seat, opening the way for Paskhon to attack again. Instead, the angry blond snatched up his share of the oars, and the two pirates rowed back toward their ship. He dodged Nightfall's gaze until they had paddled beyond the range of *The Sharius*. "You owe me a sword," he finally grumbled.

Nightfall kept his cool. It would not do to allow himself to share the pirate's anger, nor to antagonize him; but he did need to show strength to gain the advantage. "And you owe me my dignity. I'd consider us even."

It was a subtle self-insult, but Paskhon clearly failed to see the humor. "You're just lucky the crew needs you alive."

"Paskhon," Arturo warned.

The younger man turned on his companion. "Don't 'Paskhon' at me, Artu. You didn't get kicked ass over scuppers! Your cutlass isn't rusting in the ocean."

Nightfall turned his attention to the approaching pirate ship, allowing the bald man to handle his seething companion. A ragtag lot of men studied them over the rail and gunwales, dressed in everything from silks to shreds depending on their picks from the spoils, and covered with rings, necklaces, and earrings. Most wore beards, though none were long enough to trip them up or offer a handhold in battle. Rags ringed most of their brows, and many bore battle scars on their faces and hands, including a few with a patch or empty socket and one missing his right arm at the elbow. A hatchwork of riggings ran up the side of the ship.

Arturo continued to chide his crewmate. "He's worth more than a rusty old cutlass, I'd warrant. Killing him won't bring it back, nor dry you any. It'll just keep you from getting a share to buy yourself a new blade. And if you deny the others their shares . . ." He did not have to go on. Nightfall, and certainly Paskhon, knew what would happen if his irritation and impatience cost them a treasure.

Paskhon did not reply, but he did work well in tandem with Arturo to bring the smaller boat against the side of the ship. This time, they pulled up expertly to the ropes.

Clearly, these two had practiced the maneuver many times and could have easily saved Nightfall the jump and them all a soaking. Lines weighted with hooks flew toward them, hurled from above. Nightfall threw up an arm to protect his head as the pirates reached to catch them as they fell. Paskhon snatched one from the air, but Arturo missed; and the hunk of iron flailed around in reckless ovals until the bald man finally seized it. Each pirate snapped a hook around an iron ring on his seat, holding the longboat in place and allowing a means to pull it back up onto the deck when the time came.

"You first." Arturo gestured for Nightfall to climb.

Though worried about a jab in the back, Nightfall obeyed, scurrying up the rope rungs. Before he reached the top, a sea of arms descended toward him. He dodged the first few, but they came at him in numbers he could not avoid forever. He had to assume they intended to help him aboard, so he forced himself still and allowed the greasy fingers to close around his wrists, fingers, and forearms. They hauled him upward and deposited him on the deck.

Nightfall managed to keep his feet on the gently rolling planks, though he dared not rely on his talent. With so many men touching him, one might detect the change. Even a grubby pirate could be a sorcerer, and sorcerers trained themselves to notice the subtlest of oddities. His own instincts bent toward thievery, and he could not help admiring the brilliant rubies, emeralds, and diamonds strung from metal chains or embedded into rings. He could swipe a few with ease and live in luxury for months, even were he not bound for his quarters in a castle with a chest load of precious metal and jewels already in his possession.

The pirates surrounded Nightfall, turning their backs to the two men who had brought him, forcing Arturo and Paskhon to drag their own weary, sodden selves up the ropes and over the railing without assistance. Nightfall counted at least thirty pirates, nearly all grim-faced and leather-skinned, men scarred inside and out. He already knew fighting men outnumbered seasoned sailors: the planks needed caulking, the canvas was in need of cleaning, and the decks had gone slimy with the blood of what he hoped were fish. The pirates formed a human wall, all but two taller than him. Most, however, seemed leaner, especially with his pockets stuffed with treasure. They muttered to each other in a colorful dialect filled with swear words and gutturals, akin to the clipped and rapid slang spoken on the Xaxonese streets. Nightfall pretended not to understand.

A few of the pirates stepped aside to allow a single man through. The newcomer was strikingly handsome, thick with muscles despite a flat stomach and a lack of fat pads around his cheeks. A rag tied back a cascade of soft ebony hair, highlighting rugged features with a strong chin and straight nose. Eyes like clear sky held a light that hinted of a quick and deadly temper. Clothed like a noble, he wore cream-colored silks bound with an intensely blue sash; and fine boots enclosed his feet and legs, nearly to the knee. Brilliant copper buckles held them firmly in place. Like the others, he wore several rings; but his did not clash. Every deep blue gem sat in a solid gold setting. His necklace and earrings also held sapphires. Without introduction, Nightfall knew he had met the captain.

"Sit!" the captain said.

Nightfall glanced around for a box or other object on which to set his hind end. Finding nothing within the circle of pirates, he lowered himself to a low crouch on the deck.

The captain watched his every movement. "Introduce yourself, silversucker."

Nightfall met the stormy eyes with unabashed courage. "Sudian," he said. "Sudian *Silversucker,* adviser to King Edward of Alyndar." Since he had no given surname or father to credit with his birth, the insult seemed as good as any name.

The pirates sniggered. Even the captain smiled, revealing a row of straight, brilliantly white teeth. "Ah. A noble with a sense of humor."

Nightfall relished the irony. These killers found pleasure in a wit Edward and his ilk usually dismissed as sarcastic insolence.

The captain continued to do all the talking for the pirates. "Are you not also Alyndar's lord chancellor?"

Nightfall doubted a truthful, "I'm not exactly sure," would satisfy them. "I've never called myself that, but I believe it's my title."

Murmurs rose among the pirates, silenced by the captain's upraised hand. He had large, callused palms with deeply set lines. "Well, Lord Chancellor of Alyndar, why don't you tell us why we shouldn't simply kill you?"

It was a dangerous question, and Nightfall considered his answer as long as he dared. Most men would embellish their worth in response to such a query, pleading for their lives by overemphasizing their significance to their kingdoms, their families, and the world. Having done so, they would find it impossible to backpedal when it came time to put gold behind their words and barter for their lives. The truth would not serve him here. With Edward gone, Nightfall was worth nothing to anyone except Kelryn, and few would assign much value to the love of a bawdy house dancer. "Under ordinary circumstances, I'm not sure the other nobles of Alyndar would miss me at all."

The murmurs grew louder. Nightfall could read some increasing tension in the demeanors around him. The pirates were hungry for money and blood, and he did not want to stoke their fire for either. "But," he added loudly over them, and the volume of their discussions decreased. "But with the king taken and me the only survivor of his kidnap, they won't take kindly to anyone preventing them from questioning me." He reminded warningly, "Alyndar does have a substantial navy." He hoped that answer would satisfy the pirates enough to keep him alive without costing him every coin and trinket aboard *The Sharius*.

A spark of emotion flashed through the captain's eyes. Though unsure, Nightfall thought he read the same admiration one con man has for another who bests him. Nothing of that nature, however, leaked into the captain's tone. "So, Chancellor, how much money is your life worth?"

The pirates cheered, the sound thunderous enough to carry to the men aboard *The Sharius*. They broke into an awkward chant that gained in timbre and volume. "What you worth? What you worth? What you worth?" The circle tightened, nooselike. They stomped their feet in rhythm with their mantra, the sound echoing and re-echoing against planking.

Responding over the noise would have proved impossible. The closing of the circle, the readied weapons, the screaming drove Nightfall to stiffen his crouch. His heart rate quickened to a dangerous pace, and sweat spangled his palms and rolled down the back of his shirt. Terror prodded the edges of his facade, and he needed something to bring the brigands under control, to shock them to silence. If he waited much longer, even the captain would not have the authority to control them. Nightfall thrust his hand into a pocket, dug out a generous handful of coins, and flung them to the deck.

It was exactly the wrong thing to do.

The ring and clink of the money was lost beneath the hubbub, and Nightfall's low position kept the coins from scattering much. The chanting broke to a mad scramble, and the organized noise became a chaotic snarl of shouting. Once they realized he carried money, the pirates sprang for Nightfall en masse. Bile bubbled into his throat. Every sinew tensed, prepared for whatever evasive action the situation required. But, this time, even his skill failed him. The pirates sprang upon him from every side, sheer numbers slamming him against the deck. Piled under too many men to escape, he found himself dragged and tugged in every direction simultaneously. His clothing tore under the assault, jewels, gems, and money spilling onto the deck, grimy hands tossing everything onto a single pile. Bits of silk flew through the air like feathers. The stink of a crush of men filled his nostrils until he wanted to vomit; and filthy, callused fingers mauled his clothing like vultures starved for carrion. Soon, every pocket lay in ruin on the deck; but the pirates still searched, tearing and cutting the hems and linings in a rabid search for some goodie he might still have hidden.

Never helpless. Nightfall relied on a mental chant of his own. *Never, never helpless.* If the pirates did not find more soon, they might cut him to ribbons along with his clothing. Though pressed beneath them, Nightfall's hands started working. He robbed pockets with the silent ease of experience, slipped rings from groping fingers and chains from sweaty necks. The pirates clearly did not notice their own ill-gotten gains mingled freely with the ones their captive had brought aboard, did not realize in their frenzy that he was denuding them of valuables with far more skill and talent than their savage money-lust did him. Swiftly, the pile on the deck grew to the height of Nightfall's knees, far more than any man could possibly have carried on his person. As an increasing number of pirates became more interested in the spoils than their captive, they calmed to the point where the captain finally gained their attention with a well-timed order.

The pirates dropped back, panting, bits of silk clinging to their flushed and lathered necks. Nightfall lay, fully exposed, on the deck beside the ruins of his clothing and a glittering mound of treasure. His fear dissipated in increments as each man retreated, only to be replaced by a vicious and hollow anger. Nightfall sprang to his feet, eyes blazing, making no attempt to hide his nakedness. He had lost all shame in childhood and knew little of modesty. Aside from the scars, he had nothing to hide; and those only because they might serve as identifying marks between abandoned personae.

The pirates looked at the treasure, the ship, their own feet, anything except the captain or their prisoner.

The captain seized the nearest shoulder. "You! Get Chancellor Sudian some clothes."

"Yes, sir."

The captain added forcefully, "The *best*. From *my* quarters."

The man paused a moment, withering beneath his captain's touch and glare. "*Your* quarters, sir?" Then, apparently more worried about getting caught questioning orders, he finished with, "Yes, sir." Head lowered, he stalked forward.

The captain confronted his men, his features displaying a rage so raw even Nightfall had to constrict his leg muscles to avoid taking an involuntary backward step. Many of the pirates were unable to display the same control, shuffling their feet, picking at their clothing, looking more like errant boys than the brutal killers who had seemed more than willing to maul an innocent man to death moments earlier for the trinkets he carried.

"When did the Father replace my crew with wild animals?"

No one answered.

Nor did the captain appear to expect anyone to do so. "If we kill the hostage, what do we have to barter?" He stared directly at a short brunet, stouter than the rest and missing half his left ear, who then seemed obliged to reply.

The pirate spoke with a thick Xaxonese accent, "But, Cap'n, we dint 'ave to barter. 'e brought the loot with 'im."

A taller blond added, "And we didn't kill him." He gestured at Nightfall. "See, nothing worse than scratches."

Nightfall wiped his nose on the back of his wrist, leaving a trail of bloody snot. He wanted to leap upon the man and inflict one very deep and very fatal "scratch," but he remained staunchly in place. He had nothing but his hands, and those had never served him well as weapons. Casually, he eyed the riggings, the layout of the ship, the valuables gracelessly stacked on the deck. Eventually, the pirates would realize they no longer wore their prized possessions, and he would need a way to defend himself. He tried to discern the outline of a knife from the hoard of precious stones and semi-precious metals. With the pirates' attention fully on their captain, he could make a quick break for the pile or the riggings if the need arose. He wondered if the longboat still floated or if they had hoisted it on deck. Arturo and Paskhon shuffled among the others.

The captain took a menacing step forward; the two speakers melted back into the crowd. Several of the pirates retreated to maintain the distance between themselves and their disgruntled leader. "If we don't barter in good faith, who will barter with us next time?"

No answer.

"Well?"

The pirates murmured several divergent answers that mingled into an unrecognizable hum.

It seemed to satisfy the captain, however. "If you turn the hostage barter into a way to rob and execute the highest ranking individual on any ship, every ship that comes upon us will attack first and question later. The priority not just of Alyndar's navy, but of every country with a navy, will be hunting us down for destruction. The private shippers, too."

The murmurs cut off, but the shuffling persisted, more prominent than before.

"Had the chancellor not been smarter and more skilled than the lot of you combined, you would have killed him."

Nightfall fought down a smile. The captain, at least,

had not overlooked his antics, and that earned him Nightfall's admiration. One among the mob had kept his head.

The man who had gone to the captain's cabin returned with an armload of silken wear. With a tip of his head, the captain made a grand gesture at Nightfall.

Hesitantly, the pirate approached and offered the clothing to Nightfall.

Having disccerned some decent blades among the treasure, Nightfall made a show of accepting clothing from the pirate, using legitimate movement as a means to work his way closer to the booty. As he donned the clothing, he slipped two well forged knives from the pile.

Cued by the captain's words, the pirates began patting pockets and stroking their necks, seeking favorite pieces of jewelry. Many turned their attention to the loot, visually seeking the items they had lost, though none dared to touch any of their ill-gotten plunder without the captain's consent.

The captain ran a callused hand through his hair. "Under the circumstances, we have no choice but to return the chancellor alive and as well as possible." He gave Sudian a short bow, which restarted the grumbles and murmurs. "My lord, I hope you can forgive my men their shortcomings."

Nightfall feigned an inordinate interest in his new clothing. It felt soft and warm, a one-piece outfit of charcoal black, its lining quilted. Though constructed for a far larger man, it fit comfortably with the cuffs rolled and a wide amber sash to pull the extra folds snug.

"Because," the captain continued, "I'd rather have a man like you as an acquaintance than an enemy."

Nightfall knew the captain could never know how true a statement he spoke. He did notice the captain had not suggested the possibility of friendship and believed that came of the captain not wanting to sound presumptuous rather than any unwillingness to join in such a partnership. Seeing an opening, Nightfall took it. "Captain, give me the name of the man who ratted out *The Sharius*, and all's forgiven." He adjusted the sash and, secretly, the knives. "Find out who snatched King Edward and get that information to me, and I'll see you're rewarded. Alliance or payment, whichever you prefer."

The captain's heavy brows shot upward. This time, he gave a real bow, even adding an admirable flourish. "Lord Chancellor Sudian of Alyndar, we will accept that deal."

† Chapter 6 †

Attribute nothing to malice until you have ruled out stupidity.

—Dyfrin of Keevain, the demon's friend

NIGHTFALL AWAKENED as he nearly always did, without stiffening or changing his position, instinctively matching the deep in-and-out cycle of sleep breathing. His senses placed him in an instant: the warm scratchiness of a woolen blanket, the toss and rock of a ship on the ocean, the quiet enwrapping him interrupted by the occasional and distant shouts of sailors. He heard nothing to concern him in their tones, just the regular announcements and banter that kept a ship safely and properly directed upon the sea. He lay in his cabin aboard *The Sharius,* alone; and he believed he had slept for quite a long time. He also knew a closer noise had awakened him.

Nightfall opened his eyes to near-total darkness broken only by the leak of light through incompletely constructed walls. Gentle footsteps crossed the lower deck, coming toward his door. They sounded too delicate for Ragan or any of the Schizian guardsmen.

Still dressed in the black silk pirate garb, the king's

ring tucked safely into its folds, Nightfall sat up and rubbed the hard seeds from the corners of his eyes. He had indeed rested for many hours.

A timid knock sounded on Nightfall's door.

Nightfall slid from the bed and readjusted the blankets. Stretching his muscles fully awake, he crossed the room and threw open the door.

The cabin boy, Danyal, stood on the lintel. Dressed in a faded windbreaker that fell nearly to his ankles, he carried a tattered and dirty rag draped over his left shoulder. His yellow hair lay in dusty disarray.

Nightfall gestured the child inside, wondering why he had come.

Danyal accepted the invitation, silently entering and waiting for Nightfall to close the door behind him. Once he did, Danyal tossed himself into the chair.

"Busy morning?" Nightfall guessed.

Danyal nodded wearily, stripping the rag from his shoulders, wiping his hands, then dropping it into his lap. "But I didn't come for a break. I came because I was worried about you, my lord."

"Really." Nightfall found that hard to believe.

"Did they . . . did they . . . hurt you?"

Ordinarily, Nightfall would have denied any form of weakness; but he played along with what appeared to be a game. Rolling up one overlong, quilted sleeve, he displayed the nicks, gouges, and bruises left in the wake of the pirates' assault. Though superficial, the wounds made a remarkable picture.

"My lord!" Danyal stared in clear horror. "They did hurt you."

Nightfall restored his sleeve to its natural cuff. "Never get between a starving dog and food, nor between a pirate and gold." He added casually, "So, Danyal, how much do they pay you?"

"Pay, my lord?" Danyal shrugged. "I get to eat, some clothes. A place to sleep on the deck or at an inn, sometimes, when we're on shore. A toy or a coin now and then when—"

Nightfall interrupted. "That's not what I meant."

Danyal met Nightfall's eyes, then paled. "You mean—"

"Yes, I mean. I mean the pirates. I mean the men who assaulted me."

Withering under the scrutiny, Danyal drew into himself, pinching the rag between his thighs. Moisture filled his eyes. "They give me coppers, food, drinks. Just for telling them what we're hauling. It's never hurt anything—"

"It hurt me." Nightfall did not add the encounter had cost Alyndar a fortune. Money came and went too fast and easy for him to concern himself with it in a long-term way. "It nearly killed me."

Tears dribbled from Danyal's eyes; but, to Nightfall's surprise, the boy did not beg for his life. Had any adult wronged Nightfall so severely, he would not have bothered with discussion. The offender would already have filled the bellies of lobsters and sharks. Now, raw sorrow colored Danyal's features. The cabin boy truly did not worry for his own lot, only for the pain he had inflicted on someone who had been kind to him. "I'm so sorry. I'm so very very sorry, my lord," he sobbed, burying his face in his hands.

Nightfall stared, speechless. Was it possible the boy had not realized the consequences of selling information to strangers in some backwater tavern? Could a child who had only known him a few days feel such true remorse? The answer came to Nightfall in a single word: Edward. The naive king had been known to dutifully supply facts to dangerous men for no payment at all, and he had ferociously protected Nightfall from abuse, even against other nobility, even when propriety demanded severe punishment. Risking the king's own life was not reason enough for Edward to inflict physical punishment on a servant.

Nightfall had never had a similar compunction. Killing, maiming, torture occasionally remained parts of his repertoire, but he found himself incapable of harming this boy. Despite the deception, he still liked Danyal. Though he might never trust the boy again, he had no interest in hurting him either.

"Please, my lord. Do what you will with me. But please don't tell the captain. Please, my lord."

Nightfall doubted the captain could inflict anything worse than the demon. "I'm the one robbed, humiliated, and wounded. What makes you think the captain would beat you half as hard as I would?"

The tears came faster, but Danyal raised his head bravely. "I'm not afraid of any beating. I deserve that. But the captain'll throw me off the crew." Face smeared, Danyal choked out the words. "Sailing's all I know, all I ever done, all I ever wanted to do. I've suffered worse than a beating for it before. Nothing you can do to me's worse than that, my lord."

Nightfall did not dwell on the fact that he could inflict worse. He knew all the rules, written and unwritten, between sailors. "You do realize, Danyal, if anyone else finds out about this, your only hope for sailing is the pirates themselves." He studied the boy to make sure he had captured Danyal's full attention. "It's not a happy life. And rarely a long one."

Danyal's weeping became so intense, he could not reply.

Nightfall had once considered himself heartless, but the boy's plight touched him. "I'm not going to tell the captain."

Danyal sniffled, still incapable of speech.

"Or anyone else." Nightfall smiled wanly. "I'm not even going to beat you."

Danyal managed to blurt out, "You have to!"

"I don't 'have to' do anything."

"But . . ." Danyal started and stopped. "But . . . if you don't . . . I . . ." Racked by sobs, he could not continue.

Try as he might, Nightfall could not complete the sentence for the boy. It made no sense for Danyal to beg for punishment, and Nightfall had spent too much of his own early life dodging thrashings to believe anyone would want one. He waited patiently for Danyal to regain enough composure to finish.

After a long interval of intense crying, Danyal finally did. By then, he seemed to have lost his train of thought.

But Nightfall still needed to understand. "I'm not going to hit you," he reminded.

This time, Danyal took the news stoically. He twisted his rough little hands around the rag.

When that did not elicit the conclusion Danyal had dodged speaking, Nightfall pressed. "I would think that would be good news."

Danyal nodded, still kneading the cloth in his fingers. "It is, my lord. In a way." He looked up, the whites of his eyes now a soggy crimson. "No one likes getting beaten, of course, my lord. But . . ."

This time, Nightfall would not let the boy off. "Yes?"

"I'm not sure I can explain it, my lord." Danyal unclenched his hands and spread his fingers, his gaze growing distant. "When something really bad happens, I'd rather get beaten and be done with it. Otherwise, it's . . . it's like it's in my head . . . bothering me all the time. Making me feel like . . . like I'm not . . . worthy of any joy."

Now, Nightfall remembered Dyfrin describing a similar feeling, one Nightfall had never shared. "Haunted by guilt," Dyfrin had called it. It first required a functioning conscience, and Nightfall, like many of his ilk, seemed not to own one. If it worked the way Dyfrin had said, it would prove a worse burden than any beating; and it might leave the boy beholden to his victim. "I'm afraid you'll have to live with that, Danyal, because I'm not going to punish you and I'm not going to tell the captain. But I do ask two things of you in return."

Danyal nodded and made a gesture to indicate Nightfall should continue.

"First, never sell information about your ship or its crew to anyone again."

"I won't, my lord!" Danyal said emphatically. "Not ever."

"Second." Nightfall leaned closer to emphasize the seriousness of his next condition. "If you find out anything about King Edward's disappearance: who has him, who took him, where they might have gone, you find a way to get that information to me in Alyndar as swiftly as possible."

"I will, my lord."

The agreement came too fast for Nightfall to believe the boy had considered the implications. "That might mean an extra voyage for you. A different ship. Or that you pay someone to bring the message in your stead."

Now, Danyal hesitated in clear consideration. He nodded grimly and spoke through teeth gritted in solemn promise. "I'll do whatever it takes, my lord. I owe you that much."

Nightfall knew emotion and expression like other men knew their hearts. Danyal held his vow sacred. Relaxing, Nightfall sat on the pallet. "Thank you."

"You miss him, don't you, Lord?"

The question blindsided Nightfall. Most adults would simply have seen his stipulation as loyalty to a ruler, but the boy saw through it to the raw emotion that would overwhelm him, if he were not deliberately holding it at bay. "Terribly," he admitted. "I might be the only one to believe this, but Ned has the potential to become the best king Alyndar ever had."

Danyal nodded politely.

Now it was Nightfall's turn to catch his companion by surprise. "Where are your parents, Danyal?"

The boy looked at his feet, again twisting the rag in his lap. "I never knew my father, my lord. My mother died two years ago, and . . ."

Nightfall sat back and listened to a story that could have been his own.

Rain clouds scudded across the sky, muting late morning to a grayness that simulated evening. Men scrambled over Alyndar's docks like ants through tunnels, hoisting and tossing crates and boxes, drawing on lines, shouting gruff epithets at the cargo and one another. A dozen stood at the ready as *The Sharius'* sailors began the careful, all-too-familiar sequence that would steer her safely into an empty berth. Avoiding the riggings so as not to interfere with their work nor become tangled with furling canvas, Nightfall stood at the bow and scanned the docks for a welcoming party.

At first Nightfall saw no one except the men who habitually handled the docks, sun-darkened, work-calloused men with muscles hardened to steel by years of assisting ships and hauling cargo. Suddenly, he spotted a female figure sprinting up the planking, flanked by two men and a boy. He knew her at once, memory filling in whatever details distance and intervening objects hid. She ran with an unmistakable dancer's grace, short locks as white as an elder's flying, manelike, from the back of her head. Though he wanted to give her his full attention, Nightfall's wariness would not allow him to. He also noted the two men scurrying in her wake, dressed in Alyndarian colors and decked with swords. The boy appeared to be a page, clutching his hat to his head as he hurried after the others, needing two and a half strides for every one of the guards'.

Unable to wait for the ship to tie up, Nightfall sprang to the gunwale, then made a broad leap for the dock. He landed lightly, barely remembering to restore his weight in time. A startled dockhand grabbed his arm, attempting to steady him and nearly knocking Nightfall sprawling in the process. A moment later, Kelryn hurled herself into his arms with a force his already precarious balance could not handle. The dockhand let go, sparing himself, but the two lovers tumbled to the planking. Resisting the urge to roll, Nightfall scrambled to place his body between hers and the sea, surprised to find the feel of her body against him excited him wildly despite their predicament.

The two guards who had accompanied Kelryn took her arms and hoisted her easily to her feet. Nightfall scrambled up before anyone could think to help him as well. He had barely reached a standing position, when he found Kelryn filling his arms again. This time, he remained firm, taking her into his arms and reveling in her warmth. He buried his mouth and nose in her hair, which smelled of salt wind and flowers, though his eyes remained wide open and aware of every nearby movement. "I missed you," he whispered, kissing the top of her head.

"I missed you, too," Kelryn said, so softly he could barely hear her. "And I worried so much."

"Edward will be all right." Nightfall tried to reassure her, though he did not know if he spoke truth or not. "We'll find him."

Kelryn pushed Nightfall away to look him in the eye. "I worried for you."

"Me?" Nightfall laughed. "I was never in any danger."

Kelryn studied him sternly, bright blue eyes nearly lost in narrowed sockets. Nightfall no longer saw any of her imperfections; her features had become the very definition of beauty. "Don't lie to me, Sudian. You could've been killed. You're hurt right now."

Nightfall wondered how she knew, certain he had covered all of his injuries and bullied through pain rather than dare show any weakness, even when the salt air stung his myriad cuts and abrasions. She knew him with a dangerous intimacy that scared him. He had never allowed anyone, not even Dyfrin, that close; and he thought he had divested himself of any predictability. No typical gestures. No repetitive reactions. No patterns. Kelryn saw through all of it, however, just as she had recognized him the first time he had presented himself to her in the guise of Sudian. "I wasn't there when they took Edward, gods damn him."

Kelryn sucked in a mouthful of air. "Sudian!"

Anger overtook common sense. "He's the one whose damnable honor sent me off on a damnable fool's mission because of a damnable crackpot promise. If I'd've been with him, no hell-damned gang of bastards could have damned well kidnapped him."

"Is this a game?"

The question came out of nowhere. Nightfall could scarcely believe Kelryn could fail to see the gravity of the situation. "What?"

Kelryn continued, "Are you trying to see how many times you can use 'damn' in the same sentence?"

"Damn it, Kelryn!"

"And again, Sudian? You do know, there are ladies present."

Irritated by Kelryn's belittling his rage, Nightfall resorted to ruder teasing. "Ladies? Where?" He scanned the docks around her, then jerked away, certain she would slap him.

She didn't. Kelryn never resorted to physical violence. She knew enough not to use his mother's tactics against him. She lowered her voice. "Whether or not he deserves it, the king cannot be spoken of in that manner. The law—"

"Piss on the damned law." Back in familiar surroundings, Nightfall found himself more angered than upset by all that had happened, enraged by his own mistakes. He looked around Kelryn to find the guards staring at him. "There's a chest on board that belongs to Alyndar. If you can tend to it, I'm sure Kelryn and I can get ourselves safely to the castle."

The guards hesitated, clearly weighing their orders against his rank. Finally, one bowed. "Yes, my lord." They both scurried to *The Sharius* to pass words with the Schizian guardsmen.

Nightfall took Kelryn's arm and wove between the dockworkers. The page looked uncertainly from the guards to the couple before falling into step behind Nightfall and Kelryn. Nightfall wondered how far he would have to go to demonstrate their desire to remain alone. He considered starting with a passionate kiss, but decided against it. After such a long absence from his fiancée, he suspected romantic gestures would punish him more than embarrass the page. He could not afford to perform anything obscene or improper before understanding where he stood when it came to Alyndar. He knew he lived in the palace only by King Edward's grace and suspected the other nobles would thrill to see him go. "So," he said softly. "How do things stand here?" He did not mention his suspicions about a traitor ... yet. If Kelryn broached the topic, he would discuss it. Otherwise, he did not want to further burden her until it became necessary.

Kelryn snuggled against Nightfall as they walked, forcing him to guard his every step. She bounced along easily beside him, seeming not the least inconvenienced by his closeness. "A bit troubled, but no lapses into chaos that I can see. The nobles seem certain a ransom demand will arrive soon, and they're willing to await the king's return to consider the need for retribution."

The sounds of the docks grew faint behind them, replaced by the distant cries of merchants from the open market, the murmurs of passersby on the streets. "So, ransom really is expected."

Kelryn managed a shrug. "It seems certain."

Nightfall nodded thoughtfully, pleased the duke had told the truth, at least on that point. He kept to the main street, ignoring the scurrying peasants, even the ones who paused to salute the pair with bows or curtsies. "So things should go back to normal soon."

"Mmmm-hmmm."

Nightfall felt his muscles uncoil. His rage dissipated.

The sights of the city did seem ordinary, the distant spires of the castle towering over the trees. He considered the possibility he had made a mistake in reasoning that someone near Edward must have tipped off the kidnappers to his travel plans and vulnerability, but found himself unable to abandon a theory based on sound reasoning. His concern required investigation, which, however, could wait until after a proper reunion with his betrothed. "What would you say to a warm bath and a long . . . snuggle?"

Kelryn's hand slid down Nightfall's arm as she pulled away far enough that only their fingers touched. "I don't think anyone would begrudge you that bath, my love. But the rest will have to wait until after court."

Nightfall groaned at the bare thought of that stuffy pretension, with its parade of malcontents and its incomprehensible rules. "I wasn't planning to couple in the Great Hall."

Kelryn's delicate fingers enwrapped his hand. "Of course not, silly. But, as the highest ranking official, you will have to preside."

"What?" Nightfall came to a dead halt, hoping he had misunderstood.

A sudden side step saved the page. Beside him, a woman jerked into a clumsy dance to keep from running into the pair, startling a mule who reared, overturning a small cart of vegetables. The man who had led it cursed softly, careful not to aim any of his harsh language directly at the noble and his fiancée.

Kelryn cringed at the spill. "You are the chancellor, Sudian."

Though Nightfall had now heard his rank proclaimed for about the tenth time, he refused to acknowledge it. "Ned just asked me to be an adviser. Not a chancellor."

"*The* chancellor, Sudian. There's only one."

Nightfall resumed walking, though he turned Kelryn a sarcastic glare. "*The* chancellor, then. Thanks. That makes it so much better."

"I'm sure Ned didn't want to overwhelm you. He thought it might scare you from accepting the position."

"It would have."

Kelryn spread her hands, her point made for her. "But we all knew what he meant when he asked you."

"I didn't."

"He wanted you to take Gilleran's place." Kelryn gave him a sideways look that brooked no deceit. "You're not stupid, Sudian. You knew that."

"I guess . . . I did know that." At the time, Nightfall had lain in agony, seriously wounded from his battle with Gilleran. He had overheard Kelryn refusing King Edward's proposal because, she said, she was in love with him. Warmed and shocked by Kelryn's sacrifice, and the king's friendship, Nightfall had not considered the full extent of Edward's offer. "But I didn't . . . I mean . . ." The realization was frightening. "Gods above, *Ned* conned *me*!"

Kelryn laughed. "I knew you'd love the irony."

Nightfall could not help smiling in silence for several moments as they walked, hand in hand toward Alyndar Castle, the page dogging every step. An anemic glimmer of sun forced its way through a crack in the cloud cover, adding a sheen to the cobbled street. Men and women stepped aside, leaving the center of the way clear for Alyndarian nobility. Nightfall picked up the last thread of their conversation and built on it. "Not half the irony of me sitting in judgment on anyone. Can't we pass on the duty to some enthusiastic underling?"

Kelryn picked lint from Nightfall's shaggy hair. "I'm afraid not."

"Well, who's done it while Ned and I were gone?"

"By law, the members of the High Council took turns." Kelryn ran her fingers through his tangles, giving up almost as soon as she started. The sea air had turned his hair into a hopeless snarl. "And they're not underlings, Sudian. Together, they hold tremendous power."

Disinterested in such matters, Nightfall waved away the details. "Can't they just keep doing it?"

Kelryn shook her head, not giving up on her explanation as easily as on Nightfall's hair. "The most important cases have waited for the king's return. The chancellor will do in his absence."

"I will?" The words were shocked from him.

The two turned onto the rocky path toward the castle, suddenly alone. Even the page became lost on the main streets.

Kelryn steered Nightfall to a large boulder and signaled for him to sit.

Nightfall obliged by springing onto the stone, though he settled in a defensible crouch. Certain no one could overhear them, Kelryn switched to the name by which she had known Nightfall most of his life, one she dared not speak in anyone's presence. "Marak, you need to understand. King Rikard had two sons, no daughters. When he and his oldest, Leyne, were killed, that left only Ned."

Nightfall made an impatient gesture.

"Only Ned. King Edward. The king's last blooded relative."

Nightfall missed the point. "I know that. That's what released me from Gilleran's damned oath-bond. That's why I was able to attack him."

"You also know his goal was to kill Ned, too."

"Yes. Yes." The discussion seemed a waste of time. Nightfall glanced toward the reappeared page as he settled on another rock a polite distance away. "To destroy the king's entire line . . ."

". . . so Gilleran, Chancellor of Alyndar, would sit upon the throne."

Suddenly, everything became clear. The blood drained from Nightfall's face. "You mean . . . ? You mean that until King Edward returns . . . ?" He could not finish.

So Kelryn did. ". . . you are the ruler of the kingdom of Alyndar." She performed a fancy curtsy. "Your Majesty."

Nightfall sank to the boulder, speechless.

† Chapter 7 †

Beware what you pretend to be—lest you forget the game and become it.

—Dyfrin of Keevain, the demon's friend

THE WORLD CHANGED the moment Nightfall reached the castle door. Brisk and fawning servants whisked him from his salt-crusted, wrinkled pirate gear into a warm bath; and he barely managed to keep hold of Edward's rescued ring. Much to his chagrin, one man remained to scour him with ashy perfumed oil, sand, and brushes, despite his insistence he could tend to himself. He had weathered this treatment only once before, also in Alyndar Castle, just before King Rikard had assigned him his new identity as Prince Edward's squire/steward. Then, the bath had seemed as dangerous as it was symbolic, washing away the filth of his immoral past but also the protection of the many personae who had kept him alive and concealed through the years. Once fully exposed, he could never escape to anonymity again.

This time, the process seemed more invigorating and physically painful than humiliating or emotionally charged. The scrubbing opened his healing wounds as well as dislodging weeks of grime, leaving the water an ugly reddish brown and requiring three changes. When the bath attendant finished, another man coated Nightfall's abraded skin with soothing balms and sweet-smelling oils, then swaddled him in fluffy towels. A woman came after with a pouch of tools, attacking the rigid knots and snarls that defined his hair. He sensed her frustration as the tangled locks refused to yield to her usual ministrations, and she loosed occasional grunts or hissed through her gritted teeth.

The three male servants stood by with Nightfall's fresh clothing, but they would not remove the towels in the woman's presence. At length, one paced. Another hovered over her, pointing out areas that needed tending. Each time he spoke, his voice barely above a whisper, her manner grew choppier, her combing more hatchetlike. The third man inspected the court silks repeatedly: unfolding and refolding, removing invisible lint, checking every seam.

Finally, even Nightfall had had enough. "You!" He jabbed a finger toward the male servant near his head. "Leave her alone and let her work before she stabs one of those picks through your annoying, interfering heart!"

Clearly taken aback, the man retreated. "Yes, sir . . . Lord . . . Majesty."

The woman snorted, clearly a suppressed laugh.

"And you." Nightfall indicated the woman with a lighter gesture. "Stop worrying so much about hurting me or ruining something. Cut off whatever's in your way. Shear me bald, if you have to."

"But, Majesty—" the man he had first addressed protested.

Nightfall interrupted. "It'll grow back. It always does, damn it."

The woman worked faster, more heavy-handed, while the man continued to watch over her shoulder wringing his hands but no longer directing.

The pacer ceased his useless movements to approach

Nightfall. Averting his eyes from the towel-covered form, he bowed deeply. "Lord Chancellor, who would you have us fetch for the chancellor's seat?"

Nightfall turned his attention to the speaker, a thin, nervous-looking man with a long, narrow face and wispy blond hair. "Excuse me?"

The servant bowed again. "Who do you wish to advise you from the chancellor's seat?" He added carefully, "If anyone, my lord."

Nightfall hesitated, considering whom among Alyndar's staff he would dare to trust. Many of those with the most knowledge might deliberately steer him wrong to embarrass him, and he had paid little attention to court affairs in his short time at Alyndar Castle. He could think of only one person he could wholly trust. "Kelryn."

The servant blinked but otherwise made no movement. He did not even seem to breathe.

The clothier paused in his inspection, and the man who had done most of the previous talking left the woman's side to face Nightfall directly.

Nightfall got his first good look at the man. A bit older than the others, nearly Nightfall's age, he was tall and lean with curly brown hair and a ruddy complexion. "Pardon me, Chancellor Sudian, sir. Did you say Kelryn?"

"Indeed."

"As in *Lady* Kelryn?"

"Lady Kelryn, yes. Is there a Lord Kelryn?"

"No, my lord." The man shifted from foot to foot in his livery. "But, Lord Chancellor . . . ?"

When the head servant did not finish, Nightfall pressed. "Yes?"

The blond finally blurted out, "But she's a . . . a lady!"

Though Nightfall guessed the cause of their consternation, he continued to play dumb. It seemed better than the previous cautious silence. "Of that, I am very glad, seeing as how I intend to marry her."

At Nightfall's back, the woman's touch gentled, and a comb glided through his locks, dislodging dirt the bathwater could not previously reach.

"A woman as adviser?" The head servant pressed his hands together. "It's simply not done, my lord."

Nightfall could feel wetness splashing onto his scalp. When the servants finished with him, he suspected he would look more foppish than regal. "Why not? Is a woman's advice not as useful as a man's?"

The clothier paled, and the headman's movements became a shuffling dance. Those two, Nightfall felt certain, had wives. "It is just . . . softer, my lord. Bedroom advice. Kitchen advice. Not courtroom advice."

"Done!" the woman announced suddenly, stepping back to admire her work.

Nightfall shook his head. She had managed to keep his hair at a length just past his ears. Free of tangles, it moved easily, still wet from the washing and freshening oils. "Get Kelryn," he demanded, not caring if he violated protocol. "My judgment could use softening."

The staging area consisted of a small, empty room with curtained walls and two exits, including the one through which Nightfall and his new entourage entered. Dressed in doublet and hose, a protective leather tunic beneath the silver-trimmed purple silks, and pristine doeskin boots with gleaming silver buckles, Nightfall barely recognized himself. He wondered if the pretty-smelling crap they smeared on his face hid the predatory features or toned down his glaring eyes. Or, perhaps, the servants deliberately enhanced those features, believing harshness might strengthen the look of Alyndar's temporary ruler.

Me, Alyndar's king. The idea seemed so ludicrous Nightfall wanted to laugh out loud. Even if he could handle it, he did not want the job: the attention, the glitter, the responsibility. Every instinct drove him to hidden corners and solitude, and his determination to rescue Edward grew even more intense. The king belonged on the throne of Alyndar, and Nightfall felt like something worse than an imposter.

The servants had remained behind to clean up the bathing room, and three new men replaced them. Nightfall knew the first, a plump steward with stringy, dark-blond hair and pale, recessed features. Though not much to look at, he had a calm, jovial personality that had won him a charming wife and one of the highest positions among Alyndar's advisers. Named Charson, he had secured King Edward's trust, and Nightfall also liked him.

The second was Khanwar, the tall, trim man whose seat Edward had given to Nightfall at their conference prior to leaving for Schiz. Ebony-haired and brown-eyed, Khanwar bore some title Nightfall had missed, though it sounded long and impressive. He spoke little, seeming to expect his charge to already know all the locations and formalities, and frowning at every tiny ignorance or mistake. The third attendant, called Vivarick, came and went with brusque efficiency, reporting back to either of the other men at intervals. Middle-aged and -sized, he sported auburn hair shorter than the current style, which always followed the king's. Edward's locks hung to his shoulders, casually layered and hinting of curl. Few could match his natural beauty, but most of the noblemen tried. Idly, Nightfall wondered if he became king, would royalty run around with wild snarls of grimy hair falling into their faces. He found no humor in the image, which first required him to accept Edward's death.

Through the other exit wafted the sounds of myriad conversations mingled into a rising and falling hum as the spectator nobles gathered, found their seats on the benches, and awaited the arrival of Alyndar's lord chancellor. The sound of footfalls and voices just outside the entrance, sent him spinning toward the door. Kelryn stepped inside, accompanied by a male steward and a female servant. She wore an ankle-length, lace-edged dress, tailored from fine green silk that filled out her otherwise sinewy curves. Her snowy hair lay flat, brushed to a fine sheen and falling into delicate feathers at her ears. A clip studded with emeralds held the wilder locks in place, enhanced the more colorful tones in her hazel eyes, and drew attention away from her oddly shaped nose. She was the most beautiful thing Nightfall had ever seen.

The other men, too, went silent, clearly impressed. The woman beside her beamed, obviously the key to Kelryn's transformation.

Kelryn glided toward Nightfall, her movements swanlike in their graceful perfection. Her dance, her every motion, had attracted him before her appearance, and she had lost none of her nimbleness in their time apart. He could scarcely believe this vision had consented to marry him, that she had worked most of her life as a dance hall girl.

"If you open your eyes any wider," she murmured, "they'll fall out. And close your mouth. There's nothing inside we need to see."

Nightfall tried to obey.

"See," Kelryn continued with a twirl that sent the fabric fluttering. "Rich clothes can make anyone beautiful."

Nightfall said the only thing he could, "You're always beautiful to—"

"There you are!" Khanwar gave Kelryn a shove through the far exit and onto the dais. "We've been waiting—"

Faster than Nightfall could think, he had Khanwar by the cloth at his throat, dragging the noble's head down to meet his killer stare. "Don't manhandle Kelryn." He had a weakness when it came to his beloved, the same that had forced him to spread false rumors about her having the clap to end the prostitution most of the dancers took up to supplement their meager wages. The same that once drove him to hunt down any man who dared to offend her. "Don't even touch her."

As Charson and Vivarick scurried to Khanwar's aid, Nightfall released his victim and schooled his expression back to calmness.

Khanwar sprang backward, gasping in a sharp breath and readjusting his clothing. "You . . ." he sputtered. "He . . ."

Nightfall turned his back on the fuming noble, though he measured every movement by sound. He knew he should apologize, that a man of high upbringing would do so, no matter how justified he felt; but he could not bring himself to speak. If he so much as looked at Khanwar, he might do the man serious bodily harm.

Clearly trying to defuse the situation, Charson guided Nightfall toward the exit. "Time for you, too, Sire. Do you feel ready?"

To play king? Never. Nightfall doubted, if he sat upon Alyndar's throne for a hundred years, he would ever feel like more than a poor substitute for Edward. Accustomed to lying, he said easily, "Ready."

Accompanied by all three members of his escort, one looking mightily ruffled, Nightfall stepped through the curtain and onto the dais.

The conversations cut off as if choked, most in mid sentence or even mid word. Nightfall looked down over a courtroom packed with standing nobles. Usually, only the front two benches were occupied. Now, all seven rows held at least a few onlookers on both sides of the aisle. Many had come to see how a mysterious commoner turned acting-king would handle the requests of regal nobility forced to kowtow to the title such a man should never hold, to see how he judged Alyndar's peasants, or to find entertainment in his many mistakes. Nightfall's gaze went to the high peaked windows hovering above the outer aisles, the stretches between them thick with paintings and tapestries of myriad colors. A massive shield hung over the great doors, through which those who came before him would enter, striding or being dragged down the long, carpeted hallway. Nightfall had once taken the walk down that carpet to stand before King Rikard, accused of murdering his eldest son.

Guards lined the outer walls and pathway, Alyndar's colors sharp over the bulges of their mail. Three stood at the edges of the dais, including Captain Volkmier, the only one wearing the more subdued gray and lavender of the prison guards. The compact redhead looked as intent and serious as any of the standard guards, and Nightfall swallowed a lump that appeared suddenly in his throat. *Bring our king safely home,* Volkmier had warned him, the words gentle but the tone heavy with threat. Nightfall dreaded his next private run-in with the chief of the prison guards.

Charson gave Nightfall a gentle nudge. "Sire, no one can sit until you do."

Really? The conventions of the royals seemed nonsensical to him. He glanced over at Kelryn, smiling at him from in front of the chancellor's seat, then drifted toward the only other chair on the dais, the high-backed plush throne. Just the idea of placing his lowly rear end into the king's place alarmed him. A man could get executed for such an audacious act.

Kelryn lowered her head slowly, as if controlling his motion with her own. Trusting her cue, he sat on the very edge of the chair, his back unsupported and his feet still in contact with the floor.

As soon as Nightfall did so, the nobles followed suit, benches creaking and groaning beneath the sudden massive shift of weight. Kelryn also took her seat. Her attendants had not followed them through the curtain. Charson stepped to the far right front edge of the dais, Vivarick to the left, beyond Kelryn. Seemingly in full control of his composure once more, Khanwar strode from the dais to the floor, standing in front of the waiting nobles. "Alyndar's court will now come to order!"

Even the sounds of the benches desisted.

"In the absence of King Edward Nargol, our Lord Chancellor-on-high, Sudian . . ." Khanwar pronounced the name with an unmistakable hint of distaste.

Kelryn glanced at Nightfall in question, and he shrugged in response. He knew exactly why Khanwar disliked him.

" . . . will preside over the process." Khanwar made a grand gesture. "Admit the first case, please."

As if controlled by Khanwar and his words, the great doors opened to admit two well-dressed men escorted by members of Alyndar's guard. One strode down the purple carpetway, glancing neither right nor left, while the other paused to greet some of the nobles on the benches. Nightfall watched both of them, learning much simply by the way they moved toward him. Both carried extra years and weight. He guessed they were in their late forties or early fifties, and neither wanted for meals. The cut and material of their clothing, the extra buttons and trim, made it clear they came from the upper classes. The first wore a look of somber determination; he would allow nothing to interfere with his mission, whatever it might prove to be. The second seemed less comfortable in court, his friendliness an attempt to hide nervousness.

Khanwar announced, "Sir Broward Arnsbok."

The man in the lead stopped at the foot of the dais, where the carpet ended, and bowed deeply to Nightfall, removing a poofy velvet hat as he did so. The gesture revealed a prominent bald spot and wisps of graying sandy hair.

Though the second man had not yet made his way to the foot of the dais, Khanwar also announced him, "And Sir Reginald Pinkard."

Reginald increased his pace, making several dipping bows as he walked.

"Land dispute."

Land dispute. Nightfall wondered what exactly that

meant. Only nobility had the right to own property, and he knew from experience that it was expensive. Beyond that, he understood nothing.

Kelryn whispered, "Say something."

Broward bounced on his heels restively, his face scarlet with need.

Nightfall glanced at his chosen adviser.

"Say something," she repeated. "Before he explodes."

Nightfall cleared his throat. "Do you . . . ?" he started, uncertain where to go from there. "Do you need to . . . relieve yourself, sir?"

The stands burst into laughter. Kelryn winced.

"Relieve myself?" Broward seemed as put off by the laughter. He glanced around the nobility, cheeks returning to their normal color, then flushing again as he caught the meaning of Nightfall's words. "No, Sire. I just wish to state my case."

Nightfall realized his mistake. Apparently, Broward's discomfort came from a less primal unsatisfied need. Just as the spectators could not sit before Nightfall did, he had waited to speak his long-rehearsed piece until the man on the throne spoke first.

Sir Broward cleared his throat as he drew a piece of parchment from his pocket and began to read: "The Northwest Quarter of the Southwest Quarter of Section Twenty-three in the area Seventy-six North, Range Four West of the Fifth Principal Meridian excepting therefrom . . ."

The words flowed around Nightfall.

" . . . a parcel of land situated at the Southwest Quarter of Section Twenty-three in the area . . ."

Nightfall heard little more. He wondered where Edward was right now, whether he was in pain or imprisoned, and why he, himself, had bothered to return to Alyndar at all. He had worried about a traitor; but, since the moment Kelryn had forced him to realize he stood next in line for the throne, he found the possibility more difficult to accept. Surely no one would rather see

Nightfall rule Alyndar than Edward. *Unless they plan to eliminate me, too.* It seemed foolish for anyone to make such a grand and bold overthrow attempt so soon after Gilleran's had failed, while the castle and its security remained at the height of alertness. *Or, perhaps, it's the best time, given the chaos inherent in reshuffling priorities and command, the uncertainty about Edward's ability to lead a country.* Nightfall needed to find out who would inherit rulership of Alyndar in the event of his own disappearance, but he doubted the guilty party would prove so obvious or simple to find. It seemed just as likely that whoever had alerted the kidnappers to the king's destination might have done so for the same basic reason as Danyal: monetary reward, or the promise of it. One thing seemed certain: *sellout or betrayer, Kelryn was never in danger.*

Nightfall had also believed Duke Varsah, or wanted to, that a ransom letter might already have arrived in Alyndar. He understood too little of the way royalty worked to follow his own instincts in such a matter. Yet, now, he realized he had made a mistake that might cost Edward his life. Nightfall should have remained in Schiz, should have followed every lead he could uncover. Now, the trail had grown cold, and it seemed as if he had trapped himself into waiting and wondering, into the same helplessness as the rest of Edward's men. *I should have pressed. I should have done something. I never should have come home.* Nightfall wriggled on the chair. *Edward's ass should warm this padding, not mine.*

Kelryn hissed, "At least pretend to pay attention."

Nightfall straightened with a start.

" . . . commencing at the Northwest corner of the Southwest Quarter of said Section Twenty-three thence North 90 00" East (assumed bearing) 1159.02 King Leordin feet along the North line of the Southwest Quarter of said . . ."

"I would, if he'd use one of the known languages,"

Nightfall whispered back. "I don't understand a word he's saying."

Kelryn kept her words as low as possible. "He's describing the outlines of a piece of land, I think."

Nightfall glanced to the right and caught Charson's eye. He gestured subtly with his head, and the steward came casually toward him.

Nightfall waited until Charson reached whispering distance before asking, "What, exactly, is this dispute about?"

Charson kept his voice as soft as Kelryn's and Nightfall's as Broward continued his description. "It's complicated—"

"Make it simple."

". . . East 180.45 feet along the North line of said Southwest Quarter and centerline of the Road to the intersection of the centerlines of two Roads: thence South 22 25'58" West 282.16 . . ."

Charson lowered his head in thought, then licked the tip of one finger. Finally, he said, "The man in front says the man in back built a sheep fence on his property. The other man says it's on his own property."

Nightfall bobbed his head. At least now he had an idea of what was happening, even if he knew he would never manage to figure out the answers from the description of the parcel. "How much land are we talking about?"

Charson raised a hand, spreading his thumb and forefinger to about the width of a thin loaf of bread.

Nightfall blinked. "Really?"

Charson dropped his hand. "That wide, sir. Quite long."

The length seemed insignificant. A ribbon of nothing still added up to nothing. "They're fighting over this much land?" He spread his own fingers the appropriate distance.

"Yes, Sire."

Nightfall looked at Kelryn to see if she found the situation as ridiculous as he did. She chewed her lower lip, displaying no emotion.

"Why?"

"It's land, Sire. It's important to them."

Kelryn released her lip, her expression now one of stern warning. "Sudian, remember this is still Edward's kingdom. You mustn't make rash decisions."

Sir Broward continued, undaunted by the hushed conversation, ". . . along the arc of a ten-degree curve to the left side 123.16 feet, the chord of which bears South 16 16'30" West 122.92 feet through a central angle of . . ."

Nightfall guessed, "So I should rule in favor of the one more important to Alyndar?"

"Ned wouldn't do that," Kelryn reminded.

Nightfall groaned. If he had to rule the way King Edward would in any given situation, he would have to overcome too many years of experience and accumulated wisdom. "You mean I have to rule in the most guileless—"

"Sudian!" This time, Kelryn spoke loud enough to interrupt the man at the foot of the dais.

Broward looked up at Nightfall, who waved at him to continue. So long as the noble droned onward, he did not have to make any ruling at all.

"Don't say it," Kelryn warned more softly.

Nightfall understood. It was treason to speak against the king under normal circumstances. With Edward's fate unclear, it was also unseemly. Not that he meant anything insulting by the comment. Everyone knew the current king of Alyndar was a naive young man with aspirations that seemed impossible to fulfill. *Wrong, Demon,* Nightfall corrected himself. *The current king of Alyndar is . . . you.* "So I should rule for the one who needs the land the most?"

Charson shuffled his feet. "Why not rule for the one who's right?"

You mean it's possible to tell? Nightfall shifted his attention to the other man. "And that is?"

"I don't know," Charson admitted. "But the royal surveyor can go out there and work with the written description."

Broward finally stopped talking, leaving the three in quiet discussion while the nobles shifted on the benches below them.

"Is that really necessary?" Kelryn asked.

"No." Charson glanced out at the silent hall, then turned his back on it. "And it's costly, too. But neither will believe he got a fair ruling unless it's done."

Nightfall let the two talk, as they seemed to be accomplishing more than he could.

"A contingency ruling?" Kelryn suggested, and Nightfall hoped she would define what she meant.

Charson stroked his chin. "Yes. The loser pays the surveyor's expenses; and for dismantling and rebuilding the fence, if necessary."

They both looked at Nightfall, who tried to return both stares simultaneously. "What?"

Charson smiled. "Well, Sire. You're the one who has to deliver the verdict."

"Of course." Nightfall cleared his throat, glad for his two advisers and hoping he had it right. Hesitantly, and with prompting, he managed to deliver the agreed-upon decision.

A parade of nobles followed the first, their concerns mostly childish or incomprehensible to Nightfall. When he thought "yes," the best answer was nearly always "no." When he thought "wrong," Kelryn steered him to "right." When all seemed muddled, the problem had an easy answer, while those difficulties seeming straightforward usually turned into contingencies or holdovers. It felt to Nightfall as if foodless, sleepless days had dragged past before Khanwar prepared to announce the last of the nobility. By that time, Nightfall worried he would need to have a chamber pot built into the throne. If the proceedings did not end soon, he might wet his fancy purple hose.

As always, a hush fell over the spectators, though this time it seemed as weary and uncomfortable as Nightfall felt. Khanwar stepped forward. "Your Majesty, the last case in Noble Court brings an emissary from Hartrin to your presence."

Nightfall straightened in his chair. Until now, a poor judgment could do nothing worse than stir unrest or feuds among the Alyndarian highborns. A mistake here could spark war with a country as large and powerful as Alyndar, and relations between the two countries had teetered of late. The very event that had driven King Rikard to the desperate action of harnessing the demon to his son had come out of their last official dealings with Hartrin. Then, Prince Edward had killed a royal slaver in an attempt to free the slaves the entourage had brought with them to Alyndar. Edward still bore a fading whip scar across his cheek from that encounter, the very detail that had cheated Hartrin out of blood price. Nightfall doubted King Idinbal was happy that the misguided adolescent who had caused all the trouble now ruled Alyndar.

That sent Nightfall's thoughts on another tangent. He wondered if Hartrin had had a hand in Ned's kidnapping. If so, he doubted he would ever see the brash young king again.

Still standing from the last judgment, Kelryn rested light fingers on Nightfall's balled fist in warning. Though he had grown to accept it, Nightfall did not like slavery any more than Edward did. He just preferred that his charge used more subtle and effective methods to combat it.

"What are you thinking?" Kelryn whispered. As Charson had returned to his position, only Nightfall could hear her.

"I'm thinking I wish this was done. I really have to pee."

Kelryn tipped her head and turned him a stern look.

Nightfall voiced his real concern. "Hartrin would have reason to abduct Ned."

"Hopefully, you're right; and this is the ransom demand."

That thought had not occurred to Nightfall, though it became obvious once Kelryn mentioned it. If Hartrin had taken Edward, they would have no other reason to appear before him. He watched as the emissary glided down the aisle, with two Alyndarian guards in tow, then knelt in front of the dais.

Nightfall had learned he did not necessarily have to speak first if he gestured to the other to do so. He signaled the emissary to rise, noting the nervousness in the man's dark eyes beneath a fringe of short-cut bangs. The man merely looked uncomfortable. Whatever his request, it might not please Nightfall, but it seemed unlikely to hold the significance of a ransom demand.

The Hartrinian rose, displaying the white eagle on a blue-and-red tabard that symbolized his country. "Sire, King Idinbal brings his best wishes. Had I not left before the incident, I'm certain he would express his gravest regrets on the disappearance of King Edward Nargol and the tragic deaths of his loyal guardsmen." He bowed his head. "Sire, Hartrin shares your grief and offers our condolences. I am certain another emissary is on his way to deliver that very message in the king's own words and to offer assistance."

"Thank you," Kelryn whispered.

"Thank you," Nightfall said aloud, trying not to squirm. The more flowery the Hartrinian's presentation, the longer the delay until he could relieve himself.

"Sire, I also wish to thank Alyndar for the hospitality it has shown me while I awaited a chance to appear before your most august self."

Nightfall nodded, knowing he had received a compliment, even if he did not fully comprehend it. He believed the foremost intention of the line was to remind Nightfall that this man had come to Alyndar before the kidnapping so that, if his request appeared indecorous under the circumstances, Nightfall would take into account that the emissary's orders preceded the sorry event.

"What can I do for you?" Nightfall prodded. His bladder had grown uncomfortably full, but he dared not mention bodily functions twice in one sitting. He suspected most of the spectators could use a break as well.

"King Idinbal sent me to negotiate tariffs."

Inwardly, Nightfall groaned. He had no idea how to do such a thing. "Go on."

"As our coffers are currently running light, His Majesty would like to propose an increase in tariffs to twenty percent. Six months should be long enough to get our finances back on track, then we can return to the standard ten percent."

Nightfall finally felt as if he had discovered a familiar topic. As the merchant Balshaz, he had experience with tariffs, and despised them. The costs of business between the two countries was already the highest in the known world due to a series of tariff wars, the vast differences in politics, and the physical distance between them. "Twenty percent seems steep. Don't you think it might drive away some merchants?"

Murmurs rose from the gallery.

"A worthy point, Sire, and a considerate one to be sure." The emissary bowed again. "But the merchants always adjust. They pay a bit less to suppliers; they charge a bit more for goods." He shrugged. "It's only a temporary increase, a necessary one, Sire, I think you'll agree."

Nightfall did not know what to think. He supposed kingdoms did have reasons for raising tariffs, beyond simple greed. Since the tariffs would rise equally in both kingdoms, he saw no reason to deny the request and fuel Hartrin's dislike for Alyndar. "Perhaps fifteen percent would please King Idinbal and still allow the merchants to make their livings." Nightfall studied the emissary, who seemed deep in thought. The fullness in his lower abdomen had advanced to significant pain. He had to end this soon.

After what seemed like forever, but was probably only a moment, the emissary nodded. "I believe that will suit His Majesty, Sire. Thank you for your time." He made one more deep bow, then turned on his heel and trod up the carpet.

Pleased he had handled the problem reasonably swiftly, without international incident or even the need for counsel, Nightfall sprang to his feet.

The response was instantaneous. The spectators all scrambled to stand in a frenzied rush. Bench legs scraped raucously across planking, and men jostled one another wildly. The clatter and swish of small objects falling from laps joined the chorus of shoved benches and the gasps, hisses, and warnings of men attempting to follow a protocol that Nightfall had just rendered impossible. Under ordinary circumstances, he might have reveled in the chaos he had inadvertently created. Now, he wanted only to find a proper place to empty his aching bladder. He dashed past Kelryn, through the curtained partition and into the staging room. There, he paused, trying to recall the nearest garderobe and the shortest route to it.

Khanwar caught up to him. Breathless, but still immaculate, he planted a hand on Nightfall's shoulder. "Do you know what you just did?"

Nightfall stiffened, turning to face the tall slender man he had begun to despise. *Yes, but I'm sure I missed something. I'm sure you'll let me know what, in intimate detail.* He kept the thought to himself. The delay allowed Kelryn and Vivarick to catch up to him as well. He met Khanwar's glare, forcing himself to still, though he felt as twitchy as a stallion. "You can either lecture me or let me piss."

Clearly taken aback by words and tone, Khanwar did not immediately answer.

Nightfall assisted the decision. "If you value your shoes, you'll choose the latter."

"Go, go." Khanwar made a dismissive gesture. "We'll talk later, Sire." The last word emerged with a clear reluctance that Nightfall did not bother to contemplate. Brushing past the others, he hastened from the room.

This time, no one stood in his way.

† Chapter 8 †

When you choose to kill an enemy, you buy your-self many more. His friends and family will rise up to replace him, driven by a righteous anger more powerful than hatred.

—Dyfrin of Keevain, the demon's friend

THE GARDEROBE Nightfall chose had a cathedral-cut window overlooking the dead patch of ground where the waste collected. Once he finished emptying his bladder, Nightfall climbed through the window to perch on a ledge scarcely wide enough to accommodate his narrow backside. Crouched in the gentle mist that followed the rain, he gained sideways glimpses of the nobles who used the facilities after him, as well as a full view of the less well-tended grounds of Alyndar. Even Khanwar came, glancing wildly around as he relieved himself, clearly searching for the missing chancellor. Though several of the garderobe's users glanced through the window to look out upon the gloom, none thought to scan the ledges. So, while Nightfall saw them clearly, no one noticed him watching.

When the nobles had taken their turns, the guards arrived one by one, several appearing sheepish and chastised. Clearly, they were expected to know the where-abouts of the man they guarded. Lastly came the red-haired commander of the prison guards. Volkmier did his business, readjusted his clothing, then disappeared from Nightfall's sight.

With a sigh, Nightfall relaxed, staring off in the direction of the city, now accustomed to the stench of raw sewage. He enjoyed the cold pinpoints of rain hitting his face, a fresh contrast to the hot, stale air of the court-room and its stifling protocol. Now more than ever he wished for Edward's swift return. The nobility seemed to have no difficulty sitting around and waiting for events to transpire around them, but Nightfall had neither the patience nor the faith to do the same. "Ned, where are you? Alyndar needs you!" He balled his hands to fists, dropped his voice to a whisper, and lowered his head, "And so do I."

"There you are, Sire!"

Captain Volkmier's voice startled Nightfall. One foot slipped from the ledge, and he tumbled into empty air. Twisting, he caught the ledge with a hand, snapped the other one into position beside it, and levered himself back to safety.

Volkmier's pale eyes seemed to bug from their sock-ets. Though too far away to assist, he held out both hands. "I'm so sorry, Sire. Are you all right? I swear I wasn't . . ."

Nightfall grinned, though he doubted it looked sincere. "I'm fine. Don't worry about me." It felt good to have the quick and deadly captain on the defensive for once, though it could have cost him serious injury. "I knew it wasn't a safe place to . . ." He trailed off, seeking a good term to define what he had been doing. He had just settled on "think," when Volkmier finished for him.

" . . . hide."

No longer a sanctuary, the ledge seemed chilly and wet, grossly uncomfortable. Though he dreaded confronting the man inside, Nightfall stood and skittered to the window. "I wasn't hiding."

Volkmier stepped aside to allow Nightfall room to enter. "Your advisers and bodyguards would see it differently, Sire."

Nightfall leaped nimbly through the window to land on the seat of the garderobe, then hopped to the floor. He braced for the inevitable lecture, punctuated by dire threats or even violence. The chief of prison guards had directly charged Nightfall with Edward's security, and he had failed miserably. Nevertheless, he continued the charade, "Does even the king never get a moment alone?"

"Not in the middle of court, Sire."

Nightfall dried his cheeks with a sleeve, certain the dampness had destroyed much of the hard work the servants had lavished on his face and hair. "The middle of court? But I thought—"

Volkmier attended to his own garb. "The nobles are finished, Sire. There are still the commoners' cases to judge." Volkmier appeared sincerely focused on the matters at hand; he clearly had no intention of blaming Nightfall for the king's ineffective security. Surely he realized that, if a contingent of the general's best men could not keep Edward safe, one man could not have done so.

Nightfall believed otherwise. If he had been in the tavern at the time of Edward's capture, even the Bloodshadow Brotherhood would not have succeeded. Nightfall deserved Volkmier's ire, yet the chief of the prison guards seemed determined not to vent it, much to Nightfall's relief. Resigned to more hours of the drudgery of playing king, he nodded.

Volkmier smiled. Though not broad, it was the friendliest expression Nightfall had ever seen grace the captain's face. "You don't like being acting-king, do you, Sire?"

"Is it that obvious?"

"Only to another man with absolutely no desire to sit upon the throne."

Nightfall pondered the statement. "That would seem to me to cover just about everyone."

Volkmier shook his head, briefly closing his eyes. "You would be wrong, Sire. Most men crave the position, secretly or overtly. You and I are rarities."

Nightfall studied the commander of Alyndar's prison guards, seeking some ulterior motive to lumping the two of them into the same category. Scarcely a month had passed since King Rikard had called Nightfall into the Great Hall to accuse him of murdering Prince Leyne. Then, the king had dismissed his royal guards to enable him to talk directly with Nightfall without anyone learning his identity. Volkmier had refused to leave his king's side, even under threat of punishment, had insisted on guarding Rikard from whatever unknown threat Nightfall might pose. The guard's presence had forced king and prisoner to couch their conversation in euphemisms and tangents, though Rikard had ordered Volkmier not to listen. "Then you'd understand why I want someone else to handle court."

Volkmier's headshake grew more vigorous. "Impossible, Sire. You're the king."

The words enraged Nightfall. "I am *not* the king! I am a poor and very brief substitute. Ned is the king, and don't you *ever* forget it." His hands clenched to quivering fists. "Not ever!"

Volkmier stepped back, hands spread in innocent apology. "For the moment, Sire, you are the king. Provisional king, if you prefer; but, for all intents and purposes, you currently rule Alyndar."

Nightfall sucked in a deep breath. It did no good to take out his frustrations on Volkmier. He wanted the loyal and competent commander on his side, if at all possible. "What did I do wrong?"

The question did not follow the course of the conversation. "Excuse me, Sire?"

"The last judgment. The one with the tariffs, with Hartrin." Nightfall placed a foot on the garderobe seat and balanced a hand on his knee. "It seemed so straightforward, yet Khanwar sounded ready to gut me over the end result."

Volkmier gave the standard response. "Sire, I would not presume to judge the presiding ruler—"

Nightfall could not stand it. "Don't play games with me, Volkmier! And don't throw me tired servant lines. I saw you defy King Rikard, and I know you don't hold me in higher esteem than you did him."

Caught, Volkmier turned Nightfall a crooked smile. "All right, Sire. As I understand it from listening to King Rikard and Prince Leyne . . ." He made a religious gesture to honor the dead. ". . . King Idinbal is both shrewd and frugal. He likes to get the best of every deal, at least monetarily."

Nightfall nodded. He knew that from his merchanting days.

"Hartrin has better ships, and they trade in textiles, spices, and perfumes. Most of their goods come to us in the spring and summer, when the Klaimer Ocean is free of ice."

Nightfall nodded again, this time to encourage the guard to continue.

"Alyndar sells Hartrin furs and lobsters, cold weather goods. Overland."

Understanding clicked into place. "With winter coming, raising tariffs hurts Alyndar more than Hartrin."

"Correct, Sire." Volkmier seemed pleased Nightfall had caught on so quickly. "And you'll recall the Hartrinian emissary spoke of ending the increased tariffs in half a year."

"When Hartrin's trade becomes more profitable."

"Exactly."

"Ah." Now Nightfall knew what to expect from Khanwar's scolding, though he had no way to counter it. "Thank you."

"You're welcome, Sire." Volkmier bowed. "You know, Sire, it is my job to protect you . . ."

The words made Nightfall cringe, reminding him of his own botched security that had resulted in Edward's capture. ". . . even from tongue lashings."

Volkmier shrugged, the grin on his face turning evil. "And, if you like, Sire, I won't tell them where I found you."

Nightfall appreciated that. Aside from the oddity of choosing a narrow ledge for a resting place, he suspected they would not like the thought he could have spied on them performing a bodily function most people preferred to do in private. "Let's just say I was outside enjoying the rain."

"Indeed, Sire."

The two men walked together toward the staging room, joined by a growing entourage of palace guards and proper escorts. Once inside the room, the guards separated to take their places in the Great Hall, while the advisers, Charson, Khanwar, and Vivarick, remained behind. Having arrived before them, Kelryn also waited.

Volkmier departed last, explaining as he left, "You know, Sire, if you must take a break during the proceedings, you should simply tell Lord Khanwar. You shouldn't suppress a physical need until it impairs your judgment."

The senior adviser gave Volkmier's back a dark look. Clearly, Khanwar worried Nightfall would use that information to his advantage, calling for a rest between every case to hide from his duties.

Nightfall had no intention of doing any such thing, as it would drag court out to an even more interminable length. Only the realization that it would vex Khanwar even made him consider it. "Thank you, Captain." He added pointedly, "I wish someone had let me know earlier."

Volkmier waved over his shoulder, then disappeared through the curtain.

Khanwar rounded on Nightfall again. "So, Sire, would you like me to tell you what you did?"

Armed with knowledge, Nightfall confronted his steward in a placid manner pitched to irritate. "Oh, I know what I did, Lord Khanwar."

Khanwar crooked a brow and folded his arms across his chest.

Nightfall had rehearsed the words during his walk to the staging room, believing he had them exactly right, "I pleased King Idinbal by granting him temporary economic advantage over Alyndar, thereby resolving any rancor King Edward's last political interaction with them might have raised."

Khanwar's jaw sagged.

"It really doesn't matter whether His Majesty of Hartrin believes I tendered him the victory out of courtesy or ignorance. He will feel better for having won, and his outlook toward Alyndar will improve."

"Y–yes, Sire." Khanwar had no choice but to execute a respectful bow. He scurried to attend his duties.

Kelryn hugged Nightfall. "Very nice," she whispered directly into his ear. "How?"

She did not need to finish the question; Nightfall understood. He made a slight gesture to indicate he would explain the details to her later.

"Are you ready?" Vivarick asked.

"Almost." Nightfall disengaged himself from Kelryn. "Now I'm ready." But he was not and felt certain he never would be. He whispered his doubts to Kelryn as they walked through the curtained entry, keeping his voice almost inaudible as he remembered the court would go dead silent the moment he entered the room. "How can I pass sentence on people for crimes I've committed, unpunished, myself?"

The moment the question left his lips, Nightfall wished he had never asked it. Doing so placed Kelryn in the awkward position of having to justify the evil he had done. She might feel obligated to explain that he had never killed for pleasure or at random, that he had stolen mostly from necessity. But, in truth, his motives spanned a gamut. Even had he committed every crime for altruistic reasons, and he could not honestly say he had, to justify them made him a hypocrite of the worst kind. He despised men who ridiculed fallen women while breaking the vows of their own marriages or those who lambasted drunkards on their way to the tavern. Somehow, people found twisted ways to justify in themselves the weaknesses they most reviled in others.

Kelryn surprised Nightfall with a simple answer. "You'll do what you have to do. For Ned."

For Ned. A phrase that once meant less than nothing had come to encompass his world. *For Ned.* The words inspired fresh prickles of guilt. He could do so much more for the young monarch were he not trapped in Alyndar performing his duties.

This time, Nightfall did not hesitate before taking his place on the high seat of Alyndar's court. Less full, the courtroom itself seemed to breathe a sigh of relief as every constituent took his seat on the spectator benches.

Charson remained standing directly at Nightfall's right hand. Again in front of the dais, Khanwar made a gesture toward the far side of the room. This time, he did not announce the participants in the case. Commoners did not warrant that formality.

Charson explained the upcoming situation in low tones, his gaze on the shackled man staggering down the carpetway, sandwiched between two guards. "Sire, this is Griflin Fodor's son, accused of the crime of murder. It's a straightforward case. He doesn't deny the charge. King Edward would place him in the dungeon lifelong, but you have the option of execution if you prefer, Sire."

Nightfall looked helplessly at Kelryn, who shrugged.

"They bring the worst crimes first," she explained, "working down to the trivial."

Misreading Nightfall's discomfort, Charson added in less formal tones, "Don't worry, Sire. This is the only murderer you'll see today."

The guards brought Griflin to the base of the dais. He sank to his knees, head low, hands weighted by chains. Another man headed down the aisle, also accompanied by guards, though unfettered. As he drew near, Griflin watched his advance with clear hatred twisted across his features.

The second man also knelt and bowed his head, revealing a mop of hair the color and texture of straw.

"Tell them to rise," Kelryn instructed.

"Rise," Nightfall repeated. Then, as it sounded inadequate, he tacked on, "please."

Both men stood, Griflin with more effort.

As soon as he did so, the second man spat out, "That . . . *animal* . . . killed my father."

Nightfall turned his attention back to Griflin, who stood between the guards in stony silence. If he felt any remorse, he did not show it.

Charson prodded now, talking from the side of his mouth. "I believe he will confess, Sire, if you ask him."

Nightfall doubted it. To do so might prove sure suicide. "Is what this man says true?"

"No, Sire." Griflin finally raised his head. "I'm not an animal." His dark eyes blazed. "But I did kill the old man."

And, once again, I'm wrong.

"Sentence him," Charson whispered. "If you're not sure, you can always imprison him until the king's return."

Nightfall ran a hand through his hair. He had to ask, "Why?"

Griflin swallowed. "Sire, his brother killed my father."

Nightfall waited for more, but it did not come. His brows rose in slow increments. "*His* brother . . ." He pointed at Griflin's accuser. ". . . killed *your* father?"

"Yes, Sire."

The straw-haired man broke in, "The reason doesn't matter! He slaughtered my . . . !"

The guard to his right shook his arm in warning, and the man broke off in mid shout.

Nightfall still did not wholly understand. "So why didn't you kill his *brother*?"

Even Griflin seemed taken aback by the question. "I . . . I couldn't, Sire. He's in your dungeon."

"So you killed his father instead?"

"He killed *my* father."

Even with a guard gripping his forearm, the other man could not hold his tongue any longer. "Because his father killed my uncle."

Nightfall muttered at Charson, "What in bloody hell is going on here?"

"A feud, Sire," the adviser whispered. "Two families killing one another's men in revenge."

"Revenge for what?"

"Does it matter, Sire, what the original slight was? They may not even remember."

Nightfall studied the two men in front of him. Their hatred for one another felt tangible, hot, beyond reason. "You know I can order your execution."

Griflin did not even flinch at the pronouncement. "Better that, Sire, than to die at the hands of his slimy, pigshit-eating family."

"Hey!" A guard nudged the prisoner with a booted foot.

His accuser bared his teeth. "You deserve nothing better. Your family—"

The guard gave his arm a heavier shake. "You're in the presence of royalty."

That snapped the man free of hate-inspired rudeness. "Apologies, Majesty." He bent into a deep bow. "Please forgive my disrespect."

Nightfall rolled his eyes, ready to rule. "Imprison the murderer. In the cell beside his father's killer."

Now, Volkmier jerked his head toward the dais, shaking it in obvious counsel.

Nightfall ignored the chief of the prison guards. "Their sentences will be . . ." He sought a word to explain his arrangement, not knowing whether he had invented it or if such a system already existed. ". . . circumstantial."

Charson shifted from foot to foot. "What are you doing, Sire?" Though polite and very soft, the words held an undertone of warning.

"If any relation of Griflin's kills any relation of . . ." He waved at the other man, who supplied his name.

"Lanier, Sire."

". . . Lanier, then Griflin's sentence will be converted to execution." Nightfall added to strengthen his point. "Painful execution."

Lanier smiled. "Thank you, Sire."

Nightfall met his gaze. "Oh, don't thank me."

Lanier paled, withered.

"What's your brother's name? The one in the dungeon."

"Forly, Sire."

"If any relative of Lanier's kills any relative of Griflin, then Forly will be executed. By torture."

Charson's brow beetled in clear puzzlement, but Kelryn nodded. The strategy was not lost on her or, Nightfall believed, on Lanier and his kin. If one of them chose revenge, he would have to live with the realization he had killed Forly as well. And if one of Griflin's relatives continued the feud, he would have to take direct responsibility for costing Griflin his life.

Nightfall finished, "We will reevaluate this case in five years, with the possibility of a pardon if no further murders have occurred within these two families."

Silence followed Nightfall's sentencing. When it became clear he had finished, a murmur rose, then a hum, as the nobles discussed the judgment, its complexity, and its meaning. The case had seemed simple. Surely, they had only wondered if the acting ruler would have the courage to inflict a capital punishment in the absence of a king who never would. Now, they had to figure out exactly what he had accomplished and why.

As the guards led Griflin and Lanier away, even Khanwar had to huddle with Nightfall. "Sire, are you certain that was wise?" His inflection implied he already knew the answer, and it did not fall in Nightfall's favor.

Nightfall had no idea whether his plan would work, but a straightforward sentencing would only have resulted in more murders. He supposed the nobility would just as soon see these two common families totally annihilate one another. "I'm not certain of anything, except I'd rather not preside over a murder every day. If this gets them to think before attempting revenge, then I've accomplished something."

"And if not?" Khanwar had to ask.

"If not?" Nightfall shrugged. "Then we are no worse off than if I'd sentenced him to death in the first place, which I understand was perfectly within my rights."

"Yes, but—"

Charson interrupted with a concern of his own. "Volkmier won't like the 'painful execution' part. The torture . . ."

Nightfall wondered if any of these men had ever so much as heard of a scam. "It doesn't matter whether the execution is painful or not. So long as the families believe it will be."

"But, Sire—" Khanwar started again.

Nightfall looked down the carpetway to the great doors, where the guards were leading another chained man down the aisle. "Khanwar, don't you have a duty to attend?"

Khanwar glanced over his shoulder, then scurried to the foot of the dais. He gestured the party forward, though it was unnecessary. The group had not waited for this formality.

Charson recovered his own composure. "This is

Clion, Sire. Caught stealing from an Ivralian ship at the harbor."

Nightfall studied the man as he paced down the aisle, managing a swagger despite the fetters and chains. He had hair the color of winter weeds, an olive complexion, and green eyes that darted over the assembled nobles. His face seemed inappropriately wide for his medium build and smallish ears. He stopped in front of the dais and dropped to one knee with a brisk and businesslike flourish.

Nightfall stared.

Kelryn reminded in a whisper, "Rise."

"Rise," Nightfall said.

The thief did so, leaping to his feet with reasonable grace.

One of the guards explained. "Sire, this man was caught rifling crates at Alyndar port."

"I do not deny the thievery, Majesty." Clion executed an elegant bow, though his previous gesture of respect seemed more than enough for the circumstances. The chains clattered as he moved. "But you may wish to reconsider punishing me when you hear what I have to say."

Nightfall studied the thief. He knew a swindler when he heard and saw one, and Clion's voice had become perfectly pitched to draw men into a great confidence. He knew Clion would let the pause grow until Nightfall ended it, hoping the suspense would draw out his audience's curiosity to unbearable lengths, that they might feel honored he would share such a valuable secret. Reserving judgment until he figured out the man's game, Nightfall encouraged with a simple, "I'm listening."

"Sire." Clion glanced around him, as if afraid someone might overhear, though the entire court already had, along with his guards and those closest to Nightfall. Vivarick had kept his presence relatively unnoticed compared to the announcing Khanwar and the ever present Charson, but he now glided to Nightfall's side to hear and, ostensibly, assist. "I am ... the notorious ... villain, Nightfall."

A rumble of conversation followed the revelation. Nightfall looked at Kelryn.

"He's lying," she hissed.

Nightfall blinked. The statement went beyond ludicrous. Even at a whisper, he managed to convey sarcasm. "Do you really think so?"

"Of course, he's lying," Charson added. "Nightfall was executed half a year ago. Right here in Alyndar."

"I know." Nightfall reassured Charson he would not rise to the bait. Clearing his throat, he addressed Clion aloud. "Are you trying to say our own great King Rikard put the wrong man to death?"

The hum of the spectators grew louder, then dropped as Clion shook his head. They clearly did not want their conversations to drown out his response.

Clion took a step back, appearing horrified. The guards scrambled to move with him. "No, Sire. Certainly not. What I'm saying is that there is a reason the legend of Nightfall has been a part of our society for longer than any man has been alive." He lowered his voice, forcing the nobility to silence. "Because the mantle, the secrets, have been passed down from one man to the next. I . . ." He paused for effect. "I am the son of the previous Nightfall."

Sure, if I was fertile at three.

"And his successor. To me, he taught all of his tricks, the deepest darkest secrets every murderer, assassin, thief, and scammer would never want you to know." Clion leaned forward conspiratorially. "And, if you spare me, I can reveal them to you."

Nightfall sat back, amused by the scenario but hoping he looked thoughtful. The crowd remained locked in a hush, clearly as interested in his response as in Clion's declaration. He sucked in a deep breath and let it out slowly. He could match his ability with timing and bluff against the best.

Apparently believing Nightfall needed advice, Vivarick jumped in to provide it. "Sire, I don't believe him."

"I don't either. I'm just trying to figure out why he's taking such a risk."

"Sire?" Charson tried to follow his ruler's line of thought.

Nightfall kept his gaze on the thief while he addressed his assistants. "If I believe him, I might just as well execute him as accept his counsel. Surely the punishment for simple theft isn't so severe."

Kelryn remained silent, allowing the two men to usurp her position without comment. Under the circumstances, Nightfall appreciated her sacrifice. Her words or demeanor could reveal him.

"Not usually, Sire," Vivarick confirmed, wringing his hands. "But Clion has served three terms in the dungeon already. King Rikard would consider a man like him incorrigible, which would make him eligible for permanent imprisonment or death."

"Ah." The last piece of the puzzle fell into place. Nightfall sat up. "Well . . . Nightfall." The name flowed easily off his tongue, though he deliberately added a hint of distaste. He had named himself a stranger on more than one occasion in other guise. "When you use your vast and mysterious talents to escape Alyndar's dungeon and her ever vigilant prison guards . . ." He glanced at Captain Volkmier who stood at stiff attention, though a smile twitched at the edge of his lips.

Clion paled.

" . . . please return to me. I will not only accept your generous offer of counsel, I will reward you with an honored position in my service."

Clion's chains rattled, betraying trembling he otherwise hid. He gave the only answer he could under the circumstances, though it was surely insincere. "Thank you, Sire."

As the guards led Clion back up the carpetway,

Nightfall addressed the commander of the prison guards. "Does that suit you, Captain Volkmier?"

Directly addressed, the leader of Alyndar's prison guards turned. He acknowledged the chancellor with a tip of his helmeted head, his face bathed in shadow. "Sire, you will not see this rapscallion again, I assure you." His voice tightened, and his eyes grew distant. "The man this one claims as predecessor, the one who menaced the world for decades managed to get out of his cell." His tone grew even more startlingly chill. "But he didn't escape me. And regardless of what he claims to be, this one won't either."

The memory blossomed in Nightfall's mind against his will. He remembered a dizzying fall from the castle parapets leaving him dazed and battered, a warning crossbow shot that nearly grazed his ear, and looking up to the red-haired commander kneeling on a ledge with crossbow aimed, drawn, and leveled. The same assured and threatening tone touched his voice then as now. "I don't know what demon blessed you. I don't know how you survived that fall, and I don't want to know. The king wants you questioned. Hell take your wicked, ugly, disgusting, murdering soul, I'm going to see that his will is done. But if you so much as quiver . . . if you give me the slightest excuse, I'll shoot you dead and revel in it."

Then, Nightfall had lost the battle to the solace of oblivion. This time, he could only stare, a shiver spiraling through his gut. He dared not even sputter out a meaningless phrase of gratitude, afraid the tremor in his voice might give him away.

For the first time, the audience applauded Nightfall's decision as well as the bravado of Alyndar's captain of the prison guards.

Nightfall forced himself to smile.

† Chapter 9 †

*I think what he struggles with most is that deep in-
side he's a good man, fighting to become the demon
his mother and the populace named him.*

— Dyfrin of Keevain, the demon's friend

WITH THE HELP of his advisers, including Kelryn,
Nightfall's time in commoners' court went far
smoother than when he had faced the nobility. As the
last farmer skipped down the carpetway, a free man,
Nightfall collapsed into his seat. Khanwar's pronouncement that court was adjourned brought a stiff grin to his
lips, and he watched the nobles file out without bothering to move. Apparently, propriety allowed them to
stand while he remained seated, and he savored the
moments snuggled against padding warmed by his body.

Kelryn took Nightfall's callused hand. "Not so easy
being king?"

Nightfall shrugged. He felt weary, but not physically
exhausted. He doubted it would have proved nearly as
difficult had he not sailed into port just that morning
and gotten thrown into unfamiliar territory without a
hint of warning. He could see where placating nobles
and judging commoners could become routine. He only

hoped it would never become *his* routine. Seeing no reason to contradict, he only repeated, "I'm not the king." Alerted by caution to another presence in the room, he glanced up to see a young page trotting down the carpet. He groaned.

The boy removed his hat and bowed at the foot of the dais.

No one else seemed to notice the newcomer, but Nightfall's gaze went directly to him. Though he dreaded discovering what matter needed his attention now, he addressed the boy. "What can I do for you?"

The page sprang to an upright position. His voice squeaked over the general din of the advisers' conversation, "Sire, your immediate presence has been requested in the Strategy Room. The Council awaits you there."

Nightfall had no intention of going from one stodgy proceeding directly to another. He had not eaten since his arrival in Alyndar. "Tell them I'm not coming."

The page's dark eyes widened. He kneaded his hat between his hands.

Khanwar leaped in, "Sire, you can't do that."

Nightfall could scarcely believe how many people presumed to order him about like a servant. He had always thought the king had ultimate freedom, and he had never seen people treat Edward in this manner. "I think, Khanwar, I can. I really, *really* think I can." He dripped a venomous warning into the repetition.

Khanwar swallowed hard.

Kelryn stepped forward to soften the stalemate. "Sir, what I believe the chancellor is trying to say is he would like a chance to relieve himself, to get a bite to eat, to . . . to freshen up first."

Khanwar opened his mouth, then closed it. He motioned to Charson to take over the explanation.

Charson cleared his throat. "Sire." He pitched his voice to soothe.

Always willing to listen to his more temperate companion, Nightfall kept his anger in check.

"You may, of course, stop at the garderobe on the way; and the Council never meets without refreshments. They know you have spent the day in court and will see that you are . . . appropriately nourished."

Nightfall studied Charson. He seemed sincere, and Nightfall trusted a man of Charson's girth when he said the food would prove adequate.

Kelryn leaned over, as if to kiss Nightfall, then whispered in his ear. "Ransom."

Nightfall understood. Kelryn had already stressed the significance of the High Council. If they chose to meet with him at such an inopportune time, it surely had something to do with King Edward, probably the arrival of the kidnappers' demands. "All right, then."

Khanwar visibly relaxed.

Nightfall sprang from the chair, only to find his muscles stiff from disuse. He stumbled gracelessly, squirming to release the knots from sitting too long in one place. More than emptying his bladder, more than eating, he wanted a rousing dance or a sprint around the palace. His tiredness was entirely mental, and the last thing he wished to do was attempt to match wits with a roomful of Alydarian nobles. *For Ned,* he reminded himself for what seemed like the millionth time. He jumped down from the dais.

The page took several startled steps backward, then scrambled into an awkward bow to the chancellor, who now stood beside him. When he finally managed to speak, he said, "F–f–follow me, please, Lord Chancellor."

Nightfall did as the boy bade, walking back up the carpetway and out the great doors, surprised to find only the usual two inner guards dogging him. Somehow, he had expected the entire retinue of Castle Alyndar to sew itself to his hips.

Nightfall fairly skipped up the carpeted stairs of the West Tower, forcing the page into a short-legged jog and sending his armored, two-guard entourage clomping in their wake. The need for motion, not excitement or interest kept Nightfall moving so swiftly, or so he explained it to himself. He could not admit, even to himself, his eagerness to learn the High Council's business, to gain some information, no matter how small or bleak, about Edward's condition.

Though focused on business, Nightfall could not help but notice the cathedral windows on every landing. Shutters and bolts on the first three floors gave way to paned glass on the fourth. He knew from experience the upper floor windows would lie open, essentially safe from prowlers and would-be thieves; but the page stopped at a steel-bound, oak door on the fourth floor guarded by a pair of attentive sentries.

The page gestured at the door with a flourish and bow, then reached for the latch. The guards who had accompanied Nightfall stepped aside, joining their companions stationed beside the door. The page struggled to pull open the heavy, unusually thick panel, managing the feat only by seizing the ring in both hands and grunting with each mincing back step that enlarged the growing crack.

Nightfall waited only until it became an opening he could squeeze through without losing his dignity, then ducked inside the room. Five immaculately clothed men sat around a massive table that took up most of the space, and he recognized all of them from the meeting where Edward had announced his intention to visit Schiz. At the head sat the massive general who had dedicated his men to the king's security. About a dozen others stood along the walls, wearing tailored linens or fancy silks. Nightfall knew only a few of these, including Captain Volkmier in a gray-and-lavender dress uniform decorated with short ribbons and medals. Maps covered the walls, and Nightfall noticed no windows, which immediately increased his level of alertness. A chandelier hung over the table, holding eight large candles that lit the room in irregular patches and left other parts in

dense shadow. The table held papers and two silver
trays of food and mugs. The aroma of warm bread, meat
pies, fruit, and juice intertwined with several clashing
perfumes turned Nightfall's hunger into nausea.

This time, no one bothered to stand when Nightfall
entered. The enormous general at the head of the table
motioned him to the only empty chair, at the far end.

Without a word, Nightfall took his seat.

The general looked across the table at him. "Lord
Chancellor Sudian, so nice of you to come."

Like I had a choice. Nightfall lowered and raised his
head once in respectful acknowledgment. He had already decided to speak as little as possible. He wanted
to gather as much information as he could, then excuse
himself as soon as propriety allowed. He did not like
crowds, unless he could disappear into them, and he definitely did not fit in here. Even eating no longer seemed
important. Nervousness and the myriad smells combined to sap his appetite.

The man at the head of the table continued, "I am Simont Basilaered, the general of Alyndar's army." He
rose, unfolding the tallest frame Nightfall had ever
seen. Had they stood together, Nightfall would look directly into the man's breastbone. Muscled like a bull,
Simont probably outweighed one. Hair as black as ash
perched in a pile of curls on top of his head, and a thick
beard bristled from his chin connected by a dense line
of sideburns. Nightfall estimated the man's age was
close to his own, though no one else would assume such
a thing. Nightfall looked a decade younger when
scrubbed clean as Sudian, while Simont's craggy face
added years to his appearance. A large nose and bushy
brows overshadowed eyes so dark they appeared to
have no pupils.

"To my left is the top-ranked officer of Alyndar's
navy, Lord Admiral Nikolei Neerchus."

Nightfall tore his gaze from the army's giant, only to
look upon another. Though not quite as tall as his land-

based equal, the navy commander matched him for bulk, all of it hard sinew and muscle. He was blond and handsome in contrast to the general's dark homeliness. He appeared calmer, more gentle, an appearance enhanced by enormous green eyes and clean-shaven, chiseled features. Nightfall tried to memorize names and titles, knowing he had barely begun and wishing the men would stick with a single name or designation. He had an excellent memory, but the seventeen men in the room would surely challenge it.

The general indicated the man sitting beside the admiral. "And this is Sir Alber Evrinn, a knight of Alyndar and its third largest landholder."

Alber rose, and the admiral retook his seat. Though taller and broader than Nightfall, the knight looked positively tiny in the wake of the military commanders. He had a wild crop of medium-brown hair that seemed as untamable as Nightfall's own. He appeared preternaturally sad, with sloping pale brown eyes, a long face, and a small pointy nose.

The general skipped Nightfall to move to the other side of the table. "Another knight of the realm, Sir Tenneth Kentaries, second largest landowner."

Alber took his seat, and the middle-aged man directly across from him rose. Average in height and breadth, at least for a courtier, he sported sand-colored hair cut short and plastered with oil. Pale, flabby skin poked from beneath his silken garb. His straight-set features boasted of a handsome youth, but his hazel eyes had gone watery with age. He rested his hands on the table, long-fingered like a thief's but without dirt or callus. "Pleased to make your acquaintance," he said, though his tone seemed a mix of boredom and suspicion.

The general gestured at the only remaining seated man. "This is Baron Elliat Laimont, our largest landholder."

Sir Tenneth sat, and the baron rose. Fat and white-haired, his fine features widened by bulk, he still carried an aura of command that demanded respect. His dazzling outfit displayed at least five colors. Nightfall guessed he had a wife. Few men could coordinate clothing so complicated with such seamless competence. Though not a striking gentleman, he managed an air of cultured attractiveness despite size and age, and much of that had to do with his clothes.

The baron gave Nightfall a stiff nod, then took his seat.

Nightfall glanced around the table, trying to commit each name and appearance to memory. It seemed easiest to go by titles: the huge dark general, the almost-as-huge light admiral, the well dressed baron, and two knights: one sad-looking, one pale. Trying not to groan, he looked around at the remaining men, standing, sitting, and leaning against the walls.

But the general did not bother to introduce the others, instead going right to business. "Chancellor, we apologize for disturbing your busy schedule, but we have some concerns requiring immediate address."

Nightfall kept his attention firmly on General Simont Basilaered. He did not have to feign interest. The solemn and serious expressions on every face displayed the significance of this meeting. Receipt of a ransom note seemed certain. He only wished the enormous man would come directly to the point. Seeing no reason to delay by adding words of his own, he remained silent.

"As you know," the general continued, "Duke Varsah of Schiz sent a contingent of men to Alyndar."

"I traveled with them," Nightfall reminded the general, hoping it might forestall more talk of the obvious. It suddenly occurred to him that Ragan and his men should have reported to court with the rest of the nobility, yet they had not stood before him.

As if in direct answer to Nightfall's unspoken question, General Simont said, "They came straight to us, the High Council, just as the duke's earlier message did."

Earlier message? Nightfall did not let his curiosity show. He wondered how word could have arrived quicker. They had taken the shortest route to Alyndar, by sea, and had left reasonably fast. He supposed someone traveling alone might have made better time, especially if he had not fallen into the hands of pirates; but the message would have arrived only a few hours sooner, which scarcely seemed worth the trouble. *Unless it was a ransom demand.* It made no sense. *What in all hell is going on?*

"Both raised some interesting concerns and questions."

Nightfall read warning in the general's statement, bordering on accusation. Every gaze went to him, intent and unflinching. They seemed to expect some reaction to words that warranted none. He tried to analyze the matter but was surely missing necessary information the others already had. Remaining quiet still appeared to be his best course of action. Nevertheless, they all clearly required something from him. "I'd warrant so." He met Simont's gaze with a casual ease that was a sham. The growing tension in the room bothered him, and his survival instincts drove him to caution and escape. "Anything . . . useful?"

"Maybe." Simont met Nightfall's look solidly. "Perhaps we could hear your version?"

Nightfall blinked, still uncertain whether or not he faced some sort of threat. "My version . . . ?" He trailed off, hoping one of the other men would fill in the blanks. The utter lack of extraneous conversation unnerved him. Either etiquette held them at bay, or nothing interested them as much as the ongoing discussion, as one-sided as it was.

". . . of King Edward's kidnapping."

Nightfall shrugged. "I'm afraid I wasn't there." His own words raised ire. *If I had been, this never could have happened.* He did not know who to hate more: Ned for forcing him to fulfill a disingenuous promise or himself for not coming up with a better excuse for refusing Brandon Magebane. He tried not to think about the consequences of leaving Byroth alive. Brandon might well have died without Nightfall's help, and a dangerous sorcerer could still stalk the world; but at least King Edward would have remained on Alyndar's throne.

"We know," the general said through clenched teeth. The men around the table stirred, clearly wanting to speak yet constrained by etiquette and rules of order. "On some mysterious mission which kept you away just long enough to survive the kidnapping."

Nightfall did not like where the questioning was headed. "Not true. I was gone all evening and night, not just—"

This time, Simont Basilaered did not allow him to finish. "And you returned exhausted and covered in blood."

Covered in . . . ? Nightfall could scarcely believe Schiz had exaggerated his wound. "It was *my* blood." Protestation seemed futile. Only Brandon and Gatiwan could confirm his explanation; and they had promised to keep him out of the matter, swore that they would never mention his name. Even if they retracted their promise, Duke Varsah would make certain the Magekillers did not have the opportunity to assist him. Besides, Nightfall had no intention of letting large groups of distant courtiers and nobles judge what had happened that night. When the truth came out, and it surely would, it would destroy a friendship and a family; and he would face the justice of Duke Varsah for killing a child. He had no doubt that would prove as severe as anything Alyndar would inflict on him, even if they really believed he had a hand in Edward's disappearance.

"Can you explain your whereabouts?"

"I can."

Simont's brows rose in expectation.

Nightfall had had enough. "But I won't. I don't have

to. Ned traveled the world with only me for protection, and I got him through it alive. I saved him from a sorcerer, by the Father! I don't owe explanations to anyone."

The baron could no longer hold his tongue. "You owe one to us."

Simont took back the reins of control. "You would not be the first loyal servant to turn against his liege when granted a position of power. A chance at the crown."

The comparison to an evil, ruthless sorcerer enraged Nightfall. "We're finished here." He sprang to his feet.

The men at the table rose with him, the admiral so quickly his chair tumbled over backward. It slammed against the floor as the men already standing bunched toward the door, the only exit from the room.

Nightfall's heart rate quickened, but he hid his tension behind a mask of bravado. "Get out of my way."

"You still have questions to answer," the pale knight proclaimed.

"And I've already told you I won't speak of that night." Nightfall took a step toward the door, knowing he could not successfully fight his way through the crowd. If for no other reason, because Volkmier stood nearest the door. "Surely someone in the tavern overheard Ned commanding me to assist two men who came in that evening. I tried to refuse them, but he wouldn't let me."

The other knight spoke softly but with whipcrack force. "Chancellor Sudian, name your parents."

The question seemed to catch everyone off guard, Nightfall not the least. "What?"

Again Simont took control of the conversation, though no one retook his seat. "We've tried to find a history for you, Sudian, but it doesn't exist. It's as if you appeared by magic."

Nightfall resorted to sarcasm, mind working furiously on escape. He knew he could move quicker than most of the men between him and the door could think to stop him. How to open the door without interference still eluded him. "That's right. I was conjured out of the air by sorcerers. No, actually, I grew on a tree." He threw up his hands with the grandeur of a priest. "I hatched from a lost egg that fell, like hail, from the heavens." He gave a stern look to the men in front of him. "Step aside."

The men in his path glanced uneasily from Nightfall to the High Council standing around the table. It was clear that they didn't wish to ignore the chancellor's direct order, but they also felt it necessary to cater to the whims of their other superiors.

Now that most of the standing men blocked his way, Nightfall realized he was the smallest man in the room, at least by weight. Many of the Council, other than the superiors at the table, wore working purple and silver, trusted guardsmen of the inner court. The rest dressed richly, as befit land-and/or titleholders in the favor of the king.

"Stop this nonsense!" bellowed Lord Admiral Nickolei Neerchus. "And name your parents, Chancellor Sudian. Now!"

Nightfall stiffened. This charade had gone way beyond propriety. All day long, men and women had reminded him he currently ruled Alyndar. He knew even the men of the High Council would never treat Edward in this manner. Slowly, he turned, trying for a look of suppressed rage. "The nonsense is this sham of a meeting. My parentage is none of your business. You know I'm lowborn, and I've not denied it. I've never claimed an inherited right to any land or title."

The baron took over, his gentle tone so in contrast with the admiral's it seemed to beg for understanding and an answer. "Sudian, please don't misunderstand. You must realize how strange and worrisome it is to be ruled by a man who appears to have no past. We all know you were born of a woman; but, when our best searches turn up nothing before you appeared in the courtyard at Prince Edward's side, you might just as well have hatched from that lost egg you mentioned."

Though the baron seemed more reasonable, Nightfall did not like the turn his questioning took any better than the louder, more direct commanders. He wondered how long this particular line of thinking would take to get around to the demon spawn theories explaining the origins of his other persona. He tried to throw the councillors enough information to satisfy their curiosity without sending them down a path that would prove him a liar. The truth would only seal his doom. "My mother died in childbirth. I never knew her name. Papa and I just always called her Mama."

Nightfall ignored the whispers that followed this statement, needing to keep all his attention on the men interrogating him.

"And your father?" the general pressed.

"Took odd jobs to feed us."

"His name!" the admiral snapped. It seemed to Nightfall as if the man said everything in explosive expletives.

Nightfall knew he could not hesitate too long, could not give the appearance of making things up as he went along, even though he was. He said the first name that came to his mind, "Dyfrin. His name was Dyfrin." Just speaking it aloud brought back all of the bitter sorrow and anger that erupted whenever he thought of his friend's final moments. "And he's dead. Murdered by your dog of a previous chancellor, a sorcerer without a scrap of goodness in that evil, black pit he called a heart." Nightfall realized something he had never before considered. When he had first met Gilleran, King Rikard had used the sorcerer to determine whether Nightfall spoke truth or lies. Now, he knew the sorcerer had fooled them both. No careful phraseology could have rescued Nightfall from Gilleran's truth-detection spell, because it did not work the way the sorcerer had claimed it did. From the start, Gilleran had been using Dyfrin's stolen birth gift to read Nightfall's mind.

While Nightfall considered details of his encounters with the former chancellor in a whole new light, he could practically hear the nobles' thoughts clicking into place around him. Only then, in the midst of the total silence following his pronouncement, did he realize his mistake. He did not worry that they might track Dyfrin down and realize only eight years separated them in age. His cleaned up appearance made him look a decade younger. He supposed he might have to deal with the people who had known Dyfrin yet had never met his son or heard him speak of having one. But the councillors pounced on something far more important to them.

"So that's why you attacked the sorcerer." Though clearly a thought, Sir Tenneth Kentaries spoke it loudly enough for the entire room to hear.

The baron added, "It had nothing to do with saving Ned's life."

The wrong things continued to enter conversations around the room. "He only took the steward's job to get near the sorcerer who killed his father."

Nightfall shook his head. "No, no. That's not right."

His protestations became lost beneath the rumble of speculation. Nightfall stopped speaking. He saw no reason to go on. No one would listen to what he had to say. In their minds, they had already convicted him, seeking only some way to invalidate his single act of selfless courage. He had hated Gilleran, and not only for what the bastard had inflicted on Dyfrin. But Nightfall had attacked the sorcerer to rescue Edward's life. The oathbond had no longer constrained him at that time. He could have run without sacrifice, leaving Edward to face the sorcerer alone. Instead, Nightfall had risked his own life, fully intending to sacrifice it, to save his liege who had also become his friend.

General Simont pounded a fist against the wall with a mighty crash that quieted the room again. "Sudian, the evidence presented by Schiz is overwhelming. Your inability to counteract it is telling, and your explanation has overcome the last obstacle of doubt. Therefore . . ."

The stillness became a deadly silence.

". . . we, the High Council, hereby sentence you . . ."

Sentence me? Nightfall could scarcely believe he had gotten away with dozens of crimes to get imprisoned for absolutely nothing.

". . . to the punishment due all traitors: execution. The method to be decided—"

Nightfall fixated on the word. *Execution!* He froze. King Rikard had claimed to pardon him for every crime worthy of such a sentence. He measured the distance to the door again, then scanned the windowless room for other escape.

"Stop right there!" Volkmier's voice rose over the hush. "What craziness is this?"

Simont's pronouncement dropped to a directed growl. "You're out of line, Captain."

Volkmier ignored the chastisement. Though shorter and squatter, the chief of prison guards carried a frame as packed with muscle as Simont's own and commanded nearly as much respect. "Sudian is the chancellor. In the king's absence, that makes him Alyndar's ruler. Killing him is . . . it's . . ." He sputtered. "For all intents and purposes that's *regicide,* the ultimate treason. You have no right . . ."

"This gives us the right!" The admiral jerked open a drawer in the table, dug out an enormous book, and slapped it to the tabletop with a thunderous bang. "Alyndarian law itself." He flopped the book open to a marked page and began to read ". . . in the event the king is killed, missing, or incapacitated leaving no blooded heir on the throne . . ." Nikolei mumbled past the parts that did not apply to the situation. ". . . the Council is granted overriding discretion in all matters of judgment provided it has the full consent of the High Council and a majority vote of the Council in Full." He looked up from the book but did not close it, allowing anyone who wished to see the proviso access.

The crowd shifted as a few became curious enough to look.

Captain Volkmier stood in place with his mouth open. It took several moments before words emerged. "I don't recall any vote of the Council in Full on this matter."

"The High Council counts two votes each," the baron explained. "That's ten. We only needed two more votes, and we had no trouble finding them." He looked out over the mass of landowners, royal guardsmen, and titled gentry. "But I'm willing to take a formal vote, if you insist."

Nightfall said nothing as he edged toward the door. The less attention he drew to himself, the more likely he could escape unnoticed.

"I insist," Volkmier said.

"Very well." The baron retook his seat, followed by the remainder of the High Council. Though General Simont still held the head seat, Baron Elliat took over the proceedings. "All those in favor of the sentencing, raise your right hand and chant 'aye.' "

A sea of hands flew up amid a chorus of "ayes."

"Opposed, raise the left and chant 'nay.' "

The silence sounded equally deafening. It seemed as if even the chief of the prison guards had forsaken Nightfall.

"Seize the traitor!" someone shouted.

Nightfall made a wild leap for the door, caught the latch, and yanked. Heavy as pooled lead, the door jerked opened crookedly. The guards stationed outside scrambled to attention as Nightfall dropped his weight and dove through the crack.

A sea of humanity flung itself at him. One crashed against his shoulder blades, driving his meager weight to the floor. More afraid to reveal his talent than of death, Nightfall forced his mass back to normal as arms buffeted him from every direction. A hand clamped on his ankle. He kicked, scoring a solid hit, but it delayed him enough to allow a heap of men to plunge down on him simultaneously. Blinded, hearing muffled by piled clothing, nostrils thick with the reek of stale sweat, he slipped from beneath the pile as the men gouged and grabbed at one another. A final twist freed him. Crouched low, he surveyed his position, only to find the masses had confused his bearings. He had come out in the same room he had just escaped, only now his pursuers lay mostly behind him.

The knights and the baron stood beside the strategy table. A few of the Council members stood in various positions around the room. The tangled mass of bodies in the doorway blocked the exit, only just beginning to sort itself out. Nightfall saw only one way out, over the heads of the cluster. Climbing them would leave him wallowing in the heap. Instead, he sprang to the tabletop, scattering papers beneath his feet and sending the book sliding.

General Simont cursed and jumped after Nightfall, remarkably quick for such a large man. He made a nimble grab that probably would have snared Nightfall had the giant not slammed his head against the hanging candelabra. Nightfall caught the swinging holder as lit candles plunged to the table around the general. Flinging his body backward, Nightfall added to the momentum, then dropped his weight. The candelabra surged forward. Nightfall released his grip, flying over the loosening knot of men in the doorway, hit the floor headfirst, and tucked into a graceful roll. He scrambled to his feet, restoring his mass as he did so, only to find a boot thrust suddenly between his legs. A sudden move to the side only partially saved him. He stumbled a half step rather than falling, but that took him over the edge of the upper stair.

Nightfall tumbled down the steps in an uncontrollable frenzy, desperately adjusting his weight across a spectrum to try to find something to slow his descent and decrease the growing collection of bruises the edges stamped across his flesh. Pain flashed through his skull. The world juggled past in dizzying spirals. Up and down, directions became muddled and unrecognizable concepts. Then, he crashed to a landing with a spine-jarring force that left him breathless and helplessly sprawled, one leg twisted through the railing. *Get up!* he told himself. *Get up, or you and Ned are both dead.*

Nightfall managed to limp to legs feeling raw and deeply battered, the air above him filled with shouts. Then, a familiar voice wafted to him from below. "Don't move, Sudian. I don't want to have to kill you."

Nightfall looked at the landing below him, where Volkmier stood with a drawn crossbow, the bolt aimed directly at his chest. He knew the captain's damnable aim too well to resist. He froze.

The brigade above charged down the stairs toward Nightfall, careful to keep their feet. They had seen the fall he had taken, and no one wanted to repeat it.

Nightfall kept his eyes locked on the captain, obeying his command to the letter. It occurred to him suddenly he had absolutely nothing to lose. Whether Volkmier shot him, or the mob executed him, he was just as dead.

Nightfall stiffened.

"Be still!" Volkmier reminded.

Nightfall cursed himself for giving even a hint of his next move away. Without a word or other warning, he drove up his weight and flung himself at Volkmier.

Volkmier swore viciously. The string of the crossbow twanged, and agony speared Nightfall's chest. His left arm went numb. His consciousness wavered, and he lost control even of his talent. He landed on the chief of the prison guards, collapsing him to the landing. Both men toppled. Nightfall could feel himself falling, his head filled with distant buzzing, his eyes registering only a blank tan haze interrupted by spots and squiggles.

Then, silent blackness overtook him completely.

† Chapter 10 †

Time undoes the heart of every creature of this great world, excepting the Divine: the Almighty and the Demon.

—Dyfrin of Keevain, the demon's friend

"**I** KNOW WHO you are."

The vaguely familiar voice dragged Nightfall from the black vacuum of unconsciousness to painful self-awareness. The outline of his body buzzed into focus first, and agony speared the upper left side of his chest. *Am I dead?* For a moment, he could not comprehend the absurdity of his question.

"I know who you are, *Nightfall.*"

That brought Nightfall fully to his senses. He opened his eyes to a stone-walled room painted a garish blue. He lay on a mound of blanketed straw, near an empty chamber pot. A set of dull, gray bars cut the room into halves. On the other side, Volkmier crouched on a seat carved into the wall, dressed in his standard working lavender-and-gray uniform. Beyond him, the only door was closed, surely bolted from the outside. A shuttered window suggested they occupied a room on one of the three lowest floors, though not the dungeon which lay underground. The middle floors held glass panes and the upper ones nothing at all.

"I've suspected it since your meeting with King Rikard," Volkmier continued. "But I didn't know for sure until I watched you battle your way through the Council. I never forget the way a man moves."

Nightfall believed him. He lived only because the bolt had missed his heart, though probably not by much. It had passed slightly to the left and high, cutting through the muscle where his chest met his shoulder. Someone had carefully bandaged the wound, and his left arm rested in a gently knotted and surprisingly clean sling. He sat up and faced the guard, ascertaining at the same time that they were alone. "Why didn't you kill me?"

"I missed."

It was not the answer Nightfall wanted. "You don't miss."

Volkmier frowned. "When my enemy does something so unexpected, so against his own survival, even I can be caught off guard. And I do miss. Even the commander of the prison guards, even the legendary demon, makes the occasional mistake."

Nightfall had to admit he had made plenty, all of them, it seemed, in the last six months. Afraid to take his eyes off the chief of the prison guards, he tested the muscles of his shoulder. The pain went beyond anything physical he had known before, a deeply seated ache screaming for his full attention. "So what form of slow humiliating execution do I have to look forward to?"

"None." Volkmier hopped from his crevice to the floor, carefully stretching each leg.

Relief flooded Nightfall. "I've been reprieved?"

"You're going to escape."

Nightfall's forehead creased. "I am?" He forced himself not to look at the cell door. The last time Alyndar had imprisoned him knowing his identity, they had used three separate locks, each with its own key. They had also stripped him of anything he could use to open them. Instead, he met Volkmier's gaze. The quick blue eyes held desperation and need.

"You're the only one I know who can find King Edward. The only one who might have the skill to bring him safely home."

Nightfall stared, shocked speechless.

Volkmier continued to study Nightfall, from safely beyond his reach. The sword at his belt might make a formidable weapon should Nightfall manage to snatch it through the bars.

When the captain said nothing, Nightfall forced words between his teeth. "You know who I am."

"I know—" Volkmier paused to clear his throat. "I know King Rikard trusted you, and he was a man of great wisdom with an uncanny understanding of people."

"King Rikard also trusted Gilleran." Nightfall could have slapped himself. *Why in the Holy Father's darkest hell am I trying to talk him out of letting me live?*

"Yes," Volkmier admitted, rocking back on his heels. "And for over two decades, the wizard served him well, if not always . . . pleasantly. The arrangement suited them both. The king kept Gilleran safe from other sorcerers, and his vile chancellor kept ill-wishers off-balance and used his magic for the good of Alyndar." Volkmier pursed his lips, shook his head. "Then, Gilleran gained some additional powers that gave him the strength and the confidence to seek the throne itself."

"He killed another powerful sorcerer." Nightfall had learned it from Kelryn, who had witnessed the attack. Gilleran had fortuitously rescued her from Ritworth the Iceman, only to bind her to his bidding moments later. Both sorcerers had tried to kill Nightfall in their time, and both had nearly succeeded. "And took control of all of his spells as well."

"Ah." The answer clearly did not surprise Volkmier, and Nightfall suspected he only wondered how his prisoner had come by the information. "Well. It is also possible Gilleran had some magical influence over our king that thwarted Rikard's knack for appraising people, but he never fooled our Prince Leyne." Volkmier glanced at the ceiling, his gaze going distant. Like most of the palace servants and nobility, he had expected Leyne to take the throne after his father's death, had never expected Edward to do anything more than remain a life-long annoyance for his brother. "Leyne hated Gilleran, and the crown prince was the only man with an even more finely honed skill for understanding people than his father." He looked directly at Nightfall. "Interestingly, he really liked you."

"Me?" The word was startled from Nightfall. "Prince Leyne liked me? But . . ." Nightfall stopped himself from mentioning that the elder prince had barely known him. He wondered what it was about excruciating pain that was making him honest to the point of stupidity.

Volkmier dipped a hand into his pocket and emerged with a battered book, its cover dyed a rich purple with decorative silver flourishes. The guard brandished it like a weapon. "Leyne's diary. In it, he says he tried his best not to like you, not to trust you, but he wound up doing both." He slammed the book down on his other palm. "Of course, he didn't know who you really were, which makes it all the more useful. He tested your loyalty to Edward and found it stronger and tighter than he believed possible." The book disappeared into Volkmier's meaty hand, then back into his pocket. "I tested you again, when I let you go after Edward despite my own orders to detain you. You saved him from Gilleran and proved us both right."

Nightfall nodded, knowing neither man had had the key piece of information: Gilleran's oath-bond had coupled Nightfall's soul to the prince's life. If Edward had died, Nightfall's essence and talent would have passed to Gilleran, an eternal torture. Compared to that, any lesser death had seemed a blessing. He knew better

than to share the explanation. It could only dampen
Volkmier's faith at a time when Nightfall needed allies.
The situation then did not matter. Now, he would do ex-
actly what Volkmier hoped he would: he would rescue
King Edward, if such a thing were still possible. He did
still need to make one thing clear. "How did you know
I had nothing to do with Ned's disappearance?"

Volkmier smiled. "Because while the Council met
with the nobleman Schiz had sent, I talked to his entourage. The guards know and see a lot more, and it's
usually untainted by politics."

Nightfall nodded his understanding.

"Schiz' guards like you. Duke Varsah—"

"—doesn't." Nightfall completed the understatement.
He managed a grin of his own, remembering how he
had gained the men's trust with his antics at *The Sharius'* mooring. Then, it had seemed foolish, now so very
wise. "So, how am I going to escape?"

Volkmier's smile disappeared, and he back stepped.
"I don't know. I figured you could manage it." His gaze
went to Nightfall's bandaged shoulder, and the corners
of his mouth drooped lower. "Right?" The last word
sounded far less certain than the others.

Nightfall restored the confident inflection. He knew
Volkmier could not appear to assist him in any way.
Now that he had the commander on his side, Nightfall
finally looked at the lock, a basic construction he could
handle, though he would need a pick or blade. He ran a
hand through his clothing, a fresh outfit that, though not
Alyndar's colors, had no holes or patches either. Beneath it, he found the undergarments the servants had
dressed him in after his bath. The guards had not fully
stripped him, which meant he might still have a few of
his hidden daggers. A cautious touch revealed at least
three, his favorites, the slender throwing knives he usually kept secured to his right arm. The shutter latches
would yield to them as well. "Where are we?"

"South Tower. Third floor." Volkmier looked doubtfully at Nightfall's injured arm. "Are you going to be able to climb down?"

Nightfall carefully slipped his injured arm from its sling, easing it through its full range of motion. The muscles had stiffened in his sleep. Every movement hurt, but he had performed through pain before. At least, the muscles, bones, and tendons seemed to work. "No problem," Nightfall lied. He found it impossible to admit weakness, even to someone who had promised to assist him, at least indirectly.

Volkmier explained the normal procedure. "It's my job to stay with you until you awaken, to scare you into complying with the understanding that any attempt at escape will result in your death, then to let my underlings take over."

"Consider me warned." Nightfall wondered how effective such a threat ever proved to a man under sentence of execution.

"You also must understand you were situated in a low security area because of your title and status, and it would be beneath your station and unethical for you to attempt escape anyway."

Nightfall rolled his eyes. "Wouldn't want to go to my execution having done anything . . . unethical."

Volkmier snorted his amusement, then continued, "We'll keep you comfortable and well fed, and a guard will remain with you at all times, either inside this room or just outside the door." He gestured at the only exit.

At the mention of food, Nightfall remembered he had missed at least two meals. His mouth felt dry as cotton and his stomach pinched. He waited for the routine speech to end. None of it really mattered.

"If you feel we have neglected a need, you have the right to ask, though we may not grant it."

Volkmier paused, though whether because he had finished or only for breath, Nightfall never knew. "I do have one request."

Volkmier nodded curtly.

Recalling how Volkmier personally had foiled at least two of his escapes, Nightfall suggested, "When it comes time to recapture me, could you please command your guards in a way that makes sense for hunting down Sudian rather than . . . ?"

"Nightfall?" Volkmier supplied helpfully.

"Well, yes, thank you." Nightfall fixed his blue-black gaze on Volkmier. "And I'd appreciate it if you never used that name in my presence again." He softened the warning by adding, "Please."

Volkmier nodded his agreement to both requests. "And I'd ask one thing of you, as well."

Nightfall duplicated the amenable nod.

"When making your escape, don't permanently harm any of my men."

"I'll do my best." Nightfall's last dungeon break had left two guards dead, under very different circumstances.

"Then . . . I guess I'll turn you over to your regular detail." Having said that, Volkmier made no move to actually leave. He stood, frozen in place and time, seeking something Nightfall did not feel certain he could give.

Nightfall knew Volkmier wanted reassurance that he had not made a horrible blunder, that he had not just loosed the demon back against the world and doomed King Edward to the very death he desperately wished Nightfall would prevent. "I can't eliminate your doubts. I'm not even sure I can diminish them, but I am going to do everything I can to find and, if possible, rescue King Edward Nargol of Alyndar."

That confidence, spoken with innocent sincerity, loosened Volkmier's tongue, just as it had the cabin boy's on *The Sharius*. "The Council still believes a ransom note will come."

"The Council is wrong."

Volkmier jerked. "How—how do you know that?"

"I don't," Nightfall admitted, rising to a crouch. "But nobles kidnapping nobles don't kill their entire staff in the process. If it were coming, a note should have arrived by now. The abduction of a king doesn't occur on a whim." He shook his head. "There's something odd and very different about this situation that the gentry doesn't realize or understand. It's beyond their experience." He added carefully, ". . . and into mine." He shook his head, dislodging straw from his combed-out locks, already beginning to collect knots. "I should never have left Schiz. I should have stayed until I found him." That mistake haunted him more than any other ever had. "The sooner I get out there, the more likely I'll still find useful clues."

Volkmier's head bobbed again. "You're right, of course." He kneaded his fingers together in concern but did head toward the door.

Though Nightfall worried about pushing his luck with the shrewd chief of prison guards, he had to speak of the matter that had brought him back to Alyndar. "One thing more, Captain."

Volkmier froze in position. Though he did not face Nightfall, he clearly listened.

Encouraged, Nightfall continued. "The reason I didn't immediately follow Ned's trail . . ."

Volkmier turned, interested.

"The king's capture was too well coordinated to have been thrown together in a week. News of our destination traveled faster than any word of mouth could."

The corners of Volkmier's eyes twitched, and he gave Nightfall a sideways look. "What are you saying?"

"One of Ned's advisers or councillors, someone in the room the day he announced his decision to apologize to Duke Varsah, is a—"

"Don't say it," Volkmier warned.

Nightfall dropped the loaded word "traitor" from his explanation, turning obediently vague. "Either intentionally or inadvertently, someone sent word to the thugs who murdered Ned's escort." He added the qualifier that overrode the possibility of accident. "At great speed."

Volkmier strangled his reply, "Who?"

Nightfall shook his head. "I haven't had a chance to find out, but I'll bet it's the same man who contrived my arrest."

"Contrived . . ." Volkmier's voice remained strained, and he contemplated the possibilities. "A traitor among the honored men of Alyndar's High Council? Impossible."

Nightfall took the words in stride. He had hoped, but never expected, the chief of the prison guards to believe him over the nobility. Still, Volkmier seemed the only one with the willingness, knowledge, and ability to find Edward's betrayer in his absence. Nightfall had to try again. "Perhaps traitor is the wrong word." He tried to place himself in the position of the members of the Council. Though a totally foreign mind-set, he thought he understood. "More than a few of the gentry never expected Ned on the throne, and I'm certain few of the Council can stand me."

Though Volkmier's prior words had appeared to dismiss Nightfall's suggestion, his mouth remained pursed in a twist, his brow furrowed. "I suppose someone very loyal to Alyndar might see King Edward as dangerously inexperienced and you as a threat." Volkmier straightened abruptly, as if suddenly shocked. "Of course, such a person could not have known the fiends would slaughter the king's escort." He continued to mull over the details. "We all know the king would never dismiss you himself, but with him detained, that would open the way . . ." Volkmier did not finish. The evidence for his last thought stood right in front of him. Nevertheless, he shook his head vigorously. "I can't believe I'm even considering this."

Nightfall said nothing. He had committed himself to rescuing Edward. It remained up to Volkmier and those honest members of the Council to secure castle and kingdom for his return.

"I'll do what I can." Again, Volkmier headed for the

door. As he reached it, his face tipped upward, as if beseeching the gods.

No longer wholly certain of his own motives, Nightfall hoped Volkmier got the answer he sought.

Volkmier walked purposefully through the door, pulling it closed behind him.

Nightfall waited only until the panel clicked shut before scurrying to the cell lock. A practiced shift and flick brought a knife to his hand. He slipped the tip into the lock, feeling every slight vibration, each glide of steel against the mechanism. It gave with a nearly inaudible click, and Nightfall slid the door open amid a slight squeak of hinges.

Cringing at the sound, Nightfall hurried to the window. Stabbing the blade low through the crack between the shutters, he worked it gently upward until he met resistance. He flicked over the first latch, then continued the knife's journey to the second, which was just as simply disengaged. He edged the left shutter outward barely far enough to allow a hint of darkness and moonlight to funnel inside. Apparently, he had slept for several hours, though not through the entire night. He realized with a pasty-mouthed jolt he had had nothing to drink either since the previous morning.

A key rattled in the door lock to his room.

Nightfall returned the dagger to its proper place, then crouched on the sill, waiting. He wanted the guard to witness his escape, to divert suspicion from Volkmier.

The door bashed opened, and a man dressed in prison guard gray and lavender entered, balancing three bowls and the heavy door, which he held open with a burly hip. "Good night, Sudian. My name is—" The guard broke off with a gasp as he saw the empty cell. His gaze swung from the gaping cell door to the window.

Nightfall gave him a feigned look of surprise before shoving through the shutters and sinking out the window.

The clatter of dropped crockery filled the room behind him, followed by a shout. "He's escaping, gods damn him! Captain, help! The prisoner is escaping!"

Nightfall clung to the edge of the ledge, letting his boots fall to the ground. Flinging down his weight, he swung himself by his good arm in a solid arc that brought him up beside the prison window. He scrambled toward the roof, agony tearing through his left shoulder, as the guard pounded across the room. Hidden by a fifth-floor ledge, Nightfall watched the guard's head thrust suddenly through the shutters, now two floors beneath him. As Nightfall expected, the man looked down; people searching always did. Nightfall went utterly immobile, hoping the guard would not think to glance upward, hoping that, if he did, he would miss the still form hovering in the darkness.

Amid a round of raucous cursing, the head withdrew.

Nightfall continued his mad scramble toward the roof, glad for the talent he had so often cursed. His feather weight kept his injured arm from supporting too much for him to bear. Just moving it hurt, and he could scarcely imagine trusting it with its usual load. Mapping the rooms of the tower in his mind, he selected the one he wanted, on the sixth floor, and scuttled through the window like a bug.

Sleeping forms cluttered the floor, huddled beneath threadbare blankets on mounds of straw. Scarred furniture, mostly trunks and old dressers lay flush with every wall. Nightfall cautiously tiptoed around the servants, the minuscule sounds made by his clothing and bare feet masked by heavy breathing and gentle snores. Now on familiar territory, he breathed a silent sigh and set to work.

Kelryn sat on her room's only chair at a simple table that held her cold and untouched dinner: a small roasted hen, a buttered round of white bread, a mound of mashed tubers, and a mug of mulled cider. Her face felt like putty, and her hands had gone numb from supporting it. A dried flood of tears glued her elbows to the table. Pulled on hastily, her flimsy nightgown fell loosely around strong, sinewy shoulders; she could not muster the wherewithal to bother with stays and ties.

It all seemed impossible and insufferably ironic. For twenty years, Nightfall had plagued the four kingdoms of the world and every place between them. For twenty years, the demon of legend had roamed free, apparently unstoppable. Then, just as she and, inadvertently, Edward, had taught him to tap the goodness Dyfrin had sworn lived deep within him, the gentle compassion she had perceived from the day she had met him, he would face execution for a crime he had not even committed.

Trapped in a terrible limbo of grief, Kelryn found herself incapable of eating, incapable of sleeping, incapable it seemed, even of moving. She had maintained her position for more hours than she knew, tears gliding from swollen eyes that could no longer form or shed them. She had suffered so much for love. Discovering the true identity of her darling Marak had proved a shock from which she had never expected to recover. Yet, coming from him, a secret he had never shared with anyone, it had seemed almost exciting. She had adored him all the more for sharing that deadly confidence, for doing so had proved the depth of his love for her as well. He had dared to open himself to her, to trust her, as he had no one before her.

Now, he was going to die. Not for being Nightfall. His slayers would never even know his true identity, if indeed he could be said to have a real one at all. He would die for all the things he had once rejected as foolish and dangerous: friendship, morality, caring. Even if he evaded his sentence, he would always know the reason he suffered. She wondered if he might, once again, disdain those things she and Dyfrin had fought to draw out of him, those ideals they had teased and loved and dragged from the depths of his being. Decades of painstaking work destroyed in seconds by the decree of a power-mad Council.

A tap on Kelryn's door, though delicate, startled her. She jerked her head from her hands, and her face peeled painfully from her palms. Her room, though unlit, seemed uncomfortably bright compared with the closed-eye view of the last several hours. "Who is it?" Her voice emerged as a deep croak.

The soft, lispy voice of a child barely wafted to her. "Maid, milady."

"Maid?" Kelryn wondered aloud. "At this time of night?"

The other seemed put off, pausing several beats before admitting, "We thought you could use some company, Lady Kelryn."

Kelryn managed a smile despite her sorrow. *How sweet.* She rose too quickly, assailed by a sudden lightheadedness that rendered her blind and dumb. It seemed to take forever to pass in a wave of specks and spirals before she regained her equilibrium. Crossing the room, she tripped the latch and ushered a young chambermaid into her quarters.

The newcomer looked unfamiliar, long hair tucked beneath a head scarf, except for a few wispy black strands that escaped onto a young-looking face. The eyes dodged Kelryn's. The cheekbones sat high, the lips bow-shaped and darkly pink. The standard gray uniform fit well, defining the early stirrings of breasts and hip curves on an otherwise waifish body. The chambermaid glanced around the room, looking nervous and uncertain.

Though she felt dead inside, Kelryn tried to reassure her. "It's all right. I'm glad you came. I could use someone to talk to."

For a moment, the eyes stopped moving to focus on Kelryn. They were large and dark, with a hint of blue that might show fully in better light. "You look terrible."

Though words of concern, not insult, they took Kelryn aback. "I love him," she said as explanation. "I can barely imagine my life without him. I—"

Fists slammed a frenzied pattern against the door.

Kelryn gasped in a shocked lungful of breath, and the chambermaid scurried to look busy. "Who is it?"

A harsh male voice came next, muffled by the door. "Guardsmen, my lady. We need to talk to you."

Kelryn hurried to the door and opened it to reveal two large men in working leathers covered by purple-and-silver tunics.

"Lady, you—" the first started, as the second's eyes widened to comical proportions. He cleared his throat, averting his eyes.

Only then, Kelryn realized she had not bothered to fasten the lacy gown she had hastily thrown on in the hope she might sleep. Modesty meant little to showgirls who regularly doubled as whores. Nightfall had rescued her from that life, but he had no more turned her into a lady than becoming chancellor had made him a gentleman.

The second guard continued to stare, too pleased or surprised to remember his manners. The first shaded his eyes with a hand. "Lady, you . . . your . . ."

Kelryn drew the gown around her but still did not bother to fasten it. It seemed like too much work; and, at the moment, she did not feel kindly disposed toward Alyndar's guardsmen. "Did you come for a reason?"

The speaker dragged callused fingers through his hair, his helmet clenched between his arm and other hand. "We just wanted to inform you Sudian has escaped."

Kelryn's heart leaped, but she hid her excitement behind a mask of uncertainty. "He has?"

"Out a window and into the night," the man continued. "We think he's in the city by now, perhaps headed for a ship, but he might come for you. If you see him, you must report to one of us at once." He glanced at his companion, who was still gawking, giving him a hard nudge that snapped him free of his trance.

"Of course." Kelryn said, the only thing she could think of. Any other answer would make them stay longer. She wanted to be alone with the chambermaid, who might have overheard the details of Nightfall's flight. After all, the palace elite spoke as freely in front of servants as animals.

The guard swallowed hard, as if hating his own next words. "Hiding him would make you an accomplice." He lowered his head to emphasize the significance of his words, "And vulnerable to serious punishment."

"I have nothing to hide." Kelryn flung her door wide, losing her hold on the gown in the process. "You're welcome to come in and search."

The chambermaid used a rag to swat dust from a bedpost.

"Not necessary," the first guard said, cheeks reddening, gaze sweeping the room. "Just see that you tell us." His tone softened, and his gaze flitted everywhere except to her half naked body. "We know you planned to marry him, but he committed a crime against the kingdom, against the very king himself. He's desperate, dangerous, and in very real peril. If he doesn't surrender, we have orders to kill him where he stands."

If she had had any tears left to cry, Kelryn would have. Instead, she gathered her gown and lowered her head. "I understand."

The second guard finally found his tongue. "Begging your pardon, Lady, but you'd do us all a favor, including him. He's hurt bad enough he can't get far. We could collect him peacefully. He'd have longer to live, and you wouldn't have to watch him get . . . ." He paused, apparently seeking a proper euphemism. Then, he must have realized the real word would have a stronger effect. ". . . killed."

Kelryn nodded silently but, she hoped, with convincing force.

Both men returned gestures of respect, then retreated from the room.

Kelryn closed the door. Unable to move, she stood behind it, eyes closed, cheek pressed to the cold wood.

A hand gripped Kelryn's shoulder. Startled, she gasped before remembering the chambermaid. She allowed herself to be gathered into arms that enwrapped her with surprising confidence and security. She fell against her benefactor, imagining it was Nightfall who held her, his body warm, thin yet powerful against hers, his lips pressed against her scalp. She could almost hear his voice tickling her ear.

"It's all right, Kelryn. Everything will be all right."

It sounded too real. Startled, Kelryn pulled away, staring into the chambermaid's face. The youthful feminine features looked distinctly unfamiliar, but the dark blue eyes held a soulful depth of concern, accompanied by a glimmer of pain.

"It's me, Kelryn." Nightfall's intonation issued from the chambermaid, an eerie combination that sent her stumbling backward against the door.

"M–Marak?" Kelryn studied the person in front of her, scarcely daring to believe. Again, she scanned the eyes, the detail that had given him away the day he had stepped into her room as Sudian. As blue-black as tempered steel, they met her gaze, and she knew them. "Marak." She hurled herself into his arms, and he loosed a grunt of pain.

Kelryn grimaced, guilty she had hurt him just to ease her own discomfort. Slipping free from his embrace, she seized his hands and guided him deeper into the room. "You're not safe here."

Nightfall slid one of their entwined hands beneath her gown. "Neither are you."

"Stop it!" As much as she had missed him, Kelryn could not fathom thinking about sex at a time like this, especially when he held the appearance of a woman. "They're searching for you. They're going to kill you on sight."

"I heard." Nightfall reminded her he had been in the room when the guards had made their pronouncement. He glided around her to the table, tore a leg from the chicken and bit off a chunk of meat. He waved the bone at her. "They're out combing the city and the docks. They'll expect me to run as fast and far as possible."

It made sense to Kelryn. "As well you should. You're not safe here. What are you doing . . . ?"

"Right now?" Nightfall scooped up a handful of tubers and sat on the bed, stuffing them in his mouth. "Eating." He swallowed, clearly too ravenously hungry to savor the food, then addressed her real question. "I know what I'm doing."

Kelryn went silent. Despite her desperate worry, despite her every instinct, she managed a smile. If anyone knew how to perform a proper escape, he did. She had no right to second-guess him. "I suppose you must." The grin disappeared almost immediately. "They said . . ." Tears tried to rise to her swollen, stinging eyes. "They said you were shot. In the . . . in the heart."

Nightfall smiled around the food. "Which proves what so many have claimed." He took another bite of chicken. "I don't have a heart."

Kelryn did not know whether to hit him or hug him. "Whether anyone believes it, including you, you have a wonderful heart." She wanted to tear his clothes off, to see the wound the servants had called fatal, the guards had said would slow him, and clearly had caused him pain when she had hugged him. But she worried more about ruining his disguise. "Don't lie to me. How bad is it?"

"It hurts," Nightfall admitted, to Kelryn's surprise. "But it'll heal." Taking her wrist in a greasy hand, he pulled her down beside him. "I'm going after Ned. I'll get word back to you when I can, and you need to keep your ears alert for me." His expression turned earnest, even for a girlish chambermaid. "Trust no one, Kelryn. No one. Except Volkmier."

Few names could have surprised Kelryn more. "Volkmier? The chief of the prison guards?"

Nightfall nodded. He rose, tossing the empty bone to

the plate and seizing the other drumstick. He sucked down the entire mug of cider.

Kelryn stared, wanting more but knowing she was unlikely to get it.

Nightfall put aside the mug and wiped his mouth on his sleeve. "Just don't put him in a position of having to choose between us and Alyndar. We will lose."

"All right," Kelryn said, hoping that, as situations arose, she would figure out how to handle them. Though not to the extent of her partner, she, too, had often needed to survive by her wits. "I'll do my best. For you, for Ned, for all of us."

The room went silent, except for Nightfall's hasty chewing. Kelryn had seen him eat with the proper decorum of a noble and realized how famished he had become to bolt down food like a dog. "Remember the code?"

Kelryn nodded. She could not read or write, but she and Nightfall had worked out a picture language so they could understand one another from a distance or in touchy situations. Nightfall had last used it when he and Edward had escaped Duke Varsah's imprisonment. The then-prince had wanted to let her know where and why they had left without her, but Nightfall had used it to show his contempt for her. At the time, he had believed her to be his betrayer. "Of course."

"I'll get word to you as I can when I can." Using the mincing steps of a nervous young chambermaid, Nightfall dropped the half eaten second chicken leg and headed toward the door.

Kelryn suppressed the urge to run after him, to beg him to stay. The hours it gained them together would surely be his last. "Remember, I love you. Whatever else you do, come back safely."

"I'll try." Nightfall took up the bread slice.

Thinking quickly, Kelryn wrenched open the desk drawer and removed a pouch of silver, which she offered to Nightfall. "Here, have this."

Nightfall took huge bites from the bread, glancing at the offering without reaching toward it. "You keep it. You might need it."

Kelryn shoved the balled-up purse into his hand. "I don't need anything. You do. Take it."

With clear reluctance, Nightfall accepted the purse and stuffed it into the bodice of his shift. "Thank you."

Kelryn grabbed his arm. "Bring back Ned, and also ... Sudian."

Nightfall hesitated.

Kelryn wished he could promise everything would work out all right, though she knew he would have to lie to do so. He had no way of even knowing whether King Edward still lived.

"I'll do my best," he said with the force of a solemn vow. "I'll do my very best."

† Chapter 11 †

Treat others not as you expect them to treat you, not as they do treat you, but as you wish they would treat you. If you do, your wish may well come true.

—Dyfrin of Keevain, the demon's friend

THE CHICKEN, tubers, and cider sat like lead in Nightfall's gut as he slithered through the darkness. He avoided the docks, where the guards would scrutinize every traveler and probably offer the captains a hefty reward for his capture. The realization frustrated him. A boat could take him back to Schiz far faster than any form of overland travel, especially since caution restricted him to walking. Horses drew the attention of passersby and thieves, and rendered silent unseen travel impossible.

Nightfall trusted his ability to outwit any guards. He could stow away aboard a ship, but the crew would eventually find him. Once they did, he would be effectively trapped until the ship pulled into port and the sailors handed him over to Alyndar. He had suffered that fate once, and never would again. Procuring a ship, by bet, money, or theft did him little good without a trustworthy crew to man it. That left him no choice but

an overland route, even it if took him a month or more
to reach Duke Varsah's city.

Now dressed as a male commoner in well-worn
homespun snatched from a drying line, his hair in an ar-
tificially lengthened black braid, and his features al-
tered, Nightfall knew he would not stand out in any of
the nearby cities. Nevertheless, he slunk around inhab-
ited areas, preferring to lay low in the cornfields and
forests springing up around Alyndar's outskirts. Soon,
he had completely circled the city, skirting the harvested
fields to plow deep into the shadowed forests.

Though Nightfall kept off the roads, he remained
near enough to monitor traffic and keep his bearings.
Anyone traveling before sunup would appear suspicious. Hiding in plain sight usually worked better, in
Nightfall's experience. He had performed most of his
greatest thefts with the owners at home and his best dis-
appearances in broad daylight. Less cautious then, people tended not to lock up valuables and to ignore noises
that would raise alarm in darker, quieter times.

The acrid smell of fire touched Nightfall's nostrils.
Deep in the woodlands, it could only mean a campfire.
Guards, he guessed, and soundlessly followed the odor.
It seemed worth the small risk of discovery to learn the
location, numbers and, perhaps, the mind-set of his enemies. The more he understood about their hunt, the
safer he became.

No stranger to creeping through woodlands, Nightfall made swift passage despite his need for quiet. At
length, he spotted the red dot of the campfire, interrupted at intervals by the movement of figures around
it. He saw and heard no horses, which struck him as
odd. Surely Alyndar's guard force would have access
to mounts, though he supposed they might not use
them. Perhaps he had stumbled upon a stealthy force,
geared to find a lone man sneaking through the forest.

The skin between Nightfall's shoulder blades tickled
as his imagination placed unseen eyes in the brush. A

group of men trained to spy would not kindle a telltale fire. *Unless they're using it to draw me.* It seemed farfetched, yet it had worked. Perhaps these men had set up their camp knowing it would draw him, then stationed others in hidden places to surround him. Nightfall froze, wondering if guardsmen could really manage such a clever and devious ruse, then dismissed his fears as paranoia. They would have to have anticipated his timing and route with an uncanny accuracy. Even he did not know exactly how he planned to get to Schiz, and they could only guess at his final destination.

Then, a familiar loud, squeaky voice reached Nightfall's ears. "So we basically got permission to rob and kill any loner in this-here woods."

Nightfall sifted his memory for the name of the lowdown punk who owned that voice: Thumesto, a smalltime thief who worked out of Nemix. Nightfall edged closer, knowing whoever spoke next would do so at a lower volume.

"I reckon he's going to have to resemble the fellow they's looking for at least a little if'n we don't want to wind up executed or in a dungeon cell somewheres."

The shadows sorted into three human forms sprawled in front of a low and flickering campfire. The scrawny, irritatingly voiced Thumesto had his back to Nightfall, his clothing of threadbare linen and his stubbly hair cut tight against his scalp. The second speaker lay on his back, his hands tucked beneath his head as he stared at the sky. Though of medium build and coloring, most of his body swaddled in a tattered blanket, Hammaxl the Highwayman was also recognizable to Nightfall once he put together the pieces of what he heard and saw. The third sat in profile, hawk-nosed and huge, a lumbering bear of a man who served as a frequent partner to Hammaxl. His name escaped Nightfall's memory.

"They might forgive us a mistake or two." The bearlike man stretched with an enormous, noisy yawn. "Though dinnit the one guard say they perferred him live?"

"Preferred." Hammaxl restored the proper pronunciation. "But they dint offer more money that way. Why should we trouble ourselfs struggling with the fellow if'n we doan have ta?"

They all laughed, as if Hammaxl had said something wickedly clever instead of just wicked.

The bear-man poked a stick at the fire. "Ain't we got more ta eat?"

Thumesto's grating voice came next, "Ain't you be thinking 'bout nothing ought your stomach?"

"I'm hungry," the big man said. "Can't help that I am."

"You done et three quarters of what we had already." Thumesto's tone grew even more grating, if possible. "Don't see as . . ."

Nightfall withdrew reluctantly, stifling the urge to grab Hammaxl by the throat and demand whatever information had oozed to Nemix' underground. Again, his inability to act freely tied his hands. The demon would know every detail these wretched thieves did in moments, while Nightfall-turned-Sudian had to settle for whatever he randomly overheard. He might learn more by remaining, or he might lose hours listening to an inane, unhelpful recitation of highwayman strategy. He knew he could avoid them easily enough. Other travelers would have to take their own precautions, aware secluded areas seemed to breed men like Hammaxl and the others. Lone travelers were rare, and anyone who dared such a thing probably deserved what he got. Despite the viewpoints of King Edward and Dyfrin, it was not Nightfall's job to see to it that fools traveled safely.

One thing seemed abundantly clear to Nightfall. Alyndar had offered enough of a reward to stimulate at least the lower echelons of thieves and assassins to comb the world for him. Any lone traveler would become fair game, and even his disguises might not save him if desperate people in search of gold proved no more discriminating than these bandits. He saw no way to make himself part of a group without severely hampering his mission. Dressed as a female, he would stand out even more as a lone traveler and bar himself from many of the best sources of information.

As Nightfall turned away from the traveled pathways and toward the coastline, he realized he had few options. He could skulk about for a time, living off the land and laying low, but that would not gain him the facts he needed to find King Edward. Wherever he went, he had to find a way to fit in with the local populace; and that might mean employing old personae.

To Nightfall's surprise, the idea brought a tingle of excitement. Strange as it seemed, he missed some of his old friends, even if they were only himself in different guises. Finding a safe hollow, obscured by trees and vines, Nightfall snuggled into a defensible position and allowed himself to drift toward the featherlight sleep that kept him alive. As he drifted, he thought of Kelryn's last words to him: *Bring back Ned, and also Sudian.* Naturally, she wanted them both home safely, yet the phrasing confused him. *Why did she say "Sudian" instead of "yourself"?* No clear answer came; it all seemed inconsequential, distant.

Nightfall fell into restless sleep.

Nightfall awakened well after sunrise, still completely hidden by brush and trees. His mouth felt dry and sticky. The imprint of every twig and pebble seemed stamped in bruises across the soles of feet protected only by a pair of stolen cloth shoes. His head throbbed in time to the dull, pulsing ache of his shoulder. Oblivious to his presence, or his awakening, birds whistled a symphony through the treetops. A squirrel scrambled in energetic bursts across the branches overhead, sending down a shower of leaves that had blanketed Nightfall through the night. Once his senses told him nothing dangerous shared this area of the forest, he rose and forced himself to stretch through the pain. The desire to hold his left arm utterly still was strong, but he resisted. He could not afford to allow it to stiffen.

Though it meant scrambling over rocks and unkempt ledges, Nightfall spent the next several days traveling along the coast, enjoying the aroma of salt and bracken, the shrill of gulls, and the gentle bob of other seabirds on the current. Occasionally he saw ships in the distance, their masts carving perfect triangles and rows of rectangles against the clouds; but none came near enough for him to read its standard. Every time a stone or stick added to the mass of bruises on his instep, he wished he stood aboard a rollicking deck, staring out over white runnels carved by the stern. He feasted on clams and oysters washed against the bank, infant lobsters when he could catch them scuttling beneath the bracken, and handfuls of autumn berries from twisted, prickly vines. Myriad tributaries washing into the ocean supplied him with reasonably fresh water harboring only a tinge of silt and salt.

Soon, the land grew more familiar as tended rows of crops appeared to Nightfall's left. As Telwinar, he had tended his five small fields with the help of his neighbors and odd-job laborers whom he kept well paid for their services. He had made an effort to take Telwinar guise at planting and harvest and to ply his other trades and personae in winter and the growing season. He worked his own fields whenever possible, though he received little of the land's rewards, which went to the overlord owner of the land. The people of Delfor knew him as a gentle recluse, badly scarred from a plowing accident. It surprised no one that he had no wife and had to hire the children of those around him rather than make his own.

Nearing Delfor. Nightfall recalled his last visit there. A woman named Genevra, with the natal ability to heal wounds, had come to Delfor, sheltered and protected by the overlord. He kept her in a fortress, albeit a richly convenienced and comfortable one, and gave her his men and the wealthy to heal. The arrangement pleased both. Genevra sacrificed her freedom for security and believed herself the better for it. She had witnessed Dyfrin's nightmarish death: the excruciating agony of the sorcerer's attack, the flaying of soul from body; and the sorcerer had touched her talent as well. She believed any arrangement satisfactory if it rescued her from the same fate. Genevra liked Sudian. She would surely agree to heal his shoulder, but he doubted all of his silver would prove enough for Overlord Pritikis to grant him an audience with her.

Nightfall drifted landward as he examined the checkerboard pattern of hay and corn, careful not to draw near enough to discern human figures among the crops, as they might see him as well. When he and Edward had passed through, the spring planting had just started. He had missed it for the first time and knew Telwinar was now considered dead, his fields, horses, and supplies handed over to a new farmer or divided among neighbors, his meager belongings claimed by Overlord Pritikis or thieves.

As Nightfall considered the lot of a man who had existed only as a part of himself, he reconsidered his idea from the previous night. *A lone stranger will draw attention, especially if Alyndar's guards came through here.* He knew he could count on that being the case. *But the return of a familiar face, alone or not, might go unnoticed.* Though Nightfall had assured Edward he had no reason to assume any name or persona but Sudian's for the rest of his life, he believed the king would understand. He had only vowed not to take up the guise of Nightfall again, a promise he fully intended to keep. Reviving any of the others would require explanation and might entangle him in minor discomforts and interpersonal affairs, but a rebirth of the demon would result in an uncontrollable bonfire of trouble. Just one living man in Alyndar could explain what had happened, Commander Volkmier, and he had only hunches and assumptions, without explanations. The law of every country, and thousands of vendettas, would condemn Nightfall to death. The integrity of Alyndar's greatest king would become an issue of challenge, and Edward would never forgive his squire turned chancellor.

Nightfall shook the thought aside. Making himself into Telwinar did not mean surrendering to all of his past. If he could successfully manage to revive the Delforian farmer, it opened the way to normalcy in other cities as well. He would not have to dodge human contact, without which he would never find King Edward. He could become Etan the laborer in the south, Frihiat in Schiz, and Balshaz the merchant almost anywhere. He could move through the world without the need for constant scrutiny, and Alyndar's guards would never think to search for Sudian in the guise of well-known and established citizens.

Excited by this new prospect, Nightfall set to rearranging days of clinging filth into the familiar, scarred features of the Delforian farmer. Already dirtied and colored black, Nightfall's hair required little coaxing to take the proper curls. He fixed his clothes to give him the appearance of additional bulk while still appearing close-fitting. Since his staged accident with the plow, Telwinar never allowed fabric to flow where a stray tool, wheel, or misbehaving animal might trap it. The purse Kelryn had insisted he take held only silver coins, twelve in total, each worth nearly as much as Telwinar could earn in a year. It put him in a quandary. Until he changed one, he would look conspicuous paying for anything.

Dumping the contents, Nightfall hid nine of the coins deep inside his clothing, leaving the last three in the purse he attached to his belt. He studied himself in the water, which gave back a warped and colorless image of Telwinar. He practiced a limp he knew as well as breathing. The transformation hit him at that moment, deep and magical. His thoughts went to the time of year, the nearness of the approaching harvest, concerns over weather. He would need several rainless days for the hay crop. It had to be cut dry, then required a few days of sun-curing before he could store it. Otherwise, it might develop spots of rot that would poison the horses. Every raindrop dragged down its value. If it got wet once and redried well, the cows could still stomach it. After that, it became sheep fodder or went to the goats and geese, who seemed able to handle almost anything. The corn mattered, too; but the difference in the quality of the hay crop determined whether a family lived comfortably in any given year or borrowed toward the next.

Nightfall's trepidations disappeared as he approached the farm fields swathing the area between encroaching forest and the city of Delfor. For all intents and purposes, he became the quiet, gentle farmer who had made his home here for longer than a decade. Hitching his painstaking way across the fields, he met children first, the two youngest daughters of Lloowal. The girls ran geese between the cornstalks to pluck out weeds while their older brothers and sister examined the stalks and pulled up the vines, flowers, and volunteer sprouts by hand.

One glanced up and must have said something to the siblings, because the rest turned their heads toward Nightfall simultaneously. The oldest, a girl, gestured at the middle child, who dropped a handful of drooping stems, wiped his face on the back of a grimy sleeve, and trotted off toward home. The others paused in their work to watch Nightfall's approach. The geese also noticed him, honking and hissing with a vehemence that could wake the soundest sleeper.

Nightfall ignored the birds, which ranged in color from purest white to a soggy gray with speckles of black. They could raise an impressive challenge but only attacked when protecting eggs or goslings. Otherwise, they kept their distance, gliding away from anyone who walked directly toward them in a bunched and noisy protest, their paddle-feet slapping distinctly shaped prints into the loam. As Nightfall drew within speaking distance, he tipped his head in greeting. "Good eve," he said, in his tight Telwinar voice.

All of the children acknowledged him with slight bows and curtsies, but only the remaining boy spoke, "Good eve, sir." He studied Nightfall intently. "You've returned."

"I have," Nightfall admitted, his words nearly lost beneath the guttural noises of the geese. Disguised as a man of few words, he headed onward.

The second youngest girl piped in, "Billithane's done your fields."

The oldest hissed at her, nearly as loudly as the geese. "Arly, quiet. It's for the grown-ups to tell him things like that."

Hoping to put the girl at ease, Nightfall turned.

Arly huddled into herself, a hand clamped over her mouth. Brown hair dangled in strings around her face.

"I'm glad they didn't go to waste," Nightfall said kindly. "I hope they do him well." He crooked an eyebrow conspiratorially, and the little girl smiled.

Nightfall continued through the fields, slowed by his affectation. The corn crop looked good approaching harvest, the stalks as tall as his shoulder, the ears as wide and long as his middle finger. The old farmers' adage ran through his head:

> *Thumb thick:*
> *Ready to pick—*
> *Stalks hewn*
> *By Harvest moon.*

The hay appeared healthy as well, thick and brilliant green without blight or mush, though he did see occasional bald areas of ground where the land had flooded or seed failed to take hold. By the time Nightfall wound his

way around the edges and rows of a dozen fields, he found
a group of farmers and wives gathered, he hoped, to greet
him. He knew them all as neighbors, men and women
baked brown by the sun, their faces craggy, their hands
callused and work-hardened. Billithane stood among
them, a sturdily built man who had fathered ten children,
seven of whom had survived. Nightfall had hired the five
boys at various times to work his crops and keep his home
safe in the off times between plantings and harvests. They
had proven honest, hard workers; appreciating their assistance, he paid them well. He could think of few people he
would rather have take over his land. As Nightfall approached, the farmers and wives stood in silence, even as
he limped to within speaking distance.

"Hello," he finally said.

That seemed to break the others from their trances.
Billithane's plump wife stepped forward and caught
Nightfall into an embrace.

The sudden display of affection startled him and sent
pain lancing through his chest and shoulder, but he
maintained character, weathering the exuberant welcome with only a hint of surprise. She smelled of fresh
bread, herbs, and roasted chicken. Though narrow at the
shoulders, waist, and hips, she had a front to back fullness that softened her hug into what would have
seemed a comfort if not for the growing agony of his injury. "It's good to have you back, Telwinar." Though
there was still the matter of land and crops to consider,
she spoke with sincerity. It surprised Nightfall to learn
anyone had cared about his disappearance.

Grunts and mumbled agreements followed from
those less able or willing to display their emotions.

"Thank you," Nightfall said, knowing they wanted
more. They clearly itched to demand where he had
gone, what had happened to him of a nature serious
enough to cause him to miss a planting and, nearly, the
harvest. He also realized no one would ply him for information until he had a full belly and, if needed, a nap.

Nightfall did not recall being asked, yet the group herded him toward the nearest cottage, which belonged to a couple named Paisyn and Barbarah. The men scrounged up chairs, benches, and barrels, while the women squeezed into the parlor to throw together an impromptu meal. The men talked about weather and family, crops and chores left undone. Billithane edged his way to Nightfall. "I planted and tended your fields." Having said that, he went silent, leaving the opening in the conversation for Nightfall to fill. As always, the harvest belonged to Overlord Pritikis, but a small percentage of the outcome went to the farmer. The five fields were Telwinar's to work as he saw fit and reap the benefits, but Billithane's seed and effort had gone into this year's crop. It made sense for Nightfall to offer a generous portion of the proceeds or, at least, to pay Billithane for his time. "We didn't expect you to . . . I mean . . . we thought . . ."

Nightfall understood Billithane's discomfort. Nightfall was under no obligation. He had not asked for assistance, and the other farmers could simply have left his fields fallow. ". . . thought I was dead," Nightfall finished. "Of course. Thank you; and you may, of course, harvest and keep what you've planted."

It was a more than generous offer.

"Th–thank you," Billithane stammered. "But don't you need—"

Nightfall waved him off. "I don't need nothing. I'm finished with farming. Keep the field rights and whatever's on 'em. My plow, my tools . . . whatever's left of 'em."

All conversation ceased.

Finally, Paisyn stated the obvious. "You gettin' out of farmin', Tel?"

Nightfall swung his head to the young farmer. "Wouldn't you all, if you could?"

Laughter followed the pronouncement, just as two of the ladies came in with pots of juice and bowls for drinking.

"You musta come into some money," grunted Shan, a grizzled man with a permanent slouch.

Ragged Estok added, "My pa came into some money once."

Shan accepted a bowl from Paisyn's wife. "*Your* pa?" he said incredulously. Estok had inherited the rights to some of the pastiest farmland around. He usually planted late, as the snowmelt left the soil sodden, and flooding in the summer often killed out large patches of seed. "What'd he do with it?"

Estok sat back with his own bowl of juice and a lopsided grin on his filthy features. "He just kept on farming that muck till the money was all gone."

The laughter increased in volume and intensity. It was a running joke among the farmers that it cost them more to farm than they made doing it. It was an honest living, if not a consistently decent one. Most years, they could use a chunk of land for their own small gardens, which kept their kin fed and could be used as barter in addition to what the overlord let them keep for seed and sustenance.

The conversation continued over a veritable feast of pork, corn, vegetables, and tubers. Though they could not fit around the table, the women ate their own share in the parlor, and children trooped in at intervals to snatch what they could from parents' plates. Eventually, they all had enough and pushed away from the table, though the conversation had degenerated into chatter. Finally, Billithane pressed, "So, what's the secret, Telly? How do you make enough money to give up farming?"

"Hey, I know," Paisyn said, still a bit of a dreamer. "You're bounty huntin', ain't you? Lookin' for that Alyndari' fellow."

Nightfall rolled his eyes. *That's right. I'm stalking myself.* He gave an equally sarcastic answer to such foolish a question, "Sure, Pais. I'm chasin' killers 'round the world with this bum leg." He slapped his thigh.

That sent the men on a tangent. "You know, that

missin' king, he was right here in Delfor just prior to the plantin'."

Nightfall started to school his expression to show skepticism, when bobbing heads and cries of agreement followed the pronouncement. He recalled their stop in Delfor well, back when Edward perched at the height of his noble flights of fancy.

"Fell off'n his big white horse, plop, splash!" Shan described. "Right in the mud."

Snickers traversed the group.

"Didn't swear or nothing. Handled it real well, 'cept he made that squire fellow clean up the horse right then and there."

Nightfall remembered. Vividly.

Snorts erupted into giggles, and Paisyn added, "Stuff like that has to be why the fellow turned on him."

Shan made a dismissive gesture. "It's a wonder all servants don't turn on 'em. Makes me glad I'm just a farmer."

Nightfall dodged the conversation. It did no good to point out Edward's generosity. Telwinar would have no reason to have experienced it.

Shan clapped a hand to Nightfall's shoulder. "Don't suppose you'll be spendin' a bit of that newfound wealth on some friends, eh? Tonight at the trough, perhaps?" He used farmer slang for Delfor's only tavern.

"Sure." Nightfall agreed, finding a happy medium between reluctance and the actual joy that accompanied the suggestion. With a mass of farmers as cover, no one could believe him a lone traveler; and, if information existed anywhere in Delfor, it would be in the inn/tavern. "I'll meet you there after chores and buy the first round."

Paisyn groaned. "You had to mention chores." He rose, and the others followed, their grins wilting as their minds went back to the many things they had to do before calling it a night.

"Don't suppose you'd want to lend a hand," Billithane said to Nightfall as the others headed back out to their fields and livestock.

Nightfall considered. He had no wish to throw himself into backbreaking labor for no reward, especially while hiding a serious injury and maintaining the image of others. "Maybe a bit, donner. My old wounds have stiffened, and I'm out of practice."

"Women's chores only," Billithane promised. "I'd just like to hear about what's going on in the world."

Reluctantly, Nightfall agreed.

To Nightfall's surprise, he found the chores more refreshing than burdensome. He enjoyed having a companion with whom to chatter as he worked, though he had to invent most of his share of the conversation. Billithane appreciated every small thing contributed, never chiding or teasing the physical limitations Nightfall was forced to place upon himself. Afterward, they had a fresh, hot meal, over which Nightfall was made to repeat much of the news, both real and created, for Billithane's wife and children.

By the time Nightfall and Billithane reached the coarse wooden construct that served as Delfor's only inn, the sun had fully disappeared, leaving a clear night sky sprinkled with an array of stars and half a moon. Most of the farmers had already arrived, spending their own coppers on frothy mugs and bowls of ale, though a few straggled in even later than their sponsor. Billithane pulled up a sturdy wooden chair to join the others, who had saved a place for the man who had promised to buy the first round of drinks.

As the barmaid approached, Nightfall slapped one of his silvers to the cracked and beer-stained table. "Keep them coming until this runs out."

"Yes, sir." The barmaid snatched up the coin, running her fingers over the worn-smooth surface as if to memorize its feel. Surely, she had seen silvers before, though she might not have had the opportunity to personally handle one.

A cheer went up from the farmers, and the closest ones clapped Nightfall on the back. None of them would have ever had that much money to spend at one time in one place, and it would buy much more than the promised first round.

Nightfall glanced around the room, trying not to get so caught up in his role that he forgot his real mission. He knew the inn's scarred and rough-hewn beams by heart, and the old tables had weathered many a fight and accident. The pock-faced bartender smiled at the bounty the serving girl carried to him, then jerked his chin to acknowledge the table full of farmers. The common room contained the usual assortment of city folk but no travelers. Nightfall suspected the Alyndarian guardsmen had come and gone, sprinkling enough money about to spark the interest of bounty hunters and assassins.

Nightfall did as much listening as he could, trading the tales of the rumormongers and gossips for ones of his own. But stories about wandering husbands, petty vengeances, and babies did not satisfy the need he had for information. As the night wore on, and his silver ran out, the farmers excused themselves to prepare for an early awakening and another round of drudgery and chores. Several offered Nightfall a place to spend the night, but he declined all of them. The real purveyors of information would come out in the wee morning hours, and he wanted to catch them at their most talkative. He did not expect much: a lucky clue that might steer him in the right direction or enhance the information he already had, or would get, from a larger city with a stronger maze of thieves and spies. Mostly, he wanted to test the strength and validity of his various personae, to push boundaries he had never dared to in the past.

Nightfall was nursing his second and final mug when the last of the farmers headed home for the night. The others had downed as many drinks as they could for the money he had expended, but Nightfall felt comfortably full from his meal with Billithane and knew better than to addle his wits before confronting the more dangerous denizens of any town. Delfor's delinquents seemed like kittens compared to the dark and dirty killers haunting the larger cities, especially Nemix and Trillium. Nevertheless, Nightfall intended to face them with his intellect wholly intact.

Once alone, Nightfall moved to a rickety stall in the corner, leaving the enormous table for any group that might arrive in the night. Balancing the need for some change against the suspicion flashing wealth might raise, he broke a second silver on a night's lodging and another mug. The alcohol stole the sharpest edges of his thinking but also dulled the growing agony in his chest and shoulder. He was paying for the work he had done for Billithane in several ways. Exhaustion further blunted his wits, his muscles ached, and his wound throbbed an irritating and steadily increasing rhythm of pain.

Nightfall knew every man who entered the common room, deftly sorting out the ones he had made acquaintances of in Telwinar guise from those he should pretend were strangers. He dismissed the ignorant thugs, the wanna-be snitches, and the ones focused solely on thieving. That left him with one target, a pudgy, balding, middle-aged punk who had moved from Nemix to Delfor to become a bigger fish in a smaller farm pond. Named Hyrik in Nemix, he now called himself Veil in the apparent hope of sounding mysterious. He ran a junk shop by the river, claiming to buy, sell, and trade anything. Mostly, it served as a fence for thieves, a fact well-known by the overlord's men who made regular raids, which kept Veil from realizing any significant profit. Always a bit hungry for money, he spilled secrets for the right price.

Veil took a seat at the bar, and Nightfall watched for

several moments to see if the Nemixite had business there. Interrupting matters of perceived importance would work against Nightfall. In other guise, he would have bought the man a drink to loosen his tongue and win his favor. He knew how to engage a man's attention with a glance unnoticed by the other patrons. Several other possibilities crossed his mind, but none of them fit the shambling personality of the Delforian farmer. He had no choice but to stumble through the encounter, in character, and hope for the best.

Scooping up his mug, Nightfall limped to the bar in time to hear the aspiring fence order a meager dinner of whatever his day's profits might buy him.

"Good eve," Nightfall greeted.

Veil scarcely bothered to roll an eye in his direction. He grunted a "hello" that barely passed for a greeting. Clearly, he had no interest in making small talk with a poor and grubby farmer.

Under the circumstances, Nightfall thought it best to go right to the point. He might not get another chance. "I was wondering if you might not know something about the king what got snatched in Schiz."

"I might."

It was a clear plea for money, which Nightfall ignored. Telwinar would not have the experience to recognize it. "Whatcha know?"

"Depends."

Nightfall blinked, feigning confusion. "On what?"

"On how much it's worth to you."

"Oh." Nightfall paused, then repeated more thoughtfully, "Oh!" He twirled coppers around his purse with a finger. "I got . . ." He decided something grander might open Veil's mouth wider. ". . . this." He flicked the last silver still in Kelryn's purse to the counter.

Now, he had Veil's full attention. The man clamped a meaty, short-fingered hand over the coin and turned his gaze fully upon Nightfall.

Nightfall read a mixture of emotion in those eyes: desire and greed mingled with a bit of fear. That last surprised him, though he had grown accustomed enough to recognize it. Telwinar should not frighten anyone.

"The king of Alyndar is dead . . ."

Nightfall felt as if an icy hand clamped onto his heart.

" . . . murdered by his chancellor who is now on the run from her army."

Terror drained away, replaced by irritation. Veil had just repeated the official party line. Nightfall clamped his lips in displeasure. "That's what I get for my money? Unfounded rumor?"

"It's truth," Veil insisted. "I swear it. This man, Sudian he's called, killed the king of Alyndar to take his place on the throne."

Nightfall had no trouble reading through the lie, though he also realized Veil had told him all he knew about the matter. The fear he had read in the man's eyes came of the realization that he did not have the answers he had been well paid to give. He had worried not about what Telwinar might do to him, but about losing the silver. Veil was hiding nothing; he simply did not know the facts.

Nightfall wanted to take back his silver, to seize the man by the throat and shake him nearly to death for extracting the coin under false pretenses. Perhaps that might loosen his tongue or, barring that possibility, at least gain Nightfall the name of someone who might actually know something about the matter. He was tired of pussyfooting around people who ought to be groveling at his feet, begging for their lives rather than providing snide looks and answers, wasting his time, taking his money for nothing. *If Nightfall were here . . .* But Nightfall wasn't there, couldn't be because of his own vow, his own damnable honor. He discarded a line of thought that gained him nothing. "Thanks," he finally said, forcing some of the edge from his voice. Sarcasm did not fit the persona. "Thanks for . . ." *Absolute crap.* ". . . telling me what you could."

With that, Nightfall left the common room and shambled out into the night. He had one more thing to accomplish before leaving the town of Delfor, and he had every intention of making certain it worked out right.

This time.

† Chapter 12 †

*The simple absence of pain is the ultimate blessing;
too bad only the affected appreciate it.*

—Dyfrin of Keevain, the demon's friend

NIGHTFALL APPROACHED the enormous, centrally located building housing the healer of Delfor before the first pink rays of dawn touched the sky. The half-moon's light sparkled from chips of quartz in the tiled roof and highlighted every crack and knothole in the Delforian oak that formed its walls. He had taken the time to change his appearance, though becoming a lone stranger placed him at substantial risk. As Telwinar, he could never talk his way past the guards, and he knew he could not slip into the heavily guarded building in any guise given the state of his left shoulder.

Nightfall resisted the urge to hide beneath a cloak hood or a collar drawn up to hide the shape of his chin. The less furtive he appeared, the more likely the guards would trust his story and see nothing beyond what he presented to them. He kept his hair a standard brown, hiding only the red highlights. He washed away the scars and reworked the shape of face and ears, the way he held himself, scraped off any hint of facial hair. Genevra was no more than twenty-one years old, and he had to appear close in age for his deception to work. He matched his skin to the olive tone of hers.

When Nightfall had come to Delfor with then-Prince Edward, the sickest and lamest beggars mobbed the streets, hoping to ply some rich and sympathetic soul to pay for their healing. They could not have found easier prey than Edward, who blithely tossed away their silvers in a naive attempt to help the downtrodden. His generosity had incited a riot of the destitute, who had torn apart Edward's belongings, each in a desperate attempt to get his share of the bounty. Now, Nightfall noted, the beggars kept their distance from the healer's quarters. Either the overlord kept them away to prevent a repeat of what had happened to the prince of Alyndar and his squire, or the beggars had finally come to realize Genevra's talent only worked on wounds that had not yet scarred.

Nightfall kept his arm flexed, though it ached so badly it interfered with his concentration. He longed to let it dangle limply at his side, but he dared not reveal the injury. The Alyndarian guards had surely mentioned it when they spread his description and offered rewards for his capture throughout the world. Four of the overlord's men stood at the building's only entrance, wearing dark blue tunics and breeks beneath tabards of lavender and silver, which identified Delfor as a holding under the high king in Alyndar. On his last visit, they had fawned all over Edward and his squire. This time, they scarcely moved as he approached.

Nightfall cleared his throat. He tried for an aura of confident politeness that might keep him on their good side and also let them know he did not plan to accept a simple "no" as an answer. He adopted Genevra's Noshtillian accent. "Pardon me, sirs. I need to speak with Genevra."

The guards exchanged glances, then looked him over in an inappropriately long silence.

Nightfall stood his ground. He had rearranged and augmented his clothing so it displayed neither holes nor an inordinate amount of dirt. The guards would have difficulty placing his status and would, hopefully, deal with him cautiously.

Finally, one spoke, "I'm sorry, sir. The healer is sleeping. Do you have an appointment?" Dark eyes examined him more intently.

Nightfall steeled himself. If he withered under the glare, he risked raising suspicions. "I don't need an appointment."

"No appointment from Overlord Pritikis . . ." a second man said gruffly, ". . . no healing."

Nightfall knew it had far more to do with money than time. Genevra had healed him on his previous visit in apology for the mauling Delfor's beggars had given his master. Even then, he and Edward had not carried enough silver to buy the healer's services from Pritikis. He tried to sound outraged. "Do I look like I need healing?"

"No, sir," the first speaker admitted. "But it doesn't change the fact that—"

Nightfall did not allow him to finish. "Tell my sister I'm here. I'm sure she'll see me."

"Sister?" The gruffer guard's tone lost its fire. "Genevra never said anything about having a brother." He studied Nightfall again, clearly seeking a resemblance.

Having gained the upper hand, Nightfall continued, "Tell her her *lavvey* brother has come to see her." He referred to the language of the Xaxonese streets, a rapid clipped dialect peppered with slang, which they had used to communicate in private the last time they met. Even people who spoke fluent Xaxonese could rarely follow a conversation in *lavvey*.

The first guard crinkled his features until his face looked like an old, leather mask. "*Lavvey* brother?"

"Tell her," Nightfall continued without explaining, "that I have the information she wanted about our . . . sister." Concerned he might not have given Genevra enough hints to his identity, he added the name, "Kelryn." It was a dangerous move, depending on whether or not the Alyndarian guards had mentioned her. They would have no reason to do so, since she had not left Alyndar with him; but he was worried about giving the overlord's men too many clues. He walked a fine and perilous line.

"Genevra has a *sister,* too?" The second man seemed even more surprised at this news.

"Her *lavvey* brother with news about her sister," the first guard repeated.

"Yes," Nightfall confirmed. "Named Kelryn."

"Your name is Kelryn?" The second guard rolled his eyes to the last two guards, still at attention, one of whom loosed a snicker.

"No, no." Nightfall waved off the second man as too dull for his time, then focused on the first. "Kelryn's our sister. My name is . . ." He tried not to delay too long, choosing a phrase in *lavvey* that should catch Genevra's attention. ". . . Hunnidun." She would recognize it as a shortened form of "The Hunted One," following the conventions of *lavvey*. He felt certain she would see him inside if she knew him as Sudian, but proper names sounded the same in any language. He hoped she would prove quick enough to decipher his code, or caution would foil his plans. Genevra had every reason to fear strangers, any of whom could turn out to be a sorcerer in disguise.

"But she's asleep," the first guard reminded.

"She'll want to be awakened for this."

"If not?"

Nightfall let his brows rise in increments. *If not, you stupid bastard, she can go back to sleep.* He swallowed his irritation. Genevra needed and deserved protection, but simply waking her to ask if she wished to visit with him did not put her at any risk. He did not leave room for doubt. "She *will* want to see me."

The first guard looked at the second, who shrugged

and nodded. He opened the door while the other three kept their gazes locked on Nightfall, as if daring him to attempt to follow.

Nightfall remained in place, prepared to run away, if necessary. His injury would slow him down and ban him from most of his ruses, especially those involving climbing; but he still believed he could shake a group of guards. Genevra had seemed intelligent but somewhat guileless when it came to politics and intrigue. As obvious as they seemed to him, she might not put the clues together. If she did, it could place him in even more danger, depending on what the Alyndarian guards might have told her or her entourage.

The door slammed shut. The moments dragged past in an awkward hush broken only by the occasional clinking movement of one of the guards. Nightfall and the overlord's men avoided one another's gazes as they waited, their future interactions, as yet, uncertain. No one knew whether to smile or glare, to stare in curt warning or shrug in indecision.

At length, the guard returned. His tone sounded even, with a hint of bewilderment. "She says she'll see you, Hunnidun."

Nightfall stopped himself from loosing a pent-up breath and headed matter-of-factly toward the door, trying to look as if he had known the outcome from the start. A sigh of relief or a gloating grin would ruin that image. Instead, he held his neutral look as he trailed the guard into a familiar antechamber, keeping his breathing regular and his muscles limber. The second man followed him, closing the heavy door behind them. Nightfall heard a bolt snap into place.

It took a surge of will not to stiffen at that sound, not to turn and ascertain he had just become locked into a small space with two guards much larger than himself. He knew the drill but feigned ignorance.

"All weapons must be left here," the first guard said.

Nightfall nodded. "A good precaution, but I'm unarmed." It was a lie he hoped they would not uncover. He had only the three daggers, those well hidden beneath layers of clothing that a cursory search would not uncover.

As before, the guard patted him down, missing the slim, flat blades. The guard gestured toward the only other exit from the room.

The second guard drew out a key, which he used in the lock, then pulled the panel open to reveal a huge room filled with pillows. A single lit lantern dangled from one of the torch brackets lining the outskirts of the room. A hearth took up most of one wall, filled with ashes and half-charred logs. Across from it, a shelf held an assortment of knickknacks and other feminine bric-a-brac. Genevra sat near the niche in the wall that held her clothing, her waist-length, blonde hair faded and sleep-tangled, her lids droopy over her usually intense green eyes.

Knowing she would not recognize him by appearance and afraid she might cry out something dangerous, Nightfall stepped forward and spoke in hasty *lavvey,* "I'm in disguise."

Genevra blinked, long lashes gliding up and down. She rose, the lightweight fabric of her sleeping gown falling around a slender figure built for dancing. Unlike him, she used the tongue of the Yortenese Peninsula, apparently for the guards. "Hunnidun! How wonderful to see you again!" She sprang toward him, wrapping her arms around him. She felt insubstantial against him, as easily broken as a child's toy. Mouth pressed against his ear, she whispered, "Sudian?"

Nightfall embraced her, though it caused him intense pain. "I've missed you, Sister." He added under his breath, "It's me." Surreptitiously, he rubbed away clay from his left hand to reveal the scars left from her healing. It would convince her better than anything he might say. A craftsman always remembered his personal handiwork. He whispered in *lavvey,* "Would you like to see my thigh, too?" Only five people knew she had also handled a second wound: Nightfall and the four guards who had overseen the process.

Clearly convinced, Genevra pulled free and looked past him. "Please, leave me alone with my brother."

"But, Lady," the second guard protested.

"I'm in no danger from my own beloved brother!" Genevra snapped. "Am I not allowed a moment of privacy now and then?"

"Yes, my lady." The first guard grabbed the gruffer man's sleeve. Both exited with a bow and a glance at Genevra's face, as if to make certain she did not need them.

Genevra made a dismissive gesture, and the men exited, pulling the door shut behind them. Nightfall noticed in the silence that followed, the absence of a lock clicking. The guards could, and surely would, return at the slightest hint of trouble.

Though the guards had gone, Genevra used *lavvey,* "Won't my mother be surprised to learn she has a son?"

Nightfall forced a tired smile. "I'm sorry about the lie. I couldn't think of any other way to see you."

"What's wrong with the truth, Sudian?"

Nightfall cringed at the name, worried her use of *lavvey* meant the guards could overhear. "Supposedly, I murdered King Edward for the throne."

Genevra jerked away. Suddenly, all sleepiness left her. "Did you?"

"What do you think?"

Genevra shook her head and opened her mouth. When no words emerged, she shook her head again, more vigorously. "I think a squire as wildly loyal as you would never crease a hair on his golden head." She studied him briefly. "And I don't think you have the size or strength to manage it, even if you wished him harm. Although . . ."

Nightfall let her finish.

" . . . I wouldn't have believed you could come up with a disguise this . . . this . . ."

"... impenetrable?" Nightfall suggested.

"Yes. How did ... ? Where did you learn ... ?"

"Desperation makes for fast students." Nightfall tried to look sincere and a bit pitiable. He needed Genevra's help, and he had to have her on his side. He had gone with the truth, a tactic that had served him well in recent weeks. He only hoped it would not fail him now.

Genevra waited for an explanation, a direct answer.

"I would never hurt my master. Not ever. And you have to believe me; I didn't even know it was possible for a lowborn servant like me to be in line for the throne." Nightfall did not have to feign the anxious pain that entered his voice as he spoke, and Genevra clearly knew it.

"I believe you." Genevra sat cross-legged on one of the many pillows and gestured for him to do the same.

"I'm hoping he's still alive. That I can find him and bring him home." Nightfall crumpled more than sat. The agony of his wound, the rage and distress in his heart, a sleepless night combined into a numbing and all-consuming pain. "I didn't do anything wrong." The words sounded ridiculous from his mouth; but, this time, it was truth.

"You're hurting," Genevra said.

Nightfall closed his eyes and nodded. Speaking his situation aloud dragged hopelessness to the fore. For the first time since his mission had started, he wanted to surrender: to the pain, to the grief, to despair.

"Now let me see that thigh wound."

Nightfall's eyes flicked opened, and his head rose. He thought he had convinced her of his true identity hidden beneath the dyes, paints, and dirt. Without a word, he peeled away layers of clothing that added bulk to his otherwise scrawny frame to expose his legs.

Genevra scooted closer, using a rag to wipe through the olive coating to the paler flesh beneath it. Though faint and fading, enough remained of the scar to convince her, he believed. She leaned over him, smelling faintly of some clove-based perfume or soap. Her long hair tickled his face. She placed her hands directly on his thigh and caressed the skin lightly, fingers moving sensuously over the skin far beyond the treated area.

Blood warmed Nightfall's cheeks and privates. He felt himself responding to her fondling against his will.

Genevra raised her face to his, close enough to kiss. "You want me," she announced in a whisper.

Distinctly uncomfortable, Nightfall caught her hand before she could touch any place definitively improper. "Of course, I want you. What man wouldn't want a young, beautiful, talented, and clever woman?"

Genevra smiled at the compliments.

"But I can't, Genevra. I'm betrothed."

The smile wilted. "You're betrothed?"

Nightfall nodded, hoping he had not just destroyed all reason for her to help him. He had rarely used attraction as a tool before. Though women had sought him out for the notoriety sleeping with the demon might bring them, he had never worried about betraying or disappointing them. Few of his personae had much to offer when it came to appearances. Most had scars or pocks, some carried crippling reminders of previous accidents or illnesses; and he was not the strapping do-it-all most women sought for spouses. He rarely spent enough time as any one person to cultivate a healthy relationship. Only as the sailor, Marak, had he managed such a thing, the identity under which he had associated with Kelryn and Dyfrin. "I'm betrothed. To a wonderful woman I don't deserve."

Genevra withdrew with a joke clearly intended to disperse embarrassment and disappointment. "So . . . she's marrying . . . beneath her."

Nightfall tried to help with some humor of his own. "Some would say all women do."

Genevra rewarded him with a chiming laugh. "Not this time. She's very lucky."

Lucky was not a word Nightfall would ascribe to anyone who cared for him. "Thank you, but you must know how silly that sounds. My beloved master is missing, and I'm being hunted for his murder under threat of execution. I'm not known for my looks or strength. I'd scarcely call getting tangled in that 'lucky.' "

Genevra retook her position on the cushion while Nightfall casually restored his clothing. "And yet, I am. But I don't get any of the good parts of the sweet, caring, mysterious man. Those are for—" A light dawned in her eyes. "It's Kelryn, isn't it?"

Astounded by her insight, Nightfall could only swallow hard and nod.

"I should have known right away. It only makes sense I'd send a man running right to the woman who could steal him from me." Genevra smiled, though it looked forced. "She's wonderful, isn't she?"

Nightfall gave the only reply he could. Though not what Genevra wanted, it was the single one she would believe. "Yes. She is."

"And she deserves some joy."

Nightfall agreed. "More than I can give her." His words sank deep, more significant to him than to Genevra. Recalling the reason the healer had sent him after Kelryn, he added, "She's alive, obviously. Scarred by her encounter, but not damaged." Like Genevra, Kelryn had been present when Alyndar's sorcerer/chancellor had slaughtered Dyfrin for his talent. Genevra had escaped first and had been concerned about Kelryn. When she had sent Nightfall after the dancer, she had not known he already hunted her for his own reasons.

Genevra apparently read something beyond his words. "You're injured, too. Aren't you?"

Nightfall could not put the healer's words into the context of what he had just said.

Apparently noting his hesitation, Genevra continued, "I mean you're hurt physically as well as emotionally."

Nightfall nodded, hiding his interest. It was, after all, the real reason he had come.

"Would you like me to take a look?"

"Please." Nightfall unlaced garments, unwrapping some and hauling others over his head. Every movement sent fire tearing through his chest and arm.

Genevra watched him disrobe with a tight smile of amusement. "Preparing for a blizzard?"

"It's part of the disguise." Nightfall would have found it difficult to play a character skinnier than himself, so he automatically went to padding. His natal gift obviated the need for strength or bulk.

"Left shoulder," Genevra figured out before he peeled away the last layer.

Though Nightfall continued to move in such a way as to hide the injury, he could not fool a woman self-trained to notice any sign of physical weakness since birth. Soon enough, he proved her right, revealing the shredded skin the crossbow bolt had left in its wake.

All trace of amusement left Genevra's demeanor. She sucked in a tight breath. "You've been shot."

Nightfall said nothing, not needing to confirm the expert's diagnosis.

Genevra moved in to practically sit in his lap, though this time there was nothing sexual about her demeanor. "You were very very lucky."

Nightfall knew exactly what she meant, how close the bolt had come to his heart. "Most people would call getting shot very very *un*lucky."

Caught up in the seriousness of her task, Genevra initially missed the humor. "You have a lot of vital organs in that area. It could have hit a lung, a big blood vessel, the heart itself." She sat back on her heels, smiling suddenly. "I can fix this."

Nightfall knew her gift had limitations, but he had never doubted her ability to handle the wound. "Good. Will you?"

"Of course." Genevra's muscles tightened as she visibly steeled herself. She always shared some of the pain when she healed a wound, though it lessened for healer and victim quickly.

Nightfall remained still and allowed Genevra to find the best position for her own comfort. Her small hands explored the edges of the wound tentatively. Then, the healing power came in a rush of energy that tingled through his chest. She winced, emitting a muffled gasp.

Nightfall swung his attention to the door, worried the guards might have heard even that small sound and would come bursting into the room. One glimpse of the crossbow hole would surely give him away.

Genevra planted both hands against Nightfall's injury, and the pain ebbed away, replaced by the draw of healing tissues. She managed a shaky smile. "How long have you been suffering with this?"

Nightfall could barely remember. He had bullied through the agony for so long, he noticed only the crescendos. It bothered him most when he tried to sleep, when more pressing needs and concerns could not distract him. "A week or so," he said, trying to sound matter-of-fact. It was a silly charade. She knew exactly how much it pained him.

Genevra's alarm came through, though she clearly tried to hide it. "You know," she said, not quite casually. "An infection this close to the heart would be fatal."

The words themselves did not surprise Nightfall, but the implication did. "Was it infected?"

"A bit." Though Genevra had raised the issue, she seemed to want to dodge the obvious question. "With time, it would have gotten worse." She gave him a motherly look. "Not a nice way to die."

Nightfall had never expected to die nicely. Nor did he believe he could dodge death forever. He would have thought he had used up all his luck in that department. "Can you fix the infection, too?"

"No. I can't do illnesses."

Nightfall sucked in a sharp breath.

"But once I heal the wound, it should go away. It hasn't penetrated deeply—yet." Genevra emphasized the last word. "If you had waited much longer, you would have died." She added fiercely, "A grimy arrow, probably shot in practice through moldy, manure-stained straw doesn't belong in a man's flesh."

Nightfall did not bother to correct the misconception about the kind of bow that had shot him. "Next time, I promise I'll ask the guy attacking me to launder his weapons first."

"Funny."

"Thank you." Nightfall rolled his eyes to examine the wound. Though mostly covered by Genevra's hands, it already looked much better. The skin had pulled almost completely together, and the pain had nearly disappeared. He knew she had no obligation to assist him, yet she had saved his life and his mission. He only wished he knew how to properly express his gratitude. It had not been a necessary skill in his youth, when his abusive mother and her clients had treated him as an annoyance, if they had bothered to acknowledge his existence at all. He owed much to Dyfrin who, he now realized, had rescued him from becoming nothing more than the black-hearted demon whose role and name he had abandoned. He had never properly thanked Dyfrin, had barely even acknowledged the enormous service the man had done for him so matter-of-factly day by day through the years. But then again, as a mind reader, Dyfrin already knew. "And thank you for the healing. I'm . . ." The words did not come easy to Nightfall. "I'm in your debt. Is there something I can do for you?"

Almost as quickly as he spoke, Nightfall wished he had not. If she asked him to sleep with her, he could hardly refuse under the circumstances; though doing so could strain or destroy his relationship with Kelryn. If the current state of affairs had not intervened, he would already be a married man. *When did I develop scruples?* Yet, Nightfall realized, when it came to Kelryn, he had always had them.

Genevra did not look up from her work, nor did she

seem to notice Nightfall's discomfort. "Just keep Kelryn happy. She deserves it."

"I'll try," Nightfall promised earnestly, feeling as if he had dodged another crossbow bolt.

"And . . . and maybe stop in now and again. Bring me some news of the outside world."

"I will." Nightfall pitied the trade-off Genevra had made: security for imprisonment. Yet, she had made it clear the last time she preferred it to spending her life running from sorcerers. "I can't afford the overlord's fee, but you can leave word to let your brother visit."

"My *lavvey* brother," Genevra reminded. Though she kept her head low, Nightfall could see a hint of her smile by the set of her cheeks. "Hunnidun."

"Yes." The last thing Nightfall needed was another permanent personality to add to his list. "Or your sister, Kelryn." Caught up in the idea of exchanging news, Nightfall could not help begging a favor of his own. "Genevra, do your clients . . . tell you things?" He hated the word "clients," the same term his mother had used for her lovers.

"Of course. Sitting in silence makes most people uncomfortable."

"If you just happen to find out anything about the king or his disappearance, could you get that information to . . ." Nightfall could think of only one safe delivery point. ". . . Kelryn? In Alyndar?"

Beads of perspiration formed on Genevra's brow, and she sat back, releasing Nightfall. "I'll do that."

Nightfall glanced at the place where the wound had been. Barely a shade lighter than his normal skin, the scar had edges as sharp and wild as starlight. He tested his arm, stretching it in all directions at the shoulder. For the first time since he had awakened in Alyndar's tower prison, it did not hurt. "Thank you," he said again, more from relief than gratitude. Excitement filled him; and, with it, a strange desire to clamber and scamper like a monkey to assess her handiwork. "Thank you so much."

Genevra reached out her hand and brushed the wound

with a finger, more in the manner of a family member than a healer. Leaning forward, she kissed it gently.

Again, Nightfall's nose filled with the clean, pleasant aroma of spices. Knowing what she wanted, he drew Genevra into his arms and pressed his lips to the top of her head. She leaned into him, eyes closed, clearly enjoying the contact. He felt enormous and powerful with her small body crushed up against his naked chest, overwhelmed by the need to protect her.

For a long time, they sat this way before Genevra's soft voice broke the silence. "If you didn't have Kelryn, do you think we . . . the two of us . . . could have . . . ?"

Genevra did not need to finish the question, and Nightfall knew there was only one right answer. Nevertheless, he considered. To do otherwise might belittle it, making it seem forced and trite. A lot of problems came along with Genevra, owned as she essentially was by the overlord. Her own request had doomed her to a very circumscribed life that did not allow for long walks, the wind in her face, running through the rain. Her duties and obligations did not end at any set time. Injuries could occur day or night. Pritikis could not hold her husband to her bondage, but he could make his coming and going difficult. Yet, such a marriage would have conveniences, too. At least, Genevra's husband would never have to worry about her safety or her location and so could leave for long periods of time to pursue his own ventures. "I can't think of anyone else I'd rather marry, aside from Kelryn, of course. I know of many men who would treasure a wife like you, if only they had the opportunity to meet you."

"Perhaps," Genevra whispered. "Perhaps you can send them my way?"

Nightfall ignored the double meaning buried in her request. She surely did not realize she all but begged him to assault the nicest, richest men. "I'll do my best."

Genevra rose with clear reluctance. "I guess you'd better be on your way, Sudian."

Nightfall also stood, carefully replacing every layer of clothing. "Hunnidun," he corrected, knowing the importance of training the mind when it came to keeping up a disguise. If Genevra slipped and someone made the connection between the two men, his next visit would prove his last. Though he knew her loneliness, not his winning looks or personality, made him so appealing, it still felt good to be desired. He also suspected his use of *lavvey* at their first meeting, which had turned their conversation private and personal, also helped make him special in her eyes. Few of her clients would bare their souls in front of her valiant protectors. "I really do need to keep moving. At least until I vindicate myself."

Nightfall walked to the door and opened it, immediately confronted by the two guards, who snapped to attention.

"I'm fine," Genevra called out to reassure them. "My brother and I had a lovely visit. Thank you so much."

The guards made no replies other than a few curt nods before returning Nightfall to the night. Feeling infinitely better, he savored the crisp air and disappeared as swiftly as he could without appearing practiced at it or guilty. He could hardly wait to catch a few good hours of sleep.

† Chapter 13 †

Power and knowledge live in unexpected places.

—Dyfrin of Keevain, the demon's friend

AFTER HIS VISIT to the Delforian healer, Nightfall discovered an intense clarity of mind he had not even realized he missed. He could not wholly credit the absence of pain's distraction; Genevra had told him his wound had festered. A fever he had not even realized he had had affected his mind as well. With those burdens lifted, he felt like a free man, triumphant and ready to face whatever obstacles Alyndar's guards placed in his way.

Nightfall also knew he would need all his wits about him. Moving swiftly along the coast, the journey from Delfor to Trillium took two weeks. Autumn and its encroaching cold made food more scarce, but he still managed to catch small, young lobsters, made sluggish by the dwindling temperature of the water. They huddled beneath stones near the shore where they could feast upon minnows, safe from the larger fish in deeper waters that found the tiny lobsters a particularly tasty snack. Many men, it seemed to him, led the same kind of life: hiding from larger predators in the shoals, biding their time until the quarry became large and dangerous enough to stalk the hunters.

Nightfall made the decision to avoid Trillium while he walked. The city existed on land jointly owned by three of the world's four kingdoms, though most people considered it utterly independent, lawless, and ripe for any perversion or trade. Anything legal anywhere else in the world was considered fair game in Trillium, and that opened the way for a flourishing black market as well. If any place held the information he needed, Trillium did; yet Nightfall knew he would have to penetrate the darkest, most dangerous criminal dens to find the answers he sought. Even then, he had no certainty he would receive correct information rather than innuendo, rumor, or downright misdirection. Only one persona could cut to the truth, and that persona was irretrievably dead.

It made more sense to slip past the city, where every lone traveler would evoke suspicion. Men spurred by the promise of a kingdom's reward might kill a solitary stranger first and bother with his identity later, if at all. While some of Nightfall's alter egos would not be unfamiliar to some of Trillium's regular inhabitants, the shifting population and masses of visitors, usually not of the most wholesome type, might still put him in the way of many who did not know him. It seemed better to bypass the whole mess than to try to deal with it or have to worry that his frustration and temper might drive him to actions he might regret. People who hindered the demon tended to wind up dead.

That same mind-set sent him veering widely around the hidden home of Finndmer the Fence. A master seller of even the most hunted merchandise and information, Finndmer hid his darker dealings behind the image of an innocent woodcutter. At their last meeting, the fence had sold Nightfall, as Sudian, a patch of swampland that had proved useless in landing Edward. If Finndmer did the slightest thing to further irritate him now, Nightfall did not believe he could contain himself. Given Finndmer's arrogance, greed, and tendency to mistrust and mislead strangers, exasperation seemed a certainty. Finndmer was important to some of the most dangerous men in existence; by harming him, Nightfall would find himself the object of another, equally vigorous manhunt.

So, Nightfall continued hugging the coastline, avoiding roads, any sign of travelers or brigands, and towns and villages most of all. As he passed over the border from joint land to the outskirts of the kingdom of Shisen, he veered southward toward the city of Schiz. That same day, he changed his appearance again, this time to that of Frihiat, his Schizian persona. He combed and bleached out his hair to a yellow-white sheen that hung in a straight curtain. He rearranged the layers of his clothing to enhance his size and make him appear twisted and stricken. He practiced walking with a warped and off-balancing limp to display the damage he attributed to polio.

Though slowed by an affectation he dared not drop for a moment, he gained time and ground by switching to the well traveled paths and roads leading to Schiz. As Frihiat, he had right and reason to travel when and where he wished, and it would look more suspicious for him to seem to magically appear from nowhere. Frihiat would not go unnoticed on the streets, not only because of his appearance but because he was well liked among the regular inhabitants of Schiz.

The awkward movements of Nightfall's alter ego bothered him as they never had in the past. So far, he had made excellent time, zipping across the rocky coastline on foot nearly as fast as he and Edward had managed on horseback. He waved and smiled at the people who passed him, going in either direction. He could not keep up with the walkers, let alone those with mules, horses, or wagons. Though he knew he had handled the situation as well as possible, he wished he could abandon everything about the Schizian storyteller and return to the quiet existence he had known for the last several weeks. Then, he had no one to worry about but himself and his own survival, and that came so naturally to him he scarcely needed to think.

It felt like an eternity before Nightfall reached the edge of the city, and he began to appreciate the slowness he had cursed earlier in the day. As evening grayness descended over Schiz, people tended to closing their businesses, finishing those tasks that could not wait until morning, and reuniting families separated by jobs and chores. Without appearing to intentionally do so, he easily dodged the need to explain his recent whereabouts to a curious horde, one man at a time. Instead, he made his limping way past the wood scrap sign of the He-Ain't-Here to shove open the door with his right hip and shoulder.

The hinges squealed their usual noisy protest, announcing his presence to the few patrons, travelers, and those without work or family obligations. The aroma of baked bread and spitted meat wafted to him, and his gut churned in excitement. After weeks of sea plants and raw young lobsters, more shell than meat, the idea of filling his belly with a greasy array of roasted lamb or pork and vegetables became a pleasure he could not deny. He barely noticed the background odors of stale beer, fire, and sweat, though he imagined he caught a whiff of blood that soured his ardor for food. Several of Alyndar's finest had died here.

Resisting his natural urge to find a table in a dark corner, Nightfall flopped gracelessly into an empty seat at the center table. Though less defensible in this position, he savored a security born of familiarity. Frihiat always sat here, where his stories could become the center of attention. He never checked his pockets before ordering. If he had money, he would spend every copper buying drinks for himself and anyone he considered a friend, for which he had a loose definition. If he found his pockets empty, someone else always jumped in to pay.

A serving girl headed toward Nightfall. An instant later, the proprietor caught up to her and waved her aside to serve the newcomer himself. Gil eased his bulk onto a chair directly across the square table and smiled, teeth a dull yellow against his jowly face. "Frihiat! Haven't seen you in a seaman's age. Rumor was, the scourge of your childhood finally caught up to you."

Nightfall returned the smile with one of his own, instinctively keeping it a bit crooked. "You know better than to believe rumors, Gil."

The proprietor tipped his head sideways and made a dismissive facial gesture. "Rumors are usually all I get. And you've spread enough of your own to know there's usually at least a kernel of truth to 'em."

Nightfall loosed Frihiat's free-flowing laugh, so much less guarded than his own. "Well, you know I haven't succumbed."

"Unless I have, too." Gil's laugh sounded more like a throaty roar.

Nightfall glanced around the common room. "If this is where good folk go after death, I'll take the alternative."

Gil tapped his fist against Nightfall's shoulder in a manly, friendly gesture. "What makes you think you'd go anywhere good folk go?"

Though glad for the healing that took all pain from the proprietor's vigorous gesture, Nightfall seized on the paranoid notion that Gil had just tested him. *Was he checking the place Alyndarian guards told him to look for a wound?* The question seemed ludicrous. *No one in decades ever crossed my identities. Gil's not smart enough to be the one.* "So I'm in some hellish afterlife inflicted on me by the gods?" He threw another, more exaggerated, glance around the tavern. "I should have guessed that by your presence and my surroundings. I always knew there was something noxious about your drinking hole."

"My drinking hole?" Gil tipped his head in mock insult. "Are you referring to my establishment? Or my mouth?"

Nightfall passed off the rhetorical question with another uninhibited laugh. "I've spent the last several months checking out that new healer in Delfor."

Gil rested his elbows on the table, his head in his hands, and leaned forward in clear interest. "Yeah? What did you find?"

Nightfall made a disgruntled noise through pursed lips. "Every man with a scratch or ailment had the same idea. Only, it costs ten fortunes to actually see the lady. So the streets were packed with every scrofulous, pus-reeking beggar in the four kingdoms."

Gil's eyes widened. "That explains why we've seen so few. Can't say as I miss 'em."

Nightfall's brows inched upward.

Gil studied Nightfall's silent features a moment before realizing the potential for offense in what he had just said. "Oh, fie! I don't consider you one of 'em. You're not scrofulous or pus-reeking, for one. You're a decent fellow who just happened to get sick when you were young and has a bit of a limp now, that's all."

"I also won't stoop to begging." Nightfall shook his head, not having to imagine the scene of hundreds of filthy, disease-riddled beggars groping at the fortunate. He had lived it at Edward's side. "I took up any odd job offered, though I spent some time convincing those Delforians I could handle some things."

Gil rubbed his stubbly cheeks and chin. "They don't know you like we do."

Nightfall shook his head, then rolled his eyes. "Come to realize over time the healer's powers are limited. I'm doing all this hard labor, saving up my coppers, only to find she can't cure ailments like mine."

"She can't?" Gil's interest grew more intense. He thrived on the information travelers brought to the tavern, especially tidbits he could sell or share with clients who might appreciate them enough to bump up tips.

"She can't." Nightfall shook his head with a sigh. "Should have known I'm destined to live with this curse forever." He shrugged. "Guess I did something to offend a god who holds a wicked and long-standing grudge."

Gil raised a hand to make a warding gesture. His religious beliefs were more stolid than Frihiat's. "Is it because your problems came from polio? Or because you've had them so long?"

Nightfall shrugged one shoulder, then let it fall. "From what I understand, she can only heal injuries, not afflictions or illnesses."

"Ah." Gil shifted his bulk backward in clear contemplation. "Perfect for a noble with a standing army or guard force."

Nightfall nodded gloomily. "But useless for a man like myself." Dejection was such a rare part of Frihiat's character, Nightfall abandoned it. "Ah, well. Not sure I'd know what to do with right-working legs anyway. I might start going through life too fast to really enjoy it."

Still clearly considering Nightfall's words, Gil did not speak.

"So, I hear I missed some major excitement here."

Stricken from his reverie, Gil jerked. "Huh?"

"Word on the roads is the king of Alyndar and his entire entourage vanished from this very tavern."

Gil glanced around with clear nervousness. He licked lips that seemed to have gone dry in an instant. "Not exactly vanished."

"No?" Nightfall encouraged.

"The king, himself, disappeared. But we cleaned up a heap of bodies."

"Glad I missed it," Nightfall said, using a tone pitched to encourage. "What exactly happened?"

"I . . ." Gil's eyes became inordinately busy looking anywhere but at Nightfall. ". . . I . . . can't say."

Nightfall displayed his best twisted look of incredulity. "You were here, weren't you?"

"Well, yes, but . . ."

Nightfall waited; but Gil did not complete the thought, so Nightfall prompted. "But . . . ?"

Gil shook his head, barely disturbing his sweat-plastered hair. "I can't talk about it. I'm sorry."

Nightfall stared, hoping to convey his thoughts in a look. *Frihiat just bared his soul and handed that jerk the most useful piece of news he got in months, and all I get back is silence.*

Apparently getting the point, Gil drew into himself on the chair. It made him look rounder, rather than smaller. "Look, Fri. I'd tell you, but . . ."

Nightfall could not afford to let Gil off the hook. "But what?"

Gil lowered his voice to a whisper. "They'll kill me."

Nightfall also whispered. "Who?"

"They," Gil hissed. "the ones who did it."

Nightfall leaned in so they could hear one another. "How will they know?"

"They have eyes and ears everywhere."

Though tiring of the game, Nightfall continued to whisper. "Even on their bellies? Their backs? Their butts? That must make them look . . . very silly."

Gil's mouth twisted. For a moment, it looked as if he would laugh, then he shook his head instead. "This is no joke, Frihiat."

"I agree," Nightfall said. "But I hardly think the Bloodshadow Brotherhood is going to dismember you for telling what you saw to an old cripple."

Gil turned greenish. "How . . . how did you . . . know about . . . ?"

Not wanting to wait until the tavern became too busy for Gil to spare the time, Nightfall interrupted. "The Bloodshadow Brotherhood?"

"Shhhh!" Gil cautioned, looking around nervously again.

Nightfall made a stern noise. "Gil, would you stop acting like a cat dangled over a fire pit? I assumed. Who else could get you to clam up so tightly over something so interesting?"

"Then you know why I can't say anything."

"To the guards, maybe." Nightfall could not afford to let the matter drop. "But I could have been here that night, should have been. Who could I tell that would matter?"

Gil rubbed his hands over his sleeves in edgy bursts.

"Gil, you owe me. And I don't mean a few glasses of that watered urine you call ale."

Clearly anxious, Gil let the insult to his product slide. "You can't tell anyone, Fri. Not anyone."

"Have I ever betrayed you?" Nightfall could ask in good conscience. Frihiat had never duped anyone, at least not in that particular guise.

"No," Gil admitted.

"Then spill."

Gil's gaze went toward the quarters at the back, but he made no suggestions that they move. Nightfall knew he had chosen the most defensible spot when it came to people overhearing. Windows would pose the greatest hazard here, and those existed only in the back rooms. Though he had chosen the centermost table to maintain character, it turned out to have other advantages as well.

"No one can hear us," Nightfall reassured, certain of his words. "If you didn't look so guilty and anxious, no one would even know we're not discussing the coming weather."

Gil bit his lower lip. He could not afford to believe in evil spirits, given the information that regularly passed through taverns; yet he clearly worried those arisen from the blood of a demon could listen through solid walls, ceilings, and floors. Perhaps he believed they hovered around him, invisible to the human eye. Nevertheless, he recounted his story. "They slipped in like the

wind. Some were already inside, looking like regular
travelers. Others slithered through the windows in the
back, their hands and weapons already stained crimson
with the blood of the sleeping Alyndarian guardsmen.
They knew the strongest warriors, who to kill first, and
they took those men out before the others realized their
danger. Some fought, including the king himself—a surprisingly masterful swordsman, by the way. But even he
was no match for the . . ." He dropped his voice so low,
Nightfall could not hear, but understanding and lip
movement filled in the word: Brotherhood. "They
worked like a single seamless being, the reincarnation
of the demon Nightfall himself. They overwhelmed the
guards with their numbers, butchered everyone, and
took the injured king away."

Injured. Nightfall had to fight to keep from saying the
word aloud. He knew better than to distract Gil now
that the proprietor had lapsed into story mode.

"They disappeared into the night, and no one has
seen them since."

As Gil had clearly finished, Nightfall needed to ask.
"The Brotherhood took no casualties?" He could
scarcely believe such a thing possible, given the competence of King Edward's entourage.

"They took their dead and wounded with them.
Four, at least, from what I saw. And," he shivered
grimly, "we found another outside the sleeping room
window, his throat slit, disemboweled. Clearly done in
by one of his own."

Great way to inspire loyalty. Nightfall believed he
knew the young man, the one who had not managed to
steal the ring Nightfall still carried on his person.
"Where did they go?"

"What?"

"Where did they take the king?"

Gil looked at Nightfall as if he had gone daft. "Wherever demons go. They disappeared as swiftly as they
came, melting into the shadows like the demonspawn

they are. No one knows that." His eyes narrowed. "Why would you want to know a thing like that?"

Trapped by his own need, Nightfall downplayed it. He held out his hands. "I don't know. It just seemed like the next logical question."

Gil made a noise deep in his throat.

Nightfall played victim. "Now listen, Gil. Don't be aiming that paranoia of yours at me."

Gil managed a tense smile. "You're right, Fri, of course. It's just horrible to have seen such a thing and ... well, just to have seen it. To know what they're capable of."

Nightfall knew at least part of Gil's discomfort came from witnessing the most exciting event in all of Shisen, yet having no way to speak of it. He had relished the chance to tell the tale. In that respect, Frihiat had done him another favor, one he could never admit.

"Wherever they took him, the king is dead."

Nightfall's heart skipped a beat. He tried to sound curious rather than desperately alarmed. "How do you know?"

"That feisty little squire of his was behind the whole plan. With the king dead, leaving no heir, the throne is his." Gil shook his head. "Seems they need to reconsider that line of succession, or at least be more careful who they put in positions of power."

"Yeah." Nightfall concealed a relieved sigh, glad Gil's knowledge of Edward's supposed death came from false information he already knew. "Isn't that how they lost the last king, too?"

"And the real crown prince. King Edward's brother." Gil ran a hand across his face. "Real upheaval there, I'd warrant. Glad I'm not Alyndarian."

"I'd heard about the squire being involved. Not safe traveling alone, any more."

"That's what the customers say, too." The door hinges shrilled their angry chorus, and Gil looked over to watch a couple of regulars, off duty guardsmen, come in and take a table in the corner. "And the sailors say not many ships are heading for Alyndar these days. First off, the chaos makes for fewer goods. Second, the guards have taken to searching every ship to make sure the squire's not snuck aboard. Those with even a bit of illicit cargo don't want to take the chance, and others just don't like the delay."

Nightfall stared absently at the newcomers, essentially strangers, though he had seen them in the tavern when he took the guise of Frihiat in the past. He had learned what he could from Gil, and it seemed woefully inadequate. The details of the battle, even the confirmation of the Bloodshadow Brotherhood's role, added few pieces to a puzzle that seemed unsolvable.

Now on safe territory, Gil continued. "I feel bad for the boy."

Nightfall's brows dropped, and he wondered if he had missed something. "What boy?"

Gil waved away his own topic. "Oh, there's this cabin boy. He was aboard the ship that took the king's effects back to Alyndar. They also delivered the squire, not knowing he had a hand in the murders. Anyways . . ." Gil studied his companion to ascertain he still had an audience.

Nightfall tried to look interested, without revealing that his attention had been captured completely. *Danyal.*

" . . . the boy comes in every day asking if I know of any ships heading to Alyndar. It's clearly important to him he gets there, but he won't say why. I've heard him defend the murdering squire, too, though it's gotten him slapped once or twice't. Nice kid, but doesn't know when to hold his tongue."

Nightfall knew of only one reason why Danyal would want to go to Alyndar. *He knows something, and he's trying to keep his promise to get the information to me.* Alyndar seemed a silly place to look for a hunted chancellor, but Nightfall remembered he had explicitly told the boy to deliver any information there. Excitement swept the edge of his mind, but he banished it. Likely, the boy had found a tidbit Nightfall already knew, but he had to make certain. Also, it would not do to let the cabin boy go all the way to Alyndar only to get caught in the morass of bureaucracy that defined a kingdom. His apparent link to Nightfall might get him imprisoned or, at least, closely questioned, a terrifying experience for a young boy who might inadvertently reveal some snippet of information that could hurt them both. Nightfall sighed at the realization. Befriending people held serious disadvantages.

Gil eased his bulk from the chair. "I've got to get back to work. We'll finish catching up later?"

Nightfall watched a serving girl converse with the guardsmen. "Sounds good." He took an exaggerated whiff of bread-and-meat-scented air. "Smells good, too."

Gil grinned. "I'll bring you a platter. And a bowl of mead, I presume?"

"The good stuff." Nightfall jangled the remaining silvers and coppers in his purse. "I need to spend the money I earned for the healing I never got."

"Yes, *sir*!" Gil headed back to the bar with a bounce in his step.

Nightfall knew the proprietor liked it when Frihiat came into the bar with money, as it all tended to wind up in Gil's pocket. This time, however, Nightfall intended to leave before the night's rush. He needed most of the remaining silver for travel. Though, as a skilled pickpocket, he could always get more, he would have to choose another guise under which to steal and risk the possibility of capture. Leaning back in his chair, his "bad" leg outstretched, Nightfall awaited his dinner.

Crouched on a stone ledge that jutted into a pitch-dark alleyway, Nightfall watched the door to the He-Ain't-Here. Though he kept his eyes trained on the entrance, his other senses alerted him to every nearby movement. An occasional stray dog or rat nosed through the leavings, seeking whatever scraps had not gone home with the workers. Only once a human form glided across the alleyway. He seemed not to notice Nightfall lurking in the shadows, though he did leave quickly. Nightfall knew the game too well: feign ignorance, never look directly at a skulking predator, but always know his exact location.

Nightfall had seen Danyal go into the tavern, accompanied by a trio of rowdy sailors. That had not seemed like a good time to accost the boy in any guise. Now, he waited patiently, searching for the opportunity to catch the cabin boy alone. It seemed more likely than not that his patience would be rewarded, given the smaller capacity of a child's bladder and the tendency for adults to ply a young man with drinks for the entertainment value it might supply.

The moon rose higher, and the sky became sprinkled with stars. Nightfall began concocting an alternate plan, one that might allow him to slip onto *The Sharius*, where Danyal undoubtedly spent most of his time. The boy would not have the money for other shelter and was already accustomed to the rock and pitch of the ship at mooring. Then, just as Nightfall began considering costumes, Danyal slipped from the tavern and trotted toward the neighboring alley that served as the preferred relieving place of the He-Ain't-Here's patrons.

Quiet as the darkness, Nightfall slipped from his hiding place and into the other alley. He crept toward the boy as Danyal splashed the narrow, packed dirt threadway. Sneaking ever closer, he watched as Danyal finished his business and readjusted his clothing with an awkwardness that displayed the alcoholic content of at least one drink. An unexpected noise, even as soft and gentle as a whisper, might startle Danyal into a scream, so Nightfall pounced like a predator. One arm whipped around Danyal's head, a hand clamped over his mouth to muffle any sound. With the other, he caught the boy around the middle and dragged him deeper into the alley.

Danyal struggled wildly, trying to twist. Shouts gagged to silence emerged warm against Nightfall's hand, and he could feel the boy's mouth open and close as he searched for flesh to bite.

"Be still," Nightfall said directly into the cabin boy's ear. "It's me, Danyal. Sudian. And I'm not going to hurt you."

Danyal froze in position, his body dead weight in Nightfall's arms.

"I'm sorry I had to grab you, but it's not safe for anyone else to see me. Do you understand?"

Danyal nodded his head as well as he could.

"Please don't scream." Nightfall resisted the urge to ask the boy if he would comply. Whether or not he intended to do so, the answer would be "yes." Prepared to run, Nightfall released Danyal.

The boy whirled toward him but made no sound or threatening movement. He examined Nightfall through the darkness.

Nightfall allowed him to look. Now costumed as a stranger and standing in near blackness, he did not expect to be recognized.

"Sudian," Danyal tried. "Is that really . . . you?"

Nightfall hissed. "Don't call me that, all right? It's dangerous."

Danyal bobbed his head, lowering his voice. "They think you killed the king."

"I know, the fools."

"Why?" Though a simple question, it did not have an easy answer.

"Because, Danyal, it's the laziest way to handle a problem so complex and dangerous most can't or won't consider the real depth of it. If they blame me, they don't have to look for a more difficult adversary. And, if they believe he's dead, they don't have to search for him either." Though not precise, the explanation would have to do.

Danyal continued to stare into the night. "Is it really . . . you?" He finally remembered his manners. "My lord?"

"It's really me." Nightfall understood the cabin boy's uncertainty and applauded these first early stirrings of discernment. He sought to make his identity certain. "As promised, I didn't tell your captain about . . ." Though no one could overhear, Nightfall defended Danyal's privacy as well as his own. ". . . your one-time association with . . . certain people. And I didn't beat you."

Danyal shivered, though whether because of the cooling night air, or Nightfall's words, he could not tell. No one else knew about their private conversation in *The Sharius'* hold.

Having clinched his identity, Nightfall turned to business. "I understand you have some information for me."

Danyal's hands fell to his sides. "How did you know, my lord?"

Hearing attuned for the tiniest sound, Nightfall kept his methods mysterious. "What do you know, Danyal?"

Now, the words came tumbling out; Danyal seemed glad to be heard, happy to lose the burden of finding a way to Alyndar. "A ship slipped from Schiz' harbor the night the king got attacked, without colors or standard."

A ship. The information told Nightfall little. Whether over land or sea, the kidnappers had had plenty of time to reach whatever destination they chose. "Yes?" he pressed, hoping Danyal had more.

The boy did not disappoint. "From what I could piece together, my lord, it appears the ship landed in Hartrin."

Nightfall's heartbeat quickened, but he continued to hold hope in check. "You're sure, Danyal?"

"Not absolutely." Danyal's head drooped. "I–I did my best. I talked to crewmen from several different ships to track it, had to piece together their sightings, but . . ." He lapsed into silence. "I was careful," he finally said, with more confidence. "I don't think I'm wrong, my lord."

Nightfall considered. It might just take a sailor to put

the story together, especially a boy who could slip from man to man, asking questions that seemed childishly harmless. As things stood, Nightfall had no better information. "Thank you, Danyal. A brilliant bit of work. We're even now."

"Not by my conscience, my lord."

"Your conscience is a hard master."

Danyal shrugged.

Nightfall decided to take advantage of the guilt Danyal continued to suffer. "If you find out anything else, take the news to Kelryn in Alyndar. All right?"

"Yes, sir." Danyal studied his fingers.

"Kelryn," Nightfall emphasized. "No one else." Although he trusted Volkmier to properly use the information as well, he dared not take a chance someone might discover his alliance with the chief of Alyndar's prison guards. It could mean a traitor's death for Volkmier. His relationship to Kelryn, however, was already well known and established. No one could blame her for Nightfall's decision to send someone to her with news.

Danyal peered up at Nightfall, clearly trying to read a face he could barely see through the alley's darkness. "Please, my lord. Be careful."

Nightfall met the boy's gaze, surprised to discover worried sincerity stamped across the young features. He had seen such looks before, had read the emotion on other faces, just never ones directed at him. *He really cares. He's concerned about what might happen to me.* Though simperingly obvious, it unmanned Nightfall who found himself staring back in silence, without bothering to gather words. It occurred to him that the boy had not even bothered to ask if Sudian might be guilty of the crime Alyndar's guards ascribed to him. Danyal embraced the man's innocence with an exuberance that left no place for doubt.

"Please," Danyal emphasized.

"I'll try," Nightfall said, energized by the new lead

the cabin boy had given him. Though only a hair warmer than the Schizian trail, it at least moved his mission forward.

"And, Lord," Danyal added. "Though it suits your status more, you might want to avoid the upscale inn." He gestured southward.

Intrigued, Nightfall awaited clarification. He knew the Gold Lantern well, having spent many nights there in his merchant guise, and it tended to draw much safer, quieter clientele than the He-Ain't-Here.

"Them pirates, my lord," Danyal explained. "They've got themselves cleaned up and jingling with money, but I recognize them. That's their ship out in the harbor, too."

Nightfall rolled his eyes at the irony of Alyndar's money buying legitimacy for pirates. He knew they would live the high life only as long as their riches held out. Then, poverty or love of cruelty and danger would drive most of them back to the sea. "Thanks for the warning, Danyal. I really can't afford to stay in one place overnight anyway, given the size and scope of the manhunt. When I stop moving, I'm ..." He was going to finish with "dead," but softened it for Danyal's sake. "... caught."

Danyal lowered his head.

Nightfall wished he had kept his comments to himself. For reasons he could not wholly fathom, the boy cared about him. "But only until I find the king and clear myself. Now that I have a clue where to look, it's only a matter of time."

Danyal's face rose slowly.

"And it's all thanks to you. I've searched half the world for information, and you're the first one to give me anything useful."

Danyal beamed.

"Godspeed," Nightfall said. "And don't tell anyone, except possibly Kelryn, that you saw me."

"I promise, my lord."

Danyal's reply disappeared into the distance as Nightfall crept silently away.

Perched on one rooftop and shielded by another from the light of stars and moon, Nightfall hunched in puddled shadow, eyes and ears attuned to the slightest sound or movement. Though driven to reach Hartrin as swiftly as possible, he forced himself to think through the problem logically. Deep in the heart of slave country, Hartrin had little to recommend it as a kingdom or a city. He could scarcely imagine the trouble Edward could get into there. As a prince, the boy-king had killed a slaver once, the very act that had pushed his father to tie his life to the demon. *If Ned's there, he's a prisoner. Freed, he would only wreak havoc.* Nightfall only hoped that any such havoc had not gotten the valiant and naive king killed.

Once there, Nightfall had no idea how he would locate the imprisoned king. He now knew how severely losing his underground contacts hampered his ability to work. He had gotten lucky this time, tapping a cabin boy whose loyalty stemmed from friendship rather than force. He could not expect information to fall into his lap again. The closer he got to the king, the more difficult it would become to uncover any news about him. He would have to find some way to penetrate the sources he had once blithely used as Nightfall.

Nightfall's thoughts pulled him elsewhere. Kelryn could not help him unless she had at least a general idea of his destination. Of course, she could not sell him out either; but he now knew she would never do such a thing. It did little good to keep sending people who might uncover information to her without occasionally checking back himself. She or Volkmier could have learned some important bit of knowledge he could use, or they might need his help. Perhaps they had even unmasked the traitor, in which case they probably knew exactly where to find the missing king. Unable to pass the information to Nightfall, they would have little choice but to enlist the help of Alyndar's army and navy, which would invariably result in war. Nightfall shuddered at the thought. The bold tactics of the military would panic the kidnappers, who would have little choice but to murder Edward and dispose of his body.

The idea of returning to Alyndar after spending two weeks traveling to Schiz seemed insanity, but Nightfall needed sea passage to Hartrin anyway. Once he had a ship, travel time became a minor issue. The merchants had a credo that aptly described the situation between Alyndar and Hartrin, one at the northern end of the Yortenese Peninsula, the other at the same end of the Xaxonese Peninsula: *opposites by politics, strangers by land, neighbors by sea.*

A ship. Danyal had tried to find passage to Alyndar for weeks, without success; yet Nightfall believed he had found a means thanks to Danyal's other revelation. It would require caution and finesse, but he supposed he could manage both.

Nightfall shinnied down the rooftop and headed for the shops. He would need to do some thieving to make the whole thing work.

† Chapter 14 †

I'm sure we're learning something useful with this game, but doesn't it seem foolish to practice disarming ourselves in battle?

—Dyfrin of Keevain, the demon's friend

THE MOON HUNG low in the sky by the time Nightfall prepared to enter the Gold Lantern Inn. The regular patrons would have gone home and most travelers would be bedded down for the night, but pirates kept longer hours. Beneath the bulking garments he wore for the part of Balshaz, silver-trimmed green silks fit him well enough to appear tailored. He wore the customary jade-colored sash that identified him as a working merchant and matching cloth-covered shoes. He had not stolen these items at random, of course; few enough men boasted silk in their wardrobe. He had deliberately purloined them from the home of a merchant he knew routinely traded through the south each autumn.

Nightfall wore his hair stylishly shoulder length, combed to a copper sheen; and his crafted long-nosed face bore the pocks of a childhood illness. Clay and powder made his eyes appear wider set and larger, trustworthy. He walked with an upper class strut, trip-

ping the latch and pushing open the door as if he owned
the inn. Though it swung inward on silent hinges, unlike
the He-Ain't-Here's squeal, every eye still jerked toward his entrance. Bawdy laughter cut off as if suddenly
choked.

Nightfall took in the situation at a glance. Softra, the
owner, tended bar; and his wife, Darlane, played server.
Normally, the common room would have closed for the
night several hours earlier, and his hires had already
gone home. Nightfall saw no sign of Softra's two adolescent daughters.

The pirates sprawled in small groups around several
tables near the center of the room. Several still wore the
grimy, salt-rimed rags they had had on deck, preferring
to spend Alyndar's gold on entertainment and trinkets
than on their own appearances. Others sported new
silks or linens, fresh haircuts, and shaved faces that fully
revealed their sun-baked skin and multiple scars. Nearly
all wore a clashing plethora of jewelry, and spots of
color shot around the room as facets caught the candlelight with every movement. Several kept swords belted
to their waists, and gem-studded daggers lay bare on
some tables. At least one used a blade in lieu of a fork.

As before, the captain was the piece that jarred. Hair
as black as charcoal fell in thick, oiled curls to his shoulders. He wore a tasteful amount of jewelry, all sapphires
set in gold, and the sword shoved rakishly through his
brilliant blue sash looked more utilitarian than pretty.
Customized silks without a hint of frill or trim hugged a
sinewy, muscular frame, and he still wore the knee-high
boots with their shining copper buckles.

The air smelled cloying, thick with ale, sweat, and an
incompatible variety of perfumes, spices and grease.
Though several men were eating, Nightfall could not
detect the more pleasant aromas of food through the
mix. He did note the common room itself had changed
little since his last visit in early spring. The walls still
looked freshly painted, ale-colored with a zigzagging

pattern of red trim. The fireplace was bare, swept clean of ash, awaiting the winter season. The hanging lanterns held candles burned nearly to nubs. The dartboard hung in its usual place on the wall between them, though the dart cup lay empty, the darts scattered across the floor below it. Unlike the lower-class establishments, the board held only small nicks and scars; men in the Gold Lantern did not tend to launch knives and tableware in gross displays designed to prove one's manhood.

Nightfall hesitated in the Lantern's doorway only a moment. Spotting an empty space near the captain, he took a step in that direction. Then, Softra's subtle summoning gesture caught his attention. Pretending to ignore the many patrons, Nightfall crossed the room with his head held high and his walk just shy of a swagger. He chose a seat directly across from Softra, his back not quite to the pirates. He trusted his peripheral vision to catch any sudden movement before it became a threat.

Once Nightfall sat, the pirates ignored him, and their noisy chatter resumed.

Softra kept his voice pitched well below the hubbub. "Balshaz, it's good to see you."

"And it's good to see the Gold Lantern." Nightfall glanced over his shoulder at the rowdy band in the common room. "Usually."

Graying and paunchy, just shy of average height, Softra cringed. "I'd throw them out, but I'm . . ." He seemed loath to finish the sentence.

"Afraid?" Nightfall supplied.

Softra rocked his head in a gesture of reluctant agreement. "They've paid their tab, so far. I really don't have cause."

"Other than that they're destroying Schiz' only decent establishment."

"And keeping my regulars away." Softra sighed. "Yes, there's that. But they are paying customers, and I don't imagine they'll stay too long."

The last statement seemed more like a question, one

Nightfall did not have the means to answer. For all he knew, the pirates might choose to live here for months before greed and a lust for adventure dragged them back to the sea. "I notice the girls aren't working. Are they all right?"

Softra snorted, gaze fixed on his wife while she removed empty mugs and replaced them with filled ones. "They're fine, and I plan to keep them that way. I wouldn't trust this lot around them." He looked at Nightfall hopefully. "Were you planning to stay, Balshaz?"

"I was." Nightfall swiveled to study the pirates. They shouted and laughed with the abandon of drunkards. "Are they always up this late?"

Softra hesitated. For a moment, Nightfall thought he might lie, though doing so could only hurt his business in the long run. It did not take a wise man to realize this band of barracudas preferred the night. "I've given them every hint I can think of. Even outright suggested they might want to get some sleep." He shrugged. "They're determined to party." His dark eyes widened hopefully. "You've traveled a lot, right, Balshaz?" He did not pause for the obvious answer. "Do you have any experience ending such . . . um . . . festivities?"

Nightfall knew his own business with the pirates would not prove easy, but he might manage to help the proprietor simultaneously. At the least, Softra would allow him liberties that would ordinarily get him tossed from the establishment. "I might." Nightfall rose. "Have Darlane bring me a mug of ale." He added pointedly, "The fresh Keevainian stuff, not whatever horse piss you're passing off on those monsters." Snapping wrinkles from his silks, he turned his regard fully on the pirates. "Please don't interfere, even if it gets a bit ugly."

Nightfall could sense Softra fidgeting behind him. "Don't do anything that gets us killed, Balshaz. And I'd rather the Lantern stayed in one piece. Please."

Nightfall gave no reply. It was not in his best interests

to die either; but he could not guarantee the safety of the establishment, whether or not he got involved. Hands free, for the moment, he headed toward the captain, pausing only to swipe a chair from the next table, give it a graceful spin, and settle into it. Placing his left hand casually on the table, he turned the captain an expectant look. "Hello, good sir. My name—"

The captain struck like a snake, but Nightfall followed every motion. He watched a knife zip free of its sheath and speed toward his hand on the table. He also knew in a heartbeat that the blade would miss, so he forced himself to remain still, his expression calmly schooled, and watch the point slam into the wooden tabletop.

The common room went utterly silent.

The captain's pale eyes rolled upward to peer at Nightfall from under beaded brows. "A finger's breadth leftward, and you'd be missing a thumb."

Nightfall kept his gaze level and met the captain's squarely. He played a dangerous game, and he expected some reward for his courage. "With all due respect, sir. If the blade had come at me a finger's breadth leftward, I would have moved my hand." Whether or not Nightfall had anticipated the attack, they all knew nearly any other man would have jerked his hand to safety, either before or after the blade landed depending on his observational skills, quickness, and competence.

A grimy-looking man with a beard full of froth broke the silence with evident sarcasm, "Oh, you *knew* 'zactly where it would land, didja, sir psychic?"

Nightfall frowned. Had he pulled away, they would have branded him a coward. He did not mind playing games, but saw no point to them if every outcome translated into his loss. The man had essentially dismissed his bravado as slow reactions and dull wits.

"That good are you, soothsayer?" sneered Paskhon, the younger of the two men who had rowed him, as Sudian, to the pirates' ship. "Where's this one gonna hit?"

He seized a jeweled knife from the table and hurled it at Nightfall.

With accuracy honed from years of "dagger catch" with Dyfrin, Nightfall neatly snatched the hilt from midair. His "razor rebound" was just as unconscious. Nightfall managed only to curb his natural instinct to fling the knife directly back at Paskhon, redirecting it toward the familiar location of the dartboard. He did not bother to watch it land, but the solid thump told him his aim was true.

The common room grew even more silent, if possible.

Casually, Nightfall reclaimed his seat as if nothing had happened, deliberately turning his full attention back to the captain. "As I was saying—"

Chair legs scraped the floor, and weapons rasped from sheaths. Darlane screamed. Her tray crashed to the floor, splashing beer over the nearest pirates and sending mugs slamming and ringing across the tables, rolling awkwardly to the floor. Fire seemed to burn through Nightfall's veins, instantly followed by a painful wash of ice. His mind flashed back to his helpless moments on the pirate ship, filthy hands touching and tearing, eyes filled with gold lust and murder. It took a desperate strength of will to remain in place and allow the captain to control his men.

The captain raised both hands and shouted, "Enough!"

The pirates went still, some half risen, others with hands clamped to sword hilts.

"We're in a respectable establishment! Take your seats and act like human beings."

Grumbling, the pirates obeyed with clear reluctance.

The captain nodded toward Softra, who cowered behind the bar, sheltering his wife with quivering hands. "Innkeeper, I sincerely apologize for the mess. Of course, we'll pay for anything spilled or broken. Please assure your wife we mean her, and your guests, no harm."

Without bothering to see the effect of his words, the captain returned his attention to Nightfall. "You were telling me your name," he reminded.

Nightfall could not help feeling impressed by the pirates' captain, who seemed a study in contradictions. By dress and demeanor, he could move easily through the upper classes, though Nightfall had seen him glibly lower himself to the level of his men as well. He knew how to command savages and pacify nobility. His voice and expression held the perfect range, and he thought swiftly enough to use the right approach in diverse situations. Through everything that had just transpired, the captain had not even lost the thread of their conversation. Nightfall steadied his voice so as not to betray his own, mostly feigned, composure. "My name is Balshaz. I'm a merchant seeking passage to Alyndar."

"Alyndar?" The captain snorted. "Well, good luck there, donner. No one's sailing to Alyndar."

"So I've heard." Nightfall tried to sit back in his chair but found himself incapable of relaxing his guard that much. He forced an easy, comfortable expression instead. "Hunting a fugitive and force-checking every ship."

"That's only part of it." The captain leaned forward, his chiseled features boldly handsome even in the dim light. "There's a war brewing, and no one wants to be part of that."

Nightfall did not bother to hide the appropriate expression of alarm spreading across his features. Other than border disputes and battles over the shared ownership of Trillium, the countries of the world had remained at relative peace throughout his lifetime. "A war?" He dared not believe Volkmier had acted so swiftly and recklessly, though surely not alone. The chief of prison guards could hardly deal with a traitor in secret, and the High Council would have an overriding hand in deciding the subsequent course of action. Nightfall took only scant satisfaction from the possibility Volkmier might have cleared his name in the process. If Edward died, he had no future in Alyndar anyway. Few would accept him as king, even if he wanted the job; and assassination would be inevitable. Feigning ignorance, he plied the captain for information, "Who would declare war on Alyndar?"

The captain shook his head. "Not war between kingdoms. A civil war."

The revelation rendered his previous thoughts moot, and a wave of relief flooded through Nightfall. He still had time to rescue Edward.

"They've gone so far down the ascension, I'm starting to think I have a chance at the throne."

For an instant, Nightfall wondered if the captain might be serious. He demonstrated more than enough poise to have once lived among the nobility, perhaps as a displaced and disgruntled younger son.

The captain huffed out a laugh, dispelling the notion. "The king left no heirs, being a youngster himself. The chancellor's a traitor. Age-old law doesn't account for such details. I don't know if anyone's really sure who has next right, but a whole lot of people would like to believe it's them."

Jackals. Nightfall wondered how many of the pompous Council members considered themselves fit for the position. At worst, the squabble seemed certain to flush out the traitor. He nudged the conversation back on topic. "So, can you get me there?"

"Me?" The captain sounded taken aback, and a few of his men dared to laugh, earning them a quick, silencing glare. "Why should I go to that kind of trouble for a stranger?"

Nightfall had a ready answer, and he spoke it scarcely above a whisper. "Because the man I'm going there for said you owed him a favor."

The captain's sea-blue eyes narrowed, and he stroked his shaved chin with a massive hand. "Which man is this?"

"He said you would know."

"Did he now?"

Nightfall said nothing, waiting for a less rhetorical question.

"Would this man have a name?"

"He would," Nightfall said, "but he told me not to speak it. Said it might get us both in trouble."

The captain dropped into a thoughtful silence, which clearly unnerved his men. A few low-volume comments passed among them, but nothing Nightfall could decipher. He glanced at Softra, who remained behind the bar while his wife worked at collecting the dented mugs and mopping up the spill. The innkeeper returned the look with one of guarded hope. At least, Nightfall seemed to have temporarily quieted the pirates.

The captain cleared his throat. "So, what are you doing for this . . . mutual friend?"

Nightfall turned back to the captain. "He said you wouldn't ask."

"He lied."

Nightfall smiled. "All right, then. I don't suppose it can hurt to tell you. I'm delivering a message."

"What message?"

Now, Nightfall's brows rose.

Clearly realizing he had reached an impasse, the captain tried another tack. "Why are you doing this for him?"

Too much secrecy would make the pirate captain unnecessarily suspicious. He had reason to worry he might get arrested in the city he had robbed of so many valuables. Holding a noble hostage, even a fallen one, would surely have dire consequences. "He bested me in a dart game. Said it was too risky for him to travel there, so he wagered money against a boon."

The captain's head swiveled toward the dartboard. "Wouldn't have thought anyone could best you at darts."

Nightfall finally looked at his handiwork. The knife had embedded in the target dead center, a perfect bull's-eye. More surprised than proud, he tried to appear nonchalant. Countless years and hours of practice had given him that killer aim. "I wouldn't have either." He drew his hands together on the edge of the table. "I thought I was unbeatable, but that man is good."

"Won't argue with you there." The captain's pallid eyes held a strange spark Nightfall did not, at first, recognize. It looked vividly familiar. He had seen that same excitement in another not long ago. Nightfall only had to place it.

"Will you take me there?"

The captain dodged a direct answer, still gathering information. "How much?"

Nightfall knew he should expect pirates to have their minds always on money, but the captain had seemed so sincere in his desire to atone to Sudian for his men's behavior that Nightfall had not expected the question to arise. He still had nine silvers in Kelryn's pouch and intended to keep all of them. "He said you would do it for nothing. That you owed him a big favor of exactly this sort."

The captain made a noncommittal gesture.

"Nearly all my profits are tied up," Nightfall continued, "but I've traveled enough to watch plenty of sailors. Your ship needs some attention from what I've seen and heard, and I think I can fix her. Also, it wouldn't hurt to train your . . ." He cast a disdainful glance at the crew. ". . . sailors to pay some mind to maintenance."

The captain nodded, chewing on his lower lip. "I'll accept your offer, merchant. But when I asked 'how much,' I meant the amount of trade goods you planned to bring along. How much space you might be wanting."

Nightfall had no intention of burdening himself with anything, but he knew better than to sail empty-handed after taking a merchant's guise. "I'm short of cash, so I won't be taking much."

"Too bad," the captain grunted. "Things ought to sell well there, what with so few ships coming in."

"Yes." Nightfall tried to sound disappointed. "Luck never seems with me at the right times." Despite his statement, he pressed. "So, any chance you could take me to Hartrin once I've finished my business in Alyndar?"

The captain's dark brows rose nearly to his scalp. "You've got gall, merchant."

Nightfall wiggled his still-intact fingers on the table-top. "I thought I'd already proved that."

"The kind of gall that gets a man killed."

Nightfall prepared for a fight, though he gave no outward sign of it. He turned the captain a searching look. "Today?"

"Not today." The captain's face remained locked in a hard expression, but he made no move to carry through on any threat. "You caught me in a good mood, merchant. And with a favor unpaid. We'll take you to Alyndar, and your assistance will buy you passage back here. Anything further will require payment."

Nightfall shot back easily, "Half the profits on any goods I sell."

"Deal." For the second time, Nightfall and the pirate's captain came to an agreement.

For Softra's sake, Nightfall added, "And you and your men find an earlier bedtime so this poor innkeeper and his wife can get a bit of sleep before breakfast."

Nightfall anticipated anger but got a brilliant smile instead. "You drive a very hard bargain."

"Been a merchant all my adult life." Nightfall returned the grin and added a wink. It suddenly occurred to him where he had seen that sparkle before, in the eyes of the Delforian healer when she had caressed him to excitement. "Should I meet you at the ship come morning?"

The captain looked out over his men, most of whom had sobered during the long conversation that would clearly send them back out to sea with money still unspent in their pockets. "Make it just past midday. My men need their sleep, too."

"Very well." Though many of his personae had friends, Nightfall would never have believed someone like Sudian could win the hearts of so many. His last encounter with the pirate captain had seemed a bit pat, worrisomely easy. Now, he understood. He had known the captain admired Sudian's dexterity and cleverness in a crisis, but he had not realized the depth of that appreciation.

Nightfall had a knack for reading the intentions of others, one that had kept him alive since early childhood; but he struggled with those of the pirate captain. The women of a thousand villages might squabble for the chance to marry a man of such exquisite beauty and genteel manner, yet he had chosen life on the sea with a band of raucous, murderous bandits instead. When Nightfall put those details together with the glimmer in the captain's eye when discussing the subject of Sudian, he had to consider the possibility the captain had fallen in love—or lust—with the same romantic expectations as the healer. Some parts of the world accepted men coupling with other men, but most found it reason for disgrace. Nightfall wondered if the captain's fall from nobility had to do with his sexual preferences. If so, he had clearly trained to become a knight or warrior commander prior to his exile.

Nightfall shook his head, suspecting he had read way too much into a single look. He knew better than to construct a detailed scenario out of scraps, then rely on it, only to have it shatter at the most inopportune time. Nevertheless, he could not help wondering what the persona of Sudian had that the others lacked, what made him so dangerously attractive. He only hoped Kelryn had succumbed to the same eerie power, and that she would never escape it.

Nightfall appreciated the thick-walled sleeping rooms of the Gold Lantern Inn that kept him oblivious to the snores and odors of the captain's uncouth crew, though it left him without distraction from a bothersome jumble of thought. Exhaustion weighed heavily upon him, yet sleep remained at bay. Repeatedly, he questioned his strategy, weighing his options until they warped into a storm of doubts. On the surface, it seemed more logical to sail directly to Hartrin, to do everything possible to bring himself nearer to Edward as swiftly as possible. Deeper contemplation dispelled the notion. He had no way of knowing whether the king remained where his captors had initially taken him; Nightfall had traveled half the world and back in the same amount of time. Furthermore, he had nothing to go on upon arrival in the northwestern kingdom. He could no longer access his information sources, and he had used up all of his favors the previous day.

Except one. Nightfall continued to analyze his reason for choosing to return to Alyndar now. He wanted to let Kelryn know where he planned to go. More significantly, she might have come upon knowledge that could prove vital, including Edward's location, the details of this civil war, and any progress toward discovering the traitor. Nightfall had tipped Volkmier to hunt for Alyndar's betrayer, yet he had not fully considered the implications of the commander's success. Though shrewder than most fighting men, Volkmier might not take into account the far-reaching consequences of actions that appeared proper to his honor and training. Once alerted, the Council seemed certain to activate the military, which Nightfall knew from his darker experiences would assure Edward's death. At the very least, Kelryn would have some information that could help Nightfall avoid the manhunt for Alyndar's chancellor. Rumors of his condition and whereabouts would surely have trickled back to the castle.

Nightfall tried to pacify himself with logic that seemed strong and sound, but he could not quite shake the concern he might be rationalizing. He desperately wanted to see Kelryn again, to assure himself of her safety and quell any worries she might have for him. He had promised to keep her apprised of his mission, and just sending a coded message did not seem like enough.

Nightfall flopped on his pallet, the most comfortable bed he had managed to find since leaving Alyndar with King Edward on their diplomatic mission. Gradually, he dropped into the familiar light doze that managed to refresh while holding him poised on the barest edge of awakening. Despite his many worries, he spent a dreamless night.

The pirates arrived to prepare their ship well after midday and on toward evening. By then, Nightfall had secured his costume, trade goods, and necessities, and had freshly caulked the neediest planks. The captain appeared first. Without a word, he assisted with the task, burnished teeth gleaming like fresh snowfall through a taut smile. Clearly, it was not a job his men took on with glee or even stoic pride; and he apparently appreciated Nightfall's honest efficiency.

Individually or in small groups, the others arrived, most disheveled and reeking of the night's revelry. They pounded onto the deck without offering to help and settled into the necessary duties that preceded a launch. They knew enough about sailing to check and affix the sails and ready the proper lines and stays. Some assessed the winds. Others prepared the galley. A few scrambled into ratlines and riggings to assure everything remained in order. Cleanliness, however, seemed beyond their ken. They overlooked decks smeared with filth; mollusks and barnacles peppered the hull.

Ignoring the niceties did allow the ship to leave its mooring sooner; and, before Nightfall had finished his task, they skimmed out over the open sea. Wind whipping his neatly brushed hair into a tangle more familiar to other personae, Nightfall watched the coastline disappearing in the ship's wake. The time for consideration had passed. He now headed directly into the clutches of a country hell-bent on killing him, yet he knew it was the last thing Alyndar would expect. Ships coming into Alyndar would draw far less scrutiny than those leaving port. Since he arrived with the pirates, Alyndar's inspectors would think nothing of his departing with them.

Leaving the sailing to the pirates, Nightfall gathered his belongings. He had bought his trade goods in the late hours of morning, visiting shops, individuals, and markets he knew as Balshaz. Funds and space limited his purchases. He stuck with spices, cosmetics, and southern-crafted gewgaws, several clothing items by a Schizian seamstress with a delicate touch, and the tar and rope needed for patching. He passed up an expensive glass piece he would have loved to give Kelryn, a swan to replace the one he had shattered when he had believed her his traitor. It would have used up nearly all his ready money, hers to begin with; and he would not steal more while in the guise of scrupulously honest Balshaz.

"Why don't you take those things to my cabin?" The captain's voice startled Nightfall, though he did nothing to show it.

Nightfall swung the satchel full of items to his shoulder. "Your pardon, sir?"

Dressed in his usual bright silks and boots, the captain explained, "Bring your trade goods aft." He jerked a thumb toward the poop deck. "They're safe in my cabin. Anything left out might disappear. My men aren't known for their trading savvy and patience."

No, Nightfall agreed. *For slaughter and theft.* He kept the thought to himself and followed the captain aft. He did not need to deal with pirates taking or destroying his gear, not when their sale was supposed to buy his passage to Hartrin.

"You're welcome to bunk with me, too, Balshaz." The captain paused to lift the hatch and waved Nightfall through the opening.

Nightfall had years of experience sleeping among sweaty, snoring sailors. Exposed on the deck, he would also have to weather the elements; and the fresh caulk would show up as dense, black stripes across his back. No merchant would feel comfortable in those circumstances; to refuse would put his disguise in jeopardy. "A generous offer, Captain, thank you. But is there room?"

The captain's tone held pent up laughter. "Three unused bunks enough for you? Being captain has to have some privileges, or who would take the job?"

The captain had answered his own question in Schiz when he mentioned the civil war in Alyndar. Clearly men would kill themselves and their followers for the honor of leading a nation. Though far fewer, surely some would do so to take command of a ship as well.

Nightfall tossed his bag into the darkness, then shinnied down the rungs to the lower deck. He waited for the captain to snatch a lantern from a gimbal ring, light it, and lead the way through the galley, a storage room, and a mate's quarters to an area separated from the others by a door. The captain shoved that open to reveal a long, narrow berth, its neatness contrasting sharply with the rest of the ship. The forward portion contained a desk with a tidy stack of papers, a wooden sofa softened with a pallet, and a worn dresser with a pitcher and bowl on top. Beyond it, separated by a drawn curtain, the high-ceilinged area just below the elevated poop deck held two stacked bunks, a chair, a wardrobe, and an ironbound chest. An enormous window took up most of the back wall. Rafts of bubbles and swirling green slime churned past. The open wall space held paintings of fish and ships in gilded frames.

"Put your things here." The captain pointed at a spot near the dresser.

Nightfall flopped his bag into the indicated space, still taking in the details of the room.

"Come to a decision?" the captain guessed.

Realizing he had never actually accepted or refused

the captain's offer, Nightfall nodded. He would get far better and safer sleep here than with the crew. "It's very nice. Just let me know which bed's mine and how to best stay out of your way."

"I've got the bottom." The captain smoothed the blankets on the lower of the stacked bunks. "You can have the top or sleep out there." He tilted his head toward the padded couch. "If I've got the curtain drawn, you know to stay out."

The arrangement pleased Nightfall. Not only did it maintain privacy, it gave him the area near the door to come and go without disturbing the captain. "The couch is just fine. And now, I think I'll keep an eye on the crew, if you don't mind. They don't seem as concerned as I do about keeping this ship seaworthy."

The captain laughed. "They can get slapdash on the cleanliness, but they're not afraid of hard work. They'll keep us afloat."

"Nevertheless, Captain . . ." Nightfall headed toward the door.

The captain seized Nightfall's shoulder. "Wait."

Nightfall froze, uncertain what to expect. The command could not be ignored. Slowly, he turned to face the captain, freeing himself from the other man's grip. "Yes, sir?"

"How . . . did he look?"

Uncertain of the subject, Nightfall shook his head. "Who, sir?"

"Sudian. Did he seem well?"

Nightfall considered the wisest response without creating a suspicious pause. "Well enough to beat me at darts," he said.

The answer clearly did not suit the captain, who arched his brows over steely eyes and waited for more.

"Definitely tired. Somewhat bedraggled." Nightfall shrugged. "I'm not sure what he normally looks like, so it's hard to compare." He stuck with plausible truth, intended to mislead. A pirate captain might sell information to anyone willing to pay. "He wore long clothes, but I still noticed quite a few healing cuts and bruises. And I think he might have injured his left shoulder seriously at some point." He smiled. "Didn't stop him from . . ."

The captain finished, "Beating you at darts. Yes, I know. He's quick. Got good hands." He returned the grin. "Like you."

Though intended as a compliment, it sent a shiver through Nightfall. In twenty years, he had never crossed an alias. Now, desperation had made him sloppy, forced him to leave trails, and to consult with the same people in different personae. It was a dangerous strategy destined to fail him, especially if he kept associating with intelligent and capable people. Covering his tracks forced him to respond casually. "Thanks for not amputating them in the Gold Lantern."

The captain's smile broadened, revealing the straight white teeth. Before he could voice a clever comeback, footsteps slammed against the ladder rungs, then pounded across the lower deck.

"Cap'n! Cap'n!" The words preceded a wiry man with skin like leather and a wild mop of sandy hair. He skidded suddenly into view through the still open door. "There's a runner on the starb'd horizon."

"Runner" meant nothing to Nightfall. It was not a standard seaman's term.

The captain frowned. "What colors is she showing?"

The pirate rolled his eyes toward Nightfall as he spoke. "Can't see no colors yet, Cap'n. Got Caylor up top."

"Good." The captain's tone and stance shifted effortlessly into command mode. "Keep him there, stay on course, and let me know when anyone spots colors."

"Aye, Cap'n." The pirate spun with scarcely a movement of his tight-fitting linens and scurried back the way he had come.

Nightfall had to know. "What's a runner?"

The captain pushed past him and out the door. "It's a

smaller, more streamlined ship that could move as fast, possibly faster than ours."

Nightfall followed the captain, pausing only to shut the door. Even that slight hesitation put the larger man two massive strides ahead of him. Nightfall scrambled to catch up. "Are we being chased?" Another possibility filled his mind, though he could not voice it as Balshaz. A country aware pirates cruised the inlet might put their most valuable cargo on a ship capable of dashing swiftly past them.

Still without turning, the captain climbed the ladder onto the main deck. "Always." He did not elaborate, and Nightfall did not press. To do so might prove dangerous. Thus far, the crew had done nothing to reveal themselves as pirates to Balshaz. Loud, grimy, obnoxious, yes; but he doubted even they would take well to being presumed thieves and murderers, no matter how true the assessment.

As the captain strode onto the deck, the crew snapped to attention. Each man became intent on or found a job. The change impressed Nightfall, who, until that day, had only ever seen them in pirating mode. These men did know how to sail, and they clearly held their captain in high esteem. Nightfall wondered exactly what qualities earning the allegiance of pirates took: high connections, intelligence, skill with a sword, or simply bravado and charisma. From what he had seen so far, Nightfall guessed the man displayed all of those.

The captain stopped directly beneath the foremast and shouted up to a man balanced in the riggings. "What do you see, Caylor?"

The lean dark man in greasy red linens called down, "A runner, sir."

The captain's features set. "Yes, a runner, you twice damned galley-clod! I mean her colors, man. Is she struck?"

With a half smile of amusement, Nightfall leaned against a gunwale, keeping his distance from Arturo who cleated a freshly tightened line. As far as he could tell, Paskhon was not among the onboard crew this time.

"She's struck." Caylor ignored the insult. "Flags fore and aft. I can't quite make out the colors yet." After only a moment of silence, he added, "On the fore, it's yellow with a darker stripe. Red, I think."

"Red," another man confirmed, limbs balanced between the gunwale and the lines.

Caylor continued, "Aft, she's red with something on it. A figure of some kind. Looks like a . . . maybe a raccoon."

Someone laughed.

Nightfall glanced up, nearly blinded by sunlight reflecting from their own unadorned white sails. Currently, the pirates flew no flags.

Arturo looked up from his task. "What dizzy silver-sucking oaf would take a raccoon for a symbol?"

"It's not a bloody raccoon," said the sandy-haired man who had brought word to the captain. Now firmly ensconced in the forward riggings, he added, "It's something with a big, fat head."

"A lion?" the captain suggested, taking a position on the forecastle, just below the speaker.

"A lion. Lifthranian." A pirate spat over the sea. "Can't say as I ever seen one of those."

The gold lion on a scarlet background did symbolize Lifthran, an older city, strongly built, just across the Ivralian border from Alyndar. Two things intrigued Nightfall: a landlocked town like Lifthran had no need for ships at all, and the striped forward flag announced a direct connection to Baron Ozwalt.

A brawny pirate with a long facial scar pounded toward them from the poop deck. "Captain!"

Everyone whirled.

"Captain." The man skidded to a stop, smearing fresh caulk across the deck like ink. "There's another runner port and aft."

For an instant, the captain's facade cracked. He went utterly still and silent, not even appearing to breathe. He recovered so swiftly, Nightfall doubted anyone else had noticed the lapse. "Is she struck?"

"Red flags, far as we can tell, Captain."

The captain muttered a harsh oath worthy of a sailor.

The man on the foremast called down from his riggings. "What d'you want us to do, Cap'n?"

"Keep her on course," the captain said with a low growl. "And watch those runners. I want quarterly reports on their positions, plus immediate notice of anything odd."

A few cries of "aye" and "right" came from various places on the ship, some sounding disappointed. Nightfall suspected the pirates saw booty on any ship determined to outrun them. He hoped the bloodthirsty crew would not hold him personally responsible for sabotaging their fun and profit.

The captain issued no further commands, other than to gesture for Nightfall to return with him belowdecks.

A sudden flash of memory hastened Nightfall's step. Once again, he remembered collapsing beneath the weight of men reeking of blood, their hands scratching and bruising him, rending his clothing. He forced away thoughts that did not belong to Balshaz. They could only hamper a role he needed to play flawlessly.

In silence, Nightfall trailed the captain into the dank, gloomy depths of the lower deck and back into the lantern-lit cabin. The sea glided by the window, its calm gentle movement an odd contrast to the inner turmoil Nightfall sensed and the captain refused to reveal. This time, the pirate captain closed the door behind them. He flopped onto the deck chair and waved Nightfall to the couch.

Nightfall sat. The stiff, firm cushions barely dipped beneath his weight, which he appreciated. It kept his feet planted on the floor, and he could rise, if necessary, in an instant.

The captain did not mince words. "You have experience talking with nobles, Balshaz?"

"A bit." Nightfall gave a signal that was half nod and half shrug. An equivocal answer would have to suffice while he fished for more information. Clearly, the question had something to do with the two Lifthranian ships whose presence still confounded him. *Are they chasing Sudian?* The idea seemed ludicrous. Even if Alyndar had managed to track him through his aliases, they could use the power of their own massive navy to trap him. "No more experience than you, though, I'd wager."

The captain's pale eyes narrowed. "What do you mean by that, merchant?"

Not for the first time, Nightfall wondered if he should have kept his mouth shut. He could not afford to rile the captain. Trapped on the ship, he did not stand a chance should the captain find him unworthy or, worse, a threat. Playing dumb seemed just as foolish. The captain clearly valued intelligence and ability, and he might interpret any feigned ignorance or stupidity as reason to mistrust. "I just mean you have the appearance, dress, and bearing of the highborn. You look as if you've walked among them."

The captain gritted his teeth and bared them like an animal. Had he not faced off with the most terrible men in existence, had he not, in fact, been one, Nightfall would have withered beneath that glare. Instead, he returned the infamous ferocious stare that had, in its own time, cowed hardened criminals and royalty.

The captain broke first, though he showed nothing for losing. He sat back, arms crossed, as if the movement had nothing to do with the intensity of Nightfall's gaze. He huffed out a sigh, dodging the subject. "I'm going to try to outrun them."

Nightfall knew better than to press his advantage, instead focusing on solving the problem the captain had not yet directly addressed.

"But we have to prepare for the eventuality that we can't."

Nightfall played his part. He was not supposed to know he consorted with pirates. "What eventuality is that, sir? Of what peril are two small ships to us? Your crew seems plenty fit for battle, more so than for sailing, even."

"The Lifthranians will have weapons, too. Better than ours. Raising a bloody flag or tipping a black spot won't send them trembling into submission."

"Bloody flag? Black spot?" Nightfall clamped his hands in his lap, trying to appear startled and more than a bit nervous. "So you're . . . you're . . ."

"Pirates," the captain supplied. "And don't look so shocked. You had to have suspected, at least."

Nightfall knew better than to overplay his ignorance. "So, if they catch you—"

"If they catch *us,* we'll all be dancing the hempen jig." Apparently realizing Nightfall might not grasp the pirate slang, he simulated a hanging.

Nightfall stared. He had considered the risk of traveling with pirates: sparking a disagreement into a life-and-death war, offending the captain, dealing with a poorly maintained ship. He had worried about Alyndar penetrating his disguise. But these pirates had survived for years while actively plundering; it had seemed silly to worry about capture on a routine run to Alyndar. "So," he said, not certain where to take the conversation and wondering why the captain had chosen to confide in a stranger rather than some trusted member of his own crew. "What are you proposing, Captain?"

The captain studied Nightfall, eyes piercing beneath oiled black locks. "You're taking this well."

"Am I?"

"You appear to be."

Nightfall shrugged. He had been in more immediate danger. "Ranting would only waste time better spent preparing, and punching the captain might get me keel-hauled." He had only seen the procedure once, during his own brief stint as a pirate; and that had proved enough to keep him forever in line when shipbound. Pirates lived by a strict code, and violation called for severe punishment. Nothing less would keep men who lived and died as they did under control. They had tied the miscreant to a rope that ran beneath the ship, tossed him overboard, and dragged him along the hull. He had emerged half-drowned, clothes and skin tattered by rocklike barnacles and cast-off worm shells, and sharks had trailed the blood trail for nearly a day. "What good would that do me?"

The captain returned a wan smile at the threat. "Do you know how to coax some extra speed from a good ship?"

Nightfall pursed his lips. *Not as Balshaz.* For the sake of all of their lives, crossing aliases seemed moot. Marak the Nemixite sailor had known all the tricks before his capture by Alyndar had put a definitive end to that guise. "I might have an idea or two." He had tired of the game. "But, once again, Captain, I believe you have more experience. Especially with this particular ship."

"Oh, I'll use what I know." The captain continued to study Nightfall, as if trying to see through him. "But that may not be enough."

Though Nightfall still doubted he had come to the root of the captain's need, he proceeded. "When's the last time you careened her?" He cringed at the likely answer. If the pirates gave only as much attention to the hull as they did to the planking, they were in serious trouble. Caulking took no time compared to dragging the ship on land to scrape away the clinging animals and vegetation.

The captain looked away, a sure sign he planned to make excuses for his men. "She's inoperable careened."

"And your men are inoperable drunk, but I saw them downing plenty in the Gold Lantern."

The sea-blue eyes zipped back to Nightfall, and they held more than a hint of warning.

Nightfall let the point drop. A mass of flotsam clinging to the hull would slow them down, likely enough for the runner ships to catch them. He had always expected to die violently, but it irritated him to near rage to realize he might do so because of other men's laziness and incompetence. "Captain, sir, I ask again: What do you propose?"

The captain placed his hands squarely on the arms of the chair. Though he clearly intended to say something uncomfortable, he kept his attention trained unwaveringly on Nightfall. He would not miss a covered flash of emotion, the slightest twitch that might give away something hidden.

With that in mind, Nightfall schooled his expression to cautious interest.

"Merchant, I want you to take command of my ship."

Nightfall blinked, startled into silence. *Not again.* Everywhere he went, it seemed someone dragged him into the position of highest authority. And, every time, the suggestion caught him unwilling and wholly off his guard. He had never heard of any captain voluntarily sacrificing his command to anyone, could not fathom a seaman doing so for a stranger, could not imagine a man as self-assured and calculating as the pirate captain would ever blithely surrender his ship and his crew. "Sir," Nightfall finally managed, the effort of holding his shock in check drying his mouth to cotton. "I am utterly certain I misheard you."

† Chapter 15 †

*A man is most welcome everywhere if he properly
times his departure. Always, my friend, always leave
them wanting more of you.*

—Dyfrin of Keevain, the demon's friend

IN THE CAPTAIN'S spacious cabin lodged below the
poop deck, Nightfall studied the well muscled man in
front of him as though he had gone mad.

"You did not mishear me." The captain's voice remained as steady and strong as always, and he did not
flinch or look away. "I need you to take command of the
Seaworthy."

It was the first time Nightfall had heard the name of
the ship, and it gave no hint to her purpose. It could
have belonged to a navy ship or a pleasure craft, a merchant vessel or a jolly boat. It conjured no images of
sharks or warriors upon the sea, presumably on purpose. "Captain, I—" Uncertain where to go from there,
he stopped and restarted. "You can't—"

"I'm the captain of this ship. I can do as I please."

"Of course, you can, sir." Nightfall struggled to make a
coherent point. "But that doesn't mean your men will accept it. They don't strike me as a trusting and cheerful lot."

The captain rose suddenly, a quick reminder of his size, which dwarfed Nightfall in every way. "That's why we'll have to think of a way to convince them."

Nightfall tensed but otherwise did not react to the captain's abrupt change in position. It currently posed him no threat. "Why?"

Apparently starting to pace, the captain froze in mid stride. "Why?"

"Why?" Nightfall repeated. "Why is landlocked royalty hunting you? Why would you even consider turning over command of your ship to me? And why do you think I would accept such a burden?"

For several uncomfortable moments, the captain remained still, locked into an unfinished stride. Finally, he turned. "Do the reasons matter?"

"Entirely."

"Why?"

Nightfall sucked in a deep breath, then let it out slowly. He was treading on thin ice. "Because I won't do it in ignorance."

"You won't . . . do it?" The captain spoke in a mocking voice. "You won't do it, eh, merchant? You'll die with the rest of us?"

The captain was clearly calling a bluff that did not exist. Nightfall kept his tone calm. "If need be."

Now it was the captain's turn to ask, "Why?"

Nightfall stayed true to his current character. "Sir, I'm a man of honor, and my livelihood depends on my remaining an honest man. People know that when they come to Balshaz, they get exactly what I've promised and at a fair price. I need a reason to destroy a reputation it took me a lifetime to build." Spoken aloud, the words seemed like desperate irony to Nightfall, though they suited Balshaz. *No wonder no one tracks me across aliases.*

The captain's brows arched high in clear incredulity. "Your life is not reason enough?"

Nightfall continued his act of nonchalance. "I'm not

wholly convinced mine's forfeit. I've dealt with Lifthran many times, including her nobles; and the truth is on my side. I'm *not* a pirate."

"Men are rightly judged by the company they keep."

Another shrug from Nightfall. "I'll take my chances."

The captain's face acquired a pink tinge that signaled rising anger. "So, you're sure you can talk your way out of the hangman's noose?"

"Not sure," Nightfall admitted, leaving the captain a necessary opening. "Just hopeful."

"If that's your strategy . . ." The captain spoke through gritted teeth, color fanning darker across his cheeks. ". . . then you give us little reason not to disembowel you before the runners catch us."

Nightfall could not wholly suppress a shiver. He turned the captain a nervous smile meant to tread the fine line between maintaining the confidence necessary to hold the captain's respect without appearing smug. "Please, sir. I never said I wouldn't help you, only that I require an explanation before doing so." He knew he needed to say more. Otherwise, the captain might believe he had relented only to save his own hide. "I like you and what little Sudian told me about you, though right now I'd like to pound him unconscious for putting me in this position." He avoided the image of one persona attacking another and the impossibility of the threat. "I couldn't live with the guilt of sending a group of men to their deaths, even if they are pirates."

The scarlet of the captain's cheeks dulled back to vivid pink. "So you will help us."

"Only if I get my explanation." Nightfall had to insist. "Ignorance can lead to lethal mistakes."

The captain sighed deeply. He sat, shoulders drooping. He looked uncomfortably out of character in apparent defeat; but Nightfall knew it was the cornered predator, not the angry one, who was most likely to attack. "All right."

Nightfall waited in silence for the story to begin.

"My name is Celdurant." The captain paused, as if waiting for some significant sign of recognition.

It did have a ring of familiarity to Nightfall; but, as he could not quite place it, he said nothing.

"Celdurant el-Bartokus Arbonne." The words emerged rusty, as if he had not spoken them in many years and without the fluency that usually accompanied the repetition of one's own name. The "el" signified a legitimate son, and the rest of the name dawned suddenly on Nightfall.

"As in Ozwalt el-Bartokus Arbonne." Nightfall nodded, understanding. "You're the Baron of Lifthran's . . . brother?"

"Half brother," the captain corrected. "Ozwalt's mother died in childbirth, and our father remarried mine." It was a distinction only royals ever seemed to find significant. As if to directly challenge the idea, he added, "Not that it mattered to either of us in youth. We were simply brothers until Ozwalt reached his teens and the mantle of rulership crept toward him. At about that same time, Mother perished in an accident, along with our youngest brother, leaving only Father, us two boys, and our sister." He looked expectantly at Nightfall, clearly seeking a reaction to the story so far.

Now that he had Captain Celdurant talking, Nightfall did not wish to discourage him in any way. To show he was listening to the gist, as well as the details, he supplied, "An abrupt lesson in mortality."

"Indeed. Ozwalt didn't worry for his own life, but for our father's. If the old man died, it fell to the eldest son to rule in his place, and that scared him."

"Scared?" Nightfall shared an observation gleaned from Volkmier. "Most young men would relish the chance to rule a major city and its territories." He winked. "When we're that age, we're all perfect, you know."

Celdurant could not help but smile. "True. But my

brother never developed that cocky, youthful confidence, and I'm afraid I had a hand in it, along with Mother, may her spirit dwell in the highest, happiest reaches of the Great Father's afterlife." He made a religious gesture and rolled his gaze toward the upper deck.

Nightfall nudged him back to reality. "Did you fight with your brother?"

Celdurant shook his head, gaze still turned upward. "No more than brothers usually do. Perhaps less. But I had a few ... um ... features my older brother lacked." He finally looked back at Nightfall, obviously trying to frame his next words in a context that would not make him appear vain. "My father was not a handsome man. His first marriage was arranged for him, a political royal union to please the populace and keep peace between neighboring baronies. There was little love between them. As I understand it, she was homely and boorish; but she produced the requisite heir, though the process killed her. That left my father free to marry whomever he pleased, and he chose a woman of vast intelligence and beauty with whom he fell madly in love."

Nightfall supplied the details the captain dodged. "So, when it comes to appearances, you favor your mother?"

Celdurant bobbed his head, emphasizing the soft, black curls. "Being a younger son also freed me from certain responsibilities. I saw court as a game, anticipating the suggestions of my father's advisers. To Ozwalt, it was always a desperate chore. He had to be right, so he spent most of his time second-guessing his own decisions. Over time, my father turned to me for answers first, and that drove my brother fairly crazy."

Nightfall began to see the pattern. "So, you had the looks and the intelligence; and that made Ozwalt jealous."

The captain chewed his upper lip, the first nervous gesture he had displayed in Nightfall's presence. "I realize that now. At the time, it never occurred to me. He was my older brother, and I idolized him. He was going to be the baron, by the Father. If anyone should feel jealous . . ."

Nightfall let him trail off, certain his interest came through clearly enough.

"And that's where Mother made her mistake. She saw I had a knack for attracting women and commanding men; my judgments seemed clear and sound to her. She petitioned my father to bypass Ozwalt and crown me baron instead."

Nightfall cringed. "I could see where that might bother your brother."

"He wasn't supposed to know. Neither was I. But my sister overheard a conversation, and she never had much skill when it came to keeping secrets. That's when Ozwalt began emphasizing the *half* in our brotherhood, reminding me he had a full complement of royal blood." The captain shrugged, a grin pulling at the corners of his lips. "Not that it bothered me. I never really understood, or even cared about, his point. I never seriously considered I would wear the crown of Lifthran. I believed him when he dismissed the whole thing as a means for Mother to place her own bloodline on the throne." He considered briefly, the smile never making it to fruition. "It took me until adulthood to realize the nastiness inherent in that comment."

Nightfall only nodded. He had little true understanding of family bonds. His father might be any man who paid to use his mother's body, and she had kicked and belittled him. Dyfrin was the nearest he had come to having a sibling.

"Father took my mother's death hard. He gradually withered away from grief, while I trained to become commander of Lifthran's elite troops. Ozwalt took the throne without challenge, and he found a woman of standing and great beauty who agreed to become his wife." Celdurant's eyes narrowed, and his mouth twisted, betraying a revulsion stronger than Ozwalt's obvious envy. "Her name is Esmarda." He gave it a sneering pronunciation that revealed a fiery loathing.

Nightfall knew the name. "She is still the baroness." He revealed what he had learned as Balshaz. "And she has a penchant for pearls, particularly the rarer pink ones."

The captain stared a moment; then, his face relaxed. "Of course, merchant. You would know that."

Nightfall raised his hands in a gesture of clarity.

The captain's sea-foam eyes trained directly on Nightfall's face, again reading every subtlety. He had clearly come to the crux of his story. "She came to live at the barony during the wedding preparations. One night, I found her in my bed, dressed indecently. She said she was marrying my brother, but it was me she wanted. She claimed I fired a passion in her Ozwalt could never fulfill and suggested I play the secret role of keeping the baroness happy." He closed his eyes. "Devastatingly exquisite that face of hers. Her body . . ." He shivered. "But for the love of and loyalty to my brother, I resisted. I sent her back to her room, unsatisfied, and assured her I would pretend this night had never happened."

Nightfall realized he had earlier misjudged the captain's appetites and reminded himself why one should never rely on impressions. "Very noble, Captain." The details caught him by surprise. It seemed impossible a man with so much principle could become the leader of a bloody band of pirates.

"Of me, perhaps, but not of her. For the story she told my brother was one of trickery and rape."

"And your brother believed her?"

"I think he wanted it to be true; it gave him a legitimate reason to hate me. My sister warned me, and I escaped bare seconds before my own men came for me."

Nightfall needed to know. "What was your sentence?"

"Death." The captain spoke the word with far more

ease and grace then he had the name of his vengeful sister-in-law.

Now, Nightfall understood Celdurant's discomfort at the prospect of facing Lifthranian justice, but one thing still did not fit. "So how did you turn to piracy?"

The captain grunted. "You want it all, don't you, merchant?"

"If you want my help, I need to know."

The captain did not hesitate long. He had already revealed the significant story, and Nightfall guessed little in the further details could harm him. "I swore off women that day, and sailing seemed the best way to avoid their wiles. After spending my whole life as a royal and a leader, I didn't take well to the menial life as a regular sailor. Eventually, I got command of my own ship. I didn't have much experience with the sea, though, since I grew up landlocked." He made a strong, cutting gesture to indicate he had skipped unnecessary parts of the story. "It all came together here."

Nightfall filled in the obvious, significant details. "So those Lifthranian ships aren't after you because you're pirates."

"Not specifically," Captain Celdurant admitted. "But that will serve as an excuse. I'm the one they want, but they'll give no quarter to my men." He turned Nightfall an earnest look. "Nor, I believe, to you; but you're the only hope we have."

Nightfall put the last pieces together. "If they find an honest merchant commanding the ship, and you're not aboard . . ."

As Nightfall hoped, the captain finished the thought, "They might leave you all alone. They don't know the crew. Without me, they have nothing."

Nightfall sat back, running the plan through his mind. The captain had a definite point. The Lifthranians would have prepared for combat, substituting armed warriors for any form of cargo. They wanted a fight, any excuse to kill the exiled brother of the baron living under an unexecuted sentence of death. The pirates would give them that battle, and most would die as they did so. No telling what kind of horrors the Lifthranians would inflict upon Captain Celdurant. Nightfall might have the chance to talk himself out of the situation, but it would require him to survive the bloodlust of both sides first. "Captain, you're right. I have to take control of this ship."

The captain loosed a blast of pent up breath through his nose, and his aura of authority returned. "Didn't I say that quite some time ago?"

"Yes." Nightfall agreed. "But I didn't understand why, and the original problem still exists: your men will not accept me."

"If they thought I was dead—"

"—they would fight for command. That's one battle I'd avoid."

"Chaos," the captain said. "Perhaps if I pretended to be ill or injured and named you my successor."

In theory, the idea sounded plausible, but something still troubled Nightfall. "Is this your entire crew?" He already knew the answer. He still had not seen Paskhon aboard, and he definitely noticed fewer men than the first time he reluctantly set foot on the *Seaworthy*.

"We're working with a skeleton crew. We just came off a big campaign, and the men were eager to spend their spoils."

"And the ones with us now?"

"My regulars. The ones willing to put to sea with me even just to return a favor, without concern for compensation."

"So these are your most loyal men, Captain?"

"In other words. Yes."

"Don't you think they might take offense if you placed command into my hands? Perhaps they might think you had gone mad or I had injured or drugged you."

"Perhaps."

"And then?"

"They would kill you." The captain stroked his chin thoughtfully. "That would be bad."

"Bad for you, perhaps. For me, catastrophic."

Captain Celdurant managed an edgy laugh. "Ultimately, catastrophic for all of us, but I see your point." He threw the onus back on Nightfall. "So, merchant. What do you suggest?"

Nightfall could scarcely believe what he was about to say and only wished Dyfrin were alive to hear it. The only right answer came from his most recent experiences, ones he would have dismissed as flukes before the character of the demon became lost to him forever. "Captain, sir, I think you should tell them . . . the truth."

"What?" The captain finally fully lost his wicked composure.

"I think you should tell them what you just told me."

"Show weakness to a pack of wolves?" The captain's fist crashed to his armrest. "What foolishness is this?"

"These are your regulars, you said, your most trusted. Daily you place your life into their hands and never think much of it. Whether it's trusting them to pilot the ship or maintain it, whether it's knowing you have a friendly sword at your back on a hostile boarding, you hand them the tools of your destruction daily. How much harder can it be to share your past?"

The captain stared in silence.

Nightfall added nothing, allowing his previous words to have their full effect. He would never share the details of his own past with anyone except Kelryn and Edward, yet he still meant every word he had spoken. The captain had little choice. If he wanted his men's faith, he had to earn it with disclosure. It would prove a difficult decision for the captain, one that would require time, one he needed to make alone. "I'll be topside," Nightfall finally announced. "Keeping the sails at their fastest and the men honest."

Clambering to his feet, he left Captain Celdurant el-Bartokus Arbonne to his thoughts.

Nightfall found a quiet position on the fo'c'sle, steadied by nearly unconscious tappings of his talent. Heavy with sea spray, the winds slapped at his face, leaving a stinging wash of salt. The breezes tangled red locks usually held in strict and well brushed abeyance. The ocean spread out before him, a vast plain of blue-green tinged white with choppy wavelets. He avoided the other men, worried he might feel driven to join or assist them, to abandon his proper persona for the one who had dedicated his life to sailing.

The thud of a nearby footfall caught Nightfall's attention. His thoughts channeled instantly toward the sound, though he did not reveal this by stiffening or whirling. He knew the pirates would value calm alertness, so he turned slowly to face a short, bow-legged man with a stubbly, scarred face and a thick crop of sandy hair tied back from his eyes.

The pirate planted himself in front of Nightfall, speaking a thickly accented version of Xaxonese. "Begging your pardon, sir. What's happening with the captain?"

Nightfall wondered if the man was testing him, again. "I wouldn't break the confidence of any man," he said matter-of-factly, hoping the crew would not go to any extremes to prove his claim. Torture, he knew from experience, would only make him angry. "Most especially, your captain."

The pirate rubbed his brow with the back of his hand. "Not wanting you to give anything away, sir. Just wondering if he's in a mood. I've got a report to deliver."

Remembering Celdurant had requested quarterlies, Nightfall returned his attention to the water. "Bad news?" he guessed.

"Runners still gaining. Cap'n gonna take my head off?"

Nightfall shook his head. "He won't like hearing it," he admitted. "But he doesn't seem like he's on the edge of attacking the messenger."

The pirate padded away. Nightfall doubted the man truly needed the information he had requested; he knew the captain better than Nightfall possibly could. The maneuver, Nightfall suspected, had more to do with delay. He considered offering to accompany the pirate, but shook the thought away. His presence might antagonize the captain, who needed to make a difficult decision alone, without the pressure of a near-stranger dropping in at intervals to check on the process.

Nightfall clambered to the main deck, trying not to make it look difficult, or too easy. Though beyond competent with a dart, Balshaz was not known for the kind of agile sleight of hand Sudian had demonstrated on this same deck. He could not risk appearing too awkward either; not only would it risk the scorn of the pirates, but a graceful movement later might expose it as an act and cast suspicion on everything he did or said. For now, he needed as much of their respect and trust as he could reasonably earn in such a short time.

A stroll around the decks showed Nightfall what he already suspected: these men knew a reasonable amount of seamanship, some more than others, but tended to take shortcuts. They could keep the vessel seaworthy but not groomed for greatest speeds, quick but not primed for a lifesaving run. Given full command of the ship and a crew more fit for sailing than combat, he could coax quite a bit more speed from the light, narrow-hulled *Seaworthy*. As things stood, they made good time against bulkier ships, especially those weighted with cargo, but they seemed destined for a run-in with the Lifthranians.

As the wind shifted, a sheet clamp thunked against the mast and a sail luffed. The men rushed to take up the slack, to put the sail back in proper alignment as they lost precious moments. Nightfall could teach them not to miss those cues, to anticipate rather than simply respond, to use the sea to their advantage against pursuers. All he needed was complete command, a willing crew, and a year.

As Nightfall lamented the lack of skill and cohesion that might result in all of their deaths, an enormous pirate who seemed constructed entirely of muscle shoved him with unnecessary violence. Thrown sideways, Nightfall would have crashed to the deck, perhaps even toppled over the gunwale, if not for his talent. Instead, he staggered a single step, gracefully minced three more, then planted himself firmly on the planking.

The massive pirate turned to watch the effect of his push, his stubbly face puckered into a smirk. "Out of the way of the working men, lubber."

Ordinarily, when in Balshaz' guise, Nightfall would have let the incident go with a politely worded, though grossly undeserved, apology. However, if the captain intended for him to lead these men, he could not afford to back down from a challenge. He trained his withering stare directly into the larger man's dark eyes. "I would stay out of your way, were you actually working." He added, "Lubber."

"Lubber?" The pirate laughed, raising his voice to share the joke with the entire crew. "The long-clothes silversucker just called me 'lubber.' "

A chuckle rumbled across the deck, and many of the men quit working to watch the drama unfold around or below them.

Nightfall kept his joints limber, prepared to leap in any direction. At some point, this war of words seemed destined to degenerate into a fistfight he could not win.

"You don't even know what the word means. Do you?"

"Of course I do." Nightfall did not back down.

"Then you know you might just as well have called me 'girl.' "

Nightfall could not resist the opening. He glanced pointedly at the larger man's crotch. "Had I known it was apt, I would have."

Another short laugh swept the deck.

The massive pirate tensed. "Exactly my point. Both are ridiculous things to call me."

Nightfall appreciated the sudden common ground. "Agreed. But the names you assigned to me are equally absurd." He returned his gaze to the other man's face, seeking any advance warning of a physical attack. "I'm no silversucker." Though he would have liked to have given Balshaz the noble background many merchants had, he would have left himself open to a tracing of bloodlines that would have revealed the lie. "And I'm no more a lubber than you are. Even my blood is salty."

The pirate considered momentarily before coming to the obvious realization. "Everyone's blood is salty."

"But not everyone has seawater coursing through his veins."

The pirate's eyes narrowed, and a knife seemed to leap into his hand. "Well, then. Let's open one of those vessels and take a peek, shall we?"

Nightfall did not regret his words. No matter what he had said, it would have come down to the same fight. The pirate would have goaded until he could justify violence. Nightfall only wanted to force the first angry strike to come from the other man. "Better yet. Let's see who's the better sailor."

"Fine." The larger man released the ties from the ends of his tight sleeves and started shoving the fabric up his arm. "Let's see who can pummel the other to the bilge."

"What's that got to do with seamanship?" Nightfall acted genuinely puzzled. "Perhaps a race to the top of the mast?"

The knife remained clenched in the pirate's fist. "That's not seamanship either. That just shows who's smaller and rattier."

Nightfall would have preferred "squirrelier," but he understood the pirate's need to fling an insult that stuck.

"Look," one of the men called from the sidelines. "We already know Elliar's a sailor. Let's see what merchant-man can do with the mainsail."

The huge man the other had called Elliar stepped back, the smug smirk returning to his lips. He lowered the knife. "All right, let's see." He rested his bottom against the gunwale to watch what he clearly expected to be an amusing display. Like the others, he probably saw Nightfall's performance as unsupportable bluster.

Nightfall did not waste an instant. Seizing the main-mast, he shinnied upward.

The bulky pirate called up after him, "Hey! I already conceded you're smaller and more ratlike than I am."

Nightfall ignored him, rearranging shroud stays, bat-tens, and clamps with the deft practice of long years at sea. Most sailors preferred deckside duties, avoiding the riggings where most fatal accidents occurred. A shake, a lurch, or a collision could send a man tumbling to his death. As Marak, Nightfall had relished those jobs that most sailors hated, and he had become an expert at the perfect placement of every tiny contrivance. In no time, he had everything in its ideal position and the wind well-studied in the open heights of the hatchwork. Shinnying to the ground, he took over the lines, rear-ranging each to its optimal position before looping them around the proper cleat. He saved the main line for last, knowing that putting it in order would bring every one of his changes to bear at once.

The pirates who had manned the many lines stepped back as Nightfall watched the sheet burgeon like a silken cloud, without a single luff or billow. The vessel leaped forward, its speed abruptly increased by a long series of complex maneuvers Nightfall had made look fast and easy. "There," he said calmly, wiping his hands on silks that now held smears of grime.

Every pirate stared. Even Elliar was speechless.

Once again, Nightfall knew his next best move was to leave, to let the full effect of what he had done settle in and allow the pirates to talk about it, and him, without interference. The more they saw of his technique, they more they would recognize it as the simple operation of a well tended ship all come together at once. He would have preferred to go belowdecks, but that would put him in conflict with the captain, since they shared a cabin. Instead, he found an open position aft, high on the poop deck, and stared out over the water. The wake trailed them like lacy runnels; and, marked by the colors of setting sun, the steady droplets sweating from the hull gleamed like gemstones in the *Seaworthy*'s trail.

Nightfall's solace did not last long. A lean, lanky man shuffled toward him, glancing about as if afraid the other sailors might see him. "I've always heard, sir, a great tillerman feels like a part of his ship. Once in tune, he can get the ship to take direction nearly from thought alone." Green eyes went bright with longing. "Can you help me?"

Though not his strongest point, Nightfall did manage to assist, explaining the need for frequent careenings to keep the ship responsive. "For a sensitive tillerman, a single barnacle or mollusk changes the balance and the speed." He did not know if he spoke the truth or not, but it did not matter. The statement was essentially irrefutable, it made good legend, and it suited the situation. "A good cleaning, followed by a heavy coat of tar or whitewash, tallow, and sulfur will keep the barnacles from setting and the worms from burrowing. Fewer needs for cleaning, less work, happier shipmates."

The tillerman listened raptly, nodding at frequent intervals.

After he left, the lookout came, just as furtively as the tillerman, for tips on effective and safe speed-climbing. Next came the first mate; and, after him, the trickle became a torrent as the sailors arrived in quick succession for a bit more advice from a sailor they now considered a master.

The captain appeared twice, both times to oversee his men, to press the slackers, and to inquire on the progress of the Lifthranian ships. Each time, he came and went without so much as a glance in Nightfall's direction.

When darkness fell, Nightfall climbed silently into his bunk for a characteristically light sleep, awakened fully only by one of the captain's quarterly reports.

Captain Celdurant finally approached Nightfall after he had completed his morning touch-up, the seafoam eyes filled with a mixture of utter control and underlying pain. "The men have changed their minds about you."

Nightfall nodded, making certain his disguise remained thoroughly and appropriately in place. "That's good."

"They've come to like you and trust your shipboard knowledge."

Nightfall waited. He knew what was coming.

"Do you still think . . . ?"

Nightfall did not let him finish the question. "Yes." He met the captain's gaze and demonstrated that he fully understood the question. "I still think you need to tell your men the truth."

"Even though they should accept your authority now?" Though a question, it emerged more like a command.

"Even though." Nightfall held his tone as steady as the captain's. "Just yesterday, your men hated me. Some mistrusted me. What's to keep their whims from changing just as quickly a second time?"

The captain dismissed the argument. "It's natural, even logical, to distrust strangers. You've won their admiration. That doesn't just disappear."

"It can." Nightfall had many more reasons for the captain to confide in his crew, not all of which he would voice; but he also understood the man's reluctance. When it came to this issue, Nightfall only needed to consider the present circumstances. The captain would live with the consequences forever. "When they realize all I did was apply a few tricks I picked up along the way. Once those tricks become part of their own repertoire, they cease to be something worthy of awe. Their respect for me will vanish."

"Not in a day or two."

Nightfall shrugged. "You know pirates; anything can spark them. I'm sure you've had to assert your dominance more than once. Perhaps daily."

"Not daily."

"They may not like or agree with some of the things I ask them to do."

The captain's eyes widened, then narrowed with sudden wariness. "What, exactly, are you planning, merchant?"

Nightfall grinned. The captain had just proved his point admirably. "See, sir? I'm merely trying to carry out your own strategy, and I've managed to raise your suspicions—and your hackles. I don't want to have to explain my every word. We don't have time for that. If I'm going to guide us safely through this mess, I need the men to jump on my orders. If they have a basic understanding of why I'm in control, they'll respond better."

Bested by his own caution, the captain grunted. "I'll be standing right behind you to reinforce your commands. My men—"

Nightfall jumped in. "No, sir. You won't."

The captain's pale eyes crinkled further, to menacing slits. "What!" He balled his hands to fists. "You dare to command me?"

Nightfall could not afford to back down. "Sir, what good is placing me in charge if you're there for the Lifthranians to find? Why not just hang us all before the runners catch us?"

The captain's face reddened. "What are you implying?"

Nightfall only shrugged, believing his meaning was clear enough.

The captain would not let it go. "Are you saying I want my men slaughtered? Myself and you included?"

Nightfall feigned surprise. "No, sir," he said emphatically. "I would never pin motivations onto you, especially ones I know you would despise." He tried to sound bold but sincere. "You're the one who told me the Lifthranians can't find you here at the risk of all of our necks." He walked over to his sales goods. "Captain, sir, I have the means here to turn you, and even your men, into someone else." He unwrapped a parcel to reveal an array of powders. "Someone the Lifthranians won't recognize." He dropped the flap. "But for it to work, you have to play the part."

The crimson disappeared from the captain's cheeks, but he still maintained an expression of raw mistrust. "What part is that?"

"The part," Nightfall said carefully, weighing each word, "of my . . . girlfriend."

"What!" the captain roared so loud Nightfall could not help scuttling away. "Your *what*? Have you gone raving mad?"

No, but you have. Nightfall peeked at the captain around his sheltering arm. "Captain, I'm not planning to actually slice off any parts from you. It would be outrageous and ignoble of royal Lifthranians to ask my woman to disrobe."

"Your woman?"

"Who would recognize you?"

"Your *woman*?"

"Why not?"

The captain stared at Nightfall as if he were the stupidest fool in the world. "You think you can make this . . ." He made a gesture that encompassed the entirety of his well-muscled body. ". . . look passable as a woman?"

Nightfall straightened. It would not do to appear overly frightened. "I know a few tricks I'm certain will work."

All of the color drained from the captain's face, and his eyes returned to their normal configuration. "Is there anything about which you don't know a few tricks?"

Nightfall dodged the question. He had many shortcomings and a lot of ignorances, but he saw no reason to list his weaknesses. "And I can make your crew look more . . . sailorly. Less . . . piratey." He added carefully as his words fully settled into the captain's consciousness. "But I have to have their complete cooperation. And, sir, yours."

The captain shook his head. "We have a rule against women aboard. The man who sneaks her on walks the plank."

"Another reason why we have to let your men in on the details."

"And let them know I hid beneath the guise of a woman?" The captain took a broad, pacing step and flung out his hand. "Fah! They'll never respect me again."

"Better to give them a good reason, don't you think? Rather than have them believe you abandoned them at the bare thought of the hangman's noose. Or that I sneaked a real woman aboard." Nightfall pressed his advantage. "Captain, you can't expect your men to lie convincingly if they don't understand the particulars or the reason. They need to know that the moment they mention your name, and any connection to you, all of our lives are forfeit."

"Much as I hate to admit it . . ." The captain's proud head drooped. "You're right."

"I am," Nightfall said. "But don't think I take any pleasure in it."

The captain steeled himself, as if preparing to face a pit of live snakes. "Let's go."

† Chapter 16 †

The right words, the right tone, can convince most men that the moon is the sun, a dog is a cat, and a chunk of dry land is the ocean.

—Dyfrin of Keevain, the demon's friend

B Y THE TIME Captain Celdurant stepped onto the main deck to make his announcement, both of the Lifthranian ships had become visible to every eye aboard. Though he arrived with the captain, Nightfall separated himself from the coming revelation, stepping fully midships to wrap an arm around the mainmast and place a foot casually upon a massive cleat. It seemed foolish to think he could escape anything by climbing, but the position made him feel more secure. He watched how the men came to attention as their captain appeared, impressed by the deference he commanded from men more suited to riots and rabble.

"Men," the captain said, then added more softly, "friends." He paused just the right length of time before continuing in a tone that seemed to physically drag them all a step closer. "We have a problem."

"We can handle 'em, Cap'n," one man called from the riggings. "We's done in bigger ships than these."

Nightfall doubted they had ever taken two at a time and with a crew whittled down by loyalty rather than ferocity.

The captain did not directly address the comment. Doing so would require him to doom his men to battle against a larger, more heavily armed group hell-bent on murder, or to disparage them by casting doubt on their ability to win. "Those are hunter ships, well armed, well manned with warriors; and they're looking for me. Anyone they associate with me will die on the spot or hang as a pirate."

The pirates fell silent, gazes fixed on their captain. Nightfall suspected they were mulling over the words and their captain's tone rather than the issue. They risked dying for piracy every day.

Looking up to the speaker in the riggings, the captain continued, "Now, I'm ready to fight to the death, if that's what you prefer. But we have other options, slicker ones, and I'm not averse to those either."

A clamor of here-heres and ayes echoed across the deck.

The breeze swept the captain's black hair into an inky mane, and sunlight glistened through every silken strand that seemed immune to tangles. "We happen to have a merchant aboard, known for his word and his honesty." He smiled wickedly. "And I've managed to corrupt him into helping us."

More racket from the pirates. Nightfall pursed his lips into a tolerant grin. "I prefer my neck the way it is: attached and unbroken."

Only the nearest men heard him amidst the tumult, and those snickered.

A wave of the captain's hand restored the silence. "My plan requires every one of you to deny me, and you must give your total obedience to Master Balshaz. You will listen to and follow his every order, no matter how mad it might seem, without fail and without question. He will become the sole commander of this expedition, having hired you all in Schiz for mercenary wages. Let the Lifthranians look freely; we have nothing to hide. They will not find me aboard this ship."

Only a few murmurs broke the hush.

"Anyone unwilling or unable to carry through on this proposal, speak now and openly. Interference that comes later will be considered treachery of the basest sort."

The captain's last two sentences seemed pat, commonly spoken. Nightfall read between the lines. The captain was giving each man a chance to opt out of the strategy: now or never. They still risked the possibility a pirate might choose to sell them out, hoping to save his own life and gain some money simultaneously; but doing so meant death for the rest of the crew. *And the traitor had better hope no other man survives the purge, including me.*

There was a protracted hush, broken only by tense whispers exchanged between the sailors. The captain waited patiently for those to subside, then announced. "If no one speaks out against the plan, it is considered in effect. I will disappear now. *Captain* Balshaz," he made a grand gesture in Nightfall's direction, "the *Seaworthy* is yours." Though the order seemed cavalier, Nightfall detected a crack in the captain's voice, a slight bob of his shoulders that might pass for cringing. "Treat her well."

Caught off-guard by the abruptness of the change of command, Nightfall leaped to attention. He could never match the charisma of the captain, but he knew he needed to project at least an aura of smooth confidence. "You!" he said, jabbing a finger at the nearest pirate. "Change into something lighter colored, preferably without so many holes." Without checking to see if the man obeyed, he addressed the pirate nearest the jib. "Take that sail in a bit; you're spilling wind." Discovering the captain had stopped to watch him, Nightfall addressed Celdurant next. "You! Get to my cabin and prepare for the transformation of your life."

The captain gritted his teeth into a rictus. "You're enjoying this, aren't you?"

Nightfall snarled, "No back talk, lubber. You do as I say!"

Several of the men stiffened, glancing over to see their captain's reaction to treatment he would never have tolerated from any of them.

Nightfall held his position, no trace of humor in his expression or stance. How the captain responded would set the tone for the rest of the journey.

The captain swallowed hard. "Yes, sir. Right away, sir," he said in a voice that did not quite reach the level of servility. He scurried belowdecks.

Nightfall whirled to find several of the pirates staring at him. One by one, he sent them off to various tasks; and, one by one, they obeyed him.

The next half a day proved one of the most grueling of Nightfall's life. At every position, he stood over the pirates, forcing minuscule adjustments of sails and tack, of lines and men, and even of clamps. When he caught a moment, he instructed the men on fast and gross personal changes to transform them from a motley band of pirates to a less motley, less banded crew of mercenary sailors. The more difficult work came when he left them to their posts to visit Captain Celdurant, pacing wildly in his cabin.

The moment the door opened, he demanded, "Did we shift course?"

Nightfall entered and closed the panel behind him. He had hoped the captain would not notice. "A bit," he admitted. The captain had had them headed around the Yortenese Peninsula and into uncharted waters in the hope the Lifthranian ships would not dare to follow. Nightfall had other ideas, and he found the pirates more willing to comply than he expected. They, too, worried about gliding at top speed into unfathomable territory that could carry them off the edge of the world. The men on the hunter ships might kill them, but at least it was a death they understood and knew how to fight. "Don't worry. I have things under control."

"Don't worry," the captain spat out. "Don't worry, says the power-mad pretender who has control of my ship."

Nightfall broke out his kit and set to work on the captain's face.

"Surrendered command to a stranger. Headed for unknown territory. Hiding in the guise of a woman." The captain shook his head, forcing Nightfall to stop and sit back on his haunches. "What have I done?"

"Rescued your men from certain death?" Nightfall tried. "Now save your fretting like a woman until I've made you into one."

"My course was not random, you know."

"I know," Nightfall said, though he did not. To his knowledge, the seas beyond the continent were wholly unexplored.

"I have an island there that's off the maps. A safe hideaway when things get too hot or we need to careen." The captain's eyes narrowed stoically. "Not many ships are brave enough to follow us beyond the peninsula."

Nightfall drew back, prepared for an explosion. "We're going to Alyndar."

The captain sprang to his feet, bellowing, "What!"

Nightfall saw no reason to repeat himself. Though it was a dangerous position, he remained between the captain and the door.

"You fool! They'll catch us for sure!" The captain's face turned scarlet in an instant. "You betrayed us!"

Nightfall kept his voice flat and soft, a deadly contrast to the captain's fury. To wither beneath that terrible glare would be to admit a guilt that would end in his death. He could not afford to back down, to appear weak or uncertain. Clearly, the captain thought Nightfall intended to abandon the pirates to their fate once he reached his destination. "Don't be stupid, Celdurant."

"Stupid?" The captain trembled with rage. The cosmetics Nightfall had applied softened his features but could not hide the look of menace in his sharp, pale eyes. "You talk about stupid, you who plans to trap us in port. We're all dead men." His voice became a lethal growl. "And you're going first." His fist lashed suddenly for Nightfall's face.

Too close for a complete dodge, Nightfall weathered a glancing blow to the cheek that sprawled him. Pain slammed through his head and, a moment later, shocked along his spine. He looked up to find the captain towering over him, face still fiery, crimson with fury.

Angrier at himself for not getting fully out of the way, Nightfall flicked his own withering glare onto the captain. His cheek ached, and it would bruise; but nothing was broken. "Would you like to hear my reasons before you kill me?"

The captain kept his fist cocked and remained standing over Nightfall. "Talk fast."

Nightfall rubbed his aching face. "First, if they even dare to follow us into port, they won't cause any trouble in Alyndar."

"Why not?"

"Because, in the current political climate, they might spark a war they can't possibly win."

The captain's face went a shade lighter as he considered Nightfall's words.

"Second, an honest merchant has no fear of royal Lifthranian ships, no reason to go sailing into the realm of monsters, and every reason to head for Alyndar port."

The captain's fist dropped to his side. "But—"

"Third, I would rather confront Lifthranian royalty in a civilized location than on the open sea. Having an audience will force them to remain polite, which may keep them from examining cargo, contents, and personnel too carefully."

The captain huffed out a lungful of air, then offered his hand to help Nightfall up. "I'm sorry I hit you."

Nightfall accepted the captain's assistance, though he would have found it easier to tap his talent. Although he suffered unfairly for it, Nightfall understood the strain crushing down upon the captain. Celdurant had made the ultimate sacrifices: his ship and his men, and only time would tell whether he had saved them or doomed them. "I'm sorry you hit me, too." He ran a callused hand along his swelling cheek. "You're stronger than an avalanche, and quick, too. If I hadn't scrambled, you'd have broken my whole damned face."

"Sorry," the captain repeated, though he looked more self-satisfied than repentant as he studied the damage.

Nightfall rummaged through his wares, plucking out a tasteful dress and slips. "Put these on." He also passed over some wadded cloth. "And you know where this needs to go." He cupped his own chest to indicate breasts. "You have a role to play, and it doesn't involve punching anyone."

"Right." The captain took the proffered items, scowling at them. "It's just—"

Nightfall did not allow him to finish. "You have to show me the same trust you demanded from your men."

"How can I—"

"You must. This was your idea, remember?"

The captain winced, but he disrobed, revealing a slender torso with every muscle perfectly defined. "I remember."

Someone knocked at the door, and a voice wafted through the panel. "Captain. Captain!"

The captain reached for his regular clothing, but Nightfall caught his hand. "He means me."

"But—"

Nightfall crossed to the door and slipped out, leaving the captain to dress. "What is it?"

The pirate did not miss a beat. "We're outrunning the runners now."

"Great."

"But . . ." The pirate paused, gaze straying to Nightfall's injured cheek. ". . . we need to slow down if we're going to make port. What do you want us to do, sir?"

Though Nightfall knew his careful coaching would raise their speed, he had not expected to reach Alyndar quite this fast. "Prepare to dock. Remember your parts and act accordingly."

"Aye, Captain." The pirate rushed to obey.

Nightfall watched the retreating back, shaking his head. He doubted many people could distinguish sailors from pirates; both tended to become raunchy and rowdy after a long sea voyage. He intended to sell his wares rather than baby-sit their antics in the tavern, and he hoped they could behave themselves even without a captain present. Nightfall sucked in a deep breath, enjoying the salt tang of the air and even the musty odor of the hold. Quickly, he returned to the captain's quarters and began packing what remained of his wares, intending to have the merchandise all in one spot and his presence topside during docking.

The captain assisted, sorting objects with a speed that rivaled Nightfall's own. As he moved, Nightfall assessed his own handiwork from the corners of his vision. Celdurant made a strikingly handsome woman: his baby-blue eyes sparkling beneath oiled bangs, his soft raven hair brushed forward and caught with a dainty jeweled clip. The long shift hid the entirety of his legs, and a pair of supple slippers peeked from beneath the hem. Tucked in the right places, it simulated a woman's figure admirably. Nightfall diverted the handfuls of cloth he had been about to stuff into his pack to the captain's bodice. He manipulated the cups into the shape of breasts, earning a slap from the captain that flared through his already bruised face.

Nightfall recoiled. "What in the depths of the Father's hell did you do that for?"

The captain spoke in his best falsetto, "You were getting too friendly for my liking."

Nightfall cringed at the parody. "Do us all a favor and

don't talk any more than you have to." He rubbed his aching cheek. "And save the act until I'm done." More gingerly, he reached to straighten the false breasts.

"So where are we going first, Balshaz?"

Completing the task, Nightfall hefted his pack, rolling his eyes to meet the captain's gaze. "We?"

The captain nodded.

"Begging your pardon, madam." Nightfall emphasized the last word to remind the captain of the need for over-the-top caution. "But I think it's best for everyone if you stay here until we've finished our business in Alyndar, put back out to sea, and we know the Lifthranians are no longer chasing us."

The captain batted his eyes and gave Nightfall a pseudo-adoring look. "Do you now, darling?"

"I do."

Still in falsetto: "Don't you think we should test out this disguise of yours in a relatively safe place? It has to be able to fool my own brother."

The ship slowed. Nightfall adjusted his mass as the deck rocked and the men topsides prepared for mooring. "It's not my disguise I'm worried about. It's your lousy acting."

The captain's jaw set, and he dropped all pretenses. "Look, Balshaz. I've given you command of my ship and my men. I've completely surrendered my dignity. How do I know you aren't going to head straight to Alyndar Castle and turn us in for pirates?"

"I gave you my word—"

Celdurant shrugged that off as insignificant. "Yes, yes. And you assured me you're an honest merchant, but the scummiest thief from the filthiest gutter would do the same. No one admits to being a putrid, deceitful, shit-stinking pile of rat sick."

Apparently, the noble-turned-pirate had not found some of the dives Nightfall once knew as havens. There, he could find men proud of being putrid, deceitful, shit-stinking piles of rat sick. Balshaz, however, would not know those places either. "It's too dangerous." Night-fall's heart rate quickened to a flutter. He operated alone for many reasons, and the bruise on his face really limited his options. He could hide the discoloration, but the swelling would prove more difficult. It would arouse suspicion for a random page, guard, or serving girl to have an injury of the exact same type and position as a newly arrived merchant.

Receiving no answer, the captain shoved past Night-fall to the door.

Nightfall raced ahead and blocked him. "Sir, with all respect. You've already made my job much more diffi-cult."

"How so?"

"What would you think of a merchant with this?" Nightfall cupped his hand around his damaged cheek.

The captain paused, hand in midair where it would have tripped the latch had Nightfall not stepped into the way. "I'd think . . ." He grinned. "I'd think the mer-chant's last customer was . . . dissatisfied."

"Most people won't buy from a merchant with un-happy customers."

"But, perhaps, when they see you with a beautiful woman on your arm, they'll reconsider." The captain pushed Nightfall aside effortlessly; he did not dare in-crease his weight and reveal his talent just to keep the man there for a few more moments. Celdurant tripped the latch and turned his head to give Nightfall a dark look. "I am going with you." Without further warning, he shoved open the door and headed toward the ladder.

Nightfall grabbed up his pack and followed, sprinting around the captain to take the rungs first. He murmured as he passed. "Smaller steps, *madam*. And lighter. Re-member, you're a *girl*."

The captain whispered back a bitter oath that did not fit his tone or his dress, and he followed Nightfall top-side.

As Nightfall cleared the hatch, he nearly collided

with a pirate leaping for the opening. An abrupt side step saved them both, and Nightfall gallantly pulled his disguised companion to safety as well.

The captain let out a short, feminine squeal indicative of surprise, then hissed under his breath. "How was that?"

"Nice touch," Nightfall mumbled back.

The pirate drew to attention, gaze leaping repeatedly from Nightfall to the captain and back. "Um . . . sir . . . I . . ."

Nightfall tried to get him focused on his mesage, before the source of his consternation, the captain's dress, became apparent to anyone else. "What is it, sailor?"

The pirate turned his gaze directly on Nightfall. "Docking's nearly completed, Captain. Alyndar requests permission to board."

Nightfall rolled his gaze to the captain, careful to keep his voice as low as possible. "Anything incriminating aboard?"

The captain scowled. "Don't like them aboard my ship, but I don't see as it's avoidable. Let them come."

Without bothering to address the pirate, Nightfall headed forward. The captain took his arm near the elbow.

At the docks, men cleated the last of the lines, and half a dozen Alyndarian guards stood ready to board. Muted by wisps of cloud, the sun beamed down upon the dockhands, most of whom had stripped to their waists. Sweat sheened their bodies or glistened from dark tangles of chest hair, and the odor of salt and seathings receded beneath the stench of bodies in desperate need of washing. The pirates stepped aside, making the appropriate gestures of deference to Nightfall as they stole glimpses at their dolled-up captain.

Though all the guards sported Alyndar's purple and silver, the fist clutching a hammer symbol emblazoned on their tunics, only one wore a hat. Nightfall addressed him. "Good day, sir."

"And good day to you, sir," the guard returned gruffly, with none of the friendliness implied by the greeting. "Are you the captain?"

"Captain Balshaz," Nightfall confirmed. "Actually, I'm a merchant by trade, but I rented this ship to bring my wares." He gave the leader of the guards a pointed look. "Difficult to find anyone sailing to these parts."

The guardsman did not take the bait. "Docking fee's ten coppers. Paid now or on leaving. And we need to board."

"Last trip, it was three coppers; and no one boarded." It would seem strange not to remark on such an exorbitant fee. "Now I see why it's so hard to find passage here."

The leader of the guards scowled. "Castle orders, sir. We're counting heads. Making sure the same number leaves as comes. Same faces."

Nightfall suppressed a shiver. He might have made a grievous mistake if they had chosen the most dutiful and experienced guardsmen to examine everyone coming and leaving. Aside from Kelryn on one occasion, no one had ever seen through his disguises; but someone trained specifically to do so just might. Suddenly, he appreciated the pummeling the ship's captain had given him. It should rearrange his features even more than his disguise already did.

The captain's hand on his arm tightened in warning. He, too, was worried about this unanticipated inspection.

"Very well," Nightfall said, trying to sound irritated and put out by the details, rather than concerned. "But I would appreciate it if you left my gear in good order and didn't hassle my sailors. The ship is rented, and so are the men." He met the guard's stare directly, not wanting to arouse suspicion by appearing to have something to hide. "And we've had a difficult trip." He indicated the bruise on his cheek, leaving the details to the guards' imaginations. Most likely, they would assume the landlubber merchant had lost his footing in the normal pitch and toss of a sea voyage.

Nightfall turned to the sailors. "We set sail the day after tomorrow. Once the sails are furled, you're all off duty until then; but I expect you back first thing that morning in proper shape for sailing, if you want your pay."

The pirates all began talking at once.

"I'm light on coins, so I'll pay docking at castoff, after I've sold my wares." Nightfall nodded at the captain. "Zenia." He assisted Celdurant from the ship to the planks, and one of the guards steadied his arm as well.

The captain gave the man a shy smile.

The guard loosed the arm and bowed. "Madam." He turned his attention to Nightfall. "The bracelet you sold me last time, Balshaz . . ."

Nightfall tensed. He had made a lot of sales in Alyndar and did not recall each individual one.

"My wife loves it. Worth every copper for that alone."

Nightfall smiled. "Every satisfied customer is a reminder of why I do this." He appreciated having a guard who remembered him. They would see him as Balshaz, a familiar merchant rather than some stranger who might be masquerading. It would take some of the scrutiny off of the captain as well.

"Is this your wife?" the guard continued as his companions boarded the *Seaworthy*.

The captain giggled girlishly.

Nightfall shook his head. "Just courting for now."

Apparently realizing he was the only guard remaining, the speaker followed his companions onto the ship. "Hope things work out for you."

"Thanks." Nightfall headed along the docks.

The captain took his arm once more. "You had to name me Zenia?"

"What's wrong with Zenia?" Nightfall whispered back from the corner of his mouth as they walked past the few dockhands. Normally, the port would be bustling with activity, men scurrying to place and move boxes and crates. Now, the docks stood mostly empty, stained and weathered, and the few men not hovering around the *Seaworthy* appeared bored.

One jumped up from the shards of a broken crate. "Good day, Captain. Got some crates what needs unloading?"

"Not today, donner." Nightfall shook his head. "I've got all my wares on me." He realized how ridiculous that sounded, a merchant traveling across rough seas for the profit on a sack of trinkets. He had expected the real captain, and his crew, to handle their own reasons for coming to Alyndar, while he served as an incidental passenger. No matter how lame their story, he could fall back on the convenience of a ship that just happened to be headed to a country with which he wished to trade.

As they walked from the docks to the roadways, the captain picked up the thread of their previous conversation, as if no time had passed. "I would have thought a man called Balshaz could come up with something more exotic and interesting than Zenia."

Nightfall considered his next course of action, leading the captain down a twist of busy streets. "You don't look the exotic and interesting type." Caught up in thought, he tried to dodge the inane conversation. "Now shut up, and act like a woman."

The captain stopped, hands on hips in a gesture of female exasperation. "Those two statements are entirely incongruous."

Drawn up short, Nightfall could not help smiling. "You're mean."

"I'm a pirate," the captain reminded softly.

Grabbing the captain's hand, gloved to hide its size and roughness, Nightfall led him onward. "Not today, you're not."

The captain tweaked strands of his sleek black hair. "Where are we going? The market's the other way."

"I know." As they came upon an intersection, Nightfall

paused to insert them into the proper flow of pedestrians. "No time for the market. I've got a mission, and I have to accomplish it before we set sail day after tomorrow."

"You're the captain," the captain said, though it clearly pained him to speak the words. "You decide when to cast off."

Nightfall made a thoughtful noise. "You're paying the ten coppers docking, you know."

"That's not very gracious, Captain Balshaz." The falsetto was becoming more normal with every utterance.

For a moment, Nightfall could actually imagine his companion was a woman. "They're probably out there counting so they can charge us by the barnacle."

The captain huffed out a deep laugh, then muted it to a lighter, more feminine sound. "Merchants. Cheaper than misers, they are. Minds set on every copper."

Nightfall's concern with staying too long in Alyndar had nothing to do with money and everything to do with leaving alive and getting to Hartrin as swiftly as possible. "Frugality is a virtue, Zenia. At least merchants spend their own money."

The captain feigned offense. "Are you calling me a thief?"

"I'm calling you . . . a pirate." Nightfall glanced at his companion, accustomed to radical transformations, yet still impressed by his own handiwork. He only wished the captain knew the tricks that came with long practice, means to make one's self look shorter or taller, fuller or thinner, older or younger.

"Oh. All right, then." The captain made a long-fingered gesture. "Carry on. You were going to tell me where we're going."

Nightfall explained his plan. "I'm going to sell the entire lot to a shopkeeper on Arling Way. I won't get as much for it, but Moskajh will give me a reasonable price. He trusts me when I tell him what my wares will go for in his shop." He gave the captain a telling look. "He trusts me, because—"

"—you're an honest merchant," the captain filled in wearily.

"That's right." Nightfall amused himself with the thought that the world's most notorious criminal was preaching morality to a noble-turned-pirate. "I've never steered him wrong."

"Him, maybe," the captain mumbled as they headed into the shopping sector. "But you got me wearing a gods-damned dress."

After having used some of his products on the captain and the sailors, Nightfall felt lucky to get back the nine silvers he had spent. Shedding the pack of goods left him feeling oddly satisfied, though he still faced the most difficult part of his mission. He worked best with his hands and back free, and he felt shackled by anything that might hamper a sudden need for movement. He cursed the delay that had allowed the captain to bruise his face, though he now attributed it as much to the other man's swiftness as his own lapse. The pain distracted from his concentration, and the swelling rendered a disguise too dangerous. The captain already knew Nightfall had some skill at changing appearances, but to seem too adept at it, or too quick to use the tactic again, might give him away.

Nightfall knew he could not afford to sneak into the castle in Balshaz guise either. Not only could it destroy one of his best and most established personae, it might force Alyndar to take a closer look he could not afford. He would need to give the entire matter long consideration, preferably over a mug of ale and a plate of warm food.

"Where are we going now?" the captain asked predictably.

Nightfall looked up to a sky growing dimmer as the sun snaked toward the west. "To the inn."

The captain loosed a grateful sigh. "Even dressed like this, it'll be good to get back with my men."

"Oh, no, madam." Nightfall turned the captain a reproachful look. "The sailors'll be at the tavern near the docks, for sure. We need a more upscale establishment. One that caters to the traveling ladies."

The captain clapped his gloved hands over his face and groaned.

† Chapter 17 †

Greed pays in moments, kindness and fairness for a lifetime.

—Dyfrin of Keevain, the demon's friend

AFTER A BREAKFAST of leftovers from the previous evening, their disguises touched up to Nightfall's exacting standards, Nightfall and the captain headed toward Alyndar Castle amidst dense fog and drizzle.

"Gods," the captain whispered only for Nightfall's ears. "I honestly don't know how women wear this uncomfortable crap." He adjusted his skirts. "I'm getting a rash in . . . an indelicate place."

Nightfall preferred to concentrate on upcoming events, but he felt the need to give a warning. "Just don't be scratching that indelicate place in public."

The captain made an affronted noise. "I know how to act like a proper lady."

"Fine," Nightfall said as they headed up the path leading directly to the castle of Alyndar. "Just let me do all the talking, please."

"All right." The captain sounded grudging. "But I'd still like to know what this is about." He gave Nightfall a warning glare, softened by feminine cosmetics. "I don't need a weapon to choke the life out of you. If the word 'pirate' leaves your lips—"

"It won't," Nightfall reassured. "This has nothing to do with you."

"So you say."

"So I say. So I mean."

"Nevertheless . . ."

Nightfall sighed. They had gone over this all before. "Nevertheless, you intend to dog my every step and interfere with my every action."

"So, I've made myself clear."

"Abundantly." Though it hampered his every action, Nightfall understood the captain's apprehension, and even his hostility. To protect his men, Celdurant had placed himself in a position of terrible vulnerability in a way that would make any independent man fretful and short-tempered, including Nightfall. He tried to dodge the conversation as they approached the front gates and the two sentries standing at rigid attention. "Now be ladylike, Zenia. And also quiet."

The captain obeyed, trailing him in silence as Nightfall approached the men. "Good morn."

The one to the right, a squat, balding blond with a scarred left cheek and a crooked nose studied them mildly. Nightfall recalled his name as Garet. "Morn."

The other guard, a tall, well-muscled brunet, was a stranger to Nightfall. He did not speak.

Nightfall hid his own nervousness behind a mantle of false confidence. He needed to appear as if he belonged here. "I am the merchant Balshaz, and this is Lady Zenia. We'd like an audience with . . ." He cringed inwardly, refusing to display his mistake for the guards. "We'd like an audience."

Garet set aside a wicked-looking polearm to pull a scroll from his pocket. He examined it dully for several moments, then looked at Nightfall. "We can fit you in on the morning of the third day of the second month of the Great Cold."

Nightfall stared. He knew the drill from previous dealings with royalty in Balshaz guise. He held out a silver to the guard. "We need an audience today."

"Today." The guard accepted the coin, then examined his schedule again. "Perhaps after midday . . ."

Nightfall handed him another silver.

Garet brightened. He rolled up his scroll and returned it to his pocket. "Perhaps now would suit you better, sir?"

Nightfall smiled. " 'Now' sounds perfect." He had known from the start he could buy his way into court this morning. His own short stint as ruler had taught him the upper class visitors got the first slots of the day, and he doubted he had much competition. However, he had to play the game without risking offense to the man who determined the schedule. "Thank you."

"Right this way, madam, sir." Garet led them through the courtyard gardens, past two more guard posts, and into an unadorned room where two young guards hopped to immediate attention. "This is Balshaz, a merchant, and his lady friend to see . . . to see . . ." He paused in consternation, then surrendered with a shake of his head. ". . . whoever the hell's presiding this morning."

One of the younger guards smiled, but the other went even more rigid and made a stiff-fingered gesture of respect. "Sir, it's Lord Admiral Nikolei Neerchus."

Nightfall remembered the navy's admiral from his meeting with the High Council, a massive, handsome bull of a man with enormous green eyes and short-cropped fair hair. He remembered the man's quickness, despite his bulk, his cleverness at turning directly to the law book when Nightfall's fate had been in question, and his utter condemnation of Sudian. Nightfall would need to tread carefully and not reveal his trepidations.

Garet turned on a heel, leaving Nightfall and the captain with the two guards. The one who had reminded Garet that it was the admiral stepped toward them. "You'll need to leave any weapons here, sir."

"Weapons?" Nightfall tried to look affronted. "I'm a merchant, young man. What need have I of weapons?"

It was a rhetorical question, but the other guard answered anyway. "Well, sir. I would think you'd need them to protect your profits from bandits."

Nightfall whirled to face the man who had remained silent until that moment. "Are there bandits in Alyndar Castle?"

The first guard continued. "In the castle? No, sir!" He sounded as bothered by the question as Nightfall had acted. "But the roads . . . highwaymen . . ."

"I didn't come by road," Nightfall informed them, almost snootily. "I came by ship."

The second guard cringed. "Worse, sir. There are pirates about."

"Pirates, you say." Nightfall took some satisfaction from uttering the very word he had promised not to, in a safe manner and location. He glanced at his companion, as if from concern, taking note of the unladylike hostile glare he received in return. He shook off the warning. "Thank you, gentlemen, but my crew can fight. It's part of their job to handle any . . . *pirates*."

"Very well, then, sir." The guards exchanged glances but did not inflict the indignity of a search upon them. Apparently, they had orders to take highborns at their word. Nightfall carried no obvious weaponry, and he doubted anything short of a naked search would reveal his daggers. He had no intention of using them anyway. "Do you need instructions?"

Uncertain what the guard meant, Nightfall assumed he did. "Please."

The guard cleared his throat, apparently using a prepared speech. He walked a fine line; the arrogance of nobility and visiting dignitaries necessitated caution. The guards would not force them to endure a speech they felt too familiar with or important to need. However, leaving them without the proper means to find or address the court might prove equally humiliating.

"When you leave this room out that door," he pointed to the only other exit from the room, "you will find yourself right outside the court. We apologize if you find others waiting at the door ahead of you. We cannot always accurately guess the length of any particular audience. Rest assured, the order of your appearance is based solely on when we received your request rather than rank or worth."

Nightfall nodded, seeing the necessity for the disclaimer. He could just picture some duke shoving aside a knight standing ahead of him.

"The king is not currently in residence; so you will be seen by an appointee, in this case Lord Admiral Nikolei Neerchus. Please understand that any judgment, agreement, or treaty made by him is as binding as if it came from the king himself. If you prefer to wait until the king's return, you may reschedule without any loss of significance." The guard waited a moment, giving Nightfall a chance to opt out of the audience.

Nightfall doubted many men did.

"The proper title is Lord, Lord Admiral, Admiral, Sire, Your Majesty, Your Grace, or Your Highness." He paused for breath. "It is customary to bow, and it is considered a grave insult to speak before you have been addressed. Any questions?"

Nightfall could not think of any, though he knew he had received the short version of royal protocol. Nobles had written entire tomes on the topic. He shook his head.

The guard nodded smartly. "Very well, sir. You may proceed." He tripped the latch on the exit door.

Nightfall went through it, followed by the captain. They emerged in front of the familiar great double doors and found themselves the only ones waiting. The guards stationed in front of the court wore their fanciest uniforms, every crease perfect and not a stain, tear, or worn spot to be seen. They pretended to stare straight forward, though they sneaked glimpses at the newcomers from the corners of their eyes.

"You'd better know what you're doing," the captain whispered from the edge of his mouth.

Nightfall kept his reply equally below the level of the guards' hearing. "You're the one who insisted on accompanying me."

The captain made a soft hiss, covered by the sound of the doors bursting open. A twitchy, rat-faced noble in damp silks left the courtroom, escorted by two guards who looked enough like the ones at the doors to stand as twins. No longer statues, the sentries gestured for Nightfall and the captain to accompany them inside.

As Nightfall marched down the purple carpetway, he chased off the memories assailing him. He was Balshaz, and the finery of the court was a new experience that should evoke only curiosity. He had nothing to fear here. He glanced casually through the audience of nobles on the benches, which seemed as numerous as the crowd that had attended Sudian's first and only day on the throne. He wondered why so many of highborn lineage had suddenly become interested in affairs of court, and suspected it had something to do with the looming civil war. He recognized all of the other four members of the High Council in the front row and also managed to spy Kelryn, one of only a scant handful of women present. Her beauty drew his gaze, like the relentless obsession of a moth to flame; but he forced himself to give her nothing but a casual, searching glance.

On the dais, Lord Admiral Nikolei Neerchus dwarfed adviser Khanwar, who held the chancellor's seat. Nightfall's eyes narrowed at the sight of the dark and slender man who had belittled his own short time as ruling chancellor, and had shoved Kelryn and nearly lost his life for it. The other two men who had assisted Nightfall during his time in court occupied lesser places: Charson behind and to the admiral's left, Vivarick on the floor in Khanwar's old position. Guards lined the periphery, dressed in their usual colors over obvious mail. Nightfall was glad to see Volkmier among them, his prison

colors looking faded amid the sharper purples and silvers of the regular guard. He looked older to Nightfall,
as if he had gained years in the weeks since Sudian's escape. Yet he stood with proper decorum, his head high
and his expression properly schooled.

King Edward's finest fit Nikolei admirably, both men
massive examples of Alyndarian manhood; yet it bothered Nightfall to see this imposter sit so comfortably in
the king's chair and wardrobe.

Nightfall noticed all this in the daylight floating
through the high windows as he and the captain walked
down the carpeted aisleway in silence, their escort
clomping along beside them. In comparison, they both
appeared as light and graceful as women, and Nightfall
stopped the proper distance from the dais, taking the
captain's hand to bring him to a halt as well. He could
feel a callused, deeply lined palm through the elegant
fabric of the glove. Beside him, his companion stiffened
at the touch.

Nightfall made a deep bow, without the formal flourishes he had only seen and never executed. The captain
made an awkward curtsy. Though he knew the proper
formality from his early years, he had surely concentrated on the more manly gestures of respect.

The admiral studied the pair. "Name yourselves,
strangers."

Nightfall bowed again. "Sire, I am the merchant Balshaz, and this—"

The admiral interrupted, his gaze intent on the captain. "You're quite beautiful, young lady."

The captain executed a second curtsy.

"Might I know your name as well?"

Nightfall glanced fretfully at his silent companion,
then remembered he had insisted on doing all of the
talking. "Her name is Zenia, my lord."

Nikolei frowned. "I asked the lady," he said in cold
warning. The audience fell into a tense hush.

Nightfall bowed lower. "With all due respect, Sire, she

won't answer you. She's—" He wanted to say "mute," but that seemed like a bad strategy. Not only would he have to give a reason for such an odd defect, but several people had heard the captain speak on the streets and in the inn. "—paid me to do all her talking for her. You see, she has little knowledge or understanding of nobility, so she worries she might mistakenly insult someone. And she feels I should earn the money she paid me."

The admiral frowned. "Does she know it is exceptionally rude to ignore the direct address of a superior?"

When the captain remained quiet, lips stoically pinched, Nightfall sighed. "The ways of the highborn are mysteries to most commoners."

"Yes, well. I could stop my court until she deigns to speak."

Nightfall whispered to the captain, "What the hell are you trying to do to me?"

"I'm only following your orders," the captain hissed back.

Nightfall had not anticipated a stubborn match of will but supposed he deserved it. He was suffering the payback for snapping orders at the captain in front of his men and for his "pirate" exchange with the guard. "Yes, Sire, of course you could. But, in my experience, it's easier to defeat the sun, moon, and stars than win a war of wills with a lady. We may stand in stalemate for days."

"So we may." The admiral laughed, and the courtiers seemed to loose a collective breath. "Very well, then. You may perform the job for which she's paying you." He leaned forward, elbow on his thigh, chin resting on his palm. "What is it the Lady Zenia asks of me with the tongue of a merchant?"

Nightfall appreciated the return of the court to business. "She believes herself related to a man currently residing in your dungeon. She would like to check on his condition, assure herself of his relatedness, and, if appropriate, pay any fine or reckoning due for him."

Nikolei nodded at the simple request. "It seems

doubtful such a handsome woman could have scoundrels for relations."

Nightfall ignored the irony. "Every family tree has rotten limbs, Sire."

The captain elbowed Nightfall. "Not funny."

"Alas, that's true." Admiral Nikolei Neerchus glanced around his court. "And who is this lady's unfortunate miscreant?"

Nightfall chose the name of a thief he knew would spend considerable time imprisoned. "His name is Horrat, Sire. Is he here?"

The admiral frowned, the lines deeply chiseled into his rugged face. He glanced at the chief of the prison guards.

Volkmier nodded curtly.

The admiral turned back to his visitors. "Incarcerated here, yes. What does the lady wish to know of him?"

Nightfall considered his next words, needing to maneuver people into the proper positions without appearing to do so. "She wishes to see and speak with him, Your Majesty."

The captain whispered through clenched teeth. "No, I don't."

Nightfall ignored him. "To ascertain that he is, indeed, kin and to ask his opinion on his treatment."

"Do you think me an idiot?" The captain's breathing quickened, though he still kept his voice pitched as low as possible. "I'm not walking into any dungeon."

"I am," Nightfall whispered back, not liking the prospect much better than his companion. "And you're going with me."

"Make me."

Nightfall wanted to throttle the captain. Clearly, the displaced noble had experience carrying on subvocal conversations in the middle of court, but Nightfall found it dangerously distracting. "If you spoil my plan now, we're both dead."

The captain sounded more intrigued than intimidated. "How so?"

The admiral's voice seemed loud as thunder over the whispered exchange. "What is she saying to you, merchant?"

Nightfall immediately threw his attention back to the man on the dais, seeking a way to bend the situation to his advantage. "I'm sorry for the interruption, Sire. Apparently, Zenia knows someone living in Alyndar Castle who may also bear relation to Horrat. I'm trying to explain to her it's not necessary to bring up such a matter. It might embarrass the other person, and it won't gain us any special favors." Nightfall braced himself, hoping curiosity would prove more powerful than his own argument against revealing the name.

The admiral walked neatly into his trap. "Well, I see no harm in indulging the lady. As you said, every family tree has rotten branches. Who is this kin to a thief?"

Nightfall tried to sound uncomfortable about revealing a dirty secret. "Her name is Kelryn."

"How so?" the captain demanded again, as if the conversation between the admiral and his companion had never occurred.

Forced to address the captain, Nightfall did so quickly and faintly, "Trust me."

The captain muttered, "The two most dangerous words in any human language."

"Lady Kelryn?" the admiral repeated.

Nightfall shifted gears again. Bouncing between two conversations, he worried to make a fatal mistake in either. "I believe she has an uncle, named Skerrit, with an illegitimate son who is cousin to both my lady and Horrat." He chose the name of a real person, the brother of Kelryn's father. He could not afford the possibility that Kelryn might refuse to join them.

All eyes fell on Kelryn, who blushed so deeply her skin made a startling contrast to her snow-colored hair. "I do have an uncle by that name," she admitted. "I don't know anything about an illegitimate son, but I'm certainly willing to talk to Lady Zenia and Horrat about the possibility."

"I am *not* just going to trust you," the captain whispered.

Nightfall had enough to orchestrate without dealing with the captain's understandable, but exasperating, wariness. "Fine. Then you explain to the Navy Admiral of Alyndar why we traveled across the sea to lie to him."

"I will."

"And lose the only chance to examine Alyndar's dungeon from outside a cell?"

Despite his threat, the captain of the *Seaworthy* remained silent.

The admiral cleared his throat. "Your lady is still concerned about something?"

Again, Nightfall seized the opportunity. "Yes, Sire. She's worried about being a lady amongst . . ." He could not think of a proper term, ". . . dungeon folk."

Nikolei addressed the captain directly, his tone gentle. "You need not worry, my dear. The bad men are safely locked behind bars, and we have guards to keep you safe."

Not finished with his job, Nightfall continued, "Begging your pardon, Sire, but she's concerned that dungeon guards tend to be lonely men, too."

Laughter tittered through the courtroom.

Even the admiral smiled.

Volkmier's voice wafted over the laughter, without a hint of humor. His men, after all, were the butt of the joke. "May I speak, please, Admiral?"

Still grinning, Nikolei made a gesture of assent.

Volkmier bowed. "I could escort Lady Zenia personally, if you can spare me. I will keep the ladies and the . . ." He clearly struggled for the proper adjective. Down-to-earth warriors tended to see soft-handed merchants as effeminate. ". . . frailish gentleman safe from anything worrying them."

Nightfall watched his idea fall neatly into place. The

massive admiral surely felt safe enough with only the eleven elite guardsmen who would remain.

"Very well." The admiral waved his hands for Volkmier to join the guard escort that led Nightfall and the captain from the court.

The familiar odors of Alyndar's dungeon made Nightfall queasy. He breathed through his mouth, avoiding the overwhelming stench that seemed not to bother Volkmier at all. The commander brought them easily around the guards situated at various doors and openings, all of whom stepped aside diligently but continued to study the odd mixture of visitors long after they had passed. Nightfall tried to get close to Kelryn but found himself stymied by her persistent efforts to calm the obviously agitated captain.

Finally, Nightfall could stand it no longer. He hissed into the captain's ear, "If you don't let me near her, I'll never get done."

The captain whispered back, "I'm not making conversation with the commander of Alyndar's prison guards."

Nightfall did not have patience for more nonsense. "I need to talk to Kelryn. If you can't think of a way to distract him, I'll have to come up with one."

Suddenly, Nightfall had the captain's full attention. "Are you threatening me?"

He was, but Nightfall knew better than to say so. "Look, just talk to the prisoner as if you think he's kin. If you 'discover' he's not, just say you made a mistake."

"Believe me, I know how to fudge things."

"So do it, already. And get out of my way." Nightfall softened the request, a hand straying to his battered cheek. "Please."

"I'll have my revenge for this," the captain muttered as he stepped ahead to allow Nightfall access to Kelryn.

I know you will. Nightfall measured his steps to the proper casualness, resisting the urge to rush to Kelryn's side and seem inappropriately eager. It felt odd to care about someone besides himself. Love was dangerous; it had ensnared even him. And, eventually, he felt certain, it would kill him.

Volkmier paused to unlock a barred door spanning the craggy, damp corridor. Nightfall leaned toward Kelryn. "Marak," he whispered.

Kelryn stiffened. She looked up at him. "Ex–excuse me?"

"Marak," he dutifully repeated, though he knew she wanted more. The dimness of the torch-lit dungeon stole the green from her eyes. He took her hand, squeezing it reassuringly. Need made him long to gather her into his arms, but he resisted. Too many lives lay at stake. He dared not put Volkmier in the position of knowing his real identity again, of discovering the captain's. He had planned to tell Kelryn the truth, but the words stuck in his throat. She had seen through Sudian, and he had given himself up as the nameless chambermaid. But this was Balshaz, a long-standing persona with a life, a personality, a past. Every instinct screamed at him to protect the pock-faced merchant.

When no one moved, Volkmier pushed open the door with a squeal of hinges and gestured them through it. "Horrat's right here."

Nightfall glanced over to see the scrawny thief watching them from a cell down the line from the barred iron door that no longer blocked the corridor but now lay pressed against the uneven wall. The captain did not move.

Nightfall understood at once. The door Volkmier had opened served only as a second defense against a prisoner escape, but anyone who walked through it could become trapped behind a locked, barred door. He released Kelryn's hand before speaking. "Commander, Zenia got locked in a wardrobe once, for hours, as a child. She has an intense fear of closed places."

Volkmier glanced at the captain, who nodded.

"If we could leave this gate open while we're here . . . ?"

Volkmier frowned, eyes narrowing. Clearly, he mentally examined every reason why someone might make such a request, including the possibility of setting up a specific or general jailbreak.

Kelryn stepped in to reassure the chief of the prison guards. "It's all right, Volkmier. Balshaz is a friend of Alyndar."

Volkmier's quick blue eyes went to Kelryn, and he nodded. "Very well. If you please." He indicated that entrance again, gaze finding each of them in turn.

Nightfall knew the *Seaworthy*'s captain would not set foot beyond the gate without more reassurance, so he went first, trying to look wholly unconcerned, with Kelryn at his side. The act proved more difficult than Nightfall expected. The presence of that lockable portal unnerved him enough to interfere with his concentration. The prison guard's commander came next, reaching out a steadying hand to the captain, who looked positively ill.

Impatient beyond propriety, Kelryn seized Nightfall's hand and dragged him a safe distance from the others' conversation. "Tell me about Marak."

"He's . . . fine," Nightfall said, wondering if she would see through this disguise. He had always worried that his eyes would give him away. He could change their shape, hold them differently, but he could do nothing about their color. They were blue, but not the nearly white sea-foam hue that made the captain's so striking, nor the color of sunlit sky like Volkmier's. His were murkier, nearly black, and became inscrutable in shadow. He had never met another person with eyes like his and had feared their uniqueness would one day prove his downfall.

Nightfall's disguises drew attention from his eyes with protruding brows, a squint, or facial scars that attracted the gaze. Most people passed off his eyes as common, remembering only their darkness. On Night-fall, though, men called them demon's eyes, as sinister as night and as depthless as hell. He recalled the nursery rhyme that had haunted children's nightmares for ages, a warning to behave and not to wander the world at night: "Eyes darker than the midnight shade ..." Kelryn loved those eyes, saw none of the terror attributed to him, and through them she had recognized him once before. He would not lie to her. "Kelryn, it's me."

"Marak?" She stared, trying to find some hint of the man she loved in this otherwise opaque disguise. As he expected, she went right for the eyes, but the shadows of the dungeon made her job nearly impossible. "Is it really ...?"

"It is," Nightfall promised, glancing at the captain in front of Horrat's cell. He did not know how much cooperation he would get and knew his time was severely limited. "Have you learned anything I can use?"

"You have a month."

The words made no sense to Nightfall. "What?"

Kelryn took a few nervous steps, unwittingly displaying the perfect grace that always captivated him. He wanted to seize her in his arms and take her here, in full view of everyone, despite the gravity of the situation. "In a month, they will declare Edward officially dead. Then ..." She swallowed hard.

"The wars begin?" Nightfall guessed.

Kelryn bobbed her head, disturbing the gentle feathers of her hair. She looked close to tears.

"Who ..." He tried to think of the best way to phrase the question. "... wants the job?"

Kelryn pursed her lips before answering. "At least three of the High Council, I think. Word among the commoners is we'll be ruled by Simont Basilaered, since he has the power of the army behind him. But some think the navy has just as much brawn, in addition to controlling the seas." She gave him a pinched look of distress, either searching for his input or beseeching him to do something to offset the coming violence. "There's also quite a bit of money exchanging hands. I've tried, really I have, but I just can't follow it."

Nightfall knew the guards, especially the commanders, had likely become highly popular for bribes. He glanced over at Volkmier and the captain. Both met his gaze, clearly finished with their business. *Damn!* Nightfall had so much more he wanted to know and more information he had to impart. He could scarcely believe he had come so far for so little. He had just assumed he would find a way to talk to Kelryn for a reasonable length of time.

The captain spoke first, in his lilting falsetto, warning Nightfall of their approach. "It's not him, Balshaz. He's not related at all."

Nightfall continued the charade, "I'm sorry, Zenia. Very sorry. We always knew it was a possibility."

Still playing his part, the captain huddled into Nightfall's arms.

Kelryn's face seemed to collapse into itself in clear chagrin.

Around the captain, Nightfall gave his fiancée a look of resigned forbearance. He put his arms around the false-woman as social necessity demanded, but he kept his hands free in a wide-fingered gesture intended to convey that he was not enjoying their embrace.

Volkmier glanced between the three of them, eyes narrowed in clear consideration. When he spoke, he did not use the booming tone of command that had heralded Nightfall's previous captures. "If you women would excuse us, I'd like to speak with the merchant alone."

Nightfall's heart pounded. Though he had deliberately maneuvered the situation to have the commander of the prison guards present, he had not yet figured out the best way to use their relationship. Giving away his disguise to Kelryn had seemed necessary. Doing so to Volkmier meant killing off another persona, the only one that gave him access to nobler circles. Though the

prison guard had freed him once, he might not do so
again. At the moment, though, he found no way to refuse Volkmier's request, even if he wished to do so.

The captain clearly felt otherwise. "Anything you can
say to Balshaz, you can say to me as well. Right, honey
bun?" He swung around to Nightfall's side in a coquet-
tish pirouette, taking his hand.

Kelryn's jaw set.

Nightfall winced, his position tenuous. The captain
could not allow him to speak in private with Volkmier,
worried it might endanger himself and his crew. Under
threat of treason, Volkmier did not dare to talk in front
of witnesses. And, Nightfall also realized, he was close
to losing his fiancée because of a man in a dress. He gritted his teeth. Though secrets had served him all his life,
he currently faced a clash of them so spectacular they
placed him in an unwinnable situation.

For a moment, the four stared at one another in a silence punctuated by the scrape of a chain, the rattle of
a bar, the low moan of a prisoner.

Finally, Nightfall broke the hush. Though barely
above a whisper, his voice seemed suddenly loud. "Of
course I'll speak with you in private, sir." He gave Volkmier a slight but respectful bow. "If you would excuse
Zenia and myself for a short time first."

Volkmier made a throwaway gesture to indicate the
two should find a comfortable place to talk.

Nightfall led the captain back out of the corridor-
spanning gate and up against a craggy wall. He opened
his mouth, but the captain spoke first.

"You're not talking to a prison guard, especially that
one, without me."

Nightfall had no other choice that would not either
leave Volkmier too vulnerable to talk or destroy his
whole purpose for coming. "Look, there are problems
here that make yours look trivial."

The captain's grip on Nightfall's hand tightened

painfully. "Trivial to you, maybe. But my life, and those of my crew, hold great significance to me."

Nightfall jerked his hand free. "I'm not going to talk about you, or them, with Volkmier." He kneaded his aching fingers with his other hand.

"You're right, you're not." Clear threat entered the captain's tone. "Because I'm going to stay by your side and make sure it doesn't happen."

Nightfall fairly pranced with frustration. As Nightfall, he would never have had to deal with such foolishness. The demon had cowed men more powerful, far more evil, than the pirate captain of the *Seaworthy*. He was tired of playing politics, driven to madness by the need to balance the needs and feelings of others. It was all he could do not to strip off his costume and the role of negotiator, slaughtering his way to Edward and never caring for the lives of those who dared to cross his path. "I'm not going to betray you. You're just going to have to trust me."

"No."

"I need to talk to Volkmier for reasons I can't share."

"No!"

"My only other choice is to reveal you where you stand."

The captain's hands balled to massive fists, and he drew back.

Nightfall forestalled the attack. "Or you can just reveal yourself by pounding me into the next kingdom. That wouldn't be ladylike."

As if suddenly realizing the ramifications, the captain uncurled his fingers. "You bastard."

"No," Nightfall corrected, "an honest merchant trusted with a lot of secrets . . . and capable of keeping all of them." He gave the captain an earnest look he hoped would underscore his point. "I will protect yours with all the caution I'm using for theirs." He jabbed a thumb toward Kelryn and Volkmier. "But if you force me to compromise their caution, I'll have to strip you of all your rights to yours as well."

"What secrets could the commander of the prison guards have?"

Nightfall arched his brows. "To tell you that would be to reveal them."

"And you?"

"I have mine, too."

"And Kelryn?"

"The world is full of secrets."

The captain fell silent. They had reached a clear stalemate. "I'm . . . not good at trusting others."

Nightfall understood that sentiment all too well. "You can't afford to be." He paused. In the captain's place, he would not allow the conference to happen either. He had placed the other man in an impossible position, one that seemed likely to end horribly. Stripped of all control and dignity, a man as accustomed to both as Captain Celdurant would never compromise. Nightfall knew of only one way to even the score; he had to give the captain a weapon as powerful as his own. "Captain, it's time I told you. I know so much about . . ." He could not help dropping his voice still further, so the captain had to stand nearly on top of him to hear. ". . . Sudian because I am . . . Sudian."

The captain stiffened, staring at his companion with an intensity that threatened to flay him to his very core.

"I'm hell-bound and determined to prove my innocence, even if it means consorting with the very people who would gleefully tear me apart just for knowing my name." Nightfall gave the captain a study as severe as the one he was receiving. "If I sell you out, you can do the same to me. If you sell me out . . ." He met the captain's eyes directly, unleashing all of the lethal might of his demon namesake. ". . . you had best hope they kill me." Without waiting to see the effect his words had on the captain, he strode back toward Kelryn and Volkmier. To his relief, the captain did not follow.

"I told him," Kelryn announced the moment Nightfall arrived. No doubt, she referred to his identity.

Nightfall turned his attention to Volkmier.

If Nightfall was about to die, Volkmier did not show it. The squat, densely muscled redhead studied him mildly from beneath a crinkled brow. "Is it true?"

Nightfall had not intended to reveal himself, but he trusted Kelryn enough to believe she had a reason for doing so. "Kelryn would not lie."

"Why did you come back?" Though pitched low to keep the prisoners from hearing, Volkmier's question still carried clear accusation. Nightfall thought he understood. His presence and Kelryn's confession placed the guard in a position as awkward as the captain's had been. Not wanting to admit that most of the reason for his premature return had to do with concern about how Volkmier might handle confronting the traitor, he shifted the focus of his interest. "I have information, and I hoped you did, too." He hurried on, to ascertain that he received before he had to give. "I've heard you're close to civil war."

Volkmier nodded grimly. "Many a man would like to place his own ass permanently upon the king's throne."

"How many?"

"There are at least seven serious possibilities. Each one has offered me a generous sum to take his side." He snorted. "I've received several other proposals, all anonymous; but I don't know whether these represent secret contenders or are just more of the same, testing or hoping." Volkmier sighed. "I have become the most popular man in Alyndar."

Nightfall pursed his lips, feeling the guard's scrutiny upon him, as well as the captain's, though the latter was at a distance. Both sought signs of Sudian in the larger, homelier merchant. "Who are you supporting?"

Volkmier turned his gaze directly upon Nightfall's eyes with a slow movement indicative of withering disdain. "I'm in the employ of King Edward Nargol until someone proves to me he's dead. Otherwise, I serve whoever is placed and accepted upon the throne. My loyalty is to Alyndar herself." His head drooped, his expression turned hopeful, and his voice lost its brave resonance. "Please tell me King Edward will return."

"I'm doing my best." Nightfall tried for a tone as sincere and pure as Volkmier's, with little success. It came out more defensive. "But I've had to overcome a lot of obstacles, and I'm still facing mountains. If only Nightfall—"

"No!" Kelryn hissed.

Both men swung toward her.

"Nightfall is dead."

Ice prickled through Nightfall. "Well, yes. I'm not talking about committing any crimes," he hastily assured both of them, an assertion he would not, however, hesitate to break if he deemed it necessary. "I just need to tap some sources—"

"No!"

Volkmier placed his hands flat in an urgent plea for Kelryn to lower her voice. He took Nightfall's side. "If it brings back the real king, how can it be bad to—"

Kelryn had an answer before he could finish. "Because, Commander, once Nightfall returns, Sudian dies. And he *promised* he would bring Sudian safely home, as well as the king."

Nightfall tipped his head, unable to follow Kelryn's reasoning. Suddenly, the wording he had not understood while disguised as a chambermaid in Kelryn's room seemed infinitely significant. *Bring back Ned,* she had said. *And also . . . Sudian.* "Sudian won't die just because—"

Kelryn's eyes blurred to emerald pools. "Yes," she said in a calm voice that clashed with her tears. "I know you. Better than you know you." She shook her head, in clear pain. "First of all, you swore to Ned that Nightfall would never return."

Nightfall had not forgotten. It was his promise to the

king that had held him back thus far, not the vague one he had made to Kelryn that he had not really understood.

Volkmier jerked backward. "Edward *knew*?"

Nightfall bobbed his head, hating the memories that accompanied the admission. "Gilleran told him. It was a trick to demoralize him so he wouldn't fight, and the chancellor could slaughter him as easily as he had Edward's father and brother."

Volkmier considered in silence a moment before speaking. "It worked, didn't it?"

"Edward didn't fight," Nightfall admitted, a dark smile forming on his lips. "But I did."

"You saved the king's life."

Nightfall could not deny what had become common knowledge.

"And Alyndar has rewarded you with a sentence of death and a manhunt the like of which has not been seen since . . ." Even Volkmier had to grin. ". . . since we went after Nightfall."

"Fairly defines irony, doesn't it?"

Kelryn cleared her throat loudly. "My point is, you made a promise."

Volkmier tried to reason with her. "Don't you think the king would understand the need to make sacrifices to save his life and the kingdom?"

To Nightfall's relief, Kelryn turned her stony gaze, still teary, on Volkmier. "Edward would sacrifice his life rather than break his word. You both know he would never agree to let someone become a criminal to rescue him. Never."

Though foolish, it was true; and neither man could deny it.

"Nightfall is no mere act to this man." Kelryn waved a hand in Nightfall's general direction, as if he had become nothing more than a spectator to the discussion. "I've given my love, Dyfrin dedicated a lifetime, Edward poured his heart and soul into the creation of Sudian. If he goes back . . ." She slumped, looking miserable, but her stare remained locked with Volkmier's. ". . . he will never return." She took a step toward the prison guard. "And you will know you revived the assassin who haunted every kingdom."

Volkmier wheeled away from Kelryn, looking peeved.

Nightfall knew he had to speak for himself. "Give me some credit for self-control, Kelryn. I can handle this."

"No."

Nightfall froze. He had expected her to listen or to argue, not to disagree. "No?"

"No." Kelryn explained herself, whirling on him. Once again, Nightfall met the deep green eyes he loved, and they granted him no quarter. "You need to give me some credit. For intuition and perception. There are things women understand better than men. First among them: men." She raised her chin, revealing the features that defined striking beauty for Nightfall, no matter how imperfect. "Nightfall cannot live again. You have to swear it, my love."

Now, it was Nightfall's turn to surprise her. "No." He had never denied her anything before. "I can't, Kelryn. I'm already crippled by circumstance and hobbled by vows." His past beckoned: a time when he relied on no one but himself, knew nothing of mercy, and savored an absolute freedom he now sorely missed. "No matter how right, no matter how fair, no matter if I'm already bound by a similar vow to another, I cannot agree to anything."

Kelryn said nothing.

Nightfall gathered Kelryn in his arms. She felt wooden against him, frail and desperately fragile. "You have to stay strong, Kelryn. You have to believe."

"Believe in what?" she said bitterly. "The gods? Chance? Neither has ever favored such as us."

"Then," said Nightfall into her cheek, "believe in my promise to Ned. It seems the same as yours. Believe . . .

in me." He was not sure why he said it; he could not have followed his own advice. He had spent weeks tracking Edward, uncovering nothing but a vague rumor from a child that the king might have been initially taken to Hartrin. *What difference does it make if I promise Kelryn not to do something I've already committed myself against?* Still, Nightfall could not bring himself to say the words. He dared not chance that Kelryn had hidden some deep meaning behind something that seemed quite simple, as she had once before. He could not afford to add a blindfold to his shackles. "Kelryn, I love you."

Kelryn sighed. "Then why," she whispered, "are you cuddling with another woman?"

The words seemed so outlandish Nightfall could not, at once, put sense to them. He disentangled himself from Kelryn, following her gaze to the captain, who paced the corridor, his impatience clear. Nightfall laughed. "You have nothing to fear from Zenia."

"She seems to feel otherwise."

Nightfall spoke directly into Kelryn's ear, so even Volkmier could not hear him. "She is a he."

Kelryn's eyes grew wide, and a lost tear dripped free. "Really?"

"Really," Volkmier said, and they both whirled to face him. There was no way he could have heard what Nightfall had said. The commander tipped his head. "That's a man, or I'm a woman."

"How . . . ?" Kelryn started.

"Movement," Volkmier said. He gave Nightfall a significant look. "Gives everyone away."

Nightfall shivered. "Is that why Kelryn told you who I was? Because you already knew?"

Volkmier hesitated, as if he might lie, then shook his head. "I knew something was going on. You maneuvered deftly enough, but I have information the rest of the court doesn't share. You're the only one who would want her and me together, somewhere where we can't be overheard. Add the man in woman's clothing, and it becomes clear that things need . . . some clarification." He glanced at the captain. "I bought a scarf from Balshaz before. Clever of you to dress as a real person, though it could fail dangerously if the two of you showed up in the same place or you met someone with whom he shares a secret or a passion. I just assumed you had hired Balshaz as a messenger. You've got his mannerisms down. Fooled me, and that's not easy."

Nightfall thought it better not to explain.

"Of course, if you'd had to escape the guards for some reason, I'd have known you in an instant."

Nightfall did not doubt it. "It's no wonder you're so popular, Commander. Loyalty, competence, and intelligence are difficult to find in one man."

Volkmier snorted. "Anyone who knew I was aiding you might find me lacking in two of those areas. Especially intelligence. But I'm afraid my personal strengths have little to do with why all of the contenders for the throne want me."

Nightfall waited for the true explanation.

Volkmier did not immediately give it, apparently believing the answer obvious. Then, catching the quizzical looks on his companions' faces, he elucidated. "In a war against another country, a man could do no better than the king's army and navy. But when the war is internal, one wants men used to battling wily prisoners in dark corners hampered by jagged corridors and staircases and mindful of one's own comrades." He shrugged. "That's why the commander of the prison guards also has authority over the elite circle: the king's own bodyguards and the sentries of the royal court."

Nightfall had learned a detail of life in the castle he would never have guessed. "Thank you." He wanted to make it clear his appreciation extended far beyond this newest piece of information. "For not killing me. For your loyalty to Edward. For all your assistance."

Volkmier reached for Nightfall's arm.

Though seized with the instinctive urge to dodge, Nightfall forced himself to remain still.

The brawny hand closed around him, firm and solid. "Just bring Alyndar's king back alive."

"I'm trying."

Volkmier leaned closer. "I will do anything in my power to see that any crime you commit to save him gets pardoned." He let go. "Beyond that, you're on your own."

Nightfall understood the veiled threat behind that promise. In his own way, Volkmier had just sanctioned him to use any means necessary to rescue Edward, no matter how illegal, dirty, or underhanded. However, Volkmier had also taken heed of Kelryn's warning that, once loosed, Nightfall would fall inevitably back into the methods of his past, inexorably under the power of the demon.

In the leaden moments that followed Volkmier's pronouncement, Nightfall brought the conversation abruptly to the point that concerned him most, the one that had prompted his return to Alyndar when a run to Hartrin had seemed wiser. He kept the initial query casual. "Have you had any success finding the traitor?"

Volkmier's expression went even more somber, if possible. "We know the adviser, Khanwar, commandeered a courier dove shortly after the meeting, which he sent on a 'diplomatic mission' to Hartrin."

Hartrin. Nightfall's hopes soared. It seemed to confirm Danyal's investigation, and he could think of no one he would rather see executed for treason than the sneering adviser who had shoved Kelryn.

"And he's already formed a friendship with Admiral Nikolei which seems mostly based on a mutual hatred of . . . you." Volkmier heaved a sigh. "I'm guessing Khanwar is manipulating Nikolei after the fact. I can't believe the admiral would knowingly participate in any plan resulting in the deaths of some of Alyndar's best fighting men."

Nightfall made a thoughtful noise but offered no judgment on the matter. He could only go on gut feeling; and, right now, he knew nothing but contempt for every member of the High Council, including the admiral. "I fully trust you to handle the situation. All I ask is that you do the same for me."

Volkmier rolled his eyes upward as he contemplated Nightfall's words. Kelryn glanced between them.

Rescuing his words from misinterpretation, Nightfall explained them, "I'm just asking that you not reveal my destination, or the traitor, until I bring Ned home safely. Otherwise, I'm afraid we might spark a war, and Ned's captors might dispose of him to make it look as if they never had him."

"You have a month. Once the king is proclaimed dead, I will do whatever I must to keep peace in Alyndar."

Nightfall knew better than to argue for more time. He would not get it, nor should he need it. "One more thing, Commander."

Volkmier nodded warily, the movement barely dislodging a few strands of his short-cut red hair.

"Soon, you'll be getting a visit from Lifthranian sailors."

Volkmier's blue eyes widened, then narrowed just as quickly. "*Lifthranian* sailors? Isn't that a contradiction?"

Nightfall did not explain. To do so might compromise the captain's security. "Nevertheless, you will. Can you help see to it they get the following information?"

Volkmier waited, his expression locked, his mouth shut.

Uncertain whether to feel encouraged, Nightfall continued. "The *Seaworthy* is captained by Balshaz the merchant. Though he did not bring a lot of goods, he sold them at a reasonable price, and he had other business. He escorted a beautiful young lady to the court."

"So far, that logically fits everything you've done. I think all of it will come out without my assistance."

Nightfall nodded. "That's what I'm hoping. But with the rotating king substitutes . . ."

Volkmier seemed relieved the request did not violate anything that appeared truthful. "You brought her down to visit a prisoner relative who turned out not to be who she thought. She left a bit ruffled and irritated but paid you anyway."

"Exactly."

"All right." Volkmier agreed to the terms, though a frown deeply scored his features. "Do I need to know why sailing Lifthranians are chasing you?"

"No."

"Good." Volkmier's scowl lessened. "Now, the two of you look like you could use some time alone. I'm going to keep your . . . beautiful woman company."

Nightfall stiffened. The captain would not like this turn of affairs. "Please don't scare *her*."

"I'll be a perfect gentleman," Volkmier promised, and Nightfall knew he would. To do otherwise might demonstrate his complicity. The commander had no way of knowing whether any secret would remain safe with this stranger.

The moment Volkmier stepped away, all of the desperation returned to Kelryn's face. "Marak," she whispered. "You have to make that promise. If you don't—"

Kelryn's distress cut through Nightfall like a knife. He could not listen to another word, so he silenced her with a kiss, gathering her into his arms and drawing her as close as humanly possible. He explored her mouth, wishing he could place his lips on every part of her, from the top of her white-maned head to the tips of her dainty toes. Her tongue skipped through his mouth, tasting of honey, as if looking for a place to finish the unspoken words. The unique smells of her, the feel of her silky hair through his fingers, the warmth of her body, raised a bonfire in his loins.

The knee she thrust into his groin quenched the flames with sudden icy pain. Nightfall staggered back-

ward, glad their closeness had stolen most of the force
of the blow. She slapped him, hard, across the injured
cheek, reawakening the pain of the captain's punch.
Stunned, he dropped to a crouch, staring at her.

"You're a horrible, forward man, Balshaz! How dare
you!"

Volkmier called to them around poorly suppressed
laughter. "Are you all right, my lady?"

"I'm fine," Kelryn said, with venom. "I'm still mourning my once-betrothed, and this . . . this vile . . . stranger
dares to put his lips on mine!"

"Kelryn," Nightfall managed to gasp, the agony in his
loins receding.

"You should be publicly flogged, you cad!" Kelryn
added in a whisper, "Sorry."

Nightfall understood. She had no way of knowing he
had told the captain about his other identity, and she
had a point about reacting properly in front of the prisoners. Though it seemed unlikely they would tell anyone what had happened, if one of the other guards
found out, it could look highly suspicious. "I–I'm sorry,
my lady. I . . . won't . . . do it again."

Volkmier called over, "Do you need me to come over
there and remove him?"

"I have it handled." Kelryn lowered her voice. "What
the hell is wrong with you?"

Nightfall cupped his aching cheek. "By the Almighty
Father, you didn't have to castrate me."

"I'd rather have you castrated than killed."

Nightfall was not sure any man would agree.

"You're taking too many chances. You have to be
more careful."

"I'm sorry I didn't foresee my beloved slamming my
privates through the back of my spine."

Kelryn glared. "That's not what I meant, and you
know it. To anyone watching, you're Balshaz, remember? Balshaz wouldn't grab some woman and rub himself all over her like a sex-starved billy goat."

Nightfall sighed. "You're so beautiful. How could any man resist?"

Her tone did not soften, but her expression did. "They all manage somehow. All of them, except you."

Luckily. Nightfall remembered how he used to make certain that any man who harmed or slighted her disappeared. "I love you. And this could be the last time I ever see you."

"Don't talk like that."

"Fine, I won't." The last of the pain ebbed mercifully away. "But that doesn't make it any less true."

Kelryn turned away. "You promised to bring Sudian back alive."

Nightfall found the loophole in an oath he should never have sworn. "And I did. I'm here."

Kelryn whirled to face him. "You know I meant at the end—"

Nightfall did not let her finish. "And you know that's not a promise any man can keep. Even without a brutal, frustrating, nearly hopeless quest, I can't be sure illness, a fall, a poorly aimed weapon, or a runaway horse won't take me down."

"Men like you don't die from accidents."

Kelryn's words carried a grain of truth. "That's only because we die of violence first."

Kelryn reached for his hands, caught herself, and stopped. "I love you so much. I just don't want to lose you."

"I know." It took all of Nightfall's will not to gather Kelryn into his arms once more. Right now, she needed his support, his protection. At the moment, he would give her anything.

"Sudian is who you are."

"Yes." With all the grime, all the cosmetics, all the pretenses stripped away, Sudian was what remained, what he surely would have become without the influence of his brutal mother and his even crueler years upon the streets. First Dyfrin, then Kelryn, then Edward had

shaved away the layers he hid behind to find a core he
would never have believed existed.

"Nightfall is dead," Kelryn said.

Nightfall closed his eyes and nodded.

"Promise me."

The words came out without a moment's need for
thought. "I promise," he said.

† Chapter 18 †

Royalty has no permanent friends, only permanent interests.

— Dyfrin of Keevain, the demon's friend

THE *Seaworthy* jounced, rocked, and sluiced through the Klaimer Ocean on a straight course from the Yortenese to the Xaxonese Peninsula. Sequestered in the fore of the captain's quarters, Nightfall spent most of his time brooding. His mood alternated between fits of anger and a deep grieving despair. For over a decade, he had played his many parts without mistake, never once revealing himself, by intent or accident. Each persona remained safely and eternally separate, living out his role in secretive safety. Now, in a few moments of desperation, he had sacrificed his favorite. The character of Balshaz granted him a mobility few of his other guises could, and a lifetime of honest trading had gained him legitimacy and loyalty in all corners of the world. Prior to King Rikard foisting Sudian upon him, whenever Nightfall had considered the possibility of escaping his notorious life, it had always been to become Balshaz forever.

The moment he had exposed Balshaz to Kelryn, then

to Volkmier and the ship's captain, he had doomed the persona. Then, he had believed he could trust them. Now, doubts descended upon him, and the idea that he could rely on anyone seemed foolish beyond comprehension. The best intentioned of friends could inadvertently reveal him, as Dyfrin had; and Nightfall knew Captain Celdurant and Commander Volkmier had other agendas. If it suited their purposes better, either might deliberately reveal him. Alliances formed and disbanded over time, and he had no idea what the future might hold for any of them. Better to count only on himself and never hand anyone the means to his destruction.

Several of the sailors tried to coax Nightfall back onto the deck, none more than the captain; yet he refused them all. Days filled with solemn thoughts passed into nights filled with equally dark dreams, but the realization of what he had done haunted him nearly as strongly as the promise Kelryn had extracted and his frantic concern for Edward. With each passing day, his chances of finding the king alive diminished. He could think of many places in Hartrin where he might uncover information, but every one required slithering into dangerous haunts, extracting the equivalent of codes and passwords, asking the right questions of the right people. Crippled by the need to keep a plausible identity, in this case that of Balshaz, Nightfall plotted his convoluted approaches with maddening frustration. A merchant known for integrity did not belong in any of Nightfall's holes.

The captain found Nightfall lying on his pallet staring at the bottom of the upper deck. For what seemed like the millionth time since they had left Alyndar, he tried to rouse Nightfall from his funk. "A beautiful day."

Nightfall simply grunted, not taking his eyes from the overhead planking, studying a caulk line.

"Of course, you can only enjoy the weather above deck."

Nightfall made another noncommittal noise.

The single chair creaked, alerting Nightfall the captain had sat rather than continuing beyond the curtain into his own quarters, as he usually did. "We should make landfall day after tomorrow. The port at Hartrin, as promised."

Nightfall already knew their destination. He supposed he ought to say something in gratitude, as the captain could have taken his ship anywhere and Nightfall could not have done much about it. "Thank you, Captain."

"And thank you. We no longer have seafaring Lifthranians attempting to corner us."

Hearing "seafaring" and "Lifthranians" in the same sentence still grated. Nightfall rolled over far enough to finally look at his companion.

Dressed in his standard silks, this time a fine blue that perfectly matched his sapphire jewelry, the captain struck the same dashing figure Nightfall had noticed the first time they met. He belonged in a royal court, not on the deck of a ship; yet his pale eyes held an intense love of the sea. The rock and toss of the *Seaworthy* seemed to bother him no more than it did Nightfall. Despite his fancy clothing and regal manner, he looked at home here. "Not that they've gone. They're still following us, just at a distance."

That was news to Nightfall, who had paid little attention to anything but his thoughts for more than a week of sea travel. "Waiting for the regular captain to reappear and retake command."

"Appears so." The gold-colored rag holding back his cascade of ebony hair clearly came from the same scrap of silk as the sash that bore his knife and sword. As pretty as the captain had appeared in women's garb, he looked even more stunningly handsome as a man. He turned Nightfall a hopeful look. "Sudian, when you leave . . ."

The captain trailed off into what became a long

pause. Certain the other man intended him to surmise the obvious, Nightfall forced his thoughts from his own plight to the captain's. Surely he, and his men, knew they had severely shortened their lives the day they decided to ply their trade as pirates. Of course, he had done the same and still lived. Fearing death and choosing to dodge it were not the same thing. Nightfall attempted to finish the sentence. "When Balshaz leaves, the *Seaworthy* will need a new captain." Realizing his words could mean more than one thing, he amended, "In the eyes of the Lifthranians."

"Any chance you could turn me into that new captain before you go?"

Nightfall shook his head. A radical change, such as gender, had fooled them once; but no one would believe a rowdy band of sailors would follow the command of a woman. Disguising height and build came more from the act than the makeup, and Celdurant would not have the experience to pull off the kind of subtlety and detail Nightfall once had on nearly a daily basis. He propped himself on one elbow. "I would think you would have better luck staying aboard and dressing up your most respected man as the new captain. Someone who doesn't resemble you at all. That way, you can bring about the illusion without having to maintain a disguise."

The captain stroked his strong chin thoughtfully.

"Leave word the old captain died." Nightfall sat up, swinging his legs over the side of the couch. "Something no one but your own men can confirm or deny." He smiled wickedly, "Tell them the former captain fell overboard in a drunken frenzy, terrified by pursuing ships from Lifthran."

The captain glared at Nightfall. "Do I have to die a coward?"

"I find people are more likely to believe news which pleases them."

The captain waved a dismissive hand. "I'll think of something better."

Nightfall felt certain he would. "Whatever you decide, make sure to tell me. It will add credence if a visiting merchant witnessed the death. Also, I'd rather whatever story I might have to tell fits yours. Did I engage the ship because I found it leaderless or because the captain died halfway through the voyage? Remember, too, you died after we met in Schiz; too many incapable of keeping quiet saw you there."

The captain studied Nightfall. "You speak like a man with a lot of experience."

Nightfall hid a shiver. He remembered eerily similar words from a magehunter in Schiz shortly before a child sorcerer revealed his birth talent. "Clearly, I have a bit. When one's life is at stake, one learns quickly." Nightfall hoped that would quash any tendency of the captain to ruminate over the thought.

"Indeed."

Once again, shared desperation brought them together. Nightfall waited for the captain to leave; but he remained in place, still running his fingers across his stubbly chin. "Now that I've gotten you to a sitting position, perhaps you'll stand?"

Nightfall knew he ought to stretch his legs, even if only to pace the floor of the quarters one more time. As a sailor, he had never had excess energy to expend; he had spent his every waking moment hauling, climbing, or clewing something. His exile, though voluntary and deliberate, left him feeling twitchy as a bilge rat. "I'll do you better." Nightfall sprang to his feet. "I'll see that weather you raved about when you first came down here."

"Great." The captain held open the cabin door. As Nightfall walked through he added, "When I said beautiful, I actually meant cloudy."

Nightfall laughed but continued toward the hatch.

"How very clever of you, Captain. Lure me on deck with a lie."

"Not a lie," Celdurant amended. "Portents aside, I'd venture to guess anyone would find even the darkest of squall clouds more pleasant than the ceiling of my cabin."

Nightfall had to admit that was true. Nevertheless, he stopped before they reached the ladder. "Captain, I think you should keep this." He proffered the purse of silver from his Alyndarian sales, leaving himself only a scant handful of dirty coppers and Edward's hidden ring.

The captain halted in mid step, staring at the offering but making no move to take it. "Your money?" He looked down at Nightfall, frowning. "Why?" He had a right to suspicion, especially after Nightfall had vigorously bartered free passage to Hartrin.

Nightfall had given the matter long thought earlier that day. "The places I'm going to need to go for information, it will hamper more than help me." He grinned, still dangling the purse. "If I'm going to lose it to thieves, I might as well pick which thieves."

The captain's brows shot upward. "I'm not sure we've ever been quite so nicely damned."

"And," Nightfall added, "I think your men will hate me less if they don't feel their last two ocean voyages were wholly in vain." Seven silvers did not compare to the vast fortunes they could rob from a well-stocked ship, but it would buy them all plenty of drinks in any Hartrinian tavern. Nightfall shook the pouch, tired of holding it.

Finally, the captain accepted. The purse disappeared beneath his silks. With a single, agile movement, he turned to face Nightfall with his weight solidly on both feet. "And I have something for you." Seizing Nightfall's hand, he dropped something into it, then closed his fingers around Nightfall's so the objects were not visible.

Nightfall assessed them by touch, discerning a

brooch and a freestanding, faceted stone. The instant the captain's hand left his, Nightfall opened his fist to reveal both the embedded and the free gems as sapphires. He jerked his attention back to the other man. "I . . . I can't accept these." He held them out, but the captain did not even glance at the fortune balanced on Nightfall's palm.

"You can," the captain said, his tone brooking no defiance. "And you will. Because the information you need will not come cheaply."

Nightfall laughed at the silliness of the exchange. "But you just completely undid me. I gave you all my silver because it will look suspicious for me to take refuge in dives when I'm carrying that much wealth. Also, what good is it for me to try to buy the goodwill of your men if you give me more treasure than I gave you?"

The captain addressed the last question first. "I'll divide the money you gave me among my men in fair shares. Those gems were mine, and mine alone, to do with as I please." He lowered his voice so anyone coming toward them could not hear. "Balshaz . . ."

Grateful the captain had not used the name Sudian as he had in the cabin, Nightfall nodded.

" . . . those blue rocks can barter for information silver just won't buy. Believe me; you'll need them." The captain's eyes held undeniable concern. He clearly worried that Nightfall was entering a world he could not handle.

Gripped by an irony and humor he dared not reveal, Nightfall only nodded. Plans formed in his mind, ones centering on the fortune he held; yet he still attempted to refuse it. "Captain, I'm truly grateful; but remember what I said about thieves? How long do you think I can hold onto things this valuable in slimy dens overflowing with thugs and roaches?"

"I don't know," the captain admitted, "but I'll let you in on a weird secret."

Nightfall listened raptly.

"I've let these gemstones out of my hands four times:
once in theft, thrice in payment." The captain reached
out and closed Nightfall's hand around the sapphires
again. "Each and every time, they found their way back
to me." He shook his head and rolled his gaze to the
upper deck, clearly contemplating memories of thefts
upon the open sea. "I'm starting to wonder whether to
worship them or fear them." He managed a lopsided
grin, though. "No matter what happens, they'll return.
And, if they help you along the way, what harm is
done?"

Nightfall finally secreted the gems beneath his merchant's silks. "What harm indeed?" He smiled back for
the first time in days. "Now, let's go see that beautiful,
cloudy day."

Nightfall spent most of his on-deck time saying all of
his good-byes so, when the ship finally pulled into Hartrin port, he left immediately with nothing undone.
Carrying only the clothes on his back, half a dozen coppers, Edward's ring, and the sapphires, he wound word-
lessly across the docks, avoiding slaves and hired
dockhands. They barely spared him a glance either,
caught up in the extra work that came from having a
major port across the ocean nearly out of commission.
Many of the goods that would have gone to Alyndar
now came here, and the extra effort left the workers
gleaming with sweat, their tempers frayed, and their
words harsher and more biting than usual. Collars and
sagging, rather than feisty, demeanors differentiated
the slaves from the paid workers. An occasional whip
whistled through the air to warn them against slacking,
and Nightfall dodged around these with wary caution.
If one struck him accidentally, he knew he would not
react well.

They had arrived in broad daylight, the sun high and
bright, the clouds burned to rare white wisps. Still play-

ing his merchant role, Nightfall placed a hand on his brow to shade his vision. He had to concentrate to keep his legs from naturally taking him to the west side of town where the guards kept the world in proper order around the pricey shops and upscale inns. Instead, he turned southward, hoping he looked as reluctant as he felt. Balshaz did not belong here; and, when night crept over the mud-slogged alleys and crumbling buildings, he would know it only too well.

Nightfall had always hated Hartrin. None of his personae lived there regularly, and only Balshaz and Nightfall ventured into it at all. Even Sudian had never visited. In fact, he had struggled to keep the prince of Alyndar completely out of slave country during their voyage across most of the continent. Every whipcrack would have resulted in an international incident as Edward assaulted slavers and owners with his high ideals of morality, and one of those confrontations would surely have seen them both killed. Nightfall cared little for slavery; had his life turned out just a bit differently, he could easily have become one of those owned. Yet, he knew the solution was not as simple as King Edward believed.

Putting thoughts of slavery from his mind, Nightfall fell into the mental cadence that kept him alive on the streets. Without a glance in their direction, he knew who shared the alleys with him. He did not need the specifics of their identities. He could draw a pure and complete picture by the way they moved, by the positions they chose, by the intensity of their gazes and stances. He had reentered his world in the guise of an innocent stranger to it, and he sought a delicate balance that allowed him to display his uneasiness without goading the predators to attack.

The cobbled roads became mired gravel, then ended in dark, mucky paths scarred by sloppy footprints. Anything tossed into a Hartrinian gutter wound up in the southeastern part of the city. Including the people.

Drunkards flopped across every doorstep. Human shadows skulked through threadlike streets and alleyways, and rats scurried openly through the filth. Bony cats competed with the people for meals of scraps and vermin, and sometimes became dinner themselves. Nightfall had to concentrate on a cover that became evanescent to a mind focused on survival and need. Merchants did not lower themselves to marching boldly through the bleak, stinking corners of the world. Their lives did not usually depend on understanding the rhythms of city nights.

Nightfall passed several crumbling buildings abandoned by shopkeepers and men who had graduated to better parts of the city or found themselves branded as slaves. Each had a score of street people who slept there until someone bigger or more competent claimed their territory. Eyes watched his every movement, though no hunter left his cave to menace Nightfall. They measured him by his silks, by his walk, and by his size. Every one surely weighed the danger of robbing or assaulting him in broad daylight; and, to his relief, no one took the bait. The town guard still owned this place by day. By night, however, it became a decadent brawl.

Nightfall took the most direct path to the small, grubby inn at the farthest end of an unnamed street. He knew it well, a haven for poor travelers without the coinage for the safer places northward. There, he should be able to find a sleeping corner, shared with several other patrons, and a decent meal that would not leave him vomiting. The proprietor, Eldour, had connections to several underground groups, and he coordinated information and money well enough to keep his venture going while those around him failed or died. Beneath a trapdoor in the cellar lurked some of the nastiest criminals in the world engaged in everything from arranging murders, to hiding from the constabulary, to sales of illicit merchandise, including humans. Crossing Eldour sealed a man's death; too many relied upon his secret room for their business to allow anyone to place the proprietor of the unnamed inn in danger.

Boarded and chinked against the coming winter, the inn looked boxy and unwelcoming, aside from the thin plume of smoke drifting from its fireplace. A battered sign swung from a post pocked by knife slashes; only the center letter of the word "Inn" remained, its paint peeled and weathered. Nightfall opened the door and entered.

The common room looked much the same as always. The wooden walls held splotches and nicks from drunken mishaps and brawls. Stains in lavender and red-brown dappled the floor, a mixture of dragged-in filth, old wine, and spilled blood. Nine rickety tables filled most of the space, and a sturdy bar divided the serving area from the rest of the room. Behind it, Eldour looked up from cleaning a misshapen mug with a dingy rag, his lean, balding figure and sparse white beard unmistakable. Beyond him, a tattered curtain hung from an opening that Nightfall knew led into the kitchen. A set of poorly maintained steps just inside the front door rose to the sleeping quarters. Seven patrons sat at tables, one as a group of three and two as pairs. Nightfall recognized most of them as petty thieves and thugs.

Not bothering to study any of them, Nightfall walked across the sticky, uneven boards and flopped into the seat nearest the bar.

Eldour set down his mug, dropped the rag on top of it, and approached. "Good day, *uvna*." He used a word unique to the Xaxonese Peninsula, a neutral term low-borns used to address highborns of uncertain status. "What can I do for you?"

Nightfall heaved a sigh not wholly feigned, then spoke in Balshaz' voice. "How much for a week's room and board?"

"A week, *uvna*?" Eldour studied Nightfall through squinty, yellowish eyes. "Two coppers."

Though far less than the northside inns, it was twice the going rate here. Nightfall loosed a larger sigh and started to rise.

About to lose a customer, Eldour amended. "How's this sound, *uvna*? You tell me what brings you to lodging on the shady side of town, and I'll toss in an extra week, no charge."

Nightfall lowered himself back into his seat. "Deal. But bring me something to drink before we talk."

Eldour rushed behind the counter, filled the freshly cleaned mug with mulled cider, then sat in the chair across from Nightfall. He slapped the mug down in front of his guest, sloshing a swallow to the tabletop.

Nightfall took a thoughtful sip. It tasted bland and dirty, but tolerable. He gulped in a mouthful and swallowed. "I'm afraid it's not much of a story, really." Nightfall kept his tale within the constructs of the one the pirates had concocted to explain their new captain. "I hired a ship to do some trading with Alyndar."

"Alyndar?" Eldour leaned closer with clear interest. "I'd heard no one's going there."

"That's why I decided to do it." Nightfall smiled conspiratorially. "I thought someone should make some money off their need. Why not me, right?"

"Right, *uvna*." Eldour grinned along with his customer. "How'd it go?"

Nightfall took another drink. "Not so good. Pirates caught us barely out of harbor. Killed the captain and took just about everything."

Eldour's grin wilted, and he turned Nightfall a sympathetic look. He had a way with facial expressions and voice tones that made men believe he cared and tend to trust him. "That must have been awful."

"Yes." Nightfall shook his head, then lowered it. "Awful. Then, a couple of ships flying yellow-and-red flags chased us. I don't know what they wanted, but after our encounter with the pirates, we didn't wait to find out. We outran them and made our way to Alyndar."

The corners of Eldour's mouth lifted ever so slightly. "Not much of a story, you said, *uvna*. But this sounds as exciting as anything from the mouth of a storyteller."

Nightfall shrugged and put on a slight smile of his own. "I suppose one of the sailors might tell it that way. But I spent most of my time cowering in the hold."

"Who wouldn't?" With those words, Eldour turned Nightfall's admission from cowardice to simple logic. "And the trade in Alyndar? How did that go?"

Nightfall gave a gloomy shrug. "What little I had left sold for a fair price, and I found a side mission that gained me a few more silvers." He took another swig of cider. "Unfortunately, all of that went to paying the sailors. The pirates and the chase added combat wages, and that left me with only a few coppers." He tried a wan smile. "Know anyone who needs some silks?" He tugged at the emerald-green fabric of his merchanting outfit. "Because I don't know where else to get the money I need to restart my business."

Eldour winced. "Sad." His face screwed into a knot of compassion that made it seem as if he had never heard a more depressing story. "Always hard to see anyone fall this far. Why don't I bring you some food? No man has ever hit rock bottom with his belly full."

Nightfall did not protest as the proprietor whisked behind the counter. He glanced around at the other men in the common room. None appeared to be looking at him; and yet, he knew they all were. They had begun assessing him the moment he crossed the threshold, seeking weaknesses to exploit. They smelled money in the look of him, and they all contemplated a means to make any wealth he carried their own. At least one, a tall and wiry fellow at the farthest table, would not hesitate to insert a knife through his rib cage before bothering to see what he carried.

Bound by his promises to Kelryn and Edward, Nightfall suffered a growing rush of irritation. He felt hobbled and shackled, forced to perform high-air acrobatics without the benefit of hands or feet. Balshaz would and could request information, but only in a clumsy fashion. He needed the freedom only Nightfall possessed to hold blades at bay and loosen tongues. He needed the influence of the demon. Nightfall gulped down more of the cider. It felt warm in his stomach, soothing the nausea that bubbled up at the thought of what circumstance had forced him to do. He would have to take another enormous leap of faith.

Shortly, Eldour returned with a plate of chopped fall fruit, a lump of mashed tubers, a small piece of heavily salted pork, and a bit of moldy cheese. He placed them in front of Nightfall with a flourish, as if presenting a feast to a king.

Nightfall flopped his nearly empty purse to the tabletop and eased out two coppers. He passed them to Eldour. "I'd better pay you now. Who knows if I'll have anything left when I awaken."

The coins disappeared into Eldour's hand. "I'd take that as an insult to my establishment, if it weren't true." He again seated himself in the chair at Nightfall's table while his daytime regulars pretended not to watch. He glanced at the purse, which clearly contained only three or four more coppers, barely worth stealing. "So, where are you going from here?"

"Depends . . ." Nightfall flipped a bit of fruit into his mouth, trying to look competent without demonstrating too much dexterity. He continued as he chewed, ". . . on what kind of information I get."

"Information?" Eldour withheld tone from the word, clearly uncertain how to play his next gambit. His gaze went back to the near-empty purse. "That's not going to buy you much."

Nightfall wiped his hands on his shirt, then dipped beneath it and dropped the sapphire brooch to the table. "How about this?"

Eldour's eyes went enormous. Nightfall could feel the

gazes of the patrons jerk toward him as well. "I thought . . . you said . . . but . . ."

Nightfall anticipated the question the proprietor seemed incapable of speaking. "It's not mine."

"Who . . . ?" Eldour started, unable to tear his attention from the jewel.

"It belongs to whoever brings information that leads me directly to King Edward Nargol of Alyndar."

That brought Eldour's head up. "But he's—"

"Don't say 'dead.' " Though it might be true, Nightfall could not bear to hear it now.

Eldour went silent.

Nightfall suppressed his personal stake in the matter. "Or whoever leads me to . . . his . . . body." His mind refused to accept the possibility his friend had been murdered, at least not until he saw the remains with his own eyes. "And this . . ." He tossed down the second, loose gem. ". . . goes to whoever gives me valuable, useful information about the Bloodshadow Brotherhood."

A shiver racked Eldour. He glanced surreptitiously over his shoulder, but Nightfall already knew he had gained the attention of every man in the inn, whether they stared openly or not. "It's dangerous," the proprietor finally whispered, "to speak that name aloud."

Nightfall tried to look distressed by the revelation, though he suffered nothing but a deep flush of anger. The worthless group of bandits had stolen not only his name, but also his reputation, and used them as weapons of terror. *Arisen from the drops of demon blood shed at my execution, were they?* He released that line of thought. He could do nothing about it, and dwelling on it only placed his current disguise in jeopardy. "Then, I will leave these treasures with you, and you can let me know if anyone earns them."

Clearly awed by the fortune Nightfall had so blithely placed in his care, Eldour made no request for middleman's pay. Though Nightfall knew it would rightly come

from whoever passed along enough information to win
the gems, Balshaz would not. Eldour could have collected from both sides of the gambit.

The proprietor took the sapphires, then disappeared
through the kitchen curtain to hide them.

Ignoring the stares of the other patrons, Nightfall
turned his attention to his meal.

Nightfall spent the remainder of the evening in Eldour's common room, watching customers leave, replaced by more. As the night wore on, the coming far
outpaced the going, so the room became nearly full by
the time the moon and stars ruled the heavens. Though
quiet in his corner, Nightfall did not go unnoticed. He
saw many familiar faces: stalkers and assassins, cut-
purses and squealers, rogues of every variety in groups
that seldom surprised him. Every person who came in
studied him at least once, though whether out of curiosity or professional interest, he did not know. Eldour became very popular as men asked about the
merchant's presence and word of his wishes grew. At
length, Nightfall thought it better to leave the others
free to discuss him and his offer without worrying
about him overhearing. He retired to the sleeping
room early, shortly after a light evening meal.

Tattered, filthy blankets lay, rumpled or spread,
across the floor. Rolled or crumpled piles of clothing,
backpacks, and parcels created a scattered maze that
Nightfall navigated with ease. All four corners were already claimed by belongings, forcing Nightfall to the
center of the room or beneath the single window, devoid of curtains or covering. He chose the latter position. Though the coldest spot, and the least safe if
someone chose to scale the building and sneak into the
room, Nightfall liked having the option of a fast escape.
With his natal gift, he could handle the two-story drop
with ease.

Nightfall curled up on the floor and drifted into a

sleep that lasted only until the first of his roommates arrived. The drunken pair made no attempt at quiet, tripping over bedrolls and laughing hysterically when blankets skittered and tangled. Nightfall feigned sleep as he watched them. Regulars, he knew, men who slept at the inn whenever they had the money. He waited for them to settle into position. Moments later, their heavy snores permeated the room, and Nightfall settled back into a doze. He always slept on a knife's edge of awakening, his senses trained to distinguish safe background noise from danger. Now, those instincts failed him. Every new sleep mate brought him to jarring awareness, and he found himself measuring the breathing of too many men to allow him any rest. At length, he slipped through the window while the others slept, lowered his weight, and plummeted lightly to the ground. From there, he crawled into a nearby bolt-hole that had kept him safe in the past.

There, deeply chilled and pressed by stone on nearly every side, he found the comfort that had eluded him on the floor of the inn's sleeping room. Childhood emotions enveloped him: the joy of finding a haven among the predators, a place that could keep a boy alive one more night. Soothed by remembrance, surrounded by the customary sounds of alley night, Nightfall slept.

A change in the pattern of movement outside his hiding space awakened Nightfall to the first rays of the sun. Measuring the area by instinct as much as sight and sound, he determined that no one hovered nearby. He slipped from his crevice into the threadway and touched up his costume using his reflection in various puddles. His copper locks lay in disarray, and he carried more dirt than Balshaz normally would allow; yet it seemed appropriate for the situation. Making certain no one watched him climb, he clambered to the sleeping room window and peeked inside. The others slept in random poses around the room, legs flopped over mea-

ger belongings, arms akimbo. Nightfall dropped noise-
lessly into the room, picked his careful way around
them, then pressed through the door and down the
stairs to the common room. He took the same chair he
had used the night before, now cracked from some disagreement that must have occurred after he left the
previous night.

Nightfall sat alone with his thoughts for several moments before a serving girl emerged from behind the
kitchen hanging and noticed him. She appeared nearly
thirty, though she was probably several years younger.
She wore her dark hair cut short with bangs, and her
face looked drawn down toward her chin. Ruffles at the
top of her linen shirt nearly hid the scars around her
neck, which had surely come from a slave collar. She
had red, irritated hands covered with ashy scratch lines
and a scaly rash that clearly itched. She studied him in
the dull light leaking through the remaining chinks in
the inn's construction. "Oh, good morning, sir. Can I get
you anything?"

"Anything would be just fine, miss," Nightfall returned genially. He had hoped to see Eldour but knew
the proprietor had remained awake late into the night
serving customers. He would be surprised to see the
man, or any of his own roommates, before the midday
meal.

Leftovers from the previous night, the food tasted
bland and congealed, but it broke the fast and filled
Nightfall's belly. Though he had already paid for his
stay, Nightfall tipped the woman one of his last precious
coppers. He doubted he could keep hold of them long in
his current guise anyway, and he had become wise to the
goodwill that came of making the lowborn and servants
happy. She thanked him with an exuberance he found
embarrassing, and he slipped out the door as much to
escape her as to clear his head. He had nowhere in particular to go, but he had already grown tired of Eldour's
place. He doubted random street wandering would

yield significant information, but it seemed better than spending hours waiting for Eldour in the common room.

Clouds swathed the sun, shading the alleys into an ethereal gray. He made no attempt to move quietly, though it came naturally to him; and his senses followed the movement of others without conscious need to do so. He headed northwest, toward the more normal parts of the city, with no destination in mind. He needed a change, to see a piece of the world that reminded him more of Balshaz and less of his dark, ugly childhood and the demon it had turned him into.

As Nightfall headed down one of the last muddy alleys of the southeast quarter, his senses jarred him to full vigilance. His cloth-covered shoes were still mired in the same tarry filth that seemed to define the lower quarter. He knew his route. The alley mouth would open on a small thoroughfare leading to a series of smaller shops that sold stale bread, garden overflow, and secondhand clothing. The backs of cruder dwellings, storage houses, and crumbling ruins lined the alley itself, and Cronar, who sold turning meat, sometimes threw scraps of the unsalvageably rancid into this alley for the strays. Nightfall wondered how many orphans and escaped slaves stole what he tossed there from the scrounging cats, dogs, and wild doves. Uncertain what troubled him, Nightfall paused casually just past the mouth of the alley and took a full survey.

A moment after he stopped, others did also. Nightfall was immediately certain he was being followed. To confirm his suspicions, he took two confident strides forward, then came to an immediate halt. Again, the light footfalls and almost inaudible swish of cloth disappeared a spare instant afterward. Two men, his ears told him, accustomed to stalking. Not wanting to give away his knowledge of their presence, Nightfall bent down and pretended to adjust a shoe already mud-crusted past saving. Then, he continued onward at the same casual pace, without the sudden quickening that might cue them.

A voice crashed through the alleyway in front of Nightfall, not loud but full of command and menace. "Stop there, merchant."

Nightfall froze, looking for the source of the voice, pretending not to notice the two men stalking nearer behind him. "Who's there?" he finally said, not bothering to control the quaver in his reply.

Three men stepped from the shadows. Nightfall recognized only one, a scarred veteran mugger who rarely bothered with subtlety. He would rather knife a man for his purse than steal or finesse it. The other two looked hardened, though only in their teens, a short blond and a willowy brunet. They swept toward him without answer, covering the width of the alley.

Nightfall realized they expected him to turn and run in terror directly into the two men behind him. Instead, he took a careful back step, keeping stock of each man's position as he measured every detail of the alley. The poorly designed buildings gave him numerous opportunities to climb, though doing so seemed worrisomely out of character. He tried something more appropriate to Balshaz first. His nimble fingers untied his purse and tossed it toward the three approaching men. "Here. That's all I have." He did not expect them to believe him. His silks hinted at far more wealth than he currently carried. "If I had money, I wouldn't have to stay in this scummy part of town."

The purse struck the mud with a dull noise that overshadowed any clinking his last coppers might have made.

The young brunet headed toward the purse, but the older man halted him with a touch. Clearly, he worried their quarry might escape in the opening created by that distraction.

"It's all I have." Nightfall tried to sound terrified. "I swear it." He could feel more than hear the men moving up behind him. He did not have long to convince them.

The mugger took another menacing step toward Nightfall.

Nightfall whirled as if to run, then leaped to the right instead, dropping his weight as he moved. Launched sideways, he barely kept himself from smashing into the stonework. He scurried upward without hesitation, not bothering to find definitive hand or toeholds. Granite protrusions glided over his calloused fingers but sliced his toes, and he realized his sudden jump had left his shoes behind in the mud.

"Hey!" someone shouted from below, followed by an enraged string of curses.

"Get him!" another commanded.

A hand closed around Nightfall's ankle. He restored his mass, more afraid of revealing his secret than what these thieves might do to him. The lost toehold and sudden extra weight threw off his timing. A yank tore his fingers free, and he felt himself falling. More hands flailed toward him.

Nightfall twisted and tucked in midair. The hand fell away from his foot, and he struck the ground on his right shoulder, rolled, and sprang up running. Only one man stood between him and freedom. He tucked his head and charged, driving up his weight as he did. He slammed into the man with deadly force, knocking him sprawling. Breath surged from the man in a foul-smelling gasp, but Nightfall did not look back. Dropping his weight back to normal, he charged to the end of the alley, bellowing wildly for help. The men clattered after him, their curses echoing between the buildings.

Nightfall burst into the thoroughfare, all but trampling a man clutching two live chickens by their feet. A frenzied dodge saved the man, but the birds fled, flapping and squawking. A woman screamed, scooping up a young boy, and others leaped out of the way of Nightfall's frantic escape. The four remaining men followed him doggedly, their footfalls hammering the street, leaving chaos in their wake.

Heads poked from doorways. People scurried out of Nightfall's zigzagging path. A chicken darted beneath his legs. A series of quick steps kept him on his feet, but the man behind him did not prove as lucky. The chicken loosed a squeal that became a series of ear-splitting bawks, its wings fanning the air furiously. The man surged into an awkward tumble that sent him spinning into Nightfall. Legs slammed out from under him, Nightfall stumbled, then lost the battle to his failing balance. He fell backward, landing hard on his buttocks. Spinning to regain his feet, he saw another man flying toward him.

Nightfall ducked as he scrambled, but not far enough. An enormous man with a knife scar down his face crashed into Nightfall's chest, driving him supine. His back thumped against the road with bone-jarring force. He bit his tongue, tasting blood, and pain shocked through his head. He saw the flash of a drawn knife and forced himself to roll. The steel missed his left side by a finger's breadth, plunging into the soft earth of the roadway. Nightfall's epithet was lost beneath the louder one of the man above him.

Nightfall seized the man's wrist, still clutched around the knife. Strong and thick, it did not budge as he used it as a focal point to pivot beneath his attacker. The man shifted position also, dragging free his knife and arm, his bulk still pinning Nightfall's legs and abdomen.

Can't let him strike again. Nightfall made a wild lunge for the dagger, nearly catching it before he realized he would have the blade. He stopped in mid-movement, rescuing his hands but leaving his attacker free for another thrust. As he withdrew, another strong hand caught his left upper arm, and the mugger leered down at him. Dropping to the road, the larger man pinned Nightfall's arm to the ground with a knee. Another of his attackers lurched to catch his remaining arm. *No!* Once they had him pinned helplessly, Nightfall doubted they would spare him. Fierce men did not like it when their prey fought back, and this had flared from a simple theft to vengeful murder.

Nightfall dodged the third man's clumsy grab and buried his fist in the first man's face. He felt a pop, and warm blood twined between his fingers. The man's face turned purple, stark contrast to the scarlet streams gushing suddenly from his nostrils. His weight eased slightly from Nightfall's legs, and the knife raced abruptly for Nightfall's throat. He could hear people shouting in the background, but their words blended into nonsense. He saw nothing but the livid face of the man he had injured.

Swinging his free arm wildly, Nightfall dropped his weight and jerked his legs free. Instantly, he rolled, restoring proper mass. The knife tore his collar and raked a line of skin from the side of his neck. No longer squashed, he tried to run, stopped short by the grip on his wrist with a suddenness that nearly dislocated his shoulder. Agony shocked through his arm, blinding and deafening, nearly incapacitating him. He flailed in an incalculable frenzy, hoping to keep his attackers off guard long enough to regain his senses, which returned in a wash of black-and-white spots. The grip on his wrist disappeared, and he watched his attackers running back into the alley.

Nightfall looked up to find a crowd surrounding him, including two men in the official blue-and-red uniforms of Hartrin's town guard. A shopkeeper wearing a stained apron offered his hand, and Nightfall accepted. Once on his feet, he studied the blood settling into the lines of his right palm and rubbed the scrape on his neck with his left. That, too, came away scarlet.

The shopkeeper spoke first, "You all right, Balshaz?"

Nightfall shook copper strands from his eyes and hopelessly brushed the topmost layer of dirt from his silks. "Not really." He glanced around the crowd, finding them surprisingly concerned. They had not gathered just from curiosity. He saw sincere worry lining many faces.

One of the town guards took over, a massive man with a head of thick dark hair, shaggy brows, and a shadow already forming in his beard area. "What happened?"

Nightfall turned toward him and studied the eagle emblem sewn onto the chest of his work linens. "I gave them my purse, but I think they expected more." He lowered his head in a parody of shame. "I've fallen on some hard times."

The other guard spoke next, a bit smaller and younger than his companion. "So you didn't know them?"

"Never seen them before." It was essentially true. Nightfall had never met any of those men in Balshaz guise. Convinced he had run afoul of thieves, Nightfall continued futilely flicking dirt from his clothing. "Have you?"

"Probably," the older man said amid murmurs from the crowd. "But not that I recall." He shrugged, and nothing about him suggested he saw more in the situation than Nightfall did. "You're probably right. Saw you as an easy target and expected more from a merchant than they got, especially having to divide it five ways." He tipped his head, a clear sign he believed his work finished, and motioned for his partner to join him back at whatever post they had left. "Balshaz, is it?"

Nightfall nodded carefully, still dizzy from his sudden encounter with the ground.

"I'd suggest you stay away from that side of town."

Murmurs of assent passed through the dispersing crowd.

Nightfall rubbed his aching head. "I would if I could. I've already paid for room and board at an inn down that way." He gestured vaguely toward Eldour's. "It's all I could afford."

No longer needed, the town guard headed westward along the street. The remaining people all started speaking at once, mostly platitudes and suggestions.

Nightfall stayed them with a raised hand. "Thank you all for your concern. I'll be fine." He recognized many of them, though not with the same detail and need as he did the rogues and thugs in Hartrin's southeast quarter. He saw customers, some regular, and shopkeepers among the mix. The number and the sincerity of their apprehension for him surprised him.

One chubby, middle-aged woman broke the hush. "Please, come stay with us, Balshaz. Who's going to bring those Mezzinian sweets my children love so well if you're killed by thugs?"

A chorus of agreement followed, mostly from children, including two who clung to her skirt.

Embarrassed by the display, Nightfall laughed. "Surely I'm not the only one who brings those."

"No," a taller woman admitted. "But you're the only we can trust to bring good ones every time."

More mumbles of agreement swept the crowd.

A pretty blonde approached, and Nightfall forced himself still. Touches alarmed him at any time, but he felt particularly twitchy having nearly lost his life and surrounded by a crowd, albeit mostly female. She washed the wound at his neck with a damp rag, examined it, and announced, "Just a scratch."

"Good," several others said.

A lean, elderly woman with long, graying brown hair piped up, "I love those southern threads and fabrics. When you buy them from Balshaz, you know you're not getting loose weave."

"Or waxed linen disguised as silk."

"Or stains hidden beneath the fold."

A sturdy matron with short-cropped hair took Nightfall's hand. "I'm getting you cleaned up."

Nightfall started to protest, but she silenced him with a glare that countenanced no argument. Docile as a kitten, he allowed himself to be led.

† Chapter 19 †

A demon wakens with the night,
Reviling sun and all things bright.
Evil's friend and virtue's foe—
Darkness comes where Nightfall goes.

—"The Legend of Nightfall"
Nursery rhyme, stanza 1

HIS WOUNDS TENDED, his belly full, and his torn and muddy merchant's silks replaced with finely woven linen, including new shoes, Nightfall returned to the southeast corner against the protestations of the Hartrinian women. By then, the sun had begun its westward descent, and the already iron-colored sky turned leaden. Rain pattered on the rooftops, hiding the faint noises of the alleys, and turned the muddy walkways into a dark and mucky soup.

Believing Balshaz had a right to appear spooked, Nightfall kept his senses sharply attuned. He did not believe the same five men would assault him. By now, their anger at his escape had surely subsided, and they should have turned their sights on easier prey. In fact, no one bothered him as he made his way back to Eldour's inn, though he could hear movement among the eaves and shadows.

Nightfall pushed open the door to a larger crowd than the previous evening; the rain brought the regulars in early. His common clothing bought him less attention this time, and the bandage on the side of his neck would likely go unnoticed. Any bruises that appeared among the manufactured pockmarks would seem normal to the southeastern crowd, accustomed to daily arguments that swiftly turned physical. Every table had at least one customer. Nightfall headed to the one nearest the bar and pointed questioningly at an empty chair.

In reply, Nightfall received only a grunt. Though Balshaz might not know the coarse etiquette, Nightfall did; and he did not question. He pulled the chair away from the four men sitting at the table and drew it up to the bar instead.

Eldour came over almost immediately. "Good evening, *uvna*." He glanced over Nightfall's new outfit approvingly. "Can I get you anything?"

Stuffed beyond interest in anything edible, Nightfall shook his head. "Just information. Anything turn up?"

Eldour glanced around the room, then lowered his head. "Let's keep these conversations as quiet as possible, all right?"

Nightfall agreed with a nod. From habit, he had spoken too softly for anyone to overhear, but he understood Eldour's paranoia.

"I've made your offer known." Eldour continued to scour the common room with his gaze as he spoke. "Only thing's come up so far are claims the man you're looking for is dead, killed by his own slave. And the usual mystical rumors about . . . that group."

Nightfall sat back, as if considering something of little import. He did not correct the notion that he had served as Edward's slave; Hartrin made little or no distinction between paid and forced servitude. "Nothing useful?"

"Not yet." Eldour seemed distinctly nervous, which alarmed Nightfall. Accustomed to dealing with killers, the proprietor usually remained cool. "But give the news of your offer a bit of time to spread."

Acting on a hunch, Nightfall mentioned casually, "I got attacked this morning."

Eldour stiffened. "What?" he said, with just a hint of edge.

He already knew. Nightfall tried to make use of that fact, but the significance eluded him. "Muggers caught me in an alley up toward the outer shop row."

"What'd they get?"

"Everything I had." *Except Ned's ring.* Nightfall continued to measure the proprietor. Eldour sounded earnest in his concern, but Nightfall recognized a bluff when he heard one. "Less than a copper each, that was. Scarcely worth the effort."

Eldour laughed. "How'd you get away?"

It was exactly the wrong question for an innocent man to ask, and Nightfall called him on it. "Away from what? I said they took everything I had."

Caught, Eldour hesitated, then went with his mistake. "I'd heard those thugs chased you right up the main street, even after they got your money."

Nightfall raised his brows. "You knew?"

"It happened this morning. I hear pretty . . ." Eldour caught the eye of a client. ". . . much every—excuse me." He hurried off to tend the other man.

Nightfall waited, studying the other customers. Those he did not know personally, he understood as types: the swaggering young rogue seeking a name for himself, the baby-faced con man, the wiry little thief swathed in black and hiding in a distant corner. Here in the dank, filthy alleys of slave country, they lived out dreams the normal folk shunned as abhorrent or dismissed as nightmares.

Eldour returned in a few moments, and Nightfall immediately hit him with the obvious question. "So you hear about everything, do you?"

Eldour grinned. "Eventually."

Nightfall looked directly at the other man, careful not to pin him with the demon's glare. Eldour had firsthand experience with the demon, and Nightfall could not risk discovery. "Then you know who attacked me."

"Maybe."

"And why."

The smile became a smirk. "The right price might grease my tongue."

Nightfall wanted to slap the sleazy, cocksure expression from the proprietor's face. "I haven't given you enough?" He finished to himself, *you oily little weasel.*

"You paid for room and board, and I gave you a bargain at that. The rest, you made clear, does not belong to me."

Nightfall imagined himself choking Eldour until his eyes bugged out and his tongue lolled. His fists winched closed, but he kept his hands safely at his sides. *You're Balshaz,* he reminded himself. *You're honest, lovable Balshaz.*

Eldour's shit-eating grin disappeared, replaced by the false kindness he had shown earlier. "Seriously, *uvna.* What would you do with their names anyway? I don't need the town guard poking around here."

"Those blackguards tried to kill me!" Nightfall no longer worried about keeping his voice low. He had every right to shout.

"Balshaz," Eldour whispered tensely. "Please."

Nightfall glared.

"I'll tell you this. Those men were known professionals, and you're . . . well . . . not. If they'd actually wanted to kill you, you wouldn't be here talking to me now."

Wouldn't I? Nightfall kept that to himself, also. The proprietor had no idea who he addressed. Nightfall had attributed the assault to a robbery gone bad. Now, he had to wonder whether those men had actually intended to kill him all along. *Just for asking about the Brotherhood?* The level of their paranoia seemed extreme. Every scoundrel who put himself for hire walked the fine line between the notoriety that drew the highest paying jobs and the secrecy that kept the constabulary at bay.

Eldour wiped idly at an old stain on the bar. "You look exhausted, Balshaz. Understandably. Why don't you turn in early?"

Nightfall did not protest. He could use the extra sleep.

"There's a new crew staying tonight, so you should claim a sleeping spot while you can."

"Thanks." Nightfall doubted he could hear anything of use in the bar. The regulars would curb their tongues in his presence, and anyone with useful information would prefer to spill it to Eldour alone. Hunger seemed unlikely to bother him, at least until morning; and he did feel rather tired.

Eldour whisked away to tend another customer, and Nightfall ascended the stairs to the sleeping quarters. As before, he found it filled with travel-stained blankets, carelessly flung cloaks, and scattered bedrolls. It seemed easiest to claim the space directly beneath the window again. No one else would want it, and he harbored no wish to enter a shouting or shoving match with some half crocked thug who decided the corner Nightfall chose belonged to him. Taking off only his mud-caked shoes, he curled up on the hard wooden floor, alone with his thoughts. As those flooded over him, he cringed at the frenzied swirl of concerns the day's events had previously held in check. Mostly, they centered on Edward and his frustration at finding no leads as the trail grew steadily colder. No one just disappeared without someone in the underground knowing the true story, especially not a king. Yet, even vast sums of money did not seem capable of loosening any tongues.

Though desperately troubled by his considerations, Nightfall drifted off to sleep.

Nightfall awakened to a sense of dread and no idea of its source, which intensified it tenfold. Without moving or opening his eyes, without changing the pattern of his breathing, he assessed the world around him. He heard nothing except the steady drum of rain against the rooftop, but his senses still prickled with alarm. Someone had broken the invisible barrier he built around himself, drawing near enough to potentially harm him.

Nightfall slid his eyes open, still feigning sleep. The sun had straggled fully below the horizon, leaving a half-moon that, though cloaked in storm clouds, still granted his dark-adjusted eyes sufficient light. He discovered only one other person in the room, a stealthy shadow creeping inexorably toward him. Moonlight glinted from a steel object in the stranger's hand.

Nightfall's heart rate quickened, but he gave no sign he had awakened. He tracked the cautious progress of the other man, who did not stop until he crouched at Nightfall's side. The object in his hand rose, now unmistakably a long dagger.

Abruptly, Nightfall rolled toward the stranger, slamming into his shins. The impact made his assailant tumble forward. The knife crashed to the floor, skittering across the planking to land in a rumpled blanket. They lunged for it simultaneously. Then, Nightfall saw three more shadowy figures silhouetted in the doorway. He changed direction, mid-leap, toward the window.

A knife flew at Nightfall. He snagged it as he sprang onto the sill, and the "razor rebound" followed like instinct. Its wielder staggered backward with a strangled gurgle. In the instant it took the others to realize what had happed, Nightfall flung himself out the window, into the pouring rain.

"Get him!"

The men surged after Nightfall, footsteps trained to fall lightly against the planking. Nightfall clung to the sill, driving down his weight for the fall. Even as he started to let go, he saw more men beneath him in the alley. Fingers jabbed toward him, revealing him, and he converted his momentum into an upward swing. Instead of releasing, he found solid toeholds in the wet wooden construction of the inn and scrambled toward a roof of leather, mud, and thatch.

The men shouted in rage and disappointment as Nightfall scaled the wall like a spider. He caught the edge of the sodden roof and flung himself upward, realizing his mistake before he could stop the impetus. His now-meager weight sailed upward, driving him into another group of men, apparently stationed on the rooftop. *They knew I might climb?* The professionalism, the seamless way they worked as a group worried Nightfall, but he had no time to contemplate it. His own unstoppable motion carried him toward a swinging pipe in the hands of a brawny assassin. It caught Nightfall a ringing blow to the skull that shocked agony through his entire head. For an instant, the world went utterly black. Then, consciousness returned, masked behind a buzzing curtain of spots. His grip failed him, and he felt himself falling.

No! Nightfall grappled for awareness as the wind surged around him, his weight still paltry. If he lost the battle for his wits, he died. He hit the ground in a crouch, unable to muster the rationality to roll. Men descended on him. He dodged them like a fish, somehow regaining his feet. They tackled him, their combined mass driving him into the mud with a force that stole his breath and drove fresh spasms of agony through his head. He fought wildly, punching, kicking, thrusting. Someone popped a cloth sack reeking of mold over his head, and he felt rope tearing into the flesh of his wrists.

Nightfall tumbled into a large sack. He tried to save his eyes and nose but found his hands bound tightly together. He slammed, face first, into a mass of rocks piled at the bottom of the bag. The darkness became complete, then he felt himself getting dragged over muddy roadways. *What in the Father's hell . . . ?* He did not trouble himself to complete the thought, instead wriggling into a more comfortable position. He jerked at the ropes binding his wrists, managing only to tighten them deeper into his flesh. Blood slicked his fingers.

Nightfall stopped struggling, instead assessing himself and his belongings. They had stripped him of obvious weaponry, but they had not found everything in the brief period they had maintained total control over him. He twisted, folding his body, searching his clothing with his bare feet until he touched the cold metal of a knife hilt. He slid his toes around it, seeking a sure grip. He might have only one chance, could not afford to fumble it. A loose knife in the bag was a danger only to him.

Sweat dribbled over Nightfall's body, and the effort of keeping his doubled position wore on him. He dared not make any weight adjustments. His captors would notice and foil any attempt at escape. Worse, if they figured it out, they might sell him to sorcerers; he would rather die a thousand violent deaths than suffer the prolonged agony of a soul harnessed to a madman's will. The rocks flopped with the terrain, banging bruisingly against him. He wondered about the purpose of the men who caught him, imagining them gathering around the sack with clubs, howling with excitement while battering him to a bloody corpse.

Nightfall dropped that train of thought to concentrate on the task at hand. He managed to position the hilt solidly between his first and second toes and gradually work the blade free. A bit more bending brought the blade to his mouth. Fearful that a large bump might drive it into his throat, he worked it around with his shoulder and teeth until he had the hilt firmly clenched. Raising his hands, he ran the blade over the ropes. He felt the sisal strands parting, the wickedly sharp steel carving into the top of his wrists as well. Then, his hands jerked free, and he spat out the hilt. He caught it easily, thrilling to the sensation of the warm hilt in his grip. Armed with honed steel, he no longer felt helpless.

Only then did Nightfall start worrying about his destination. Belatedly, he concentrated on the sounds around him: the patter of rain against the canvas, the low and indiscernible talk of the men, and the squish of their boots on mushy back roads. Devoting all of his attention to hearing, he made out one more noise, the distant muffled slap of waves against wood.

Nightfall stiffened, suddenly intensely aware of the plan. They had dragged him to the docks with the intention of dropping the rock-weighted bag into the ocean. With the bag firmly tied shut, it would sink to the depths. By the time his drowned corpse found its way to shore, it would be bloated and fish-bitten beyond recognition.

Hoping the darkness and positioning hid his action, Nightfall made a small X-shaped slit in the underside of the bag. With the thick canvas breached, the garbled voices of the men finally reached him.

"Gods this bag is heavy."

Exasperation colored another's tone. "How many times do you plan to say that?"

"Of course it's heavy, you addlepated pile of chicken shit," another man hissed. "It's full of rocks."

Nightfall squeezed one of the stones through his makeshift hole. As it left the sack, he raised his weight to correspond with its loss, then tensed for someone to notice.

Undaunted, the first man asked, "Couldn't we have put the rocks in at the docks?"

Someone snorted. "You going to open the sack and take a chance on losing that snarling dog?" The forward movement stopped, and Nightfall held his breath. "You explain it to the bosses; after all that work, he gets away."

"He's not getting far without hands."

The voice that had growled out the string of insults added, "You don't need hands to run."

The reply was garbled.

Nightfall sneaked out another stone, again driving up his weight to counter it.

Their walk continued.

One by one, Nightfall emptied the bag of ballast until he felt the more regular jolting of docking through the cloth of the sack. Here, his would-be killers would notice stones strewn about on the planks. He only had a few left; he believed he could handle those in the moments he had to maneuver before he had to get himself to air. He felt certain they would take him to the southernmost dock, not only the most shadowy but also the one that opened onto the deepest water. Experienced captains shunned the south dock or tied every spare rope to the anchor.

"Made it."

That was all the warning Nightfall got before the sack flopped into empty space. Water seeped through the porous cloth already soaked by rain, and his added weight dragged it down faster than he expected.

Holding his breath, Nightfall jettisoned the last few rocks, then seized the fabric and attempted to tear it fully open. The thick, wet cloth resisted his efforts. For several moments, he strained futilely against it as the need for air assaulted his mind, driving out more logical thought. A string of swear words raced through his thoughts as he searched wildly for his knife, displaced by the rush of water into the bag. Wasting only a moment to the search, he found another knife, groped it free, and stabbed it through the opening. He tried to slash the cloth, but it slid limply around the blade. His already aching head seemed to grow heavier, both from the lack of breath and the pressure of water all around him. He felt the ocean's bottom through the cloth beneath his feet. Fighting panic, he further increased his weight, which allowed him to pin the cloth with his feet. He held the slack taut with his free hand. Now, the knife glided easily through the fabric, freeing him.

Desperation drove Nightfall toward the surface, and he jettisoned weight until his clothing bogged him down more than his person. The bag tangled around one arm.

He held it there; he could not risk it floating to the surface and revealing his escape. That thought brought another just as significant. *They're surely watching. Can't let them see me surface.*

Nightfall's thoughts reeled. His lungs spasmed, and it took an effort of will to keep from gasping in a lungful of seawater. Still, he forced himself to move sideways as well as up until he entered the safety of the dock's shadow. Then he launched himself to the surface, breaking water just as need forced him to give up the battle. Air funneled into his throat, painfully thick with salt and bracken. No water accompanied it, to Nightfall's relief. He doubted he could have stopped himself from coughing had it entered his windpipe.

Only then did Nightfall notice the night chill of the water. A sudden shiver racked him, its intensity an agony all its own. With it, raw rage awakened from his core. Balshaz was dead, murdered for his curiosity, a good man killed by fools and their goons. Nightfall's anger erupted into a bonfire he could scarcely control. The water seemed to disappear; the cold no longer bothered him. All that existed was that fiery fury seething and boiling inside him. It did not matter that Balshaz was not real, a figment of his imagination. The Bloodshadow Brotherhood had taken something from him that mattered far beyond the charade. They had taken King Edward.

Attentive only to his grief, Nightfall had fought for over a month within the vows that constrained him, promises made to those who mattered most. Edward would never forgive a rescue that revived the demon who had haunted the nightmares of the world's bravest warriors; but Edward no longer had a choice. Alyndar needed its king. Hampered by too many rules, Nightfall had barely gained ground in his search. Now, he glanced upward, seeing only the darkness of the docks and the meager light it admitted through the cracks. Beneath its shadow, he swam, without a splash, to the rain-battered shore. From there, he watched the men who had murdered Balshaz straggle back toward town, memorizing their walks and demeanors, every line the shrouded moon revealed of their faces. They executed the almost imperceptible congratulatory gestures of the underground, their grins broad, their demeanors high. They relished the slaughter of a popular merchant whose only crime was asking questions.

Nightfall headed for the coastal cliffs and one of the deep, all but unattainable hiding places where he kept his special gear: his clothing, his cosmetics, the tools of his trade. Just getting there would tax all of his talents and skills, and only he even knew where to look. The moment he arrived, his life, the world itself, would irrevocably change.

Nightfall had returned.

Lightning slithered through the cracks of the shuttered windows of Eldour's common room, and the door slammed open beneath a horrific explosion of thunder. A lone figure appeared at a lintel darkened to pitch in the wake of the storm. Wind whipped filthy black hair into a tangle; and the long, wickedly scarred face tapered to a short-cropped beard. As he stepped across that doorway, he seemed less to physically move than to separate from the squall and blackness. Huge, menacing, he claimed the room, owning it as fully as he had the violent night. It took a while for every eye to find him; but, once they did, they stared, unable to turn away. Whispers followed, everyone speaking the name Eldour's mind had already conjured: Nightfall.

Eldour stood gazing with the rest, utterly incapable of movement. He clutched a bottle of soured wine in one hand, an empty drinking bowl in the other. Deep down, he had known Nightfall would return; demons did not die at the whim of mere mortals, even be they kings. Like the others, he watched the creature glide silkily toward him, spawned, it seemed, from a tempest that now seemed more than natural. He wore a black leather doublet studded with metal that buttoned up the front. The sleeves were paned above the elbows, and skirt tabs hung over close-fitting breeches. He wore daggers lashed to his wrists and thrust through a sash of brilliant lavender, many with the skull hilt designs he sometimes left in warning. These were not dark garments made for skulking through gloom like most of Hartrin's thugs. The shadows seemed to cover him as a special favor to one of their own. In torchlight, he showed his colors like a threat, in the manner of a poisonous insect or reptile.

Nightfall moved like the wind: silent, deadly, and sudden. Before Eldour could think to do or say anything, he found the demon in front of him. Eyes like blackened steel met his and pierced him to his soul. He read anger there and hunger before the intensity of that stare sent his own gaze dodging wildly. Seized with the sudden urge to beg for his life, he bit his lips closed. He could not appeal to a heart that did not beat, that held no mercy. "What . . . ?" he finally managed, his voice a squeaky parody of normal. "What can I get for you, sir?"

Nightfall's voice was gravel. It emerged softly; Eldour doubted anyone else could hear it, but it held a commanding edge that all but forced him to comply. "Who is in the safe room?"

Two answers stood at the ready, depending on the questioner. The first, total denial that such a place existed, for strangers and town guards. The second, a blithe reminder that an army could not force him to surrender such information, followed by a quick warning to whoever met below. Neither found its way to Eldour's lips. For Nightfall, and Nightfall alone, he did the unthinkable and whispered, "The Brotherhood."

Nightfall disappeared into the storage room. Eldour felt sweat slick him all over: wetting his fingers, trickling along his spine, beading above his upper lip. The others in the common room watched him, perhaps to see if he would try to stop the demon from accessing places anyone else would need permission to enter. He glanced toward his bouncers, both of whom avoided his gaze. They would tackle the most massive town guard, or a giant of a killer, without a moment's hesitation; but neither wanted the job of trying to stop Nightfall. The patrons fell to whispering, and Eldour went back to pouring drinks. Even the pretext of interfering with the demon's business was not worth a horrific death or the rending of his soul.

Hidden behind the myriad crates and barrels of Eldour's storage cellar, flush with the floor and perfectly blended with the planking, the trapdoor yielded on well-oiled hinges. Nightfall descended the familiar dark staircase, careful to bypass the third step, which usually creaked in warning. Below, he could see the circular edge of lantern glow and hear the murmuring voices of a group of men. Still in the shadows of the stairwell, he studied the layout just below him.

A single rectangular table took up most of the space. Currently, all nine chairs were occupied, and three additional men crouched or sat on the floor. Nightfall recognized several of them, including the silk-swathed, coldhearted assassin who led them. Named Antrin, he had coveted Nightfall's position as the sovereign of crime, bragging he would one day organize it into a powerful network that would harass kings from their castles. Though he rarely spoke the thought aloud, he hated that the populace attributed most of his crimes to Nightfall, nearly as much as Nightfall did himself. Antrin killed with a bestial pleasure, often playing his victims like mice beneath a cat's paw. He thrived on their terror; it made him giddy with power; and, from what Nightfall had heard, served as an aphrodisiac as well. After every kill, a conquest followed.

The others ranged from lithe-fingered or honey-tongued con men to nimble thieves and hard-core murderers. The only unifying thread seemed to be skill. Like

Nightfall, Antrin had an eye for professionalism. Either that, or those of lesser ability who joined had already lost their lives to the Brotherhood. It would not surprise Nightfall to learn Antrin punished failures with death, though it would also follow that successes achieved great riches. Otherwise, no one would dare to join him.

Nightfall knew five of the men from a more recent association, memorized at the edge of the docks after his escape from the ocean. These exchanged smug glances, though the topic of conversation had surely changed in the time it had taken Nightfall to rappel to his cave and recover daggers and clothing carefully selected to enhance an appearance of menace. He had applied the proper scars, the filth that blackened his hair, and the false beard and mustache, which would take at least a week to grow honestly.

Antrin was finishing a lecture on how to maintain the mystique of the Bloodshadow Brotherhood, which mostly involved flawless execution of his own brilliant plans, terrorizing witnesses with senseless and brutal slaughter, and killing anyone who seemed too close to or interested in their organization.

Nightfall waited only until he had positively identified the group. Freeing one of his specially crafted throwing knives, seamlessly balanced and decorated with leering skulls, he hurled it at Antrin.

The knife soared soundlessly through the air, embedding, as aimed, in Antrin's throat. The assassin broke off in mid-word. His head jerked backward. His hands flew to his neck, and his eyes went wide with shock. Blood striped his knuckles, winding down his collar. Then, suddenly, he crumpled to the floor.

For an instant, nothing happened.

Nightfall used the silence to step grandly from the shadows, his expression schooled to reveal nothing but an ominous aura of lethal danger. "Now that I've introduced myself, I want some information."

Daggers zipped toward Nightfall. He dodged the first

with an effortless spin, and it clattered against the wooden stairs. Snatching two more from the air, he rebounded them from lifelong practice. Their wielders fell, mortally wounded. Two men drew swords, though the confines of the room gave them no way to swing without injuring companions. A grubby little con man made a leap for the escape hatch, crashing into the barrel Nightfall had placed there earlier. A moment later, his head reappeared in the opening, and he scrabbled to escape from this new prison.

Four more blades hurtled through the air. Less coordinated, these came to him in pairs that he again rebounded. Three met their mark, and the fourth went wild, leaving its thrower pawing at his neck anyway. He made a furious charge for the escape hatch, only to find it full of barrel and conman. In a move more desperate than considered, he slammed an arm against the lamp, spilling glass and burning oil across the tabletop. The old wood, saturated with years of spilled alcohol, ignited like a torch, filling the room with roaring flames and suffocating smoke.

Nightfall swore, forced to retreat. He could hear men thumping around the room, blinded by the blaze and aware their only viable escape lay behind the demon. Dizzied by the fumes despite his superior position, Nightfall knew they would all die in moments. He could not afford to allow that to happen. Catching a deep lungful of air, he plunged back into the room, seizing the first arm the flames revealed. He felt the man stiffen in his grip. A flash of red caught his eye. Before he could think to identify it, the sword in the man's other hand slashed wildly, tearing through Nightfall's doublet and underlinens to slice the flesh just above his left wrist.

"Hell take you!" Half blind himself, Nightfall trebled his weight and slammed a fist against the other's head. The man stumbled wildly, straining Nightfall's other arm and nearly tearing free from his grip. The sword crashed to the steps. Nightfall dropped his weight to normal and dragged whomever he held safely through the trapdoor. Not caring who tried to follow, he kicked the door closed and stood upon it.

Frenzied screams emerged from beneath him, muffled by wood. Their plight worried Nightfall's conscience in Dyfrin's voice, then Edward's. He ignored both. The Bloodshadow Brotherhood had sealed its own fate when it hid behind murder and when one of its members chose to start that fire. Hardening his heart, Nightfall played his part as he had trained himself to do. He flung his captive toward the shambles of the storeroom. "Don't move!" Using his shoulder, he shoved a heavy barrel over the exit. With any luck, it contained water, which might help douse the fire once it ate through the layers of wood.

The moment he finished, Nightfall turned his full attention to the man he had rescued. Cowering in a corner, the young thief had lost all of his earlier fight. He stared at Nightfall through eyes that fairly radiated terror, his face and clothing darkened with soot. Nightfall knew this man, too. He went by the nickname Roach and had a knack for petty thievery. The fifth or sixth son of a handmaiden who served a duke's daughter, he had learned sword craft from a real tutor, until his sticky fingers had gotten him tossed from the castle before he reached his thirteenth birthday. Now well into adolescence, he had surely looked attractive to the Brotherhood because of his ability to fight. No doubt, he had had a hand in the slaughter that resulted in King Edward's disappearance.

Nightfall rounded on the young thief. "Talk."

"No," Roach said, though it sounded more like a question than the defiant refusal he clearly intended.

Nightfall closed the distance between them in an instant. "Fine. I'm putting you back." He grabbed a handful of shirt at Roach's throat with a movement so quick, the boy never thought to dodge it.

"What?"

"I'm putting you back with the others," Nightfall said, indicating the covered trapdoor with a tip of his head. "I'll save someone with a glibber tongue."

Roach's eyes followed Nightfall's gesture, then widened. Terror flickered through them. He met Nightfall's gaze, a bigger mistake. What he found there had quelled nastier, more capable assassins than himself.

"Please," Roach whispered, though the grip at his neck could not be suffocating. Yet. "I have gems. Expensive ones. You can have them. Just let me go."

Nightfall had no interest in valuables, but curiosity got the better of him. "Let me see."

Roach's hand disappeared into his shirt. Nightfall prepared himself for the dagger the youngster might retrieve, surprised to instead find the two sapphires the captain had given him, balanced on the young man's palm.

Despite the looming fire, despite the desperation that had driven him to this position, Nightfall barely suppressed a laugh. The captain had warned him those items always returned. "I'm not here to rob you. I'm here for information."

Roach licked his lips, attention still on the trapdoor beneath the barrel. The screams had lessened nearly to nothing, but the crackle of flames became all the louder for their lapse. Soon, the entire inn might collapse into an inescapable bonfire.

Though not unaware of the danger, Nightfall refused to show it. If it came to will and guts, he would have no trouble outlasting Roach. "Where is King Edward of Alyndar?"

Roach's tongue flicked over his lips again.

"I know your so-called Brotherhood slaughtered a mass of guards and innocents. I know you were there." Nightfall forced his stare upon the boy, adding distinctly, "Roach."

The young man gasped. "How . . . ?" he started. "How did—?"

Nightfall did not let him finish. He avoided explaining his knowledge whenever possible. The mystery unnerved people more than grandiose claims, and it obviated the need to justify why a demon with supernatural knowledge needed to bully out information. "Do you really want to chat while the floor grows hotter beneath our boots?"

Clearly, Roach had not considered that. He shifted his feet nervously, as if the planking had already risen to an unbearable temperature.

"Now." Nightfall released Roach but did not step backward, neatly trapping the younger man against the wall. "What have you done with King Edward?"

Roach's features lapsed into terrified crinkles. He continued to clutch the sapphires, as if uncertain what to do with them. "Do you know," he said, barely above a whisper, "what the Brotherhood does . . . to traitors?"

"No," Nightfall admitted, hardening his scarred features. "But I know what I do to those who don't tell me what I want to know." He moved a step closer, placing himself nearly on top of the frightened youngster. "After I'm done tearing their bodies apart slowly with my own teeth and nails, consuming their still-beating hearts . . ." He smacked his lips as if savoring the thought of a favorite meal. "I drag them to the darkest, dirtiest corner of hell and gleefully rend their souls for eternity. Then, I start in on the family. For example, the mother who works as one of Duchess Hermollie's handmaidens. The brothers and, most especially, the sisters." He met the boy's gaze again, all innocence. "Is it worse than that?"

Roach swallowed hard. "They sold the king to the House of Xevar."

A slaver? The answer confused Nightfall. It made no sense for a gang of thugs to risk their lives slaughtering royal guardsmen to capture a king, only to sell him for a handful of silver. "I want the truth!"

Roach shrank against the wall, a wet stain spreading across his hose. "I swear it."

Nightfall studied the young man, reading panic and desperation but no deceit. He had always known when his mother's tears were giving way to rage at her lot, because she usually vented on him. He knew which of her clients he could rob with impunity and which would take vengeance on him, or on her. He knew when to approach for a proffered bite of food and when it served only as bait for a man as eager to find vicious pleasure in a small boy as in his prostitute mother. Alone on the streets at eight, he had learned to notice the tiniest details that inadvertently broadcast a person's every hidden intention. His survival had depended on it. Now, Nightfall realized, Roach spoke the truth. "Why?" he asked. "Why would the Brotherhood sell a king into slavery?"

A light flickered through Roach's eyes as he considered the question. "I just do as I'm told. No one tells me the reasons."

Nightfall believed that, too, trying to make sense where none existed. Someone had paid a phenomenal sum for Edward's capture, engineering wholesale slaughter to do so. To do nothing more than sell him into slavery seemed a madness so far beyond logic that only a lunatic could devise it. He raised a hand in sheer frustration.

As if it were a signal, the barrel over the trapdoor blasted into flames with eye-searing suddenness. Apparently, it held spirits, not water.

Roach shrieked, head jerking wildly, eyes measuring the walls for an escape.

Nightfall knew he had to get them out. And fast. "Go! Go!" Grabbing the youngster's arm, he shoved him toward the only exit, the one into the common room. Even then, he could not overcome his thieving instincts. As Roach stumbled blindly forward, the sapphires went from his clenched fingers to a secret pouch sewn into Nightfall's skirt tabs. Nightfall steered Roach around the conflagration, ignoring the heat as easily as he had the blood dripping along his left wrist and hand. Focused on Edward, he had not spared a moment for the wound.

Tearing through the curtain, both men burst into the common room to find the patrons on their feet. The fire had not yet reached them, and they knew only that someone in the storage area had screamed in raw terror. Just the barest hint of smoke funneled out here, lost in the haze of the storm and amid the warm, acrid odors of the hearth.

"Fire!" Roach screamed. "Fire!" He raced for the exit.

The response was immediate. Men lurched, ran, and staggered toward the door in a leg-tangling mass. Nightfall did not join them. Instead, he took the more dangerous route, up the stairs to the sleeping rooms and out the familiar window. Doing so eliminated the need to shove his way past flustered men wild for escape and ultimately got him out of harm's way faster. It also allowed him to maintain the illusion.

To the drunkards in Eldour's inn that night, it would seem as if the demon, Nightfall, had simply disappeared.

† Chapter 20 †

Wait out storms of emotion; act only with deliberate thought.

> —Dyfrin of Keevain, the demon's friend

THE STORIES OF NIGHTFALL'S RETURN were immediate and explosive.

Disguised as a nondescript traveler, Nightfall heard them as the primary topic of conversation in every tavern in Hartrin and even on the street. Not only had the demon destroyed Eldour's inn in a violent conflagration arising directly from his fingertips, he had also, apparently, murdered several innocents, including Balshaz the merchant. The rumors now suggested Nightfall, not Sudian, had slaughtered the king of Alyndar in retribution for his own execution. Demons, it appeared, never actually died. They just re-formed their bodies in some foul pit in the deepest confines of the Father's hell.

Though his ability to menace relied on this infamy, Nightfall took no satisfaction from the stories. As usual, they far overestimated his activities, in Balshaz' case to the point of paradox; but the populace needed that exaggeration. Better to believe all evil the work of a demon than of human beings like themselves.

After washing and bandaging his wound, which turned out to be deeper than he expected, Nightfall found a dark corner in which to doze. He knew better than to seek out the House of Xevar with his temper at its height and many hours shy on sleep. Those things might make him desperate or careless.

Once rested, Nightfall had donned his traveler's disguise, relieved a wealthy shopkeeper of a handful of silver and copper, and scanned the local taverns for food and gossip. With daylight, the embellished tales of his return brought the guilty pleasure that had eluded him earlier. The citizenry, from lumbering thugs to glib minstrels, from commoners to kings, had missed Nightfall. He shared the sentiment. He felt as if invisible chains had fallen from him, leaving him as light and free as air. The pall of ignorance had lifted; the world's secrets could no longer hide from him. He did not have to suffer surly nobles who dismissed him as a servant or shoved him into roles that fit him like child's clothing: wrong, tight, suffocating. No one dared to ridicule or dismiss Nightfall, and those who attacked him would die. Unencumbered by duties or relationships, he ruled the continent's nations with terror and intimidation.

The sensation of ultimate power lasted seconds, and realization returned to dispel the illusion. The burdens society placed upon him may have disappeared, but not those he had willingly taken onto himself. Nightfall had a job to do, a duty to fulfill. King Edward could never forgive Nightfall for taking up a role he had sworn never to revisit, and the pardon the young man's father had granted Nightfall lasted only as long as he shunned the demon character. By becoming Nightfall again, he had willingly taken the liability not only for every crime he had ever committed, but for the many more wrongfully attributed to him. He had broken the most sacred of promises, to those he loved. He could not lose sight of why he had sacrificed all of those things.

Ned sold into slavery? It still made no sense. *Why?*

Only after Nightfall had rested, his belly now full of tavern chicken, bread, and boiled leaves did he finally discover a plausible explanation. He recalled a story he had only heard secondhand, the one that had forced King Rikard's hand against his dangerously idealistic youngest son. As Nightfall understood the story, an emissary from Hartrin had visited Alyndar's court bringing a host, including several slaves. High-minded Edward had, at first, interrupted the proceedings, trying to get his father to break off relations so long as Hartrin continued to sanction slavery.

When that approach inevitably failed, Prince Edward had called on the Hartrinian camp to preach understanding and tolerance. He had attempted to free the slaves by simply removing their collars, only to find himself in a confrontation with their master. Ultimately, Edward had killed the slaver, and only the whip mark the man left scarred across the prince's face saved Alyndar from paying blood price. Diplomacy between the two countries, never good, had seriously suffered.

Now, Nightfall guessed, someone's need for revenge had gotten the better of his purse and common sense. Perhaps a relative of the dead slaver, or a well-connected friend, enraged a man he considered a murderer sat upon the throne of Alyndar, had hired the Bloodshadow Brotherhood to kidnap the king. Because the slaughter of the elite guards satisfied his bloodlust, or because he had made a promise to his informant in Alyndar, or because he stopped short of regicide, he had chosen to take King Edward alive.

Nightfall glanced around the tavern at its few occupants. No one seemed to notice him or pose him any danger. Certain he was in a safe place, a new thought struck him. *Maybe, the kidnapper preferred torturing the target of his anger to killing it.* Nightfall could think of nothing more heinous to Edward than slavery, no punishment more cruel and ironic than forcing him into it. The image of the king beaten into tossing boulders from some dank mine, the icy sodden air chilling his lungs to sickness, sent a bolt of heat through Nightfall. He could hear the rattle of the shackles, feel the sting of the lash gleefully cutting again and again across Edward's back. *No!* It was an evil even the demon could not contemplate committing. Despite his bold words to Roach in Eldour's inn, he had never found pleasure in another's misfortune. Nevertheless, Nightfall discovered a bright spot in his own imagery. At least, if he was right, King Edward still lived.

Nightfall threw down a copper, leaving his drink half finished. Now that he had a reasonable idea of what had happened, he felt ready to face Xevar and his House. As Nightfall.

Nightfall had chosen a deliberately plain appearance, and his study of the slaver's home and business in broad daylight did not take long. Xevar's house had previously belonged to one of the richest families in Hartrin, a two-story stone-and-brick monstrosity curling around a central courtyard that had once served as a magnificent, fenced garden. Nightfall remembered it as an attraction for every tourist, its heavy wrought-iron fence painted black and bent into pretty flourishes. Some passerby was always peering through the struts at patterned flower beds and healthy vegetable stalks weaving hypnotically in every breeze.

Now, a wall nearly as tall as the main building blocked any examination of the garden from the main road, turning the building and grounds together into a bleak oval. The House of Xevar took up an entire block, bounded only by roads and alleys. Slaves performed the lesser jobs, dressed in poor but well mended clothing. They wore the requisite collars and appeared thinner than the citizens but, for the most part, unscarred and reasonably comfortable. The paid help seemed to consist mostly of burly, well muscled men with coiled whips and or swords at their belts.

It did not take Nightfall long to identify Xevar ushering the occasional patron through the front door. The grown version of a youthful con man, he had worked a few scams with Nightfall early in both of their careers, before Nightfall had merged reputations with the centuries-old demon from a children's nursery rhyme. In his youth, Xevar had proved hard to fathom, his lies more believable than most people's truths, his features malleable and well schooled. Likely, he had honed that talent as a salesman, becoming whatever his customers needed at the moment. Bullying information from Xevar might not prove difficult; knowing whether or not to trust what he received just might.

Nightfall examined the exterior of the House of Xevar, from the shape, construction, and neighbors to the presence of handholds in the stonework and the strength of the roof joists and tiles. He turned his attention to the interior, which he could handle in one of two ways. He could make an excuse to enter the building, perhaps posing as a client; or, he could force the information from one of Xevar's various slaves. Though the former would glean him firsthand knowledge and details others might not think to provide, it would require him to play a role he knew little about. He lacked Edward's zeal for the subject, but he still disliked the whole concept of slavery. A prospective buyer who knew nothing of the trade would look suspicious, and it would gain him access only to the most superficial areas of the House.

Nightfall waited until dusk to don his demon gear. Self-tailored for intimidation, it required padding and coordination, meticulous detail, and the proper demeanor. The demon rarely appeared before his namesake time, waiting until darkness stole the colors from the world. He cursed Roach's wild sword stroke; it had left a large and irregular tear in his sleeve that revealed the bandage wrapped just above his left wrist. He wore woolens beneath his outfit, allowing for a quick change should he require a disguise to help him escape. To blend into the corridors, he had found himself a collar as well and hoped he never needed to use it.

Nightfall hid amid the alleyway barrels, some placed to catch rainwater and others filled with food scraps for some farmers' dogs, poultry, and pigs. Memories descended upon him of his childhood on the streets, when a swiped handful of greasy peelings, seeds, half chewed leftovers, and hard, withered fruit served as a meal. Often, the slop left him with vomiting and bellyaches, but even those seemed preferable to the dull, empty ache of hunger most times.

Hunkered down in the alley, Nightfall watched the normal internal workings of the slave house from an alley overlooking the back door. He could not study the comings and goings of the traders, buyers, and sellers; but those did not interest him at the moment. He took his cues from the slaves, mostly women of widely varying ages who came nearest to his vantage point. Some scooped water into pots and buckets, careful not to spill or waste a drop. Others scraped plates into the barrels of leavings. Most did their jobs without supervision, trusted slaves secure in their lots; but a few warranted burly overseers who watched their every move.

Nightfall let all of them pass unbothered. Though women usually made better squealers than men, for the most part easier to frighten and better observers, their absences tended to be more noticeable and alarming. They also proved harder to silence. Admitting to having caved under duress came harder to men, trained to defend self and hearth, while women seemed eager to discuss their ordeal. Some even embellished their trials, claiming rapes that never happened or bearing an infant from some indiscretion they later bragged was demonsired.

Nightfall's opportunity came later, when the male slaves arrived to empty bathwater used first by the clients, then the paid staff, before the slaves put it, and any remaining warmth, to their own uses. By the time it reached them, it would have turned gray or brown from the previous bathers, but it still stripped off some of the filth and stench or relieved their itching. After a few weeks, Nightfall knew from experience, a mud puddle seemed better than another day of stewing in one's own dirt, scales, and sweat.

The first two slaves eluded him by coming out together. The third and fourth were closely guarded. By then, the steady stream of women had ended as well, and it seemed as if Nightfall might have to give his scrutiny one more day. The idea raised a flash of anger. Edward had already suffered this long; even a few more weeks did not seem critical. Yet, the thought of the king spending one more day as a slave boiled Nightfall's blood. The urge to slaughter every man who had had a hand in the kidnapping almost overwhelmed him. He had destroyed a big part of the Bloodshadow Brotherhood, but certainly not all of it. He might spend the rest of the year tracking down every individual who had dared to join or support them, reaping all of them until he found the last, cowering man. And cower, they would, he felt certain, once they saw what he inflicted on the other members.

Then, Nightfall saw him, the lowliest of the low, a boy not yet in his teens emptying chamber pots. He seemed unbothered by the inherent ghastliness of his job, humming tunelessly as he dumped their contents into the manufactured gutter that carried waste away from the House of Xevar and toward the southeastern part of town. His hair hung in a sandy fringe of tangles, dirt showed on his neck above and below the collar, and he reeked of urine, which he had probably grown accustomed to spilling over his clothes as he walked. Glancing around to be sure no one traveled the nearby roadways, no neighbor chanced to look in his direction, Nightfall caught the boy. He wrapped one arm around the small face, hand pressed against his mouth to silence any screams. He snaked his other arm across the boy's abdomen and dragged him into the shadows behind the barrels.

The boy never struggled. Apparently accustomed to manhandling, he went limp in Nightfall's grip, dropping the chamber pot with a muffled clang, and allowed his back to be pulled tight against his captor.

Nightfall poked the potboy's side with a fingernail to simulate a menacing blade. "Don't yell," he whispered.

The boy nodded as well as he could in Nightfall's grasp.

"I'm not going to hurt you. I just need some information about your . . . master."

The boy nodded more briskly, clearly eager to assist.

Trusting his assessment, Nightfall eased his hand from the other's mouth. He spun the boy toward him. "Do you know who I am?"

As he came face-to-face with the demon, the boy bit a scream into a sharp squeak. Lips tightened to a white line, he nodded. He apparently did not trust himself to speak.

"Who is your master?"

The slave trembled. "Are you gonta kill me?"

Nightfall did not have time to waste. "Horribly."

The boy turned white as bleached linen.

"But only if you continue to dodge my questions. If you give me the truth, and tell no one of our meeting, I won't harm you."

Suddenly, the boy could not speak fast enough. "My master's Xevar. Xe-var." Apparently worried to leave anything out, he added, "Unless'n he sells me. Or trades me. Then, I belongsta whoever he sells or trades me to, and—."

Nightfall put a stop to the worthless and unnecessary flow of words. "Where does Xevar sleep?"

"In—in his bedroom, my lord."

Nightfall kept his attention on the boy but did not use the stare; that might terrify the slave into silence. He could not, however, keep a growl from entering his voice. "Which is where?"

"Jus' ou'side the forbidded courtyard, my lord."

"Forbidden courtyard." Nightfall mulled his first piece of useful information. "Forbidden to whom?"

"Ta everone, lord." The boy wiped his hands repeatedly on his britches. "Everone 'ceptin' Master Xevar an' his sister, Mistress Jacquellette." He dropped his voice still further, so Nightfall had to strain to hear. "No one else what go in ever come out. Alive."

Now, the boy had Nightfall's full attention. "What happens to them?"

The boy shrugged. "Nobody knows, my lord. Any slave what so much as claimsta catch a glimpse a wha's there gits taked in there by the master or mistress."

"And?"

The potboy stopped his hand rubbing to swipe his fingers across his nose. "Never come back, my lord. Not ever." His eyes turned liquid. "Word's they winds up in nex' night's stew pot, but I doesn't believe it."

"Why not?"

" 'Cause the master ain't mean otherwise, my lord. Can't believe he'd make us eat people, 'specially ones we knowed."

"And the mistress?"

The boy hung his head. "She ain't so nice, lord. She might kick or slap someone what gets in her way, but she mostly jus' ignores us so long's we stay 'way from her."

"So what happens in the courtyard?"

Small shoulders heaved upward, then fell again. "Can't say, my lord. Like I tole you, no one who goed in ever comed out."

Nightfall had not forgotten. "Surely someone has seen something. Through the windows, maybe?"

The boy shook his head vigorously, dislodging bits of twig and leaves from his sandy hair. "No windas, my lord. Master had 'em all bricked up 'ceptin the ones from his own quarters and the mistress'. No one sees in, and I don't know as anyone would look even if they could. That might get 'em taked into the courtyard."

The information about the courtyard seemed more like a strange curiosity, unless Xevar hid Edward there. More importantly, Nightfall had learned the master's quarters sat on the inner part of the ground floor. Most merchants lived in rooms atop their businesses. Xevar, apparently, had arranged his shop opposite the norm. On a hunch, he asked. "Does Xevar use a guard at night?"

"Three, my lord. They stand ou'side his door, 'lert and ready. I hear he's got dogs insi'e with him, too." The boy returned to the nervous ritual of rubbing his hands against his pants, though whether to clean his filthy hands on the fabric or the grimy, urine-soaked home-spun onto his palms, Nightfall could not guess. "If they's the same an'mals what begs bones and scraps from the kitchen staff durin' the day, they's big and toothy."

Nightfall frowned. He had learned long ago that the cover of darkness was not always the most important consideration. People tended to take more precautions at night, when they felt most vulnerable, placing guards and locks on things readily available during the daylight hours. Some of Nightfall's most spectacular heists had occurred the day before the theft got noticed, enhancing the stunned belief that Nightfall could confound the most sophisticated security. Surely no one human could steal a gem from a chained iron box with thirty keys and twice as many guards. As often as not, they never realized the item had left the box before the safeguards were applied.

"Is there any other time when your master tends to be alone?"

"Other times?" The boy glanced around the barrels, then shivered, as if suddenly aware he was chatting amicably with a demon. "He's not always 'lone at night-time, my lord. He's like to take one of the girl-slaves with him to bed. Likes the new ones best, 'specially if they's young."

Nightfall's opinion of Xevar plummeted still further. "Alone times?" he reminded.

"He 'bout always takes midday meal in his room, my lord. By hisself." The boy started trembling with the uncontrollable intensity usually attributable to cold. He spoke his fear aloud. "Now you gots what you wants, my lord, could you kill me nicely 'stead of horribly?"

Nightfall did not allow himself to smile, which might ruin an image he had cultivated for decades. "I keep my promises. I said I wouldn't harm you, and I won't. Not so long as you tell no one about our conversation, at least for the next week."

The potboy looked nervous. He clearly wanted to believe the demon's words yet worried for his back. "No one, my lord." He bowed deferentially several times. "Never even happened."

Nightfall reinforced the superstition. People claimed they merely had to whisper their needs upon the wind for Nightfall to hear them, that he would take those jobs he considered worthy of his effort and demand payment afterward. Few dared make such requests, however, since they also believed he exacted high payment and brutally murdered those who frivolously wasted his time. "I'll know if you break that promise."

The boy nodded in zealous and obvious faith. "Yes, my lord. Of course."

Nightfall dismissed the other with a flick of his fingers. "You may go."

The potboy did not wait for a second invitation. Grabbing up the dropped chamber pot, he scurried back toward the mansion.

An evening breeze twined through the alley, carrying the odors of woodsmoke and grease, of urine and damp. It riffled through Nightfall's hair like a brother's hand, and the smell seemed right, the very definition of city night. Alone and free, he had gained in a single day what he had not managed in weeks in other guise. The darkened streets and alleys belonged to him, and the citizenry of every class bowed before the demon lord who had survived the wiles of courtiers and kings, of assassins and thugs, of death itself. Borders came and went, illness struck down the good and the wicked, feuds and diplomacy ran their fiery courses. Only one thing remained constant, terrifying and unpredictable, yet always real. The demon of centuries of legend.

He was Nightfall. The power inherent in that persona, the pure and absolute freedom in that name, was at once staggeringly awesome and hideously vile.

Nightfall moved silently, fusing like liquid with the shadows, and became the depths of city darkness. Finding a quiet corner, he slipped into it and fell asleep to the natural fragrance and harmony of Hartrin's alleys.

Nightfall awakened with the sun and donned his traveler's disguise long enough to buy a satisfying breakfast with his stolen money. He spent the rest of the morning as the demon, though no one saw him. He remained high above the city, crawling among the beamed and tiled rooftops with the quiet ease of long practice, rarely scaring up the roosting doves. He carried a hook better suited to fishing on a long thin line, all he needed for the most difficult climbs. His weight-shifting ability obviated the need for heavy ropes and grapples. Below him, guards crisscrossed the city in packs, apparently seeking him. They carried obvious weaponry, loosened in their scabbards, and the same folk who had treated Balshaz so kindly would sell out the demon at a single glance if they thought they could get away with it.

A mansion on the next block afforded him the best overview of the House of Xevar. Four stories tall, it sported spectacular stonework in the form of gargoyles, crenelations, and spires. Pressed against the cold stone, Nightfall gained a bird's-eye view of the richest quarter of the city. Massive homes with the capacity to house a hundred commoners sprang up in every direction, all dwarfed by the castle, yet palatial in their own right.

From above, Xevar's building was a half circle of bulky brick and granite wrapped around what was once a delicate and fertile garden. A huge stone wall blocked any view of the courtyard from the street, and the house served the same purpose from every other angle. A wooden barrier bordered the entire garden, taller than a man, to prevent anyone who was repairing tiles or scraping muck from atop the slave house from catching a peek inside it.

The rooftop of Nightfall's chosen perch did not afford him a reasonable view either, because of distance. Only when he clambered down the ornate levels to a ledge slick with decaying leaves and fungi did he get a good look inside that mysterious place, surprised to find nothing of interest. No flowers or herbs grew within those walls, though the deep brown dirt appeared to have been turned over multiple times, as if in preparation for a planting. A few scraggly trees rose from within, their boughs haggard and broken; it looked like children had spent hours swinging from them. Even the trunks appeared beaten down; and one had a split, perhaps from a direct strike of lightning. A pile of shattered crockery and wood filled one corner, and bits of debris littered much of the remaining space. The only nod to wealth was a bench carved from a single piece of white stone that sat, positioned at a fashionable diagonal, at the opposite end from the bulk of the mess.

Nightfall could only guess at the purpose for the courtyard. With no slaves or servants to tend it, it had withered into disrepair; and the master clearly would not lower himself to the chore of rendering his sanctuary comfortable. He supposed it made sense for a man who trafficked in humans to need a place of solitude. Unlike a smith or a craftsman, Xevar's wares could report and gossip on his every utterance, location, or mistake. They had needs that crops, crafts, and clothing did not. He had to deal with food, illnesses, and injuries, with fights and escapes, with guards as well as clients.

Once, Nightfall suspected, Xevar had used the courtyard as a fragrant and beautiful getaway from the stresses of his day. As the flowers and fruit withered, Xevar had not bothered to replace them; and his personal refuge became more symbolic than real.

Realizing he had put the most pleasant perspective on the matter, Nightfall considered other uses for a devastated garden. The potboy had mentioned Xevar's appetite for young slave girls. Perhaps he preferred them outside or in groups his quarters could not accommodate. He might host orgies, hidden from the eyes, though probably not the ears, of his neighbors. That did not fit the boy's claim that no one other than Xevar and his sister emerged alive from the courtyard, but it still might happen. Since the only entrances into the garden apparently came from the rooms of the master and mistress, who could know for certain whether Xevar took the women into his bedroom or the courtyard? Fearing for their lives, the female slaves might vehemently deny having gone there. Or, perhaps, the disturbances in the ground represented the unmarked graves of those who squealed.

Another idea crinkled Nightfall's nose in disgust. Most adult unmarried brothers and sisters did not live in the same house. It seemed possible Xevar and Jacquellette did something together that required privacy, since the laws of most countries forbade incest. Even in Trillium, where any object or act allowed by any kingdom was legal, most people hid such liaisons. In fact, no matter its legitimacy, any behavior that disgusted at least a significant minority of citizens tended to occur behind closed doors, especially sexual acts beyond the conventional norm.

The appearance of Xevar in the courtyard, just before midday, interrupted a chain of thought growing wickeder by the moment. The slaver entered alone, a bundle dangling from one hand. Sunlight sparked gold highlights through a receding crop of oiled brown hair.

The face was lined and angular, having lost the fullness of youth, but not yet etched. Nightfall could not assess height from his angle, but he already knew Xevar stood nearly a head taller than he did and weighed easily twice his natural weight. Unlike Edward, Xevar's extra bulk was not all muscle. Though he clearly performed enough menial work to pack some sinew onto his frame, he also carried the soft overlap that accompanied a life of luxury.

Nightfall waited until Xevar settled onto the bench, setting the parcel beside him. He unwrapped it to reveal cut fruit and cheese, chunks of roasted meat, and a covered bowl. Then, Nightfall tossed his hook. It looped in a neat downward arc, landing against the wall of the courtyard. He tugged gently, measuring each movement, feeling the metal scrape over irregularities until it caught unsteadily. It would not hold long, but it would take more than a stiff breeze to dislodge it. He wound his end of the line around the nearest gargoyle, then dropped his weight to its lowest. Seizing the light line, more thread than rope, he glided soundlessly to the top of the wall. Relying more on friction than handholds, he slid into the courtyard with Xevar.

Apparently taking no notice, Xevar stretched luxuriously, then tipped his head back to catch the warm rays of the sun. A breeze ruffled the plain pale-blue cloak he wore over silks of rich design, deftly patterned with gold stitching wound and flourished into animal shapes. He sat enjoying the weather for several moments, while Nightfall crept silently nearer. The chill in the air clearly did not bother Xevar.

It was over in an instant: a leap, a swirl of cloth, a shift of weight, and a flash of steel. A bewildered and terrified Xevar lay in the dirt, gagged by his own cloak and pinned by the enhanced bulk of the demon, a dagger at his meaty throat.

"You scream, you're dead," Nightfall said.

Xevar nodded, eyes wide and broadcasting his fear.

Nightfall flicked the cloak from Xevar's face with one deft movement. "Where's the king?"

"W–what?"

Heat rose to Nightfall's face, but he stifled the anger that accompanied it. No matter how liberating it might feel, he could not afford to carve Xevar into steaks. Yet. "Where is King Edward of Alyndar?"

"King Edward of . . . ?" Xevar was stalling, trying to regather wits the unexpected attack had scattered.

Nightfall pressed the dagger more firmly against Xevar's throat, not caring that he drew blood. "What have you done with him, you obnoxious, lying bastard? Tell me, or I'll free your shoulders from the burden of your ugly head."

Xevar closed his eyes, mumbling incoherently.

Nightfall allowed the man several moments of what seemed like prayer. No gods would come to his aid; they never did. And, despite his methods, Nightfall actually held the moral high ground.

Finally, Xevar stopped muttering. "I don't have him."

The rage Nightfall had endured moments earlier drained away. Suddenly, he looked upon his old memories of Xevar fondly and felt compelled to give the slaver the benefit of his doubts. He seemed like a decent man, the kind he might have befriended under other circumstances. "You had him." It was not a question, and it left no room for a denial. "The Bloodshadow Brotherhood sold him to you."

Presented with Nightfall's knowledge, Xevar could hardly deny it. "I did."

Though many questions plagued him, Nightfall jumped to the only one that mattered. "What did you do with him?"

"I sold him." Xevar met Nightfall's eyes, apparently attempting to read any emotion betrayed there, but he soon glanced away. "To another slaver. A man named Cherokint."

Nightfall examined every aspect of Xevar's face,

searching for truth. He usually had no difficulty reading men, but Xevar puzzled him. He found himself liking the slaver, wanting to believe every word he uttered, though his expression revealed nothing but understandable dread. The inconsistencies of his appraisal bothered Nightfall; but, as always, he went with his instinct. "And?"

"I warned him." Xevar's features screwed tight against remembrance. "I told Cherokint a man like that one never makes a decent slave—too accustomed to giving orders to obey them. But Cherokint saw only the potential uses: the youth, the strength, the virility." Xevar shook his head. "Cherokint is not a patient man."

Though impatient himself, Nightfall listened. He somehow knew Xevar meant well, was trying to help. "What happened?" He did not lessen the weight restraining Xevar, but he did withdraw the dagger. He noticed now what his higher vantage had not allowed him to see. Three windows overlooked the courtyard, and two doors opened onto it, apparently those of Xevar and Jacquellette. "What happened to King Edward?"

"I'm sorry to inform you . . ."

Nightfall felt his entire insides clutch.

" . . . he . . . was killed."

"Killed," Nightfall repeated dully. Though he had known the possibility existed from the start, he could barely believe it. He had come too far, given up too much, to hit such a severe and final dead end.

"Cherokint has a wicked temper, though he doesn't display it often. As I understand it, he had the slave chained to a pole by his collar: half starved, regularly beaten with poles and whips."

Nightfall found himself incapable of movement or speech. A flush crept up his face, warming every part of him.

Apparently encouraged by Nightfall's silence, Xevar continued, "Once he became weak enough for Cherokint to safely handle himself, he personally took an ax to the fallen king." His voice became syrupy with a sympathy that seemed raw and genuine to Nightfall. "I heard it took twenty chops before he died, and his screams could be heard all the way to the docks."

No. Strength drained fully from Nightfall. It was all he could do not to collapse onto Xevar. The flush that had suffused him grew into a bonfire. *No.* He felt alternately cold as ice and hot as hellfire, his thoughts bounding off in a thousand useless directions. Then, abruptly, it all came together into a single encompassing emotion. Hatred seared through him, burning deeply and desperately, hatred directed against Edward's slayer. He could deal with the details later. Xevar's hands were not clean, yet Nightfall found himself incapable of laying blame on the slaver held fast beneath him. Cherokint had slaughtered Edward, his methods incalculably brutal and utterly merciless. *No!* He wanted to shout it to the very bowels of hell. *No. No. No! Not Ned. Not sweet innocent Ned.* He had long ago stopped believing the world had any gods, any justice, any logic to its chaos; yet he still found it difficult to contemplate how a man like Edward could die in such a fashion.

Caught in an internal conflagration, Nightfall realized his hatred bore a name. And that name was Cherokint.

† Chapter 21 †

Vengeance serves no master. Its rage steals even the most ingrained judgment, and it consumes the one it claims to serve.

—Dyfrin of Keevain, the demon's friend

ATOP THE TALLEST MANSION in Hartrin, Nightfall crouched amid gargoyles ravaged by mildew and time, staring at the heavens but seeing nothing. The world could have collapsed around him, and he would never have known it. Nothing seemed real but the staggering, unbearable dread clutching his heart and soul. He had no idea where to go, what to do next. He could not even find the strength to cry, to howl his grief at the heavens, to curse the gods and men and demons that steeped the world in such insufferable evil.

The force that had driven Nightfall for months had disappeared, leaving nothing in its wake. His emotions cycled like a windmill caught in a summer gale until hatred regained its fiery hold, filling all the empty places. Slaughtering Cherokint might soothe some of the vast loathing threatening to consume him, just as killing his mother's murderer had eased the pain. Stabbing the man who had tried to rape him as a child had aroused a pure and innocent joy, a vengeance that had satisfied not only his need for payback but brought the realization the depraved thug would never inflict his evil on another helpless child. What held Nightfall back now was not doubt or conscience but the realization of what such an act would mean to the man he avenged. No matter what evil someone inflicted upon him, Edward would never approve of returning it in kind. In an irony almost too bitter to contemplate, it would sully the king's memory to kill the man who had murdered him.

Nightfall knew his own life was over the moment he slipped back into demon guise. He had destroyed the trust of those he loved. He had betrayed Kelryn and Edward in the name of speed and gleaning information that, in the end, had gained him nothing but more sorrow. His mind conjured images of Edward, still trusting in the decency of every human being, an arm raised to rescue his vitals even as the ax blade slammed into him again and again. Nightfall could not help seeing the handsome features ravaged by the blade, the blood and gore thrown by each enraged hack, the absolute and excruciating agony that must have consumed the king in his last living moments. And those would have stretched to an eternity. Twenty strokes, Xevar had claimed. Half an hour or more of unmitigated pain.

Nightfall bit off a howl of rage and grief. *Not Ned. By all the world holds good, not Ned.* The thought did not fit in the demon's repertoire. He had known from childhood the world held nothing good, only a vast and unconquerable torment that scarred every man until it weakened him enough to kill him outright. Vulnerability was the ultimate weakness. A man could only be predator or prey; and Edward was the very definition of prey. In the world's alleyways, Edward would not have survived a day.

Guilt assailed Nightfall, too. If only he had not gone off to assist the Magebane in Schiz. If he had taken up demon guise the moment he discovered the carnage at the He-Ain't-Here Tavern, he might have found Edward in time to save him from death, if not from capture and humiliation. *I failed him. I failed Kelryn. I failed everyone and everything that matters.* The self-loathing Nightfall had cast off in childhood returned to haunt him now, every bit as ugly and bitter. He was not sure how he knew his mother had named him Sudian. She had never called him that, only "boy" or a litany of insults and swear words depending on her mood. For his first eight years, he had served as everything from her pimp to her pillow, from a supplier of food to a punching bag, with only brief glimpses of any love she might have felt for him. Only Dyfrin's friendship had allowed him to find the humanity within himself, had shown him comfort and caring and the way a parent should feel for a child.

Now, Nightfall cursed Dyfrin. It was the fault of his childhood friend that Nightfall was suffering now. Left to his own devices, he would have discarded his conscience in youth, and Edward's death would mean nothing to him. He would still see his feelings for Kelryn as an insupportable liability and jettison her without a care for her heart or his own. By reviving Nightfall, he had willingly placed himself back into an endless game of hide and attack and hide some more. Soon, the guards of every country, town, and city would begin their deadly hunts for him again. He would rule the underground by terror while the rest of the world feared and despised him. He could never return to Alyndar, not without King Edward to vouch for him, not with his only useful aliases killed or exposed.

Nightfall no longer cared who he betrayed: Edward was dead, and he had already lost Kelryn. Sudian could not resurface, forever linked to Edward's murder, though he had had no hand in it. Balshaz was drowned. Marak had been executed by Edward's father. Telwinar had given up his farm. Nothing remained but the demon and a scant handful of petty guises: a polio-stricken storyteller, an illiterate laborer, an itinerate drunkard. And one man was responsible. One man who had taken his best friend and ally away from him and left him fatally exposed and choiceless.

One man who, despite Edward's final wishes, was going to die horribly.

Nightfall rose, only then realizing twilight was descending around him. He had lain there half a day wrestling with his thoughts, without a bite of food or a sip of water. He could not have consumed so much as a mouthful without losing it, and the time of day did not matter. Despite a million of Dyfrin's warnings, despite his own innate caution, he surrendered to the murderous swirl of rage that had gripped him since his conversation with Xevar. What happened to Nightfall no longer mattered, so long as he took that hell-damned slaver with him.

Nightfall slid more than climbed down the building, not bothering with individual handholds. He touched down on a neatly cobbled roadway, scarcely aware of how he had gotten there. Instinct had taken over completely, guiding him to safety without a modicum of conscious effort. The graying streets yielded to their dark master, and he received no challenges; neither the vile denizens of the night nor the town guard impeded him. He never stopped to wonder whether his own knowledge and experience guided him to reflexively choose the best paths or they wisely chose to avoid confrontation. In either case, he easily reached the House of Cherokint and studied the structure without any conscious intention of doing so.

Blocky and dull, it had little to set it apart from the other buildings on the street, aside from a gaily painted sign hanging from the balcony. On it, strong, placidfeatured men and curvaceous young women clambered over the letters of the words: "House of Cherokint." Though it made no mention of the nature of the business, no one who knew the conventions of the trade needed more information. The slavers kept a low profile, so as not to offend visitors from those kingdoms who found the practice abhorrent.

Nightfall saw only one light. It blazed through a massive, stained-glass window on the lower level, a gaudy monstrosity that revealed the wealth of the establishment in a way nothing else but its location did. The colored glass displayed a scene of ships on open ocean, sails filled with wind. A pair of Hartrinian courier doves intertwined in play amid a friendly slash of sunlight. Sun dogs gaped in rainbow patches through breaks in puffy clouds. The artist had worked in a striking number of details, probably over several years. It would be Cherokint's greatest expense, his pride and his joy.

From its position in relation to the chimney and the root cellar, the window clearly opened onto the main dining hall. It seemed late in the day for a meal, but Nightfall could see occasional shadows moving along the colors. The thickness of the glass and density of its color did not allow him to pick out any details of the room or its occupants. The guise of Nightfall relied on stealth and quiet intimidation, but he had an eye for the grandiose when it fit his purposes. Now, he did not even consider the best option. He wanted the one that caused the most suffering.

Nightfall scaled up the neighboring building with quiet ease, examining angles with a professional eye. The sun sank farther toward the horizon, leaving a spectacular wake that put the artist's window to shame. The remnants of sun touched the horizon in an explosion of fire, and it backwashed hues in blossoming bands that spread through a startling, dazzling array of colors, closing down a day, a mission, and an era.

Nightfall tossed his hook. It sailed with the deadly precision of his daggers, trailing its nearly invisible line. He jerked it into place against the tiles of the rooftop. Seizing the line in both hands, dropping his weight so only enough remained to counter the wind, he swept, feet leading, toward the window.

As Nightfall struck, he restored his mass, losing the support of the rope. His feet thumped against the glass. For an instant, he thought he might bounce harmlessly from it and collapse in the dirt, unnoticed by the reveling guests inside. Then, the glass surrendered beneath his onslaught. It shattered, chunks and shards spraying into the room. Nightfall landed on a long table, driving up his weight to help overcome momentum. Women's screams rose over the frenzied slam of chairs being pushed from the table and the quieter tinkle of glass raining down on crockery and floorboards.

Nightfall skidded into a soup tureen, overturning it, and the wash of hot liquid added to the din and chaos. Shrieking people ran in all directions, dressed in peasant clothing and most wearing collars. Cursing his clumsiness, Nightfall slid over the far side of the table before regaining his balance. He hit the floor running. Two exits led from the room. He dashed after the figures fleeing in the direction of one of these and managed to seize the last, a girl, by the back of her simple dress. Yanked off her feet, she fell with a yelp, and Nightfall found himself supporting her. She stared up at him through eyes enormous with fright, and scream after scream ripped from her throat. The door slammed closed, leaving the two of them alone in a great hall that looked as if an army had fought a battle there. Amid the shards of glass lay hunks of crockery broken in the mad dash for cover. Cold air funneled through the window, now a jagged edged hole with unidentifiable triangles of glass still clinging to the frame.

"Quiet!" Nightfall yelled.

The girl ignored the command, still screeching in wild abandon.

Realizing the slave had no control of her mouth whatsoever, Nightfall dropped her. He bashed open the door to find a huge kitchen. An iron kettle still hung over the ashy remnants of the hearth fire. Utensils ranging from wooden spoons as long and solid as his leg to delicate bowls lay in dirty disarray. People, mostly women, had squeezed themselves under the chopping tables and into every corner, and the lid to the wine cellar lay ajar.

Nightfall grabbed the nearest by the ankle, dragging a girl of about eleven years from her hiding place. She stared with moist eyes and clear terror stamped across every feature, but at least she wasn't screaming incoherently. The others drew themselves in, crawling deeper into every crevice. The only other exit from the room, other than the clear dead end of the wine cellar, stood on the right-hand wall. "You!"

The girl assumed a fetal position.

"I'm not going to hurt you. Just tell me where to find Cherokint."

The girl did not move.

Nightfall considered slapping her; but, even in his current state of mind, he could not bring himself to raise a hand against a child. "Cherokint," he repeated, throwing the name out into the air.

For an instant, nothing happened. Then, a fat, shaky hand emerged from beneath a table and pointed toward the door. The finger jabbed a second time in the same direction, perhaps to indicate a door directly across from this one, then rose into an upward slant.

Stairs, Nightfall guessed. Loosing several daggers from their sheaths and palming six skull-headed throwing knives, he headed through the door.

He did find a door directly across from him, sporting a sign that read: "Do Not Bother the Master." A hallway opened to his right; and he saw a mass of armed men rushing toward him.

Nightfall flung the knives with practiced speed, one after the other. Each blade embedded in the floorboards a finger's breadth from the previous one, until they stood in a perfect line, every grimacing skull facing the oncoming men. He stepped out into the hallway to face them, wearing the glare that had made him famous. Despite his graveled voice, he enunciated each syllable of unaccented Xaxonese: "Next one's in the throat of whoever dares to cross the line."

The men in the front came to a dead stop, staring nervously from the row of daggers to Nightfall, who deftly flipped another knife to his hand. A few men in the back pushed forward. The crowd separated for them, but even they came to a halt at the low-lying barricade, losing their courage when the threat became close and real. Any of them could step over the hilts with ease, but no one dared.

Nightfall wished they would. His bloodlust begged slaking, and he could justify the slaughter of fools. A graphic demonstration was more likely to keep the others at bay, even after he turned his back. "Who among you is paid enough to die for your master?"

Apparently, no one was. Most looked nervously at their shuffling feet. Some glared with a defiance that proved all bluster. Not one accepted Nightfall's challenge.

Nightfall turned his attention to the door. Though this meant taking his regard from the men in the hallway, he gave no sign that dropping his guard bothered him. Doing so might invite an attack. His other senses told him what his eyes could not. The pantry door creaked open and curious peepers watched his every move with the same intensity as Cherokint's armed male slaves, servants, and guards. The sign remained in place. The door held no bolt or lock on the hallway side, but Nightfall suspected he would find one on the other. Likely, the master of the house had assured his solitude, and Nightfall would look doltish if he tried to barge through, only to slam against a door wedged firmly in place.

Instead, he drove his weight upward and slammed a sturdily crafted knife across the latch. The suddenness of the well aimed blow, the added mass of his now boulderlike arm, smashed the latch. It sagged crookedly from the frame. Restoring his proper weight, Nightfall thrust his fingers through the hole and deftly raised the bolt. The thick oak door opened with ease, and he slipped through it, drawing it closed behind him. *Thick.* Nightfall smiled as he carefully replaced the bolt. Though he doubted anyone behind him would have the dexterity or experience to work it the same way he had, he bought himself some reassurance by driving a dagger through the wood to hold it in place. *Thick enough to block sound.*

Nightfall found himself at the bottom of a staircase leading to another door. He climbed to the top, then paused there, heart pounding, rage like fire in his veins. Uncertain what he might find on the other side, Nightfall eased the door open and discovered a small library. In the center of the room, a table held a lamp and a single volume. A man bent over the book and did not look up at Nightfall's entrance, seemingly oblivious to everything but the yellowed bundle of pages in front of him. His arms rested on the table, on either side of the book, his hands holding it to the table. The last dying rays of the sun leaked through two small, high windows on either side of the room, and the back wall was comprised of a three-tiered shelf holding several more books, a few scrolls, and sheaves of scrawled paper. The room held the odors of ink and mildew.

Nightfall studied the man, who turned a page, then settled back into the exact same position, without once glancing up from the book. He did not look the sort who could wield an ax with enough power to cleave a man, even in twenty strokes. Flesh with just a hint of wrinkles sagged from his neck. His sleeves had worn through, revealing calluses at the elbows. He had a long, lean face coarsened a bit by age. Freckled and stiff, his ears jutted a bit too much, as did his generous nose. Dark hair liberally sprinkled with white spilled over his forehead and even onto his lids, falling just short of his eyes, which were brown. They did not hold the predatory glimmer Nightfall usually attributed to a man capable of the evil Xevar had described. He wore silks of a brilliant blue with just a hint of green, a color Nightfall had never seen before. This could only be the master.

Surprised by the man's appearance, Nightfall had allowed his anger to slip. He resummoned it with a name. *Cherokint. Edward's murderer.* He hurled a knife that jabbed through the man's right sleeve at the wrist, pinning the hand to the table.

Cherokint jerked his head up, just in time to watch the second knife glide through his other sleeve. He saw Nightfall, and his eyes filled with sudden and abject terror.

Nightfall liked that look.

Cherokint made no attempt to move, attention locked on the demon. "Nightfall," he whispered.

Two more throwing knives stabbed the fabric of Cherokint's tunic, affixing each shoulder to the chair.

Low on knives, Nightfall stopped with one still clutched in his hand.

A tear rolled from Cherokint's eye, followed by another familiar look, one of resignation. He knew what such a confrontation meant. In his mind, he was already dead. "Please," he said softly. "Just let me say 'good-bye' to my wife. My daughters . . ."

The request enraged Nightfall. "Did you extend the same courtesy to Edward?" The point did not fit quite right, which forced him to amend, "Did you let him say good-bye to his friends?" He had to fight to keep his own anguish from showing.

"Edward?" Innocent confusion accompanied the word, in tone and expression. "I know no Edward . . . except . . ."

Nightfall waited for the man to finish, in no hurry. Usually, he preferred to perform his dirty work and leave before anyone, even his target, knew he had come. Taunting rarely accomplished anything besides delay, and that worked only to the victim's advantage. This time, however, he wanted Cherokint to suffer the same slow agony he had inflicted on the king. If the whole of Hartrin's guard force broke through the door, so be it. It was worth a near-miss escape, a few wounds, to torture Edward's killer. It was worth his own imprisonment and execution to see Cherokint dead.

" . . . well, it's a common name among kings in Alyndar."

"Edward," Nightfall snarled. "The large man on the other end of the ax."

Cherokint stared, his expression still rife with genuine bewilderment. "Are you saying I fought with this Edward? That he tried to hit me with an ax?"

Nightfall wanted to slice off one of those jutting ears and hand it to the slaver, but his puzzlement seemed so raw, so real, he found himself doubting Xevar's story instead. He could not help liking the other slaver and that, in itself, struck him as dangerously odd.

Before he could contemplate further, a movement at one of the windows caught his attention. Nightfall continued to talk to Cherokint, giving no sign he had noticed anything unusual. "Don't play with me." Nightfall walked around the table, mincing his steps as if fully focused on his prey. He kept his every movement deliberate but casual, working his way toward the window. "You know what you did, you filthy coward! Binding a man so he could not fight for his life while you brutally slaughtered him." Nightfall noticed the irony of his words as he taunted the man he had restrained for the sole purpose of torture and murder. He spoke only to distract as he positioned himself directly beneath the window where the one he had glimpsed could not see him.

"What?" Cherokint fairly shouted the word. "I swear I don't know what you're talking about."

By lowering his weight, Nightfall managed to climb the nearly smooth wall without hand-or toeholds. Even slight and invisible irregularities held him in place when he had almost no mass to press against them. He had to keep Cherokint outraged. Otherwise, the slaver might accidentally give away the oddities of Nightfall's actions, the clear incongruity with his words. "You butchered King Edward in cold blood! Admit it, you bastard!"

"What!" Cherokint watched Nightfall from over his shoulder, not daring to struggle against the embedded knives. Though light, the silk would prove strong, and his efforts would certainly gain him more of Nightfall's wrath. "I did no such. . . ! I never. . . ! I don't even know. . . !" He sputtered, clearly uncertain in which direction to go first to proclaim his innocence.

Nightfall watched the window. As he expected, the spy had become uncomfortable with Nightfall's position, invisible and directly beneath him. A small head poked through the opening, eyes focused on the ground where Nightfall should have been.

The instant it appeared, Nightfall caught a handful of sandy hair and drove up his weight. They both fell, the boy screaming, Nightfall clinging to his prey and dropping lightly to the ground. He clutched the boy around the chest, pinning long, skinny arms against a wiry body.

Stunned by the unexpected fall, the boy barely struggled, and that lasted only until Nightfall hissed a threat into his ear. The boy went still, and Nightfall turned his attention back to Cherokint. "Are you, indeed, the master of this house?"

Sweat beaded on the man's upper lip. He clearly weighed his options.

"I'll know if you're lying."

"I haven't been lying." Cherokint trembled, though he seemed unable to decide whether he was outraged or terrified. His expression wavered, and his lip quivered, beyond control.

"I know that, too," Nightfall finally admitted, rage diminishing to make room for irritation and confusion. Xevar had clearly manipulated him, a near-impossible feat in the best of circumstances; and he needed to know why and how. "I still want an answer to my question."

The boy's breath heaved, but he did not fight or speak.

"I am Cherokint," the reader said. "But I don't know any Edward." He amended, as if afraid any tiny misstep might read as a lie to the demon. "Well, I've heard of the missing king, same as everyone. But I don't personally know—"

Nightfall ignored the rest. Usually, he appreciated that fear made people talkative, but now he was more concerned about keeping to the issue at hand. "Who is this?" He tipped his head toward the boy in his arms.

"That's Delmar." Cherokint's gaze went from the boy to the window through which he had unceremoniously entered. "A servant. He fetches things from the market and performs other odd jobs."

Nightfall did not understand. "Isn't that what your slaves are for?"

Cherokint clearly appreciated the change in Nightfall's manner. "Are you still going to kill me, Nightfall?"

The boy tensed, and Nightfall readied himself for a new round of struggling that never came. Clearly, Delmar had an interest in the answer to that question.

"It depends."

Cherokint asked, "Depends on what?"

Delmar held his breath.

"Depends," Nightfall said, still feeling the vestiges of an anger currently lacking a target. "On how quickly and honestly you answer my questions." He added pointedly, "And how much time you waste questioning me."

Cherokint paled. Apparently realizing Nightfall still had an unanswered question, he rushed to put it to rest. "Usually, the slaves do all the servant jobs; but it's hard to find real loyal ones, since all of them are ultimately for sale. Neither they nor I can afford to become too attached. Sometimes, it's just a matter of not having the right slave around when I need him. Or I can't get them dirty because someone's coming to look. So, I keep a few servants around to fill in the gaps. You know a servant's coming back if you wait to pay him till he's done the job."

Delmar nodded.

Nightfall tightened his grip. "Do you pay them to spy on you?"

Cherokint squirmed a bit, clearly uncomfortable with his atypical bonds. "Not on *me*."

It was not the answer Nightfall expected. "But you do pay them to spy?"

Cherokint sighed, as if loath to admit a vice to the prince of darkness and evil. "Our rivalry with the House of Xevar has gotten dangerously intense. We both hire spies to keep tabs on one another. I'm guessing Delmar, here, might claim his pay from both houses. Now that I think of it, it's possible others do, too. Don't know why I never considered it before."

Delmar drooped.

Nightfall looked at the boy in his arms who now appeared thoroughly defeated. If Nightfall did not kill him, Cherokint surely would.

Nightfall caught Delmar by an arm and spun him. Studying the features, he realized that what he had mistaken for a boy was actually a young man, lean and lanky but every hand's breath as tall as Nightfall. Seizing the other arm, he pressed them both against Delmar, again locking him in position.

Delmar dodged his stare.

"Why did Xevar send me here on a vicious lie?"

Delmar swallowed hard. "He said . . . he said . . . it didn't matter whether you killed Cherokint or he killed you." He cringed, clearly worried the messenger would suffer for the master's words. "Either way rid him of a nuisance."

Cherokint pursed his lips, features hardening. "Ah, so Xevar's taking this to a new level, is . . . ?" He choked off the last syllable, apparently remembering Nightfall's admonishment. Though he had directed the question at Delmar, not Nightfall, he still feared the demon's threat.

Nightfall paid no mind to Cherokint's slip. "So, slaver. It would appear we have a common enemy." He wondered why he could not muster the same rage against Xevar as he had for Cherokint and guessed it had to do with a mind-bending natal talent. He still wanted the other man dead, but the intense and overpowering emotion did not overcome reason this time.

Nightfall put his face directly into Delmar's, not allowing the boy to avoid his killer stare. "Where is King Edward, Delmar? Do you know?"

"I'm not . . . no."

The answer did not reveal everything. Nightfall forced the young man to meet his eyes directly, though it incited a yelp of pure terror.

Now, the words poured out. "A bunch of ruffians brought him in the middle of the night about a month or two ago. Xevar told us he sold him, but no one saw him go. Since then he's had someone or something in his private quarters that eats a whole lot. I don't know, but maybe . . ." He trailed off suddenly, eyes closed, shivering.

Edward might still be alive. Joy blasted through Nightfall so it took sheer force of will not to cry out in excitement, not to grin like a drunkard. There was no telling what Xevar might have done to the king; but, if he lived, there was still hope for a rescue. When he trusted himself to speak without revealing his emotions, he simply said, "Why?"

"I–I don't know." Delmar clarified, apparently worried Nightfall would not believe him. "Really. Honestly. I truly don't know."

Nightfall did not press. Even if the youngster knew something, it would as likely prove innuendo as truth. "What does Xevar do in that courtyard of his?"

"I don't know," Delmar said again. He whimpered, clearly afraid he had used up his quota of that particular reply. "No one knows. Only him and his sister . . ."

"*I* know," Cherokint said quietly.

Delmar whipped his head over his shoulder to look at the slaver, and it was all Nightfall could do not to look equally eager.

"Years ago, when Xevar first opened his shop, I tried to help him." Cherokint snorted at the idiocy of the statement, at reliving the realization he had created a rival who now wanted him dead. "He promised me an insane sum for any slave, no matter how weak or ill or homely: elders too old to work, suckling infants, anyone who did anything creepy."

"Creepy," Nightfall repeated, a sick feeling growing in the pit of his stomach.

"Inexplicable." Cherokint openly measured the effect each word had on Nightfall. "Anything that seemed dangerous or impossible; anything that made me uneasy."

"You mean," Nightfall forced out the last words, "the talented."

"Yes." Cherokint lowered his head. "I got wealthy on the three I sold him, more gold than twenty years of hard work brought me."

Nightfall winced.

"Then I figured out what Xevar and Jacquellette were doing."

Nightfall already knew the answer, but he let Cherokint speak it.

"He was selling them to sorcerers." Cherokint shook his head, clearly repentant. "I'm a moral man, and I've heard all the arguments for and against slavery. To continue in this business, I have to believe slaves are better off in servitude than immersed in squalor, poverty, and ignorance. Regular meals and a warm place to live, security and safety are worth the price of labor and even an occasional whip stroke." He sighed, changing tack.

"I'm not naive enough to think every master treats his property with the care I do, but the same is true of parents and a man doesn't choose those either."

A chill suffused Nightfall at the analogy. He would have no choice but to put his mother in the same category as the cruelest masters.

"If we did not keep and care for them, nearly all of these slaves would die on the mean, cold streets." It was a rationalization, yet not wholly untrue, and it clearly appeased Cherokint. "But I couldn't get past the fact that Xevar and his sister sold those slaves' very souls to . . ." He spat the word, ". . . sorcerers."

Nightfall found the association particularly shocking given that Xevar himself apparently harbored a secret ability. He supposed the slaver might be feeding a sorcerer in exchange for his own life. Or, perhaps, selling souls kept a dangerous enemy at hand, closely watched, and in his favor. A sorcerer would never expect one of the natally gifted to shower him with favors, even well paid ones.

"A baby who dragged storms from sky to ground. A man with a knack for talking the others out of their fair share of food. A sweet child who foolishly confessed her talent to a servant who sold it." Clear, gut-wrenching anguish entered Cherokint's tone. "Their sales haunted me as no others ever had. I couldn't sleep for the nightmares, couldn't eat for the guilt. It was only after I talked things through with my wife, with a priest of the Holy Father, and gave all the tainted money to the church that I finally found peace."

When Delmar showed no reaction to Cherokint's confession, Nightfall pressed. "Do you know what sorcerers do to their victims?"

Cherokint's eyes blurred.

"They cut their eyes out with blunt knives, beat them with salt-drenched chains, stab them with red-hot sticks cut to jagged forks."

"Stop," Cherokint sobbed.

"All through the desperate, searing agony which seems beyond bearing, the sorcerer laughs and taunts them." Nightfall needed to speak his mind, needed Delmar to understand the abject evil of what Xevar had done and was probably still doing. Nightfall's only small comfort came from the realization that King Edward had no natal talent to steal. "The means of the torture doesn't matter, so long as it causes the worst possible physical and emotional pain. For only then does the soul draw to the surface for the sorcerer to claim."

Delmar's eyes widened with realization.

"Please," Cherokint wept. "Please."

"It's never quick. The sorcerer has to keep his victim at that excruciating level of agony while he performs the foulest of rituals." Nightfall gazed at his captive audience, his face displaying the memory of his own encounters. Pain had filled his life, yet it had all seemed to come together and intensify beyond the worst agony he could imagine in the moments before the Iceman attempted to tear his body and soul apart. "Once you've seen it, you will never forget it; and the peace you found through talk and tithing becomes unattainable. This world contains nothing of more consummate and absolute evil than its sorcerers." Though it might diminish him, he had to say it, "Even me."

The silence that fell after his speech seemed more complete than death. No one even appeared to breath.

Then, a shuddering sob ripped from Cherokint's throat, followed by accusation. "Why did you do that? Why?"

Nightfall saw no reason to admit he had to. His righteous hatred for sorcerers could not have let him leave without Delmar understanding the brutality of one of the men he served, without Cherokint fully realizing the depths of his own mistake. Nightfall had not quite finished, either. "Even then, it doesn't end. The soul remains bound to the sorcerer for all eternity, and the owner of the soul suffers a repeat of the inflicted pain every time it gets tapped for the sorcerer's use."

From anyone else, the words would have seemed like pure speculation. The men Nightfall confronted believed him because a demon might actually know what happened to a soul bound by evil, even after death. Dyfrin had seemed so certain of the fate of those gifted who became linked to sorcerers that Nightfall had accepted his description without question, and it had become internalized as truth before he ever thought to wonder how Dyfrin could possibly know. Now, he understood. Dyfrin's mind reading ability had granted him an insight into sorcerers no one else could fathom. It was a talent as dangerous as the one Byroth had stolen from another child. With it, a sorcerer could scan minds until he found one belonging to one of the natally gifted. Irritated at himself for opening a raw wound of his own, he added in a harsh whisper, "Until, finally, the soul gets fully tapped out, snuffed forever."

"Forever?" Delmar asked, whispering himself. "Can't the soul ever reside for eternity in the paradise of the pantheon?" He quoted a common line of scripture.

Nightfall could never remember having believed in an afterlife, or even in the gods themselves. "There is no haven for the victims of sorcery."

Tears filled Delmar's eyes, and Nightfall released him. Though he followed a dangerous path, evil had not yet corrupted the boy of emotion. Nightfall doubted Delmar would try to run; he would find no solace in the House of Xevar now.

The room fell into another hush, this time punctuated by the sniffles of two men attempting to regain composure. In the lapse, realizations pulled together: one a description, the other a feeling. Cherokint had described one of the talented as "a man with a knack for talking the others out of their fair share of food," and Nightfall still had no explanation for why he had trusted a lying bastard like Xevar, why, even now, he could not dredge up the necessary outrage and abhorrence to butcher Xevar like the pig he was. *Xevar isn't natally gifted. And he wasn't selling slaves to sorcerers; Xevar* is *the sorcerer.* Nightfall considered how such a talent could serve a man like Xevar, to raise trust where none should exist. It would help in so many ways: soothing those he ruffled, convincing clients to buy at unseemly prices, lulling innocent gifteds to slaughter. Xevar had the perfect cover for a murderer as well. A master had every right to kill a slave of any age or type, no reason required.

Understanding sent a chill through Nightfall. "Cherokint, Delmar," he spoke words that had never before come out of his mouth in demon guise, "I'm going to need your help."

The two men stared, offering no commitment.

"To rid the world of a sorcerer."

A light shone in Cherokint's eyes, despite the tears. Still held in place by Nightfall's knives, he clearly saw his cooperation as atonement. "Just let me know what I can do."

Delmar formed an uneasy smile. "I'll help, too. If I can."

Surely both men knew refusing Nightfall was not a viable option, yet they both clearly appreciated the chance to help him. Their eagerness seemed sincere, and Nightfall trusted his ability to read people. It had failed him only once, and he now knew exactly why: sorcery.

As the plan took shape in Nightfall's mind, he instructed his willing helpers. "Cherokint, we'll need your most able assistant. And your wife, if you're absolutely certain she can play a part and keep a secret. They will have to convince your House, and everyone associated with it, that you're dead."

Cherokint looked aghast, but he nodded.

"I'll also need to know as much as I can about the talents of those gifted you . . ." Nightfall bit back the word "sacrificed," as it seemed too cruel under the current circumstances. ". . . sold to Xevar." Nightfall did not wait for a reaction before addressing his other conspirator. "Delmar, from you, I need details. The specifics of the House of Xevar, names as well as places."

Delmar nodded.

"I'll also need to know . . . you."

That obviously caught the youth off guard. "Me?" Delmar squeaked. "I don't understand."

"You will," Nightfall said, planning out his disguise. "Soon enough, my young friend, you will."

† Chapter 22 †

Kill enemies when you have to, but do so with calm dispatch. Uncontrolled violence is doomed to failure, in its consequences as well as its actions.

—Dyfrin of Keevain, the demon's friend

RAIN FELL IN A COLD and lazy drizzle that warped vision to a gray haze. The citizenry of Hartrin bustled through the streets, cloaks wrapped tightly and held in place with fingers wound through the fabric. Most hid beneath their hoods, and many grumbled epithets about the weather. No one seemed to notice Nightfall, huddled into Delmar's cloak, as he headed through the masses toward the House of Xevar.

Nightfall had waited as long as he dared, allowing Cherokint, his wife, and his most trusted to set up the situation in his House while Nightfall grilled Delmar on every aspect of the boy's life: from his interactions with Xevar's slaves and other servants to his mannerisms and routines. Nightfall had regathered his many knives and daggers. They had even managed to snatch a few precious hours of sleep before Nightfall became concerned about arousing suspicions at the House of Xevar over Delmar's long absence. Late morning found him in the sodden streets, wishing, along with most of the populace, that either the sun would emerge or the rain would come down in proper pelting sheets. Experience had taught Nightfall that the rain no longer bothered him once it completely soaked him. A sprinkle, especially one as dreary as this, tended to hold him in a chronic state of damp discomfort.

Fully ensconced in his disguise, Nightfall gave little consideration to Edward for the moment. Assuming the sagging posture of a typical adolescent, he knocked on the door several times with knuckles whitened from the cold.

For several moments nothing happened. Water dribbled from the roof in a steady trickle onto Nightfall's head, soaking his hood and the unkempt, now sandy hair below it, cut to Delmar's length and style.

The door edged open to reveal a man tall enough to scrape his head on the ceiling, with enormous hands and a remarkably coarse and homely face. "Hi, Deek," Nightfall said tiredly in Delmar's voice, using the nickname for the giant that the young man had told him.

"Hi, Del," the man returned in a booming voice. "You look awful."

"Thanks." Nightfall stepped into the entry room and stripped off his hood, prancing into a nervous sidle designed to look adolescent awkward. "Where's the master?" Peeling off the sodden cloak, he dropped it on the floor beneath an overburdened rack of hooks.

"He's with a client." Deekus jabbed a finger as big as a sausage toward the next room, one of several bargaining areas, Nightfall now knew.

Nightfall headed in the indicated direction, feigning exhaustion and fright. Slaves huddled around both entrances, trying to discover the fate of whoever had come up for sale. Nightfall ignored them, slouching into the entryway so Xevar could see him around the client. He waited several moments as the slaver spoke calmly, making an occasional smooth gesture to punctuate his words. Finally, Xevar looked up, returned his gaze to the client, then suddenly glanced at Nightfall again.

Nightfall dodged Xevar's gaze, as Delmar would do.

Xevar made a motion around the client to indicate Nightfall should wait where he stood.

Nightfall did so, assuming a state of perpetual edgy motion. Though what little he could make out of the quiet conversation became lost beneath the whispers of the hovering slaves, the body language and movements of the two men told him enough. The client seemed comfortable, and Xevar's smile, though clearly contrived, formed the perfect bow of friendship.

The men rose, their business concluded. En masse, the slaves scurried in various directions to attend the duties they had forsaken during the bargaining. Nightfall stepped aside to let the client leave, watching him head toward Deekus and the door. Xevar went directly to Nightfall and reached for him.

Though the idea of a sorcerer touching him made Nightfall's skin crawl, he pretended not to notice. The hand fell to his shoulder, and Xevar's voice filled his ear, "What did you find out, Delmar?"

Nightfall jumped as if stabbed, whirling to face the master of the House with an expression of abject terror.

Xevar took a step back and raised his hands in peace. "You're a trifle tense."

Nightfall nodded vigorously, still crouched and feigning a slow recovery. "It was horrible," he whispered. "Absolutely horrible, Master."

Xevar used a soothing tone. Again, he mumbled incoherently. Last time, Nightfall had attributed those subvocalizations to prayer, but now he knew better. Dyfrin had surmised that the best way to tell sorcerers from gifted was to watch how they used their talent. Those who came upon their abilities honestly tapped them with barely a thought, but sorcerers relied on words or gestures to stimulate the captured souls. *He's using magic on me again.* The thought awakened the rage that had previously eluded him. He reminded himself he faced a sorcerer with the ability to befriend men who should mistrust him, and that brought another realization to the fore. *I'm about to confront a sorcerer.*

Nightfall had known that before he arrived, of course; but the understanding of exactly what it meant only reached him now. He recalled all three of his previous encounters with users of magic. Even his battle with the wounded child, Byroth, had not proved easy. Gilleran would certainly have killed him had he not carried one of Brandon Magebane's spell-breaking stones at the time. Ritworth the Iceman had all but taken Nightfall's soul, and only Edward and luck had rescued him. This time, he planned to take on a sorcerer alone, one whose known powers seemed awesome enough. From what Cherokint had told him, Xevar had the power to call down lightning from the sky and understand any language, as well as the uncanny ability to make anyone like him. Nightfall could only guess at what other spells Xevar had slaughtered and tweezed from innocents cursed with a natal talent.

Xevar studied a discomfort Nightfall no longer had to fake, then turned his attention to Deekus. "Get the mistress," he commanded. "Tell her to meet me in my quarters as soon as possible. It's important."

Deekus bowed. "At once, Master." He headed into a neighboring room.

Xevar led Nightfall in the other direction. "Horrible, you say?" Though his tone sounded only quizzical, a small smile played about his lips.

"Yes, Master." Nightfall felt the bonds of Xevar's spell fall away, found himself perfectly capable of hating the large, greasy man in silks who led him purposefully toward the center of the house.

Slaves scurried out of their way, heads low in respect as they passed, some murmuring greetings Xevar did not bother to return. Shortly, he stopped in front of a fine wooden door, cleaned to a sheen and decorated with scrolling woodwork that someone must painstakingly dust with an art brush. Xevar produced a key, used it to unlock the door, and placed it back in his pocket.

More from instinct than thought, Nightfall purloined the key, two others, and a pouch of silver between the time the lock responded and Xevar pushed open the door. A mingled aroma of perfume, wood chips, and oil greeted them, and the master of the house ushered Nightfall into his quarters.

Nightfall followed, still concentrating on appearing anxious and uncomfortable. Plush couches and chairs, perfectly matched, formed a circle that broke in three places for doors, including the one they had entered by. The center of the room held a combined piece of furniture that could serve as a desk, a wardrobe, and a riser of display shelves holding fancy ornaments and bric-a-brac from around the world. Tapestries and paintings overfilled the walls, clashing terribly, each demanding immediate attention. From its position, Nightfall knew which door led to the courtyard. The other likely opened onto Xevar's sleeping quarters.

"Sit," Xevar said, more command than request.

Nightfall perched on the very edge of a chair, but only for a moment. Still feigning fretfulness, he bounced to his feet, paced a few steps, then lowered his bottom to the chair again.

Xevar had no trouble settling deep into the left-hand cushion of the largest couch. "Delmar, I want you to save the details till Jacquellette can hear them. But I have to know now. Was there a . . . death?" Though he latched a look of concern onto his features, he spoke the last word with the tone of a man enjoying a favorite meal. He seemed to savor the sound of it.

Nightfall nodded. "Yes, Master, sir. A death."

Xevar glanced sideways at Nightfall, who had already risen again. He clearly tried to contain himself, but had to ask. "Whose?"

Nightfall paced, driven nearly to paranoia by his own

performance. A sound touched his ears from the next room, the one he assumed served as Xevar's sleeping quarters. He stopped in mid step, cocking his head to try to catch the sound again.

"What?" Xevar demanded.

Caught listening, Nightfall incorporated the caution into his act. "There's someone there. I hear him."

"Where?"

Nightfall pointed at the door. "In there."

Xevar laughed reassuringly. "Delmar, my bed isn't a 'him.' And, I assure you, it isn't making noises."

Nightfall refused to allow words to soothe him. "There's someone there."

"Oh, by the Father . . ." Xevar tapped the latch and shoved the door inward. "See? Just my bed."

Nightfall took in the room at a glance. It contained an elaborate, canopied bed with the curtains drawn back to reveal freshly spread blankets. A massive wardrobe filled one wall, and a chest lay at the foot of the bed. An opening led to a small area that held an empty chamber pot, a hand mirror, and a washing bowl full of clean water. A window overlooked the courtyard, stippled glass admitting only scant sunlight through the drizzle. Nightfall noticed only one oddity, a closed door in the opposite wall. He wondered where it led.

"See, Delmar. Nothing to worry about."

Nightfall barely heard another shifting noise beyond the second door. *Edward?* His heart hammered. He knew from Delmar's description that the House of Xevar had a deep lockup where they kept the most unruly slaves and punished those who earned a lashing. Delmar said a newly purchased, young male slave lived down there now, though no one knew what the boy had done to deserve his confinement. Nightfall believed Delmar when he said he had never seen a man fitting the king's description in the dungeon. "May I look under the bed, Master?"

Xevar laughed, then waved an obliging hand. "If you wish."

Nightfall dropped to his knees and lifted the bed skirt, finding only a slimmer chest and a pair of satin slippers. In an effort to maneuver nearer to the mysterious door, he examined the underside of the bed from every angle. Lying on the floor out of Xevar's sight, he turned to glance at the crack beneath the door. He could see nothing specific or solid, but shadows shifted at intervals, denoting movement. He rose to a cautious crouch and slid one of his stolen keys into the lock, masking the click of its tumblers beneath an artificial sneeze.

Impatience entered Xevar's tone. "Are you quite finished, Delmar?"

A knock came from behind them, at the main door.

Startled for real this time, Nightfall nearly brained himself on the door latch. "Yes, Master," he managed.

"Then come out of there so I can attend the door."

Nightfall rushed to obey, pausing only long enough to glance into the smaller room and ascertain it contained nothing other than the chamber pot, toiletries, and washing bowl. "Yes, Master. Sorry. I'm just jumpy. After what I saw . . ." He hurried out of the room.

The moment he came back into the main quarters, filled with its plush furniture, Xevar closed the sleeping room's door behind him. "Now sit," he said firmly as another round of knocking rattled through the room.

"I'm coming!" Xevar hollered at the door. He wrenched it open to reveal a woman nearly as tall as himself; the top of Nightfall's head might reach her eyeballs. She had the same medium-brown hair as Xevar, but she wore it long and thick, without the receding hairline. Though minimally coarsened by approaching middle age, her features remained attractive in a slightly masculine, heavy-handed way. Her lips were full, her nose just shy of bulbous, and her jaw square and well defined. Large, green eyes with sweeping lashes might have gentled the image had she not held them in an angry squint often enough to have etched crow's-feet at their corners. Her generous

breasts did not sag, and she had well defined curves softened by a healthy layer of fat. "Ah, Jacquellette."

Nightfall bowed.

Jacquellette marched into the room. "Don't 'ah' me,
Brother. You called me here." She caught sight of Night-
fall and stopped, her wide lips pulling into a cruel smile.
"Delmar."

Nightfall bowed again, not allowing himself to feel
the intimidation he tried to show. He already knew
Xevar was the sorcerer, yet his sister had the sleek
overconfidence and regal bearing down even better
than he did.

Jacquellette sank into a chair. "So, what happened?"
She pinned Nightfall with her emerald stare.

Glad his character allowed for coyness, Nightfall
looked away. He did not want to enter a staring con-
test with her. For once, his demon glare might not win.
He licked his lips, looking desperately at Xevar for assistance.

The master obliged. "Delmar's nervous. Says he saw
something horrible, but I waited for you to get the details."

"Horrible, was it?" Unlike Xevar, Jacquellette did not
even try to hide her smile.

Nightfall understood why Xevar, rather than his sister, met with the clients. The potboy and the real Delmar had said the slaves feared her worse than him, but
Nightfall had found their claim difficult to believe. Now,
he understood why. She clearly espoused the sorcerer
cruelty Xevar hid so well. Nightfall wondered if some
sort of magic allowed Xevar to shove that part of his
personality onto her. If so, she did not seem to notice or
mind. Nightfall supposed it might be worth the cost to
have a sorcerer brother at one's beck and call.

"Horrible," Nightfall repeated, hugging himself as if
to disappear. "Truly horrible."

Xevar explained, "Delmar's become so haunted by
what he saw, he thinks he's hearing noises from my bed-

room." Nightfall detected a hint of warning in Xevar's tone.

"Is he now?" Jacquellette twisted her features into a grim parody of thought. "Well, then. Perhaps we should hold this conversation elsewhere. Somewhere absolutely safe."

Nightfall did not like the sound of that. Not only did it seem certain to drive him farther from the place where he believed they might be hiding Edward, but he did not want to wind up in some dungeon cell or, worse, in Jacquellette's quarters. He pictured human heads dangling like trophies from every wall and images of blood and death in tapestries and paintings. Thoughts of her living space brought another worry home. Perhaps the door he had seen in Xevar's quarters led, not to Edward, but to Jacquellette, a secret way for the two of them to come together. Once again, he suspected them of having a closer relationship than just brother and sister. So long as it produced no offspring, no one would know. Perhaps Xevar had some magical way of preventing pregnancy, or they sold off the results of any union as slaves.

That thought sickened him more than the scenario he had created about the meeting between Nightfall and Cherokint, so he abandoned it. If the door in Xevar's bedroom did not lead to Edward, Nightfall would have to find another one. To do so, he suspected, he would have to rid the slaving house of Xevar and his sister. Neither seemed likely to prove an easy battle.

"You mean the garden?" Xevar guessed.

"Where better?"

Realizing their destination, Nightfall went utterly still. "Please, Master." He appealed to Xevar, certain Delmar would. No one would expect mercy from Jacquellette. "I can't go there. No one ever comes out of there ... alive."

Xevar tousled Nightfall's hair like a child's. "Don't worry, Delmar. You'll be the first. Right, Jacq?" Though he pronounced her full name as JACK-let, with only a hint of a third syllable in the middle, the shortened form sounded more like Jayk.

This time, her smile seemed more tolerant, almost kindly. "Boy, if you tell us what happened last night, you'll be the first survivor. We decide who comes and goes from the garden, understand?"

Nightfall bowed again. "Yes, Mistress."

Jacquellette made a gesture toward the door. "Xevar, lead the way."

Xevar obeyed, opening the garden door and heading out into the same dank drizzle that had assailed Nightfall on his walk to the House. None of them wore a cloak, and the droplets left darker circles on Xevar's silks. Not seeming to notice, he walked across the shattered garden to the same bench where Nightfall had caught him eating. As he approached it, he turned suddenly to Jacquellette, and Nightfall had to leap aside to keep from treading on Xevar's heels. "Perhaps this isn't such a good idea. You-know-who might be watching."

Jacquellette reached for Nightfall, and it took all his will to allow her to touch him. Like Xevar, she chose the shoulder, gripping so tightly her fingers gouged his flesh. She turned him toward her. "You saw Nightfall kill Cherokint," she guessed.

Nightfall wanted to slice every feature from her face, beginning with her insolent, pouty-lipped smile. "Yes, Mistress."

"Where did Nightfall go when he finished?"

Right here, you hideous, sniping bitch. Nightfall held his tongue; she made his role nearly impossible to play. "He . . . he just melted into the darkness. Became a part of it. Disappeared." It could not hurt to follow the conventions of his reputation. He had already ascertained from Delmar that Xevar seemed to have no magical way of detecting lies. "He said he had business on the other side of the world. In Alyndar."

"There. You see!" Jacquellette shoved Nightfall away like so many rags. "He's gone."

Xevar rubbed his throat, revealing a bandage beneath his collar.

"I told you that mind-power of yours would work on him, too."

Xevar finally lost his calmer facade. "Only after I already told you it did."

"But you thought it might wear off quicker. That he might see through it."

Xevar shrugged. "He's a magical creature. A demon—"

Jacquellette made a huffing noise. "A man masquerading as a demon, you mean. He fell for it as easily as any other dupe."

The urge to damage her became stronger, and Nightfall kneaded his fists at his sides. He wondered how Xevar could stand a lifetime of her and began to doubt his earlier thoughts of an illicit union.

"Jacq, please." Xevar rolled his gaze to Nightfall. "Let the boy speak. I want to hear what he has to say."

Brother and sister sat on the bench and turned their attention on Nightfall. Raindrops clung like diamonds to their hair, wiry from the dampness.

Nightfall cleared his throat. "The demon came, like you said, and he was angry. He smashed right through Cherokint's stained-glass window."

Xevar grinned. Jacquellette fairly howled. "So much for the slaver's treasure."

"Raged through the servants' dinner, and all of the guards, without a scratch."

Xevar raised a brow. "Still think he's just a man?"

"Quiet," Jacquellette said, attention wholly on Nightfall. "Go on."

Nightfall obliged. "He caught Cherokint in his library. Pinned him in about an eye blink. Said he was returning the favor for someone named Edward."

They both listened raptly now.

Nightfall swallowed hard and winced, as if to dodge a memory. "He killed him, then."

"You mean Nightfall killed Cherokint," Xevar supplied, though Jacquellette had already gotten Nightfall to acknowledge that detail.

Nightfall nodded. "Yes, sir."

Jacquellette was leaning so far forward, she seemed likely to fall from the bench. "Don't skip the good parts, Delmar. How did he kill the old bastard?"

Nightfall whimpered. "He—he—it took hours. He used knives, sometimes. Also his—his hands, and—his—his teeth." He covered his face. "I couldn't watch most of it. It was horrible. It was like—like—" He forced tears, sobbing.

"Like what?" Jacquellette demanded.

Nightfall peeked at her through his fingers. She was leaning toward him, practically drooling with anticipation. Even Xevar seemed excited by the description.

Monsters. Nightfall summoned the most gruesome image he could, though only a sorcerer could act in such an evil fashion. "It was like he was eating the man alive. Cutting off an ear here, a finger there, gouging out eyes, bathing in the blood and laughing like a fiend."

"And Cherokint?" asked Xevar, now as eager as his sister. "How do you know he was still alive?"

"He was screaming." The tears trickled down Nightfall's cheeks. "Begging and pleading, but the demon showed him no mercy. All that blood—I couldn't believe he was still alive, still conscious. But he just kept on screaming."

Jacquellette clapped her hands in glee.

If possible, Nightfall hated her more. He tried not to contemplate what these two animals might have inflicted on Edward. Doing so might drive him to a fury he could not control, one that would surely leave him dead. For, despite his demonic description of Nightfall, he was in fact, as Jacquellette had stated, only a man. Worse, a man with a natal gift. If Xevar only killed him, he would have to consider himself lucky.

As always, Xevar remained the more professional of

the two. "Delmar, did you find out who will take over the operation of the House?"

Nightfall wiped his eyes on the back of his sleeve. "I did as you bade, Master." Though he usually liked to confront his greatest danger, Nightfall avoided looking at Jacquellette, playing his part. "One of his guards, sir, a man named Davvi, is restoring order there. But the wife plans to take over once he does."

"The wife?" Xevar looked and sounded taken aback. "Cherokint's widow?"

"Yes, sir."

Jacquellette laughed.

"But she knows nothing—"

Jacquellette threw an arm around Xevar's shoulders. "Which is why, my dear brother, you must marry her."

"Marry her?" Xevar leaped to his feet, and Nightfall shuffled a few steps backward. "Marry Cherokint's wife?"

Jacquellette did not bother to stand as well. "You have the means to convince her."

"Yes, but—"

"And as owner of both main slave houses, you'd be the richest man in Hartrin. Richer than the king, perhaps."

Still playing Delmar, Nightfall retreated farther, edging toward the door. He would have preferred to place himself in a position of escape near the wall, but that would risk his role-playing. He also knew that, if Edward still lived, he was inside the House of Xevar.

"But our plans!" In his outrage, Xevar seemed to have completely forgotten Nightfall. "If I'm here managing two businesses and a family in Hartrin, how can I go to Alyndar?"

That got Nightfall's attention. He tried to disappear among the holes and shattered trees of the garden.

Unlike Xevar, Jacquellette clearly had not forgotten their audience. She glanced at Nightfall, then switched to the tongue of the Yortenese Peninsula, one he knew every bit as well, though Delmar would not. Nightfall would have to remain on his guard and not react to anything they said. "I've been thinking, Brother."

"Yes," Xevar said with clear impatience. His tone contained warning.

Jacquellette raised a forestalling hand. "Hear me out. It's a good idea."

Xevar remained silent, but he did not take his seat.

Jacquellette's gaze went from Xevar to Nightfall at intervals, but her brother seemed to have forgotten their guest. He had his back fully turned toward the house and Nightfall.

Jacquellette curled her fingers together. "If I take the soul of the new boy in the dungeon, I'll have control over the king of Alyndar."

Nightfall almost stopped breathing. If Jacquellette could steal souls, she was the sorcerer. Yet, he had personally experienced Xevar's ability to make people like and trust him, a power he knew had come from the soul of one of Cherokint's slaves. *Unless* . . . Nightfall's mind took off in another direction. *Is it possible Xevar's power is a practiced ability or even a natal gift, coincidentally the same as the slave's?* He frowned, doubting the possibility; but the only other explanation seemed equally impossible. *Two sorcerers? Working together?* He believed Brandon when the Magebane had said sorcerers could never organize, since greed eventually drove one to slay the other for his powers. *Could the sibling bond overcome that appetite? Was it possible these two actually managed to work together?*

Apparently as struck by Jacquellette's words as Nightfall, Xevar shouted, "If *you* take it? That soul is mine!"

Xevar's reply diffused any doubt. Nightfall's heart pounded so hard, none of his tricks could control it. To remain outside in the rain left him vulnerable to the lightning spell he knew one of the sorcerers controlled, and he now understood the purpose of the frightened child penned in the deepest part of the House of Xevar.

Apparently, the boy harbored a powerful natal gift that allowed him to fully control a grown man's mind. The sorcerers must have known of the boy's existence but only just captured him; otherwise, they would already have killed him, extracting his soul to dominate the king of Alyndar. Nightfall forced himself to breathe without panting. He was not supposed to understand their conversation. He needed to get inside and quickly. No one could fight two sorcerers at the same time and hope to live past the first spell.

Jacquellette sprang from the bench. "I found that soul!"

"But I'm the one who talked the boy's parents into selling him. You couldn't have gotten past the greeting without me." Xevar took a menacing step toward his sister, though the few fingerbreadths he stood taller could hardly be considered towering over her, and their weights seemed nearly comparable.

"It's my turn!" Jacquellette's volume rose to match Xevar's. "You have more souls than I do!"

"That's because you got all the power spells," Xevar shot back. "I only agreed to that arrangement because I knew I'd get more."

Nightfall took a few more hesitant, retreating steps. If the sorcerers would just stay focused on one another, he might manage to slip into their House unseen. With any luck, they would go to war, killing one and weakening the other enough to gain Nightfall the upper hand. He tried to think of a way to drive them to battle, seeking the proper words to inflame them without drawing their combined might onto himself.

The two appeared not to need Nightfall's assistance. Jacquellette's voice turned shrill. "Being able to control a king's mind *is* a power spell. By rights, it belongs to me!"

Xevar threw up his hands. "Any talent used well is a power spell. By that logic, all souls are yours."

"Maybe they should be."

Xevar's nostrils flared. "Are you challenging me?"

Though she clearly held most of the might, Jacquellette attempted to defuse the argument. "Look, I'm just saying we can both be happy. Me as the queen of Alyndar, and you as the richest man in Hartrin."

Far from pacified, Xevar drew himself up even more. "Both rich, yes. But you steal a soul belonging to me and lounge as royalty, while I work my fingers to the bone for wealth here. No! You can still be queen; I'll make him marry you. But I deserve the chancellery of Alyndar, at least."

Nightfall saw his chance. The two now seemed nearer to accord than battle, and he had gathered all the information he could from them. He sprang for the door . . .

. . . and nearly impaled himself on a massive spike that grew abruptly from the wood.

A twist saved Nightfall, and he found himself facing a door suddenly bristling with wickedly sharp, thornlike protrusions as long as his arms. One jutted from the latch, effectively preventing him from tripping it. He spun to face the sorcerers.

Xevar crouched near the bench with a strangled look on his face. Clearly, he had initially believed himself the target of Jacquellette's undeclared attack. The woman stared directly at Nightfall. "Where are you going, Delmar?"

"N–nowhere," Nightfall stammered in Delmar's voice. He suspected the young man would have fainted from terror, but his own instinctive dodge made that reaction impossible now, even if it might have helped him. "M–m–mistress." He suspected the sudden violence had as much to do with intimidating Xevar as preventing Nightfall's escape.

As if to confirm his suspicions, Jacquellette raised a hand, then snapped it downward. Lightning slashed the sodden clouds and hurtled toward him.

Nightfall had only a split second to think. Delmar would cower, but Delmar would also die. He needed to move, but sideways would not prove enough. Electricity traveled, especially on wet ground. Seizing the conjured thorns, he scurried upward, using them like a ladder. The bolt slammed the ground where he had stood, trembling it. Grass turned black in a wide circle. A nearby tree listed. Nightfall's nose filled with the odor of ozone, but the attack missed him.

Survival took precedence over disguise. Before he could think, Nightfall drew a knife and hurled it at Jacquellette. It flew true, directly for her throat.

Still crouched, Xevar coughed out a guttural.

A quivering hand's breadth in front of her, the blade struck something unseen and plummeted harmlessly to the ground.

"Thank you, Brother." Jacquellette calmly bent, picked up the knife, and examined it.

Only then, Nightfall realized he had used one of the skull-headed hilts that served as his trademark. An item meant to intimidate had now given him away, an unforgivable and unsurvivable mistake.

"Well, well, well." Jacquellette grinned at Nightfall. "Look what we have here, Chancellor Xevar." It was her way of letting her brother know she had accepted his version of the plan, to assure they continued to work together.

Nightfall weighed his options. He could continue to climb the stone face of the building, leaving himself fully open to attack, or he could descend back into a battle he had no chance of winning. For the moment, he remained in place. So long as he did so, Jacquellette seemed in no great hurry to attack him again.

"Could this be the great Nightfall himself masquerading as a lowly servant?" Jacquellette glanced toward the spot where Xevar had stood, but he was no longer there.

Though unwilling to take his eyes from the sorcerer who had confessed to having the dangerous magics, Nightfall glanced around for Xevar as well. He turned his gaze toward the twisted trees still standing in the battered garden; but, unless Xevar had learned to blend with them, he was not there. *Where is he?* Losing sight of an enemy boded more danger than Nightfall could tolerate. For a moment, he glanced anxiously around the garden. *He's a sorcerer.* That reminder brought so many possibilities with it. Xevar might have the ability to move unseen. Upon further inspection, Nightfall's first thought proved the correct one. When he focused on movement rather than appearance, Nightfall found Xevar, now colored a mottled brown and green, creeping quietly through the foliage.

As if an attack by two sorcerers were not enough, Nightfall felt the crawling sensation of unseen eyes upon him. He caught movement from the corner of his vision. His attention jerked back to Jacquellette in time to see her make an arcing motion. He released his hold on the spikes, leaping toward her as he did so. It was exactly the sort of response no one ever expected. This time, lightning did not streak from the heavens, and no sound indicated anything magical had resulted from her gesture. Nightfall landed as lightly as a cat, seized by the sensation of nettles stinging his legs. Certain he must have jumped into a nest of hornets, he glanced down, only to find himself standing on firm, wet ground. The pain intensified, running up his legs to encompass his entire body. *It's magic. She got me.*

Jacquellette could not help gloating. "Hurts, doesn't it, *Nightfall*?"

Goading seemed his only hope now. Ignorance would prove his downfall. "I've felt worse."

"For now, perhaps. But it will worsen by the moment. Perfect talent for a sorcerer, wouldn't you say, Nightfall?"

Nightfall had to admit it was. As the pain increased, it would eventually reach the point of no bearing, dragging his soul to the surface. She only needed to cause emotional torment as well, and she clearly enjoyed that part of her work. Already, it felt as if a thousand wasps stung him simultaneously, injecting poison into every part of his body. He suffered a stab of dread. If he allowed the agony to overcome him, she would discover his talent and steal his soul as well. *No!* He concentrated on Xevar's position, on finding Jacquellette's weaknesses, on anything but the growing pain. Whatever magical shield had stopped his thrown knife could have myriad properties. It might work only once or remain in place for hours. It could prevent only knives, or airborne weapons, or it might make her utterly invincible. It all depended upon the talent of the soul Xevar had stolen, and Nightfall's only hope lay in discovering how to break through it.

In quick succession, Nightfall flung three more knives, two at Xevar and another at Jacquellette. Each slammed hopelessly against a barrier, bouncing back toward him; and he caught them from ingrained habit. The magical pain worsened incrementally. It now felt as if an army of bowmen had shot him full of arrows. He gritted his teeth against the sharpness, against the agony threatening to steal what little concentration remained to him. He could not last much longer.

Jacquellette's laughter struck nearly as hard. "You're helpless, Nightfall. Helpless and dead. And not nearly as scary or powerful as the ignorant commoners believe."

Nightfall bullied through the pain, grounding his reason on one last hope. He rushed Jacquellette, daggers flashing. No barrier foiled his physical charge. He slammed into her, driving her to the ground. A wild slash tore through silk and flesh.

Jacquellette screamed a curse.

The pain became excruciating, a blinding, deafening swirl of agony. Nightfall gasped for every breath, his assault driven more by mindless intensity than will.

Then, suddenly, the pain disappeared. Nightfall opened his eyes to see Xevar and Jacquellette in front of him. Still the color of trees and grass, Xevar grinned wickedly down at Nightfall, who realized he had fallen to his hands and knees. Jacquellette had a tear in the thigh of her hose, and blood dripped from it in a steady stream that scarcely seemed to bother her. It was not a lethal strike.

Nightfall tried to rise, to fling himself bodily upon the sorcerers, but found himself incapable of movement. Once again a prisoner of magic, he had become rooted to the ground as firmly as any tree. Other than his eyes, he could not move any part, not even his lips to speak.

Jacquellette's laughter hammered Nightfall's ears again; and, this time, Xevar joined her. "So," she taunted, "the great and powerful demon dies crawling on his belly like a bug."

Nightfall could not have spoken had he wished to do so. He knew Xevar's magic imprisoned him and it had displaced the pain Jacquellette had inflicted on him. There was no doubt in any of their minds they would kill him. He had not dared to tap his own talent when he attacked Jacquellette. That, combined with the pain, would surely have told her of its existence. This way, at least he might die with his soul intact.

"Any last words, Nightfall?"

"Just finish him," Xevar fairly growled. "You know he can't talk."

Motion at the corner of Nightfall's vision grabbed his attention. If he could only turn his head ever so slightly, he could see.

"Then I will speak for him." Jacquellette circled Nightfall, a hungry look in her eyes. "I will say the demon died begging for mercy and screeching like a little girl." She raised an arm suddenly.

As before, the clouds split open, and lightning shot from the heavens. Nightfall watched helplessly as the bolt streaked toward him, noticing, with grim satisfaction, that Xevar had not moved far enough to protect himself from any backlash.

A deep male voice filled the courtyard. "NO!" A

shadow appeared suddenly between Nightfall and the conjured spell. The lightning crashed into the new-comer, driving him, spasming, into Nightfall. He toppled backward over the grounded demon and lay still. Pain burned and quivered through Nightfall, then disappeared. Without another thought, without bothering to see who had saved him, he drew a dagger in each hand and threw himself onto Jacquellette. Nightfall jabbed for the vitals and tore. Jacquellette managed a single scream before the blade severed her windpipe, but that did not seem enough. Seven more times the blade rose and fell before Nightfall recovered enough presence of mind to remember he had a second enemy.

Nightfall found Xevar on the ground, caught by the wet spray of the lightning. Blisters covered half his face and body, the flesh charred black. For a moment, Night-fall wondered if Jacquellette had planned it that way: to strike before her brother managed to stand clear, to kill him at the same time as Nightfall and rid herself of two nuisances at once. He discarded the possibility. No sor-cerer would waste the spells Xevar had carried. Some-day, she would have murdered him, but she would have done so with the proper amount of excruciating torture to claim the souls he harbored.

Though Xevar showed no signs of life, Nightfall drove a knife through his throat to the hilt. Twice. Then touched each staring eye. Only when he received no re-sponse did he dare to relax and finally turn his attention to whoever had sacrificed his life to save a demon.

It was Edward. Though gaunter and dressed in peas-ant's rags, his features were unmistakable: ungodly handsome, golden hair matted and dirty, his round gen-tle face so peaceful and still. A smoldering hole in the fabric covering his abdomen was the only sign of the lightning strike.

"No," Nightfall said. Then louder, "NO!" He dove onto Edward, pressing his fingers to the muscled neck, willing a pulse to thrum against his touch. He felt nothing. Nothing. "No, no, no!" Anguish clotted his throat until even that single word could not escape it. He had come so far, through so much, and found the king alive. *Why did you do that, you stupid, blithering clod! Why would you give up your noble young self for a worthless villain like me?* Tears stung Nightfall's eyes, as painful as the sorcerer's spell. He despised the morality that had driven Edward to such a sacrifice. With both fists, he pounded against the dead man's chest. "You hell-damned oaf!" He slammed again. "You guileless dizzard!" He hit the corpse hard enough to shatter ribs had Edward not developed so much muscle from his years of weapons' training. "You blitheringly ignorant, overmoral, naive pretty-boy!"

Edward coughed.

Nightfall fell on his ass.

For an instant, he could do nothing but stare, his hands aching, his eyes like saucers. Finally, he brought shaky fingers back to Edward's neck. A strong steady pulse beat beneath his touch. *What the hell? What the goddamned hell!* His gaze went naturally to the sky, and his unshakeable belief in a total lack of higher powers wavered. Then, he remembered a story someone, probably Dyfrin, had told him. It concerned a man struck by lightning, declared dead. Moments later, another bolt hit him, and he sat upright as if nothing had happened. Lightning often killed by stopping the heart, and a second jolt could start it just as suddenly. Apparently, a solid blow to the chest by a fist worked as well.

Edward groaned, and his lids fluttered open. His eyes rolled, without focus.

"Ned," Nightfall tried. He knew lightning could kill a man, leave him unscathed, or any of a variety of conditions between. He had heard of paralyzations, memory loss, ruined hearing, headaches, blindness, burns that ran the gamut from minor to severe. Any of these might last a day, a week, or forever. It seemed foolish to ask if Edward was all right when, just a moment earlier, he had literally been dead.

The king sat up, wincing as he did so, and a grimace of pain crossed his face. He groped in front of him. "Sudian?"

No more lies. "It's Nightfall, Sire."

"Nightfall?"

Nightfall lowered his head. Jacquellette's spell had left him aching all over, and he could feel the soft squish of blisters on his knees. Kelryn had been right; she always was. Now that he had taken back the mantle of Nightfall, he could never return to Sudian. He did not belong in Alyndar, had no right to friendships with kings and commanders of prison guards. He was the lowborn child of a prostitute mother, unworthy even of her love, let alone the trust of nobility. All the crimes, once pardoned, belonged to him again. He had broken his promises to Edward and Kelryn, had actually reveled in the power of a demon who ruled the nights by murder and intimidation. As Kelryn had stated, once he took back the title of the demon, he could never return to Alyndar; but it was not because he found the role irresistible, not because he loved the power and status that came with the title. He simply deserved nothing better.

Edward licked his lips, moving stiffly to his feet and managing to touch, then catch, Nightfall's arm. "Nightfall," he repeated, "let's go home."

† Chapter 23 †

A wise man learns to turn small details to his advantage.

—Dyfrin of Keevain, the demon's friend

NIGHTFALL WASHED AWAY the last remnants of his shattered disguise in the basin in Xevar's makeshift garderobe, then studied his reflection in the hand mirror. It was Sudian's face staring back at him beneath a mop of hair that still retained the sandy coloring of a young slave house spy. It seemed wrong, out of place. He knew what lurked beneath all the dyes and dirt, all the mud and putty, the manipulated expressions and molded features, yet it seemed impossible he could ever again see the fair skin, the strong chin, the straight nose and ears that defined Sudian. The character had died within him, and it seemed grossly wrong to see it so clearly and easily reflected. He tossed the mirror to the bed, where Edward sat in silence, still gathering his strength.

"What's the matter, Nightfall?"

Nightfall whirled to face the king, though the grandiosity of the maneuver was wasted. Edward could not see a thing. "What's the matter?" he repeated incredulously. *"What's the matter?"*

"It's rude to echo royalty like a deranged parrot."

Nightfall went stock-still, scarcely daring to believe Edward was blind and obviously in agony, freshly clawed back from death, but could still find the strength to lecture him on manners. "Do you understand who I am?"

Edward fixed his sightless gaze far to Nightfall's right. "I'm dizzy, not addled."

"I'm Nightfall. Not Sudian. Not Balshaz." Nightfall added, "He's dead, by the way. Not any of a dozen others. *I am Nightfall.*" He waited for some reaction from Edward, a dawning of understanding to sweep across his face, a spark to flash through those unseeing eyes. Anything but the lack of reaction he had so far gotten.

"I know who you are. I heard Jacquellette. That's why I came out when I did. That's why I put myself between you and her lightning."

The king's words struck Nightfall dumb. He could do nothing but stare.

Edward broke the awkward pause. "I can practically hear the stupid look on your face."

"When you . . ." Nightfall finally managed, though it required him to lick dry lips a dozen times to continue. "When you said, 'Let's go home,' did you mean . . . ?"

"Yes."

"Me?"

Edward rolled his eyes, though even that small movement seemed to hurt him. "I'm not going back to Alyndar without my adviser. You tracked me over at least half the world, and only the Holy Father knows what you suffered to find me."

"You want me . . . I'm still your . . . ?" Nightfall shook his head. He could not make sense of this. "I traveled the world to find King Edward Nargol of Alyndar. I have no idea who you are."

"I am King Edward Nargol of Alyndar."

"No." Nightfall sat on the edge of the bed. "King Edward is a grand and glorious man who lives by immutable law and rigid scruples. King Edward would never associate with a lying, thieving, murdering demon."

"A wise man once told me the world has grays. That sometimes it's necessary to stretch one's honor, one's ethics, if the end result is a far greater good."

"Who told you that?"

King Edward heaved an exasperated sigh. "You did, you simpering moron."

"Ah." Nightfall finally found his sense of humor. "So I'm a wise moron."

Apparently cued by the feel of the bed beneath him, Edward faced Nightfall directly. "Look. I'm not going to lie and say I prefer the company of the demon Nightfall to that of my loyal adviser, Sudian. But, if that's the identity you insist on taking, I'll take my advice from the demon and defend my choice to anyone who dares to challenge it."

"Even if it means abdicating the throne?"

Edward never hesitated. "Even if."

Nightfall smiled. "Now, I see it. You really are the same underexperienced, overprincipled lunatic I escorted around the world."

"You know you can't talk about the king like that." A frown scored the handsome features. "Nightfall, don't make me pardon murder, only to have you executed for treason."

This time, Nightfall rolled his eyes. He could imagine guileless Edward doing exactly what he threatened. "Sire, forgive my rudeness." He rose to make a formal bow, then sat again. "I just find it hard to believe you would give up the rulership of Alyndar for a thug."

"Nightfall, didn't I just get finished saying I can put you to death for insulting nobility?"

Confused, Nightfall squinted, though Edward could not read his expression. "I used 'Sire,' I bowed, I begged for clemency. I'm sorry, Your Majesty, but I fail to see the insult this time."

Pain turned Edward's answering smile into a grimace. "First, we're alone; it's Ned. Second, I didn't say you insulted me. I said you insulted 'nobility.' I believe you called my chancellor a 'thug.' "

"But—"

Edward did not let him finish. "By now you surely know what the position you accepted entails."

"You mean the position *Sudian* accepted."

"Sudian, Nightfall. They're one and the same."

Though technically true, the words stunned Nightfall. "But—"

"Stop 'butting' me."

"Is it rude?"

"No. But it's irritating." Edward continued making his point, "You call me unworldly and guileless; yet you don't understand the most important lesson of all, one that, from what Kelryn told me, your friend Dyfrin tried to teach you your entire life."

The king had Nightfall's full attention now; any mention of Dyfrin did that. Nightfall had made comparisons between the two men before, both dangerously caring and instinctively virtuous in a way even the most pious rarely achieved or truly understood. It did not seem possible Edward could grasp something in a single conversation that Nightfall had not done in decades. Such a thing would have to come of that same natural bent shared by two men who had never met.

"You can change what you look like, how you move and act. You can't change your heart or soul. Inside, where it truly matters, Nightfall and Sudian are one and the same." Edward's grin turned playful, almost to the point of evil. "You know, I've got a mind not to return to Alyndar at all. That would leave you king, Nightfall, king of Alyndar. Did you know that?"

Nightfall studied his hands. The washing had cleaned them satisfactorily, and the scrubbing had opened some of the blisters. Angry and red, they oozed a clear liquid.

He had sustained burns in the places where his body contacted the ground at the time of the lightning strike. "Not anymore. I'm under order of execution."

"What? Why?"

"As Nightfall, for hundreds of murders. Not that it matters, but very few of which I actually committed. As Sudian, for killing . . . you, Sire."

"But I'm not dead."

"Alyndar believes you are."

"But—" Edward seemed to have too many words vying for his tongue at once. "But—" Apparently realizing he had become the one "butting," Edward forced himself to say something coherent. "You should have been the acting-king. What arrogant courtier dared to believe he had the authority to pronounce sentence on the king of Alyndar?"

Nightfall tried to recall the words that had condemned him. He had always hated politics; yet, to his surprise, he recalled the quotation verbatim: ". . . in the event that the king is killed, missing, or incapacitated leaving no blooded heir on the throne . . . the Council is granted overriding discretion in all matters of judgment provided it has the full consent of the High Council and a majority vote of the Council in Full." He studied Edward. "Apparently, that comes from a book of Alyndarian law."

Edward appeared stunned. "You—you memorized it?"

Nightfall shrugged, not fully understanding it himself. He always did have an exceptional memory; without it, he could never have maintained so many facades for so long. "I tend to remember words that condemn me to death." Suddenly realizing he had not directly answered Edward's question, which usually annoyed the king, he added, "Your Admiral, Nikolei Neerchus, is the one who read that passage, and the general of Alyndar's army sentenced me." He did not add his concerns about Khanwar. By now, Volkmier had the situation well in hand; and he saw no need to further burden Edward.

Nightfall could add the significant details on the journey home, after the king's pain faded and his vision returned.

Edward's face purpled. "That sounds like a law in need of changing."

Nightfall smiled. He could see the crusading spirit reawakening in a king no longer quite so naive and dead-on righteous. Perhaps Edward the Enthusiastic would become Edward the Just after all.

Still hunted under Sudian's description, Nightfall had no choice but to don another disguise as he led the blinded king of Alyndar to the docks of Hartrin. He made only one stop, to release the boy held in Xevar's dungeon and suggest he find a way to Schiz and the protection of Brandon Magebane. After only a dismal day or two in the lockup, the boy seemed more determined to return to his home and parents, a decision Nightfall did not attempt to sway. Though he could not understand running back to the mother and father who had sold their son, Nightfall supposed he might not have a full grasp of the situation. Xevar's magical ability to sway emotions could have driven even the most loving parents to an act of foolishness, especially since they could not possibly know the slaver was a sorcerer intent on stealing the boy's very soul. Unlike King Edward, Nightfall harbored no illusions he could save the entire world from its own folly.

Nightfall settled King Edward at a table in the Dockside Inn and ordered a hot meal consisting of roast mutton, chalky tubers, and early winter melon. Before taking a single bite from his own plate, Nightfall carefully cut up the king's portion into bite-sized pieces easily speared by a fork. Edward would never stoop to eating with his hands, and Nightfall could just imagine him cutting off his own fingers in an attempt at self-sufficiency. Weeks of captivity and recent injury overcame the king's legendary grandeur and zeal, at least for the evening. They ate slowly, and most of the conversation consisted of describing the inn room scenery to Edward. The specifics of each man's ordeal could wait until they had safely boarded whatever ship they found to return them to Alyndar. This time, Nightfall doubted he would have any trouble finding transportation. Surely every captain, from the Hartrinian admiral to the lowliest fisherman would be thrilled to have the king of Alyndar aboard.

Nightfall frowned, preferring to maintain a low profile for reasons he could not wholly explain. Though he had not disguised Edward per se, he had dressed him in simple linens rather than attempting to cram him into Xevar's tailored silks. The usually soft golden hair now hung in too-long dirty strings, and he had not shaved in several days. The unseeing eyes had lost their glow and focus. The subdued and aching king little resembled the grand and glorious prince who had championed every moral cause with a passion bordering on stupidity and sometimes, in Nightfall's opinion, crossed that line.

Nightfall did not know enough of politics to guess whether King Edward might face danger in his own country. He trusted Volkmier to handle the traitor; but, last he knew, a number of individuals eyed the empty throne. Nightfall did not know if things could go far enough to drive once loyal courtiers to regicide. Less than a week remained before the kingdom declared Edward dead, and Nightfall had no idea what might happen if he returned after that proclamation. Perhaps every man and woman of Alyndar had taken a side, and the true king's return would interfere with plans too far along to put to rest. Once they pronounced him, was his murder a crime or a foregone conclusion? At best, Nightfall and Volkmier would have to weigh the allegiance of every man in Edward's employ, which might result in many changes, from the lowliest servants to the High Council. Those who loved Edward could not afford to allow his drive to forgive and forget, to afford second, third, and fourth chances, to put his very life at risk.

The king reached awkwardly for his mug. His knuckles caught an edge and would have upended it had Nightfall not steadied the base. Edward readjusted his hand properly around it and drank, never realizing his chancellor had saved it from a spill. That, Nightfall realized, was the way the regime would have to work as well, with men like himself behind the scenes to keep the kingdom running smoothly, and apparently seamlessly, to protect Edward from his own well intentioned actions.

The edges of Nightfall's mouth rose to neutral, then a slight smile. He wondered what King Rikard would think of the arrangement he had initiated as a way to save a son and destroy a demon. The old king could not have borne the thought of his grotesquely idealistic youngest son upon the throne, let alone aided by a combination of his most loyal guard and most notorious criminal. It was not a life Nightfall could ever have imagined for himself, let alone wanted. Yet, now, it just seemed right: marriage to his beloved and a lifetime of quietly rescuing the bold young king from himself. At least for the next few days, he had to believe the king's blindness was as temporary as his soreness.

The door leading to the inn rooms opened, and a wiry man dressed in ragged, close-fitting sailor's garb entered. Recognizing him, Nightfall sat up straighter. He was from Captain Celdurant's crew, which meant the *Seaworthy* had not yet left port. Nightfall's smile broadened. "Ned, would you mind if I left you for a moment?" He once again saved the king's mug from a spill. "I'm working on a ride home."

"Go." Edward politely set aside his tableware to address Nightfall directly. "I'll be fine."

Nightfall could not help worrying. The king had a way of getting himself into trouble, even when he did nothing to deserve it. It might take days for the slaves and guardsmen to discover Xevar's and Jacquellette's bodies, perhaps longer as none of them dared set foot in the garden. Even then, Nightfall doubted anyone would come after them. The sorcerers would not have shared their plans. Even if they had, no one would have reason, let alone the foolhardy guts, to pursue anyone who could kill two sorcerers.

Rising, Nightfall paused long enough that Edward might believe he had executed whatever proper protocol applied. Then, he headed toward the pirate, who had taken a seat at the end of the bar.

Nightfall approached without preamble. Small talk might give the man opportunity to react with hostility. "Where's the captain?"

In the time it took for the pirate to turn his head toward Nightfall with a slow disdainful sweep, Nightfall leaned casually against the edge of the bar. "What?"

"Your captain?" Nightfall said. "Where is he?"

The man's gaze rolled inadvertently toward the door into the inn rooms. "Who wants to know?"

Though not in words, Nightfall had received his answer. He turned and headed for the main exit.

The pirate watched him go; but, when he did not head toward the inn room doors, turned back to the barkeep to place his order.

Once outside, Nightfall swept into the alley behind the Dockside Inn. Gray with twilight, it swallowed him. Instinct told him he was not alone but also not in danger from whatever drunkard or petty thief lurked there. He easily scurried up the wall, glancing through one window before recognizing the *Seaworthy*'s men and gear in a second. Captain Celdurant sat on a rickety chair, discussing something with several of his men while others milled around the room sorting packs and blankets. Dressed in silk, as always, his hair combed to a sheen, he fit about as well among his pirate followers as Edward did in a house of slavery.

Nightfall sprang through the window, landing lightly in the room.

An instant passed in chaos. Then, swords rasped from sheaths, and a ragged line of men formed between Nightfall and their captain.

Nightfall ignored them. After fighting two sorcerers at once, swordsmen hardly seemed a menace. He looked directly at Celdurant. "Captain, I'm seeking passage for myself and a friend to Alyndar."

The pirates tensed, awaiting a command from their leader. Nightfall now appreciated that the rowdiest of the men had remained in Schiz; otherwise several might have broken ranks to assault him.

"I can pay," Nightfall added, thrusting a hand into his cloak and seizing the sapphires Celdurant had given him when they first made Hartrin Port. He displayed them on his open palm.

The captain grinned. His pale eyes danced like whitecaps on a playful ocean. "And what, pray tell, is the name of this . . . friend?"

"Edward," Nightfall said, now also smiling.

Captain Celdurant laughed. "Welcome aboard, Sudian."

They launched the next morning, with full bellies and calm seas, the pirates trimming sails and checking lines like old hands. They seemed calmer, more competent, since Balshaz had trained them, sobered by their near run-in with the Lifthranian ships. As Nightfall discovered as they set out to sea, the crew had remained in Hartrin these past few days to careen the ship, as he had suggested. Now, with the hull cleaned and coated, the planks properly caulked, the *Seaworthy* had finally become more than worthy of her name: fast, sleek, and impressively maneuverable. The pirates, too, seemed better groomed and more committed to their captain and their ship, less consumed with gold and greed.

To Nightfall's surprise, the captain and crew required

no warnings about watching their tongues and manners around King Edward. The words "plunder" and "pirate" were never uttered, and they treated their guest like the royalty he was. The captain gave over the main part of his cabin, while he and Nightfall bunked in the outer area near the door. Not once did any man suggest the king of Alyndar, or his companion, was an unwelcome burden; and Nightfall listened, in vain, for someone to so much as whisper "silversucker."

Once safely out to sea, Nightfall abandoned his disguise and answered to Sudian. Only Edward questioned this choice, as they stood alone at the stern. Nightfall watched Hartrin disappear into the distance while Edward enjoyed the feel of the spray against his face.

"So," Edward said, his voice carried away on the wind. "What would you have me call you now?"

Nightfall flushed. His rage seemed long ago and far away. "Sudian is fine, Sire."

"Are you sure?"

Nightfall smiled. "A wise man once told me Nightfall and Sudian are one and the same. That they share a heart."

Edward also smiled. "A good heart." The wet air had stripped the dirt from his locks but left them in a hopeless yellow tangle. He was still strikingly handsome, even windswept and filthy, even without vision. "And you listened?"

Nightfall modulated his tone to sound mockingly defensive. "I do . . . sometimes."

Still grinning, they both stood in silence for several moments. Nightfall turned, allowing the breeze to strike him full in the face. It felt cool, damp, and soothing.

"If Kelryn found out I had spent time as Nightfall, she would dismember me." It was as much a plea as information. He would not dare directly ask Edward to lie for him; it would affront the king's honor. He could choose, however, to refer Kelryn to her betrothed for answers about the rescue.

"She was afraid you wouldn't come back if you did."

Though stunned by Edward's insight, Nightfall did not remark on it. Many things about this man continued to astound him. He had once dismissed the prince as stupid and incompetent, only to discover both of those images false. Edward was indeed innocent and coddled, ignorant of the day-to-day life of the underclasses, but keen-witted and a master swordsman nonetheless. "She was right."

"But you are coming back, Sudian."

"Only because I got the right words exactly when I needed them."

"Mine?" Edward also turned toward the ship, balancing one leg against the gunwale, looking remarkably comfortable for a man who had strained every muscle in his body. "I was half dead and not in my right mind. What could I possibly have said that made so much difference?"

Fully dead, Nightfall corrected silently. *And never in your right mind.* "Sire, I figured if the most moral and ethical person in the world could forgive me for breaking the same vow, Kelryn could, too."

Edward nodded.

"I only wished I had broken it sooner. Then, you would not have suffered for so long."

Edward's grin evaporated, replaced by a deep scowl. "Sudian, you don't understand."

Nightfall's brow furrowed. He had no idea what Edward meant. "What?"

"A man's word is everything. Without it, he is no better than a street thug. Than an animal."

Edward was right; Nightfall did not understand. "What?"

"You had no right to break one vow made in good faith until the moment it came into direct and unavoidable conflict with another." Edward groped for Nightfall's fingers, and he gave them. The king's huge, wet hands felt warm against Nightfall's cold flesh. "To fulfill your vow of fealty to me, you had to rescue me. There came a point when you realized that to keep your word, you had to break your promise to never resort to your . . . evil persona. At that precise moment, you had no alternative but to place one vow over the other."

"Yes," Nightfall admitted. "That's exactly how it happened. But how did you—"

Edward's smile returned. "Because I know your heart, and it is good."

Nightfall made a noncommittal noise, actually considering the possibility.

"Did your vows to Kelryn come into similar conflict?"

Nightfall did not have to consider. "Yes, Sire. I promised her I would bring both Edward and Sudian home."

Edward's brows rose. "A rash promise."

"True." He wasted a wicked grimace. "But I'm doing it, aren't I, Ned?"

"Indeed. And what have you learned from all this?"

Struck by the question, Nightfall stared. It never ceased to amaze him how the naive little pup dared to treat the world-wise demon as a student. Of course, since Edward could not see his expression, the king could only assume the silence came of consideration. Nightfall decided to oblige. "What did I learn, Sire?"

"Yes."

"I learned to stop making so damned many promises."

Over the ensuing week, Edward's vision returned, first as blotches and shapes, then as stripes of color, and finally back to normal. As his muscles overcame the damage from the lightning-caused convulsion, his spirits returned as well. He accepted the silks Captain Celdurant gave him, cut, combed, and oiled his hair back to its normal shimmering gold, and the crusading spark returned to his functioning eyes. Once worried the damage might prove permanent, Nightfall found himself wishing it had lasted a bit longer, just long enough to bring them safely to Alyndar's docks.

Early one morning, frantic footfalls awakened Nightfall. Even as he sat up, frenzied pounding on the captain's door brought Celdurant to his feet as well. The captain opened the cabin door to find nearly a quarter of the crew standing in wait.

"The Lifthranian ships, Captain," one man shouted. "They're back!"

Another glanced at Nightfall, then back to the captain. "Should we initiate evasive action, Captain?"

Celdurant heaved a heavy sigh. "No."

The men went utterly silent, every eye directly on their captain.

"I'm sick to death of running."

"But, Captain," one man started, silenced by Celdurant's raised hand.

"Ready a jolly boat. It's me they're after and me they'll get."

"Captain, you may be ready to die, but we're not ready to give you up. We'll fight for you, to the end, if need be."

A great cheer rose up from the men, and they lifted their curved swords.

Nightfall schooled his features, driven to smile. It must be nice to garner such loyalty, especially in a ragtag lot of pirates.

"No!" Celdurant spoke to the men as if to errant children. "Do as I say." He slammed the door on their protestations.

King Edward poked his head through the curtain. "What's going on?"

The captain dressed swiftly, pulling on his silks. "I'm sorry to involve you in this, Your Highness." He bowed deeply. "It's a personal matter between me and the barony. I'm not going to be able to accompany you for the rest of the trip, I'm afraid; but Sudian and my men will get you back safely to Alyndar."

Still in sleeping clothing, Edward placed his hands on his hips. "Do you really believe we will let you sail to your death alone, Captain Celdurant el-Bartokus Arbonne?"

The revelation shocked both men silent, but the captain recovered first. "Who . . . told you?" He turned his intense blue gaze onto Nightfall, who gave a shrug of innocence.

Edward rescued the only man on board who had known the captain's real name. "No one told me, Celdurant. I'm a studied man, and your own admission made it obvious."

The captain nodded resignedly. "Then you know why I must go alone. I'm under sentence of execution. My men are innocent." Though not strictly true, they did have nothing to do with the crime for which the baron had sentenced him. "I don't want anyone harmed because of me."

"I won't allow it."

Celdurant bowed. "I had counted on that, Your Majesty."

Finally, Nightfall believed he fully understood. Celdurant chose to surrender himself this time because he had an advantage that had not existed before. Edward would see to it his crew went free or, at worst, received fair trials for their piracy. It would prevent Lifthran from hanging them all simply for their association with him.

"Captain," Edward said. "If you could just excuse us for a few moments, please." He waved Nightfall to the inner area of the quarters.

Celdurant bowed, exited, and closed the door firmly behind him.

Wondering what King Edward had in mind, Nightfall followed him into the main quarters, stared at the ocean bubbling past the window, and waited for him to speak.

"Sudian, did he do it?"

Nightfall shook his head, confused. "Do what?" he asked uncomfortably. He had lied to Edward often, but it had become more difficult over time.

"Did he commit the crime of which Baron Ozwalt has accused him? Did he . . . you know . . . the baroness . . ." Edward's cheeks turned bright pink. Matters of sexuality embarrassed the young man, a hard-core virgin still ensconced in his adolescence.

"No," Nightfall said. "He says the baroness came to him, that he refused her, and she lied in vengeance."

"And is he telling the truth?"

Nightfall's eyes narrowed to slits as he tried to out-think the question. "Ned, my birth gift . . ." He did not like even mentioning he had one, but Edward already knew. "It's not truth detection."

Edward closed and opened his eyes. "I must admit I wondered. You have the same gift for reading people my brother had." He choked out the words, his grief over the elder prince still raw. "You can find . . . the meaning beneath their words. That's why I wanted you to advise me. You see what's in . . . in their hearts."

Edward's words surprised Nightfall. He had always believed his promotion came strictly from gratitude, a title bestowed by a king with more compassion than common sense. *If I'm so great at reading people, why do I keep underestimating this man?* Still thrown by the use of "good" to describe his own inner being, Nightfall spoke the obvious irony. "Every heart but my own, apparently."

Edward would not be diverted by self-deprecation. "Is Captain Celdurant telling the truth?"

Nightfall knew the answer, and the only heart he could not read told him not to doubt its veracity. "He did not sleep with his brother's wife."

The follow-up seemed inevitable. "Then, Sudian, we are obligated to save him."

The *Seaworthy* maintained its course straight eastward, and the Lifthranians caught up to them the following day. One set anchor directly between the ship and Alyndar, showing her broadside, while the other steered a course that would bring her directly beside them. Both flew two flags: the golden lion on scarlet of Lifthran and the striped flag that announced direct service to nobility, in this case Baron Ozwalt. A third flag flew between them, solid white with a black figure of a longboat.

Every man aboard the *Seaworthy* stood on deck, some weary from the night shift. Arturo approached, dark eyes fiery beneath the rag he wore to cover his bald head. He studied the broadside of the ship in front of them, rubbing his hands. "Any chance we could just ram 'em, Captain? Any ship what puts herself in that position deserves it."

It was the first pirating comment anyone had uttered since Edward's arrival. Though spoken in jest, it met an awkward silence, swiftly broken by Caylor's announcement from the crow's nest. "She's demanding an 'us-to-them.' "

At the bow with Captain Celdurant, Edward nudged Nightfall. "What does that mean?"

Nightfall put the request into standard terminology. "They want an ocean parley." Edward would understand that from his studies, with all its implied rules, conventions, and details. It required that a jolly boat or longboat carry representatives from one ship to the other for a discussion. No matter the outcome, the men in the small boat would get safe passage to and from their ship.

The captain seemed to take no notice of the whispered conversation. "Strike the parley flag."

A pirate rushed to obey.

King Edward frowned. It was a look Nightfall knew well . . . and hated. "An 'us-to-them' your man said? Does that mean they expect *us* to row to *them*?"

The captain continued to watch the other ship. "Yes, Sire."

Edward stepped up beside the captain, full of his usual vigor. Together, they made a formidable pair, the captain nearly as tall and broad-shouldered as the massive king of Alyndar. Each carried himself with a regal posture that denied insolence and demanded strict obeisance. Nightfall idly wondered if the classes highborns took included learning to strike poses of command. "The rules of parley clearly state the men of lesser status bow to the greater. It is they who should send the jolly boat."

Nightfall could not see the captain's expression, but he replied in a sober tone. "Quite right, Your Highness, but we're sailing unstruck. Without Alyndar's colors, or the royal stripes, we have no way of letting them know you're with us."

Edward looked up the whiffling sails to the top of the mainmast, where no flag flew. "Then, I suppose we have no choice but to forgive them their lapse in protocol."

"Yes, Sire."

Nightfall did not add that it did not matter. They could have carried all the world's kings and struck the proper colors, but no one would believe them. The Lifthranians would assume their claim a pirate's trick. "I'll go."

The captain and the king turned simultaneously, both wearing the same arch look.

"What?" Nightfall asked defensively.

The captain spoke first. "You seem to have quite forgotten you have a price on your head. One of sufficient value to make even Lifthranian nobility abandon the rules of parley."

Nightfall could almost hear Edward's mind working, logic warring with the need for justice. "Then I'm going with him. To see no rules get broken."

"Sire!" The captain glanced between king and minister. "Wouldn't it be better if neither of you, if . . . ?" He trailed off. None of his lowborn crew could handle this matter with the necessary decorum and propriety. ". . . if I went?"

"Fine." King Edward strode toward the readied jolly boat. "You can join us."

The captain glanced at Nightfall, who shrugged and shook his head. Once Edward decided something, changing his mind took an act of gods. Nevertheless, Celdurant tried, "Sire, most people believe King Edward of Alyndar is dead. It's possible they won't believe you're who you claim, especially accompanied by a pair of men they consider scalawags."

Nightfall jogged after Edward, not liking the suggestion that seemed certain to follow. "He's not going anywhere without me." Nightfall did not care what etiquette he broke by referring to the king in the third person in his presence nor subsuming his command. "I searched the world for him, and I'm not going to lose him now."

The captain trailed them. "I'm not saying we shouldn't go. Only that we need some way to prove the king's identity."

Edward climbed into the boat, taking the center seat. "They'll know who I am."

"They'll know," the captain said, joining him, "who you look like." He took his seat in the bow, murmuring. "If only you had your signet, Sire."

Edward shivered. "You sound like my captors. They said it sixty times, if they said it once. I'm not sure what good it would have done them, though. Neither could have passed for me with the best disguise, signet or no."

The captain rolled his gaze to Nightfall, who shrugged. With all his skills, he might have managed to make Xevar resemble Edward; but without the proper words, attitude, and mannerisms, the impersonation would have swiftly failed. He took the last seat, in the stern. The pirates assembled, preparing to lower the jolly boat into the sea.

"How'd they miss it, Sire?" Celdurant asked, almost conversationally. "They seemed to have everything else figured out well enough from what you've told me."

"They thought I'd be wearing it. When I wasn't, they sent a man to take it from among my possessions." Edward shrugged. "For some reason, he failed."

Nightfall's mind went back to the morning after Edward disappeared, when he foiled a thief scrounging through the inn room. He had carried the ring he discovered since that day, secreted among his knives and clothing. He pulled it out now, examining it once again: the drizzled and engraved Alyndarian symbol in its center, flanked by its two purple stones, the fine gold of its construct. He had heard the word "signet" before, in reference to a seal impression meant to authenticate a document, but he had never heard it in relation to something worn on the king's person. Now, he put the two together. "Sire, would this object you're discussing happen to be the ring you wear in court?"

Edward jerked his attention to his adviser, then to the object in his hand. His mouth fell open, then curled into a smile. He reached for it, and Nightfall dropped it into the king's palm.

"How?" the captain said. "How did you . . . ?"

Edward slipped the signet onto his finger. "Celdurant, I've found that, when it comes to Sudian, I'm usually happier not knowing."

† Chapter 24 †

Nightfall and Sudian are one and the same.
They have the same heart, and it is good.

> —King Edward Nargol of Alyndar,
> the demon's friend

O N THE DECK OF THE Lifthranian ship, a crowd of
hired sailors, many of whom Nightfall had had acquaintance with as Marak, mingled with more than a
dozen Lifthranians in colors. Most appeared to be warriors. Though they wore scarlet-and-gold linens instead
of armor and tabards, they ranged toward larger, more
muscular sizes, and straight swords swung at their belts.
On the closed hatch stood three men in silken long-
clothes: red pants too baggy for sailors, yellow coats with
buttons and the Lifthranian lion on the chest, and black
stockings in gold-buckled shoes. The smallest stood half
a head shorter than Nightfall, though he wore thick-
soled boots and a massive, wide-brimmed hat with a
feather that gained him the appearance of height. A
fringe of brown bangs peeked out from beneath it, and
his shadowed face revealed deep-set eyes of indetermi-
nate color, an elongated nose, and a broad, lipless
mouth. Dark curls topped the tallest one's head; and the

last, a close-cropped graying blond, carried a lion-headed walking stick.

Hoisted to the level of the rail, the jolly boat still hung in midair when the captain of the *Seaworthy* shouted, "Halt!"

The sailors heaving up the lines stilled. Their gazes went to the nobles on the hatch.

Captain Celdurant did not wait for them to speak. "I'm exiled from Lifthran. So long as you fly both flags, this ship must be considered an extension of the baron's lands. Therefore, I cannot come aboard."

Nightfall looked down. Droplets trickled from the bottom of the jolly boat, pelting the ocean below in widening rings. He would survive a fall, since he could lighten his impact, but the others might risk having the boat, or shattered pieces of it, strike them. Even alive, a man did not last long without provisions in the ocean. "Uh, Captain . . ." he whispered.

Celdurant ignored him.

The smallest of the nobles spoke. "You have nerve, Black Celdurant. Surely, you know you're the one we've come to bargain for. You're already under sentence of execution, so it does you no further harm to come aboard."

King Edward rose, dangerously rocking the jolly boat. "Who is this little man, Lord Celdurant?"

"His name is Johan, Sire, a hand-me-down from my father's reign." Celdurant never took his gaze from the Lifthranians, even as he addressed the king. "I was training to become the commander of my brother's elite guards. When I finished, I had always planned to give this man a greatly deserved punch in his ratlike face."

Johan's chest puffed up, and his face purpled. Clearly, he had not noticed the title of respect for Edward hidden amidst the threat, but others on the ship had. Whispers spread among the sailors and soldiers.

"Ah." Edward sprang over the rail before Nightfall could think to stop him. Forced to give his full attention to the rollicking jolly boat, he did not immediately follow. "It's the lot of younger brothers, I guess. I, too, was training to become my brother's general." His gaze swept the deck, and Nightfall noticed that most of the men shuffled backward. "Until I became *king* instead."

The effect was immediate. Those who had already recognized him nodded sagely or dropped to their knees. Others, clearly too focused on Celdurant to notice anyone else stared in shocked surprise, shifting nervously from foot to foot and taking their cues from the nobles.

Nightfall bounded to the deck more lightly, careful not to unbalance Celdurant in the dangling jolly boat again.

The other two examined Edward only a moment before sinking down to their knees as well. Only Johan strode forward, a sneer twisting his features. Now that Celdurant had compared him to a rodent, Nightfall could not help seeing the resemblance. "The true king of Alyndar traveling with pirates? I rather think not." He looked over the sailors and Lifthranians with clear disdain. "He's an imposter, you fools. He has to be—"

Following the lead of the nobles, nearly all of the remaining soldiers and sailors sank to the deck, leaving only Johan and a few uncertain followers.

Johan reached for Edward's hand, and only the king's warning look at Nightfall kept him from burying a knife in the nobleman's throat. "See, he hasn't got . . ." The Lifthranian caught the hand with the signet and raised it for a closer inspection. Sunlight struck the stones, sending purple highlights skittering over the ship and the gathering; and the gold seemed to glow. "The signet," Johan whispered, dropping Edward's hand and falling to the deck as if someone had cut his legs out from under him. "Your Majesty, I'm so sorry. So sorry for doubting. I—"

Don't forgive him. Sentence him to death. Nightfall did not bother to speak the words aloud. He knew exactly what King Edward was going to say.

"Your error was understandable." Edward gestured for every man to rise. "Now, please, I need news of Alyndar. Tell me what's happening there."

The men aboard stood, but not one made an effort to attend a line or take a post.

One of the nobles on the hatch, the blond, replied. "Well, Sire, they believe you're dead. Without a blood heir, and with your chancellor under sentence of execution . . ." Every eye glided to Nightfall, and there were nods throughout the company. They had finally recognized him as well. ". . . I'm afraid several men are vying for the crown."

"Who?" Edward demanded.

"More than a few have submitted their names," the man continued. "Your cousins: Abnar, Sweenar, and Honar Kolias, for example. Your Council leader, Baron Elliat Laimont."

The other noble on the hatch added three more names Nightfall did not recognize before the blond took over again. "But, Sire, the one who seems likely to claim the throne is Lord Admiral Nikolei Neerchus."

"My admiral?"

Johan finally dared to speak again. "Yes, Your Majesty. He's commandeered several smaller armies, and all ships of significant size in your kingdom. It's said he'll take ours, too, such as they are, once we dock."

The third noble added his piece, "Sire, from what I can tell, the admiral is still trying to win over your castle guards. I've heard there's a high-ranking officer who refuses to support any of the candidates. Still believes you will return."

Nightfall smiled. *Volkmier.*

"And rightly so," Johan added.

"General Simont hasn't publicly thrown his support behind anyone yet either, Sire," the blond continued. "Says his men's loyalties are split, and he doesn't want his troops to fall apart. But it's widely believed he'll eventually support the admiral's bid."

"Of course," the first noble took back the conversation. "None of this will matter once you return. Your father was a great and powerful king; and you, Sire, are much beloved."

Edward's cheeks gained a pinkish hue.

Though Nightfall would not put self-serving flattery past any of these men, he also knew they spoke the truth, and that relieved him of several worries. Though some of the nobles rolled their eyes at a youthful simplicity that often bordered on the absurd, they appreciated Edward's kindness and forgiving nature. The peasants loved his justice and his eagerness to champion the poor and the downtrodden. Once the true king returned, the bids for the crown would stop.

Johan cleared his throat, apparently loath to raise the matter that had brought them here. "Your Majesty, I apologize for bringing up such an issue now, but I am under the command of Baron Ozwalt of Lifthran." Though not directly stated, the words also served to remind them that Lifthran was a holding of the kingdom of Ivral, not Alyndar.

Edward gestured graciously at Johan, granting him the floor.

"That man . . ." Johan jabbed a finger toward the hanging jolly boat, where Celdurant had sat quietly throughout the long discussion. ". . . is a traitor to the barony and a fugitive. We were charged with the duty of returning him to justice, Sire."

Despite the condemnation, Celdurant sat up straighter in the boat. "I will go, if the King of Alyndar commands it; but I maintain my innocence now and forever. I did not commit the crime for which I am condemned to die."

Nightfall held his breath. If the give-and-take proceeded much longer, Celdurant would surely lose. Even if he had not slept with the baroness, he was still a traitor to Lifthran, and Alyndar, from his piracy. Nightfall nudged Edward.

The king's eyes narrowed at the impropriety, but he did not chastise his chancellor in public. "Johan, you shall inform Baron Ozwalt he no longer has any claim over this man, Celdurant, whom I now name Supreme Lord Admiral of Alyndar's navy." He swung his head toward Celdurant. "Assuming he will accept the title."

Every gaze followed Edward's to a stunned Celdurant, who managed only a strangled noise.

Then a nod.

The sailors, and many of the soldiers, erupted in cheers.

Johan bowed so low, his hair touched the deck. "Your Majesty," he said, in a voice filled with concern. "Sire, you must not be aware this man is also a notorious captain of pirates."

Edward rounded on Celdurant. "Is that true?"

Celdurant glanced at Nightfall for guidance but did not wait for a response before admitting, "I was, Sire."

King Edward barely missed a beat. "Once I place a man into my High Council, in a position of nobility, any past crimes become pardoned by law."

"But—" Johan started.

Edward did not allow him to finish. "And I've found that a man who knows the enemy makes the most formidable ally." He headed back toward the jolly boat. "Supreme Lord Admiral Celdurant, where do your loyalties lie?"

With grand flourishes, Celdurant placed a hand over his heart and saluted King Edward with the other. "To Alyndar, Sire! For now; for ever." He knelt, lowering his head, the black curls falling in a thick cascade of silk.

Though overdone, the gesture was unmistakably sincere. Nightfall knew both men well enough to foresee a happy and loyal merger that might or might not include many of Celdurant's crew. He hoped Edward did not intend to make a habit of surrounding himself with murderers and thieves.

Edward said words he had surely rehearsed, official

and binding despite the oddness of the location of their speaking: "Lord Celdurant, once of Lifthran, now of Alyndar, I officially name you Supreme Lord Admiral of Alyndar's navy, to serve until such time as I, or my successor, release you, forsaking all competing loyalties until the end of time. Lord Celdurant, do you accept your assignment and all the responsibilities inherent upon it from this day henceforth and swear your fealty wholly and completely to Alyndar?"

Celdurant kept his hand poised over his heart. He looked up, his face a mask of sincere promise tempered only by joy. "I do, Sire."

King Edward stepped back into the jolly boat, this time with more caution. Celdurant took his seat in the bow, and Nightfall rejoined them in the stern. At the king's signal, sailors set to the ropes and pulleys that would send them gently back into the water.

Edward called out as they drifted downward. "Lord Johan."

The noble's head appeared over the rail. "Yes, Sire?"

"I believe my admiral when he names himself innocent. Please tell Baron Ozwalt that the King of Alyndar says to watch his lady. And his back."

Johan made a formal bow. "I will do as you ask, Your Majesty. But I must confess . . ." He fixed his gaze on Celdurant and Nightfall. "It's your back for which I worry."

When the *Seaworthy* made port in Alyndar three days later, they found a mass of soldiers and citizens on the docks. Word of the king's return had preceded him, brought by the Lifthranian ships. Flanked by his chancellor and his new admiral, the king disembarked amid a deafening cacophony of cheers. Held back by a swarm of warriors in Alyndar's colors, the crowd accompanied the king all the way to the courtyard gates before dispersing.

Though Nightfall appreciated Edward's popularity,

he breathed a sigh of relief when they finally entered the castle and even most of the guards returned to their posts. Servants bundled Celdurant off to his new quarters, finally opening the way for Kelryn to hurl herself into Edward's arms. "Oh, Ned. I'm so glad you're back. So glad you're all right."

The guards averted their eyes from the reunion in the castle hallway.

Edward embraced Kelryn for several moments, savoring the contact a bit longer than Nightfall liked. The king had, after all, once requested her hand in marriage. At length, though, Edward pulled her far enough away to talk. "Kelryn, I wouldn't be here if not for Sudian's courage, effort, and persistence."

Kelryn's gaze went to Nightfall, and her green eyes danced with a fiery love. She thrust herself against him so violently she nearly sent them both tumbling before arms found their proper positions around one another. "I knew you could do it. I knew you'd bring him back ... and Sudian, too. Thank you."

Nightfall kissed her, growing weak-kneed with desire. The hallway, the guards, the king himself seemed to vanish, and he might have ravished her right there had he not suffered a sudden prickle of warning. Even his passion for Kelryn could not keep him from recognizing danger. He shoved Kelryn aside as two guards with drawn swords drew up beside him.

"What's the meaning of this?" demanded Edward.

The guards cowered but remained in place. "Sorry, Sire. Forgive us. We've been dispatched to confine the traitor."

"Traitor?" Edward threw a weary glance around the hallway. "I see no traitors here."

"Sudian, Sire." Dressed in the lavender and gray of the prison guards, the two bowed repeatedly. "I'm afraid he's under sentence of execution, Sire."

Kelryn clung to Nightfall. He kept his own hands free, saying nothing, trusting the king to handle the crisis in his own palace.

"This is nonsense," Edward bellowed. "I've placed no sentence upon my loyal chancellor. Who sent you?"

The bows become deeper, and the voices lower and tremulous. "The High Council, Sire. They're meeting in the Strategy Room. I'm sure they'd welcome—"

"Stand down and return to your posts." Edward seized Nightfall's wrist, and Kelryn stepped aside. "Leave this man alone."

"Yes, Sire."

Edward thundered through the castle, and Nightfall had to jog to keep up with the king's massive strides. "We'll see who dares to command my men!"

Nightfall cast a longing glance behind him, but Kelryn had chosen to remain behind. They swept through the familiar hallways and up the stone staircases, Edward mumbling the entire time about gall and insurgents. Finally, they reached the Strategy Room. Memories flooded back to Nightfall, of his interrogation, his sentencing, the attack that had sent him tumbling down the hard stone steps and ended with a crossbow bolt lodged in his chest. His footsteps faltered, but Edward did not appear to notice as he half led, half dragged Nightfall to the door. "Open!" the king bellowed.

The guards obeyed neatly, managing to bow and handle the door simultaneously. No one commented on his return or his long absence; his mood came through in his tone.

The door opened on the same windowless room, its walls covered in maps. The eight-armed chandelier swayed in the breeze created by the opened door; and the five men of the High Council sat around the table, which now held only the heavy tome of Alyndarian law. All rose at the sight of Edward to bow deeply and formally.

Edward did not wait for them to rise before shouting, "What is this nonsense about confining my minister?" He jerked Nightfall suddenly forward, releasing his wrist.

Nightfall had to raise his mass to keep from stumbling into the table. In his rage, the king had lost track of his own strength.

Baron Elliat spoke first. "We're thrilled to have you back at last, Sire! The Father has granted us a miracle."

The others nodded, speaking their welcomes and expressing their joy. No one addressed the king's question.

A profound silence followed during which propriety demanded Edward respond to their greetings and take a seat at the table. He did neither, instead glowering over the group and forcing them to remain standing.

At length, the admiral, Nikolei Neerchus, spoke, "Your Majesty, we share your chagrin, but *former* Chancellor Sudian has a sentence of death over him that should have been carried out some weeks ago."

Edward took a menacing forward step. "Well, *former* Admiral Nikolei Neerchus, I've pardoned the man who saved my life. Twice now."

"I'm so sorry, Sire." Tenneth Kentaries' face looked even paler than usual, ghostlike. He knuckled his fingers nervously into his beard. "But you can't . . . pardon . . . him . . ."

"What!"

The word was pain in Nightfall's ears. He imagined the entire castle could hear it.

"I'm the king. This is my castle. I can pardon whomsoever I choose."

The entire council looked down at once. Clearly they had more to say but wished to do so calmly, sitting in discussion over mugs of mulled cider.

Dread chilled through Nightfall, despite Edward's strident support. An obscure law had undone him before.

Edward looked at Nightfall. "Have they all gone daft?"

To Nightfall, they all started out that way. Much about nobility seemed so to him. He merely shrugged, knowing the question was rhetorical anyway.

"Sire," Nikolei took over again. "I'm afraid the law . . ." He paused, his tone going from commanding to quizzical between one word and the next. "Did you just call me *former* admiral?"

Nightfall suppressed a smile.

Now, it was Edward's turn to dodge the direct question. "What about the law?"

The other military giant, General Simont Basilaered reached across the table and pulled the book toward him. He carried it to the king. "Here, Sire."

Edward glanced at the indicated passage. "Yes, yes. I've heard that one about the Council. Overriding discretion with unanimous vote of the High Council and majority of the Council in Full. My chancellor quoted it to me." He studied the writings. "Verbatim. Very impressive, Sudian."

Uncertain what else to do, Nightfall said, "Thank you, Sire."

Edward looked at the huge general who dwarfed even the king. "What does that have to do with pardons?"

"Here, Sire." The general leafed through to another marked page and tapped his finger on a passage. Edward read, lips moving, an occasional word slipping out. "When pardoning a formerly sentenced . . . not within the realm of . . . even if the . . ." Intent, he took the nearest seat, resting the heavy book on the tabletop.

Now that the king had seated himself, the council members took places around the table as well, leaving only Nightfall standing.

Edward looked up. "But it's not the intended purpose to prevent . . ." He studied the passage again. "It refers to overruling former kings."

"And here, Sire." Again, the general found a marked page and opened it for the king to peruse.

Nightfall tried to read over the king's shoulder, but the words made little sense to him, full of flowery language and gross repetition.

"But those laws were never intended to go together." Edward looked sallow, and all of the anger left him. "They were passed at very different times." He gave his attention to each Council member in turn, none of whom spoke. "Sudian did nothing wrong. Can't you overrule yourselves?"

The general rose again, to point out one more law.

Reading, Edward slumped in his chair.

Nightfall swallowed hard, wishing he had never returned. If only the king of Alyndar had not forgiven him, he would have slipped Edward aboard the *Seaworthy* and disappeared, back to a life in the shadows as the demon, Nightfall. Once again, doing the right thing, taking the moral course, had undone him.

Nikolei Neerchus rose, opened the door, and gestured the two guards sent to arrest Nightfall through it. Arrayed in Alyndar's prison colors, they stood at attention, awaiting a direct order from the king.

"Those laws are poorly written."

"Then you can change them, Sire," Baron Elliat said.

Tenneth sighed. "But they won't apply retroactively, I'm afraid."

The guards shifted nervously, still waiting.

Edward remained quietly in place, turning pages. Finally, he stopped. And smiled. "I'd gotten so caught up in pardonings, and all the rules surrounding them, I forgot the most obvious and important thing of all."

The members of the Council sat straighter. Nightfall could tell at least some of them actually wanted the king to succeed, to see Nightfall go free rather than suffer execution. It was an epiphany for Nightfall, who realized the men who had condemned him were not necessarily bad, just blind and foolish in their own way. He truly believed every one of them wanted what they felt would best serve Alyndar. Unfortunately, most seemed convinced that meant relieving the king from the advice and presence of his lowborn chancellor.

"Sudian doesn't need a pardon." Edward rose, and the others scrambled to do the same. "The crime for which he was sentenced was never, in fact, committed." He pounded a fist on the page to which he had opened the book, then spread his hand to indicate the other pages. "There can be no guilt, no innocence. And, by one of the oldest of all laws, no one, not even the king, can sentence a man for murdering someone who is still clearly and obviously alive."

Nightfall rolled his eyes. Had these nobles not insisted on following every word and letter jotted in some moldering book, they would have seen what was obvious to a ten-year-old. "So, I'm a free man?" he tried.

"Not exactly, my lord," said Tenneth, and Edward frowned. "You are still bound into the service of Alyndar as her chancellor." He winked. "And I understand you're shackled by a young lady, too."

Laughs swept the room, dispelling much of the tension.

Nightfall shook his head. *Royal humor.* He wondered if he would ever understand it.

Baron Elliat put the matter into the proper, haughtier terms. "Without a crime, the sentence must be abandoned. Aside from your duties to Alyndar . . ." He dipped his head toward Tenneth, ". . . and as a man betrothed, you are, indeed, free."

Nightfall let out a pent up breath.

King Edward waved at the waiting guards. "Chancellor Sudian is no longer under sentence. Report back to Captain Volkmier. You're dismissed."

To Nightfall's surprise, the guards appeared even more uncomfortable. They shuffled in place until rescued by the general.

"Your Majesty, this seems like the best time to regretfully inform you that former Captain Volkmier is . . ." Simont measured his words, slowing them to an irritating crawl. ". . . detained . . . under . . . sentence . . . of . . ."

". . . execution?" Edward filled in. "You'd better be joking."

The silence that followed said otherwise. Edward threw up his hands, and Nightfall had to duck to avoid getting accidentally struck in the face. "It's a wonder the castle walls are still standing." He paced, his tread heavy with reawakening anger. "Which other of my loyal servants have been sentenced to death by a High Council gone mad with power?"

The last member of the Council, Sir Alber Evrinn, finally spoke. "Your Highness, I can understand your chagrin, but please show some forbearance. The Council did not act in haste, or without reason. We believed both men a credible and imminent threat to Alyndar."

Baron Elliat added swiftly, "And there are no others, Sire."

Khanwar. Nightfall harbored no doubt the adviser-turned-traitor had manipulated Volkmier's arrest. Likely, the chief of prison guards had approached Khanwar in private, to grant Nightfall the promised time to work before publicly revealing Edward's betrayer. Khanwar had used the secrecy of their meeting to his advantage, relying on his connections to the admiral to get Volkmier arrested before he could reveal Khanwar's crime. It would not surprise Nightfall to learn Khanwar had also pieced together the circuitous and ancient laws that had made his pardon impossible.

Edward ignored the baron, attention fixed on the quiet and homely knight. Alber had reason for choosing this moment to speak. "Captain Volkmier served my father faithfully for as long as I can remember." He glanced pointedly at the general and the admiral. "Longer than either of you. What could he possibly have done to deserve such a sentence?"

For once, Nikolei Neerchus had nothing to say. Denied the opportunity to sit by Edward's decision to stand, he hovered with both hands firmly on the tabletop.

Without a cryptic reference to the loss of his command, Simont Basilaered proved bolder. "Sire, he confessed to assisting in a prison break."

Edward's brows rose. "Volkmier? Assist a prison break? Never!"

Nightfall leaned in to whisper, "Sire, is it still a prison break if the one he assisted did not commit a crime?"

Edward's brows jumped higher, nearly into his hair. "You, Sudian?"

Nightfall clamped his mouth shut, hoping he had not just made things worse in his attempt to rescue Volkmier. His insistence on secrecy had probably proved the guardsman's downfall.

"I'm sorry, Sire." Tenneth said tiredly, guessing what Nightfall must have said. "But Sudian's guilt or innocence now doesn't matter. Volkmier knew the sentence at the time, knew he was committing an act of treason."

"No!" Nightfall could not take any more. "He never helped me. No one helped me. I escaped by myself."

Several of the Council stiffened. Alber shook his head. "I'm afraid Volkmier has confessed." He sighed. The skin beneath his sloping eyes sagged darkly, making them appear even sadder. His lids drooped over his muddy eyes. "Since the Lifthranians brought word of your return in the company of Sudian, I've spent every moment trying to find some way to save your chancellor with a pardon. Volkmier, I'm afraid, falls prey to all the same constraints as Sudian did." He indicated the book with a weary wave. "Not a word in there I haven't read, not a single rule I didn't study." He sighed. "If I could take my vote back, I would. I'd change history itself for Alyndar. Sire, I'm afraid it's hopeless."

"Hopeless," Edward repeated, sinking into his chair. Something familiar flashed through his eyes, a zealous fire Nightfall alternately loved and dreaded. "Nothing is hopeless." He flopped the book open to its first page. "Get out of here, all of you. I need some time alone to read."

The members of the High Council filed from the room, followed by the pair of guards and, lastly, by Nightfall. He could do nothing to help here, and he knew the servants of the castle would see to any need Edward might have. He would have to approach the problem in his own way. He headed toward the prison guards, intending to demand they take him to see Volkmier.

The two knights on the High Council, Alber and Tenneth, caught Nightfall before he framed his request. "A word, please, Sudian."

Nightfall weighed his options, then gave the men the benefit of his doubts. He watched the commanders and the baron descend, flanked by the guards, leaving the three men alone on the landing. He turned to face the knights.

As usual, Tenneth spoke first. "Sudian, sir, we just wanted to let you know how sorry we are about the way we treated you."

Not quite ready to forgive men who had blithely sentenced him to death, Nightfall merely nodded.

"We badly misjudged you." Tenneth looked to Alber for help, but continued talking, "We have many legitimate reasons for our mistake, including the mistrust King Rikard and Crown Prince Leyne had for you."

The words sounded strange after Volkmier's claim that the two royals' deep trust for Nightfall had influenced his own feelings for the king's unlikely chancellor. He also knew Volkmier was privy to information these knights never had, such as Leyne's journal; and the king and prince had changed their opinions of him shortly before their deaths.

"I'm afraid our views were also colored by the deceit of Alyndar's last chancellor."

Excuses.

As if reading his thoughts, Alber took over. "But those are rationalizations. All that matters is we condemned the only man willing and able to save King Edward, and we're eternally sorry."

Nightfall supposed he could forgive them, but his own fate no longer hung in the balance. Another good man's did. "What about Volkmier?"

Tenneth sucked in a deep breath, then loosed it in a huff, his shoulders slumping. "That was, clearly, another mistake. We thought Volkmier was a traitor when, in fact, he saw what no one else did."

Alber added, "The world tends to condemn its geniuses along with its demons."

The words touched too close to home. "I trust King Edward to find a way to save Volkmier. The way he saved me."

The knights exchanged looks, Tenneth's expectant. Alber's puppy eyes could not have looked more dejected. "Sudian," the quieter knight said, "you were saved by a technicality that does not apply to Volkmier. His only hope really is a pardon."

None of it made sense to Nightfall. "The king can do as he wishes, can't he? The king's word is law."

"True." Tenneth leaned against the wall beneath a tapestry depicting a great and ancient battle. "But once that law is spoken, it is written. And, once written, future kings are bound by it."

"Forever?"

"Only until they change it. But doing so does not negate its previous existence. To do so would require restitution to every man, or his descendant, affected by that law through the ages."

Nightfall had enough trouble allowing the current and regular laws of any kingdom to bind him. He could not imagine having to live by every proclamation through the ages. "It's not as easy being king as most would believe."

Both knights bobbed their heads. "That's one reason neither of us sought the position."

Tenneth added confidentially, "That, and I sure wasn't going to compete against those two giants." He tipped his head toward the stairs, though the general and the admiral had long since disappeared from sight.

Alber brought the conversation back to its point. "The king will not find a way to pardon Volkmier. I read that book cover to cover. Twice. It isn't there."

The situation made no sense to Nightfall. "If the king doesn't want him executed, if even the men who sentenced him don't want him executed, surely there has to be a way to make this right."

"One would think so," Tenneth said.

"It's a definite anomaly in the law," Alber continued. "One I'm sure our Edward will rectify."

"But not in time to save Volkmier?" Nightfall guessed.

"That's the problem," Tenneth agreed.

Nightfall would not accept the inevitable. A man to whom he owed his own life, and Edward's, would not die because of an antiquated book. "How does such a thing happen? How can the laws of supposedly just kings drop a faithful guard into a sink hole?"

Tenneth grimaced. "I don't think it was deliberate. Just an accident of how laws came together through the years. This is the first time in any history I've ever learned that the council was in the position of passing sentences. Of course, it must have happened at least one time before, or at least someone foresaw it. Otherwise, we would not have any law to cover an incapacitated king without a legal heir."

Nightfall could not help aiming his irritation at the men in front of him. They had, at least in part, caused the problem. "So why are you telling me this? Even I can't stop the king from spending night and day combing that wretched old book for a solution."

Again, the knights glanced at one another, this time with clear nervousness. Tenneth cleared his throat. "Sudian, Volkmier's crime was assisting your break from prison."

Nightfall nodded, wondering where this was going.

"We were hoping," Tenneth added softly, "you would do the same for him."

And so, Nightfall found himself, once again, a visitor deep in Alyndar's dungeon. Torches guttered in only a few of the sconces; the guards bothered to keep only enough light to safely perform their duties. The dank darkness seemed to close in on Nightfall, and the odors of long unwashed bodies, sweat, vomit, and urine brought a throbbing pain to his head. He found Volkmier precisely where the guards had steered him, set apart from the other prisoners in a cell fit only for animals. Stripped of his colors, he wore unadorned linens of simple cut and sat on a pile of clean blankets his men had undoubtedly provided. Weary sadness touched his otherwise proud features. His red hair looked freshly washed and combed, and he only had a day's growth of beard. Apparently, the guards accorded him more amenities than the other prisoners.

As Nightfall came into view, Volkmier rose and moved to the front of the cage. "Sudian. I knew you could do it." The disgraced captain appeared more upbeat than Nightfall.

"I wish you hadn't known." Nightfall slammed a fist against the bars. "I didn't need your help escaping." He pounded the bars again, ignoring the pain flaring through the side of his hand. "I didn't need your stupid, gods-be-damned help at all."

Crouching, Volkmier studied Nightfall through the bars. "You're welcome."

Nightfall refused to be pacified with humor. He was angry, and he meant to stay that way. "You're a moron, you know that? The stupidest man I ever met. Why in the Father's deepest pits did you confess?"

"The king will pardon me."

His hand already aching, Nightfall switched to kicking the bars. "The king can't pardon you, you dim-witted ass." He slammed his foot against metal again, barely controlling his real urge, to swing between the bars and kick some sense into Volkmier.

"He can't?"

"He can't! Some ridiculous law thing. I don't get it exactly, but he can't."

Volkmier slumped to his haunches.

Nightfall finally reined in his own rage, lowering himself to Volkmier's level. "Why did you confess?" he asked more calmly.

"Because it is the truth."

"So?"

"And I was asked directly."

Nightfall stared. "You're not above deceit, Volkmier. You once sent all your men chasing me in the wrong direction when I needed to find Prince Edward."

"Yes. Because I believed it in the best interests of Alyndar, her king, and her prince. And I was right." Volkmier added smugly, "As usual."

Nightfall emphasized each word. "Not . . . this . . . time."

"I can't subvert the law for my own gain." Volkmier rose and turned away. "I can't expect you to understand."

It was intended as insult; and, yet, it was the truth. Nightfall did not understand, though he had a grim certainty that it had something to do with honor. "I understand you're going to die."

Volkmier said nothing.

"Unless you let me help you the same way you helped me."

"You mean . . . prison break?"

"Yes."

"No."

Nightfall rolled his eyes. *Nobles and their ridiculous rigidities.* "Why not?" He braced himself for some long-winded speech on ethics, full of references to simplistic ideals and unwritten rules of propriety.

Volkmier heaved a heavy sigh. "Because I'm not going to exchange my freedom for yours."

Nightfall had already explored the same concern. "Actually, that's handled, Volkmier. First, I'm not stupid enough to confess. Second, as you well know, I'm legally pardoned for anything I've done from the day I promised you I'd bring back Edward till the official ceremony in court tomorrow. You were a captain of guards and member of the Council when you made that pledge to me, and the entire kingdom is beholden to your vow." He smiled wickedly, "I could murder every member of the High Council tonight, without a single consequence."

"You couldn't . . ."

"Oh, I could."

"But . . . you wouldn't," Volkmier tried, swallowing around an obvious lump.

"Of course, I wouldn't."

"Not that they don't deserve it." Volkmier came back to the bars and again dropped into a crouch. "How did you know about the ceremony and the significance of my vow?"

Nightfall laughed. "Some members of the High Council told me."

"After what they did to you, you believed them? Didn't you worry they were setting you up to take another fall?"

Nightfall shivered; Volkmier did know him dangerously well. "And I confirmed it with the king, who has the book of law in his hands at this very moment, scouring it for some way to pardon you."

"Ah."

Nightfall held Volkmier's pale stare. "Which he won't find. Which is why I'm going to get you out." He stood and began to examine the lock.

"No." Volkmier sprang to his feet.

Nightfall threw up his hands. "What is it this time?"

The ex-captain put a hand over the lock, blocking Nightfall's view. "I've served my post loyally for more than half my life. It's all I know."

"A man can change, Volkmier. Believe me, I know."

Volkmier paced, head drooping, arms and shoulders sagging. "I can't become a fugitive, Sudian. I can't hide from those I've pledged to serve. I'd rather die with honor than live like a rat in shadows."

That insult Nightfall got. "It's not as bad as you think."

"Sudian." Volkmier began his walk back toward the bars. "I envy your ability to adapt and change at will, but I'm too old to learn it. I don't want to learn it. I always knew I would die in the service of Alyndar, and nothing has happened to change my mind."

"Not even an unwarranted death."

"Not even."

Frustration drove Nightfall to hurl himself against the bars until they shattered, then throttle some sense into the onetime chief of prison guards. "Nobles," he muttered. "They're all a bunch of inbred, silversucking, incomprehensible, brainless idiots."

Volkmier moved closer. "What?"

"Never mind." Nightfall shook his head. It seemed crazy to try to liberate a man who refused to be saved. "Khanwar did this, didn't he?"

Volkmier sighed. "He may have steered the High Council to me, but I confessed." He gave Nightfall another of those looks that foretold an explanation he might not understand. "Khanwar should never have sold information about our king and his activities. For that alone, he should be severely punished."

Nightfall stared without blinking. So far, a three-year-old could comprehend the former captain's words. "But . . . ?"

"I do believe that, to his own warped way of thinking, he thought he was acting in—"

"—Alyndar's best interests?" Nightfall snorted. "I'm growing tired of that phrase. How could anyone believe that getting many of her best and most loyal guards slaughtered and our king sold to slavers could ever be in Alyndar's best interests."

Now it was Volkmier's turn to stare. "Slavers?"

Nightfall refused to be sidetracked. "I'll explain those details later." He waved a hand for Volkmier to continue. "We were talking about Khanwar."

With clear reluctance, Volkmier returned to the tale. The bold chief of prison guards was not used to being commanded. "Khanwar believed it would be a simple hostage-and-ransom situation. The Hartrinians would hold the king a bit, money would exchange hands, and we would get our king back: unharmed, wiser, perhaps a bit more worldly and understanding of our neighbor across the sea. In the meantime, it would separate you and Edward. If he could not get the High Council to remove you entirely, at least the king might have gained the experience and distance to see you the same way Khanwar does."

"You mean as a danger to Alyndar."

Volkmier shrugged. "That's Khanwar's opinion, not mine."

Nightfall saw no reason to argue the point. He knew the highborn tended to dislike him, and their concern was not entirely inappropriate. He would see to it that Edward pronounced sentence on Khanwar for his treason. Nightfall doubted he could talk the king into an execution; but, at least, Khanwar would lose his position in the castle and whatever title he held. To the royal adviser, that might well prove a punishment worse than death. Not yet ready to discuss his own ordeal, Nightfall maneuvered the conversation to Volkmier's. "So, how long have you been rotting down here?"

"Two days."

Nightfall laughed. "Well, give it a week, at least, if you aren't slated to die before then. You'll change your song when—" The answer slammed Nightfall with the abrupt and brutal power of Jacquellette's lightning. "Volkmier, stay here."

Volkmier blinked, obviously believing Nightfall had

finally slipped over the brink into madness. "Where would I go?"

"I'm getting you that pardon."

By the time Nightfall had gathered his friends and raced to the Strategy Room, the members of the High Council were already milling on the landing outside the door. No one had tried to enter thanks to the last command given by the king; he had warned them not to disturb him. Nightfall waited with them for the last of those summoned to arrive.

Baron Elliat leaned against the rail, looking out over the stairs. General Simont Basilaered stood at crisp attention just outside the door, the massive admiral beside him. The two knights gave Nightfall looks more quizzical than hopeful. Even Kelryn and Celdurant had no idea why Nightfall had brought them there, though they stood patiently in silence, apparently trusting him.

At last, two prison guards arrived with Volkmier chained between them. The red-haired warrior kept his head high, though his cheeks flushed with shame. He gave Nightfall a look that said everything: *You'd best have reason for parading my humiliation.*

Nightfall returned a smile. "Ready?"

Everyone nodded, some enthusiastically, others with clear misgivings.

Nightfall knocked on the door, then opened it a crack. Edward looked up from the book on the table. Around him, Nightfall could feel the men cringing, anticipating the king's anger; but Edward did not yell. He seemed glad of the interruption. "Did you need me again, Sudian?"

"Yes." Nightfall opened the door wider and ushered the others inside.

Only one man spoke as he entered. Sir Tenneth Kentaries whispered, "I'd give half my fortune to know what you're thinking."

"In a moment," Nightfall replied, "you'll know. And it won't cost you anything."

Nightfall waited until every man and Kelryn had taken seats around the Strategy Room table. Only the guards remained standing, on either side of Volkmier's chair. "Sorry for disturbing your reading, Sire."

Edward made a dismissive gesture.

"And for pulling the rest of you away from your duties."

Everyone except Kelryn, Celdurant, and Volkmier mumbled something that rejected the notion Nightfall had inconvenienced them. Those three remained silent.

"Sire, would you do us the honor of rereading that point of law? The one granting the High Council right of sentencing."

"Of course, Sudian." Edward flipped toward the proper page, and Alber leaned in to help him. "Though you have it memorized."

"Nevertheless, Sire, if you will indulge me."

Finding the page, Edward placed his hands upon it. "In the event that the king is killed, missing, or incapacitated . . ." He paused, clearly seeking whatever loophole Nightfall might have found. ". . . leaving no blooded heir on the throne, the Council is granted overriding discretion in all matters of judgment provided . . ." More consideration, then a headshake. ". . . it has the full consent of the High Council and a majority vote of the Council in Full."

Also trying to anticipate, Baron Elliat said, "We did get a majority vote, if that's what you're wondering. The double votes of the five High Council members count ten, but we only needed two more. The Council was nearly unanimous." He glanced toward Volkmier apologetically. "The captain did confess."

Nightfall refused to let speculation derail him. "Now, name the High Council for me, please."

Nikolei Neerchus frowned. "You know that's us." He indicated the general, himself, the two knights, and the baron.

What a time to suddenly go casual. Nightfall looked down his nose at the larger man. "I mean the definition by law, Lord Admiral."

King Edward jumped in, speaking thoughtfully, still clearly trying to second-guess his minister. "It's the three largest landholders, besides the king, of course. And the highest ranking officers of Alyndar's army and navy."

Nightfall delivered his coup de grâce. "And I would declare that the vote you took to convict the chief of prison guards did not result in full agreement of the High Council, thereby rendering it null and void."

"On what grounds?" Simont asked, more hopeful than demanding.

"On the grounds . . ." Nightfall circled the table. ". . . that at the time of the decision . . ." He came to a rest behind Celdurant. ". . . Supreme Lord Admiral Celdurant was not present to cast a vote."

"What!" Admiral Nikolei sprang to his feet, then turned his stricken expression to the king. "Is this true, Your Majesty?"

Edward laughed, too thrilled with the outcome to worry about Nikolei. "Lord Celdurant took his oath three days ago. In front of many witnesses."

Nightfall finished, "And Captain Volkmier received his sentence only two days ago. Which means the High Council was missing a member . . ." He trailed off.

Tenneth finished in a wondering whisper, "Which means the vote was indeed null and void."

Smiles ringed the table, on every face but those of Nikolei and the general, Simont.

King Edward looked at the prison guards and said simply, "Free him."

The guards set to work immediately, quiet but unable to hide broad grins of excitement and relief.

The chains fell away from Volkmier, and his grin was the largest of all. He executed one of the most flourishing and exquisite bows Nightfall had ever seen, full of grace, dignity, and poise. "Your Majesty, if it pleases you, I'd like to return to my duties at once."

Nightfall's grin broadened. He knew those duties included detaining a real traitor to Alyndar.

Edward gave a formal nod. "I'd appreciate that, Captain Volkmier."

Signaling his men to follow, Volkmier headed for the door, only to stop with his hand nearly on the latch. "Your Majesty? I would also request permission to embrace your chancellor."

Nightfall froze.

"Your request is granted."

Oh, great. Don't even bother to ask me. Before Nightfall could fully turn toward Volkmier, he found himself crushed into a hug worthy of a bear. Sucking air into his lungs became impossible, and he croaked out a breathless, "You're welcome."

Releasing him, Volkmier whispered. "How's the shoulder?"

"Fine," Nightfall responded as quietly. "At least it was until you crushed it."

Still grinning, Volkmier and his soldiers took their leave.

The former lord admiral of Alyndar's navy swallowed, surely wondering if he would ever get an answer to his question. Nightfall knew Edward would not leave him waiting long. He also knew the young king well enough to realize the admiral would keep a command position in the royal navy. Likely, he would get an interminable lecture about his behavior and find himself answering to Celdurant. Otherwise, Nightfall realized, little in Alyndar had changed.

King Edward raised his hands. "I'd like a word with my Supreme Lord Admiral and my Lord Admiral. The rest of you may go."

Nightfall let all of the others file out first, leaving only those chosen, himself, and Kelryn. "Ned," he cautioned, "we'd like to see you all before breakfast."

King Edward smiled.

Nightfall took Kelryn's hand and led her from the room, then closed the door behind them. Once on the landing, he spun her about, sending her short white locks into a radiant dance. She moved with all the grace he loved, her dancer's body a treat for attention too long focused on evil and death. "I love you," he said.

Kelryn sprang into his arms. He carried her down the staircase, and she seemed light as a shadow, as bright and beautiful as a spirit. "Thank you for keeping your promises, Sudian."

"I didn't," he admitted. At the next landing, he twirled her to the floor in an agile dance. "Nightfall had to return. Without him, I could not have rescued Edward."

"And yet, you're here." She smiled, her features the very definition of beauty. "Sudian, I'm proud of you."

"I'm stronger than you thought."

"Yes."

Nightfall leered. "And, the moment I get you to your room, I intend to prove it."

Kelryn giggled as she ran down the next flight of stairs. "And I, Sudian. I intend to let you."

Mickey Zucker Reichert

To Order Call: 1-800-788-6262

Melanie Rawn

"Rawn's talent for lush descriptions and complex characterizations provides a broad range of drama, intrigue, romance and adventure."
—*Library Journal*

EXILES
THE RUINS OF AMBRAI	0-88677-668-6
THE MAGEBORN TRAITOR	0-88677-731-3

DRAGON PRINCE
DRAGON PRINCE	0-88677-450-0
THE STAR SCROLL	0-88677-349-0
SUNRUNNER'S FIRE	0-88677-403-9

DRAGON STAR
STRONGHOLD	0-88677-482-9
THE DRAGON TOKEN	0-88677-542-6
SKYBOWL	0-88677-595-7

To Order Call: 1-800-788-6262

Tanya Huff

The Finest in Fantasy

To Order Call: 1-800-788-6262

DAW 21